THE LADY'S SLIPPER

It is 1660. The King is back, but the wounds of the Civil War remain. Alice Ibbetson is captivated by the rare lady's slipper orchid growing on the land of converted Quaker, Richard Wheeler. Determined to capture and preserve its beauty, one night she steals the flower. Fired by his newfound faith, the former soldier Wheeler feels bound to return the orchid to its rightful home. But others are equally eager to lay hands on it. Margaret Poulter, a local medicine woman, is seduced by the lady's slipper's mysterious medicinal powers, while Geoffrey Fisk, Alice's patron, sees the plant as a way to cure his own agonizing illness.

THE LADY'S SLIPPER

THE LADY'S SLIPPER

THE LADY'S SLIPPER

by

Deborah Swift

Magna Large Print Books
Long Preston, North Yorkshire,
BD23 4ND, England.

British Library Cataloguing in Publication Data.

Swift, Deborah
    The lady's slipper.

    A catalogue record of this book is
    available from the British Library

    ISBN   978-0-7505-3545-8

First published in Great Britain 2010 by Macmillan New Writing
an imprint of Pan Macmillan, a division of Macmillan Publishers Ltd.

Published in Large Print 2012 by arrangement with
Pan Macmillan Publishers Limited

Magna Large Print is an imprint of Library Magna Books Ltd.

Printed and bound in Great Britain by
T.J. (International) Ltd., Cornwall, PL28 8RW

For India and Karen

LADY'S SLIPPER

GOVERNMENT AND VIRTUES

A most gallant herb of Venus, now sadly declined. A decoction is effectual to temper and sedate the blood, and allay hot fits of agues, canker rash and all scrophulous and scorbutic habits of the body. The root drank in wine, is its chief strength, to be applied either inwardly or outwardly, for all the griefs aforesaid. There is a syrup made hereof excellent for soothing restlessness of the limbs, hence oft times goes by the name of Nerve Root.

VICES

Be wary of this herb, for surfeit of it calls forth visions, fancies and melancholy. Take it not with strong liquor. If giddiness, sickness of the stomache, dullness of the senses ensue, or drowsiness withal ending in deep sleep, straightway desist. In women and children, safer it being tied to the pit of the stomache, by a piece of white ribband round the neck.

Gargrave's Herbal 1646

Westmorland 1660

Chapter 1

Alice tiptoed into the hallway. Perhaps it was a blessing she was still in mourning, for there would be less risk of being seen. Wheeler would be watching out, and his eyes were sharp as pikes – he would spot any movement, any slight shift in the features of the landscape.

She reached up to the peg for her black bonnet and put it on, pulling the lace veiling down so it hid her face. Regretfully, she looked down at her narrow feet, shod now in pale yellow sateen. This was her favourite pair of shoes, in a style considered far too fancy these days. They were one of the few pretty things she had saved from the fire and she was loath to get them wet and muddy. But her leather bootees made too much noise; even on tiptoe the irons would clang against the flagstones in the hall. These shoes were silent, and outside would leave hardly a trace if she was careful to tread where it was dry. There must be no mishaps. This was the only night with no moon, and the orchid would fade fast, so it had to be tonight.

The basket stood ready by the back door. She had prepared it earlier with a lining of soaked green moss and dampened sackcloth. A bunch of fresh herbs was waiting in the pantry for her return: parsley, salvia, rosemary; they would be her excuse if Thomas were to wake and ask her where she had been. She glanced over towards the fireplace where he snored lightly, his mouth drooping open and his arm dangling over the edge of the chair. As usual, his boots were almost in the embers.

At the door she leaned her shoulder against the jamb, to ease the latch out of its socket; the door swung open silently and she stepped out into the night air. She heard the latch clack gently into place behind her.

The night was a soot-black tunnel. She listened, senses quivering. Her heart beat loudly as if caught in her throat; her breath came in sharp little puffs. She gathered herself. Soon she would have it, and though Wheeler might suspect her, he would never be able to prove it.

She felt her way down the path with an out-stretched hand on the fence, for Wheeler must not see any glimmer of her presence, and a lantern would surely draw his eye like bait to a fish. Her foot stubbed against a wooden milk churn and she momentarily lost her balance. She lurched for the gate with her hand and shuddered as she felt the wet body of a slug on its night-time foray for food.

Her eyes strained to accustom themselves to this new, lightless world. Thank the Lord she had re-hearsed the route. In the daylight she had prac-tised with eyes closed, opening them again as she passed close to Wheeler's house, for in the dark of the moon she knew it would be hard to find her way. Becoming more sure-footed, she followed the smell of wood-smoke from the village chimneys until she saw the lights of Wheeler's house and the barely perceptible outline of the kissing-gate to Helk's Wood.

The house lay directly next to the gate, with a window that overlooked the path. From here Wheeler could keep watch on anyone coming or going. Lights flickered in the downstairs room. She stopped short.

He was awake – and probably at his vantage point at the window.

A lozenge of yellow light slanted across her path. She reconsidered her route; she dare not risk passing the window. Instead, she felt along the hedge for a gap.

A bramble wound its thorny teeth round her ankle and she winced as she tore free. She stumbled forward and found herself in a cut cornfield. She walked faster, despite the scratchy stubble, which snagged on the silk of her shoes and caught at her underskirt. The dew was already heavy, her dress damp – the sodden hem swung over her ankles.

Above her the stars were fixed points of light, too faint to reach the shadows under the stooks, too faint to touch the flurry of a hare as it leapt into the hedge's black underbelly. She felt for the wall to the wood. Here, she could hide and keep away from Wheeler's gimlet eyes. The wall had substance, solidity – so she kept her hand there. As she listened, the ancient presence of the woodland loomed beyond; the trees were watching, and the grasses, even the stones in the wall. They were conversing with each other in an unknown silent language. She shivered and withdrew her hand.

Beyond the wall the trees were shapes distorted by the dark. Each one grew into the next; one dim shape concealing another, brooding. A crawling

sensation curled at the top of her spine. From nowhere a chill breeze swept through the branches
making the mounds of creamy meadowsweet float
like ghostly clouds against the hedge. In the night
air their smell was sickly and cloying.

But there was another smell, fainter, more
familiar. Alice sucked in her breath. It was a smell
she knew, something sweet and musty, like peat.
Instantly she dropped down behind the wall.
Tobacco. There was someone smoking close by.

Her back pressed against the stones, she pulled
the veil of the bonnet down over her face and
undid the ribbons, straining her ears for the least
sound. A cough, and then the sound of boots
approaching. She heard the ring of them on the
stones, and the slight squelch as they landed in the
muddy wheel tracks. With consternation Alice saw
a light getting closer. From her hiding place she
saw the leaves of the trees in the canopy flare into
colour and then disappear into the dark. She
shrank further into the shadow of the wall. She
knew only one man who smoked that tobacco.
Wheeler.

He must be guarding the wood.

The footsteps got nearer, until she heard what
must be the buttons of his long coat scratching
against his boots.

Silence.

She put a hand over her nose lest the steam of
her breath should betray her. She heard a dull
hiss as a taper caught light. The corn near her
feet was illuminated as he drew on his pipe. She
crouched low, head bent forward, hands now
clutching the fabric of her gown about her. The

smoke drifted over the wall and fogged above her head, like the creeping mist near the river.

What would he think if he knew she was only inches away, spying on him from behind the wall? The situation struck her suddenly as absurd. She suppressed an unaccountable urge to laugh. Mirth began to bubble up inside and she had to quash it by stuffing her sleeve over her mouth and nose.

Wheeler must not see her here. He was such a serious man – so serious he made her feel like a fool. If she were to give herself away, he would know straightway what she was about, and would have none of it. He would be incredulous to think she could consider doing such a thing.

Presently the footsteps moved away up the path. She listened to them fade away and let out a long exhalation. All desire to laugh had disappeared. When she was certain he had gone, she stood up stiffly, aware that the hour was passing and she must hurry if she were not to make trouble at home. Finding a place where the wall had tumbled down, she hitched up her skirts and climbed over, landing softly on the path below. She walked until she felt the ground become springy under her feet – a mossy clearing.

A breeze blew up again, a soft muttering of leaves, a swing of shadows, the branches moving silver-limbed against the sky. Her eyes had opened out to the dark. She stopped a few feet away and looked.

The pale globe of the flower shone out like Venus in the night sky. She tiptoed closer. Indeed, silence came easily. It was a natural response to something so exquisite.

She knelt down in front of the plant so she could look inside the fragile petal bowl and see the tiny stigmata of maroon and pink, appearing blue-black in the darkness. Reaching out a finger, she caressed the edge of a fleshy leaf.

'*Cypripedium.*' She whispered the Latin name softly, caressingly, as if calling for it to come home, feeling the taste of the words on her tongue.

Squatting down she started to dig around it, her movements precise and delicate, careful not to disturb the roots. She worked quickly with the trowel to prise away the heavy soil, not noticing that the dirt was forced up into her fingernails. In one deft movement she plucked the whole plant and lowered it gently into the basket of damp moss.

A movement made her startle. An owl flew overhead, pale faced, wings beating quiet as breathing. Again she shivered and looked over her shoulder. There was nobody there, yet she could not shake off the feeling that someone was watching, unseen in the cold shadows.

She stood up and regarded the empty hole, wondering whether to fill it in or disguise it in some way. But then she had an idea. She reached into her handkerchief pouch and pulled out a few coins. She tossed them into the hole, hearing them chink at the bottom. There, she thought, I have paid you for it. She repressed a small chuckle as she imagined Wheeler's face when he returned in the morning. He was always so keen on the idea of everything having its price.

She picked up the basket and, confident now,

followed the same route she had come. She turned to look back. Behind her, another dark human figure melted into the shadow of the undergrowth.

When she passed Wheeler's house she trod softly, for although his lights were still lit, it was even more vital to be invisible now. But the only sound was the *chek, chek* of the corncrakes in the meadow and the distant lowing of a cow.

She went straight to the summerhouse and gently took out the orchid to stand it upright in a small pot of earth. It looked small and insignificant, almost insipid, next to the pink curling papers of the flowering geraniums. She felt a pang of remorse. The orchid looked somehow less, out of its woodland setting.

It was for the best, she convinced herself. She knew she had the skills to divide it, whatever Wheeler might think; soon there would be lady's slippers growing in abundance. She watered it, just a few drops. Not because it was dry, but because she wanted to tend it – to make amends for uprooting it and bringing it to a strange place. After hiding it out of sight under the table, she locked the door with the little bronze key and crept into the house.

She need not have worried. The fire was barely aglow, and Thomas's wheezing snores told her he was still sleeping. Only now did she allow herself a sigh of relief. She thought of her dear sister, Flora, and her delight if she could have seen it. She could not wait to tell Geoffrey, and looked forward to his expression when he saw it for the first time. He would understand her excitement, and she knew she could trust him to keep her secret.

Her cuffs were brackish-brown and there was a quantity of dirt under her nails, so she washed in the scullery, out of Thomas's earshot, by the light of a lantern. She soaped and drubbed the cuffs until the water ran clean; they would dry overnight. Looking down at her shoes she could see they were ruined – the fabric soaked through and scuffed with mud, but worse, the deep scratch on her ankle had bled and dribbled over the embroidery in a dark red stain.

She carried the shoes to the kitchen and wrapped them in brown paper. It would be difficult to explain their condition to Thomas so they would need to be disposed of. She dare not pass him, in case he should wake. For the moment she pushed the shoes right to the bottom of the turnip sack. Her bare feet padded softly on the stairs as she made her way to bed. Thomas slept on – his snores loud above the ticking clock, while the embers grew cold.

Chapter 2

When she heard the cry she threw back the sheets and was out of bed before she knew it, despite the chill. Instinctively, she picked up a small earthenware cup, half filled it with water from the jug on the stand and crossed the creaking boards of the landing in her bare feet.

The morning light slid over the whitewash in pale strands. She rubbed the grit of sleep from her eyes and pushed open the door into Flora's room. Her knees buckled anew at the sight of the bare room and the empty pallet.

It was the cockerel, and not crying after all, that had woken her. She slumped against the doorframe; the little cup dripping from her fingers. She took in the mattress, thin and grey without its covering of white linen and blankets, and tears swam into her eyes. Moths had already started to eat away the cushion on the chair where she had kept her nightly vigil. How many nights had she spent, sleepless beside Flora's waxen face, watching and praying? She turned away, ignoring the dark stone of grief that weighed in her stomach, shut the door again on all the memories. She took a deep breath; she must pull herself together. Life goes on.

Alert now, she cast her mind back to the night before, and the orchid. Had she really stolen it? The remembrance of it seemed strange, like a dream. Everything was unreal since Flora died — dark and watery, as if she were drifting aboard a rudderless ship.

She made her toilet quickly, glad of the icy water in the bowl. She rubbed her face hard with the muslin cloth and a tingle of warmth crept back into her cheeks. She picked up the looking glass and saw a woman, white as alabaster, stare back at her through troubled pale blue eyes. Seeing herself, she blushed. She had stolen the orchid.

For the first time since Flora's death she felt a rush of excitement, an appetite for the day. Her breath clouded the surface of the mirror, so she hurried to layer heavy underskirts under her gown, smoothing down the dark taffeta folds and pressing the black lace-trimmed collar against her shoulders. Downstairs, she added a shawl and hastily tucked her unruly copper hair under a white coif. She stepped into her black bootees, not bothering to fasten them, and opened the door into the garden.

The tongues of her boots flapped as she hastened to the summerhouse along the grass so as not to waken Thomas with the noise of her wooden soles on the path. Under the apple trees windfalls had already made green trails in the white of the dew. The dogwood stems – red stripes against the scullery wall – naturally caught her attention, and the whirl of a snail-shell caught in the leaves of the periwinkle. Her passing eye took each small detail and stored it as a future vignette to be captured in paint.

The sun had just risen, but the air was damp as a wet stocking. These days she did not sleep well and her restless wanderings in the night often led her out to the stone summerhouse, her private place where she could breathe easily, a place she found comfort in the familiar, solace in her paints and pigments. Her portraits of Flora were there; she had hung them along the walls, like a living presence. The octagonal shape of the building meant that, whichever way she turned, Flora's face smiled down on her.

She lifted the lady's slipper onto the table and stared at its strange, almost unearthly appearance. It was essential to catch the moment before the flower faded. She could not quite believe she had done it. She, Alice Ibbetson, was a thief.

There were thieves in the stocks on the green – people who were rough and dirty, covered in slops. Like everyone else she ignored them, but felt a sting of guilt as she went about her business.

Of course, this was a little different; she was not really a thief but a rescuer preserving nature's wonders. She was perspiring slightly and wiped her fingers down her skirt. Nobody had seen a lady's slipper flower for more than twenty years. If her skill was enough, in future times little girls like Flora would be able to pick them and put them in water with the buttercups.

She must find a better hiding place, for word would soon be out that it was gone. People called her eccentric because of her passion for plants, but she was not the only person who would be interested in the orchid. The botanists would want it – the new breed of men, men like Geoffrey, who traded in foreign and unusual specimens. It always surprised her how news of a rarity could travel, as if somehow it was carried like a scent on the air. Plantsmen have a sixth sense; like homing pigeons they know by instinct when something calls them home, and this orchid would certainly draw them.

She positioned the plant on the table, where the pearly light from the long casement windows lit up the flower petals and showed off their delicate transparency. The need in her to fix its beauty on paper was urgent. Her fingers itched to take up the brush. She would just make a quick sketch. It was barely dawn – Wheeler would not be awake yet, and although he might guess who had taken it, she doubted if he would have the effrontery to come to the house.

She remembered the first time she had been introduced to him, at Lady Swainson's house. She had been curious to meet him then, for she had heard about these odd followers of George Fox, men who quaked in their boots at the word of the Lord. She had been ready to scoff at him, but found him so unlike what she was expecting that she was quite unable to do so. She had imagined a small tremulous mouse of a man, not such a tall, energetic, capable-looking person.

Alice repositioned the plant to face her. Just one turn of the sandglass, that should be enough time to capture the rhythmic line of the petals. She drew quickly, then began to grind the pigments in a stone bowl, adding water drop by drop from a small flagon. A dribble of gum was added next, imported at great expense from India. The scrape of the grindstone and the motion of stirring the paint was soothing. It was a ritual she had always enjoyed; the sound of the spatula turning in the bowl took her back to her childhood. She saw again her father's lace-cuffed hand weigh down on hers as he showed her how to press the gum into the soot.

She traced the forms and spaces of the stems and leaves, sketching the outline in fine sepia brushstrokes. Soon she became engrossed in a world where the only sounds were of sable on paper, the tinkle of rinsing the brushes, and the rising and falling rhythm of her breath. The flower took life on the paper, blooming out of the ivory spaces, waxing slowly into existence. But the light shifted imperceptibly, and she failed to notice that the sand had long since trickled away in the glass.

She did not hear the knocking for a few moments. A rapping on the front door. When sound suddenly cut through her reverie, her brush jumped and skidded across the page. Alarmed, she placed the board silently on the table and tilted her head round the corner of the door. From this position she could not see who was there; the caller was obscured by a topiary box tree. The person stepped back to look at the upstairs windows, and with a jolt Alice recognized the solid dark figure. It was Wheeler. She shrank back inside the summerhouse.

He was at her door already. She cursed her own stupidity. The hour must have grown later than she thought. She regarded the painting with panic-stricken eyes. Hastily she moved the paint water onto the side table. She concealed the watercolour behind a stack of boards against the wall and piled a good few more unfinished paintings in front of it. Her head tilted to one side and straining to hear, she pulled out a picture of a dog-tooth fern, and gently placed it on the stand on the table.

She heard Ella answer the door and some muffled discourse. The click of the door being shut. He must have gone inside. She scoured the room for somewhere to hide the orchid, dithering with the pot in her hands. Her eyes darted round the whitewashed shuttered walls, the wooden panelling, the tall domed casement windows. There was nowhere safe to hide it.

Thinking quickly, she peered through the window to check no one was looking, then crept round the back of the summerhouse, pressed flat to the wall, out of sight of the house. Cradling the pot under her shawl, she ran to the rhubarb patch. This new, odd-looking plant with its ruby-red stalks was being grown in darkness under wooden buckets. She thrust the flower into the muddy hollow under the nearest plant and lowered the bucket back over it. Back round the side wall and inside to the table, where she quickly positioned a fern.

Just in time, for Wheeler and her husband were already walking up the path.

'Oh, there you are,' Thomas said. 'I told Mr Wheeler you would be out here. I know you hate visitors, dear, but he was most insistent to see you.'

'Good morrow, Mr Wheeler. It is a lovely morning.' She stood up, aware that she was still breathless. Her voice sounded high-pitched and distant.

Wheeler nodded to her by way of courtesy, but then waited silently, filling the doorway, making no attempt to remove his brown felt hat.

'Is there something amiss?' She smiled at him, although her hands were wiping mud surreptitiously off her fingers and onto her painting rag.

'I think thou knowst what brings me here.' He looked penetratingly at her shifting hands.

'And what might that be?'

'The lady's slipper orchid has been stolen in the night.'

'Stolen?' Thomas looked at him questioningly.

'Someone has dug it out and removed it. It is a rarity. I have come to ask Mistress Ibbetson if she knows anything about it.'

'Are you accusing my wife?'

Wheeler's eyes dropped. 'She is a flower artist –

28

she may know of someone who would want it so badly they would come in the night to steal it.' He looked directly at her.

She moved towards the windows, feeling sweat gathering on her palms. The room had grown warm. It was oppressive with the three of them so closely confined, as if the walls were boxing them in.

'No one of my acquaintance would do such a thing,' she said, 'although, of course, reports of the orchid's discovery will have spread abroad by now. This is dreadful news. Are you saying the plant is gone completely, not just the flower?' She felt obliged to carry on with the charade.

'I left my guard of it for only a half-hour. In that time the whole plant was taken.' He was still staring at her. She wondered if there was mud on her sleeves.

'Surely, anyone could have taken it,' Thomas said. 'Were there any footprints?'

'No footprints. No iron marks or patten marks at all.' Wheeler fumbled in his bag. 'But whoever it was, they left these.'

Alice's stomach clenched and her collar seemed too tight. He held out the few coins, displaying them on the flat of his palm. His hand was broad and strong, the colour of a brown hen's egg. The coins appeared tiny in his grasp.

'How strange,' Alice murmured.

Thomas took the coins from Wheeler and counted them. Alice wished she had not been so reckless. She flushed and moved away. Picking up a jar of ground pigment, she began to empty it into a dish; her hands were unsteady and she scattered green powder upon the table.

'If I hear anything I will let you know,' she said. It was a kind of dismissal. She was feeling stifled under her thick petticoats. She willed Wheeler to leave.

'Yes, I'm sure my wife will keep you informed. I'm surprised anyone would bother. After all, it's only a plant.'

Alice bristled. How typical of Thomas. Why could he never understand her passion for flowers, or her need to express them in paint?

Wheeler ignored her hint that he should leave. His eyes raked the summerhouse, taking in the pile of paintings, the table with pestle and mortar, the rows of jars with their vivid array of minerals and powders. He approached the boards where she had hidden the painting of the orchid and picked up the first one. Alice held her breath.

'I like this,' he said. It was a study of flowering honeysuckle, shown just as the flowers were turning to berries.

'Yes,' she said, coolly, 'the honeysuckle is over now. That one will be wrapped and sent to the Low Countries. It is a commission for a friend.'

Wheeler examined it for a few more moments before returning it to the front of the stack. Alice maintained her distance as he walked over to the work on the table. The fern was many shades of green, from the palest moss to deepest sage. He studied it closely, looking at it from several angles.

'But this is deftly handled,' he said with enthusiasm. 'The way thou hast caught the light in the layers of leaves.'

Alice had always found his old-fashioned

Quaker speech strange, and although she had heard rumours that he had been educated, Alice was surprised he should have any appreciation of the arts.

He added, 'People have told me of thy talent, but I did not expect such fine work.'

She felt exposed, as if he had caught her undressed. She did not want him to admire her work. She did not want anything to do with him. She could not make him understand the flower's importance. He would have left the orchid to be eaten by deer, or die unnoticed in the winter frosts. She did not want any more of his conversation, she just wanted him to go.

'My wife has achieved a measure of success of late with her paintings,' Thomas said. 'She never stops painting – she paints morning, noon and night.'

Alice was embarrassed. When Thomas talked of her this way it made her feel like a prize exhibit at a fair.

She followed Wheeler's attention as he looked from the plant to the painting. The painting did not match the position of the plant and she hoped he had not noticed. Evidently not, for he turned away and moved towards the door. He gestured to the paintings of Flora. 'Is this your daughter?'

'No,' Thomas said, not waiting for Alice to reply. 'It is Alice's sister. She died less than twelvemonth past.'

'I had heard it. On the day I moved into my house, I passed the cortege going to the church.' He turned to Alice and removed his hat. 'I am right sorry for thy loss.'

31

'My wife took it hard,' Thomas said. 'We have no children, and Alice misses her sorely.'

Alice remained silent. She had marvelled at Thomas's noisy outbursts of tears, and then how easily he had found it to put his grieving aside. Alice still had found no way to express her grief and it disquieted her that Thomas trespassed upon it. She felt Thomas's presence in the summerhouse to be a kind of intrusion into her private world, the world where Flora's laughing eyes were still indelibly preserved, for Flora had been the last of her family.

Her mother's face swam into her mind, weakly entreating her to take care of her new-born daughter. Over the years since her mother's death, Alice had struggled with the task until she had become almost a mother to Flora herself.

Alice caught sight of Flora's face watching. Anger rose in her chest. How dare he barge his way in here? Wheeler's presence in this special place was an imposition. Alice placed the little mixing dish down with a bang.

'Well, good day,' Wheeler said, replacing his hat. 'I regret disturbing thy painting. I am concerned that the plant may be lost to us. It is the only one, as far as I can discern, and should remain in its natural habitat, the place where God intended.' This last part was addressed directly to Alice. She smiled politely.

Thomas acknowledged him with a nod and strolled with him towards the door. It was then that she noticed the glass jar of water on the side table, with the brushes still resting in it. The water was pink. Her heart jumped in her chest.

32

Wheeler paused and took it in. He swivelled round and their eyes met. She felt as if he could see inside her soul. Even if he had not suspected her before, in that moment he knew.

'Goodbye to thee, Mistress Ibbetson.' He gave a slight inclination of his head, but his lips were pressed into a hard line. 'But have no doubt; I intend to pursue this further through the law.'

When he had gone, Thomas returned. He tapped on the wooden door to the summerhouse.

'What a strange man,' he said. 'God's breath, I thought he was going to break the door down. Thee-ing and thou-ing all over the place. Getting me up out of my bed at this unholy hour for some business with a plant!' He shook his head. 'For some reason he seemed to think you must have something to do with it. Naturally, I told him straight I would not permit you to be out wandering abroad at all hours. You don't know anything about it, do you, dear?'

'Of course not.' It slid out easily, but it felt awkward to lie to Thomas. She patted his arm. 'It is a pity. I was hoping he would let me make a proper study of it.'

'Well, there are plenty of other things in the garden. Is Sir Geoffrey's commission finished yet?' He glanced at the painting on the table. She was glad to have a chance to change the subject.

'Almost. But it is a set of three – different varieties of ferns to hang in Earl Shipley's dining room. His house has been redecorated in the Dutch style, and Geoffrey has persuaded him they will look fine against his dark wallpapering. It is a good commission. Two are finished and here is the

33

third nearly done. Geoffrey is still overseas in the Americas so I have a little more time.'

'How much longer will he be away?'

'As a matter of fact, his ship landed the day before yesterday. But I do not expect to see him for a few more days. He has pressing business on his estate. Jane Rawlinson told me. Apparently he will be busy arranging for his men to deliver the shipment of bulbs and flowers to the gardeners at Hampton Court.'

Thomas nodded his approval. 'Take care that you do not catch a chill out here.' He walked away down the path, with his lopsided rolling gait, and she watched him go with relief. He would be riding out to the counting house soon, and she would be left at her own pleasure, to paint and potter, and make plans for the lady's slipper.

When she retrieved the orchid from the rhubarb patch it looked perfect, thank goodness, despite its stay under a dirty bucket. It made her shiver to look at it. She looked a long time, taking in its shape and texture. It was so fragile, so un-sullied. As she sat in contemplation, Flora's dancing eyes surveyed her from the walls, looking down with her perpetual smile. She would never grow old, would always be seven.

The feeling of Flora's immobile hand with its perfect shell-shaped nails still haunted her, the unchanged texture of her hair even in death. Alice swallowed hard; she would not succumb to the dark memories. Instead she recalled Flora's warm body nestling next to hers as they looked at the heavy picture book together.

Gargrave's Herbal was the only book with pictures, apart from Aesop's Fables, and she and Flora had often sat together, marvelling at the life-like woodcut illustrations, turning the heavy fan of pages with their familiar metallic smell of ink, that is until Alice began to tickle her and they rolled over and over screeching with merriment.

They looked for their favourite plants from the book on their daily walks. Flora was entranced by the name of the 'lady's slipper', imagining she would be able to put the little slippers on her pet cat's paws. She looked everywhere, hoping she would find it one day. Alice had joined in the game, half serious, not having the heart to tell her she never would – and yet, here it was. She could hardly believe it. But now Flora would never see it. A tear dropped into the dust on the table. The flower remained locked in its own stillness as she wept.

In the scullery Ella the housemaid was preparing a broth for the midday meal. As usual she took her time, and helped herself to small pickings. She was always hungry. Today it was a bit of boiled ham, along with potato, turnip and a few yellowing leeks. As it was the cook's day off she would not be there to call her a rivyrags if she wasted anything, so she threw the big rooty ends in the swill bucket. She did not bother to wash the vegetables but rubbed the earth off with her hands before chopping them and adding them to the pot with the ham. For good measure she threw in some salt from the crock. She crossed herself and tossed some over her shoulder; she

35

didn't want to leave room for Robin the Devil or his bad luck to enter.

As she scraped at the potatoes she stared glumly at the wall. She counted all the unwed men she knew in the village, at least 'them that aren't ugly or kettled'. She was born for better things than to be scrubbing carrots and carrying coal for the fire. A young man with a fat purse – that was what she needed.

She wiped her hands on her rump and went into the pantry for more turnips. The shelves were well stocked. She could sneak enough oats for two bowls of gruel or enough wheatflour for a large loaf if she was wily and didn't do it too often. Once she had even managed a small pot of clover honey.

She ran her hand along the shelf of preserves with its jewel-like jams and jellies. In some households these were kept under lock and key, but her mistress was daft enough to leave them out in the pantry. She peeled back one of the muslin cloths and poked her finger in, bringing it out with a large globule of golden plum jam. She stuck her finger in her mouth and sucked, before doing the same with another jar.

It was redcurrant jelly; sour and tart. She coughed and spat it out, ground the stain into the flagstone floor with her clog. She arranged the muslin covers again as if they were untouched, and pushed the jars to the back of the row.

She peered into the gloom under the shelves and dragged out the sack of turnips, but it tipped over, spilling them at her feet. She cursed, bending down on hands and knees to pick them up. As she dropped the first turnip back inside the sack, she felt something soft. She whipped out her hand with a little shriek. Rats had got into the pantry again. Gingerly holding the neck of the sack open with thumb and forefinger, she squinted inside.

Something butter-coloured was poking out. She reached in and drew out a damp satin shoe, partially wrapped in brown paper. Mouth open, she held it aloft in the light for a better look. It belonged to her mistress, of that she was certain – she had seen it in her chamber. But what was it doing in the turnip sack? It was a moment or two before she thought to look in the sack for the other one. When she had recovered its twin, she sat on the stone step by the kitchen door and contemplated them both.

The thought of putting them back did not even cross her mind. It was 'finders keepers' as far as she was concerned. She slid off her wooden-soled clogs and tried one of the shoes on. It was too small, but she admired the look of her cold red foot encased in something so fancy. Of course such brightly coloured clothes showed that you were ungodly and vain, but she liked the feel of the soft material, the cream lining against her calloused toes. These were the sort of shoes she deserved, not roof-beam clogs. It was a shame it was so dirty. She looked at the other one and rubbed at it with her hand. There were some dark brown spots that wouldn't come out. She spat on it and rubbed again – even now the marks did not shift. It looked like blood. How could you tell the difference between blood and paint?

She licked her lips and thought hard. Mistress would not bother to hide paint-spattered clouts – most of her clothes were spotted already. It had to be blood. A delicious shiver ran up Ella's spine. There was something going on, and she smelt a profit in it somehow. She stuffed the shoes into her bonnet, and jammed it uncomfortably on her head. Furtively, she glanced out of the kitchen door and down the garden, in case Mistress should be looking, then set off down the lane at an ungainly trot. Within a few minutes the shoes were hidden away under her mattress. When she got back, out of breath but exhilarated, there was as yet no sign of her mistress – no doubt she was still in the summerhouse, painting.

As Ella rang the bell, the summons for the midday meal, she was almost twitching with excitement. The mistress must have been up to no good, to hide her best indoor shoes in an old turnip sack. She had a good look at her to see if she could see any other suspicious signs, until Mistress said, 'For heaven's sake, what are you staring at? Go and fetch the butter.'

Alice took the risk that Wheeler, having made his enquiries, would go to market as usual and not return the same day. She would finish the painting today, then hide the lady's slipper somewhere much safer – a permanent hiding place. Once the flower had faded it would be much more difficult to identify.

As she emptied the jar of pink painting water and refilled it from the wooden butt, she puzzled over Richard Wheeler. He was certainly eccentric

38

– choosing to take his leisure up at the Hall with Dorothy Swainson and her trembling farmers. They all spoke in the same manner, addressing everyone with 'thee' as if time had flown by and left them stranded in a bygone age. Wheeler had said he would not let the matter of the orchid drop, and she could believe it; something about him was unbending, like forged iron.

A week ago when she had met him coming out of the apothecary's and he had told her about the flower, she had thought he must be mistaken.

'A lady's slipper? In your wood? Are you sure?'

'I thought it would interest thee, thou being so keen on nature study. Come and see for thyself.'

So she sent a boy to fetch Ella the maid to act as a chaperone. Then she put on her cloak and followed him to the woods, and there it was. Not half a mile from her own front door – the elusive orchid herbalists had thought never to see again. It was flowering out of season, probably because it was another cold wet summer, as if they had not had enough – with the winter so severe, and the failed harvest of last year. She examined the flower with shaking hands, barely able to suppress her excitement. She knew straight away that it was vulnerable and that she must have it. It might be the only one. She told Ella to wait by the kissing-gate. Ella looked surly but retreated up the path.

'Who else knows that it grows here?' she asked, in a low voice.

'I mentioned it to a few friends up at the Hall.'

'Was that wise, Mr Wheeler? It is rare and it could even be valuable.' She bit her lip and tried

39

not to show how disturbing she found the thought of others knowing about its whereabouts. She recalled the tulip craze of a few years before, and the fortunes that had changed hands over the more unusual varieties.

He laughed. 'Well, it is valuable to me. It's a delight. I take pleasure in its growing there. And thou art welcome in my woods to come and look at it at any time.'

'Oh no, Mr Wheeler,' she said, crouching over the orchid. 'Any rogue or vagabond might come upon it. It could be damaged. You must let me remove it, and forthwith, for safekeeping.' Seeing him unmoved, she became more coaxing. 'Come now, Mr Wheeler, we have a duty to make sure it is properly cared for and conserved.'

'I think nature is quite capable of taking care of her own, Mistress Ibbetson.'

She stood. 'With respect, Mr Wheeler, this species is most uncommon. As far as I am aware, this is the only plant in England.' She recognized that her tone was becoming indignant, and took a deep breath. 'I've heard tell it is also a medicinal plant. Herbalists and physicians will want to ensure it is available for future generations.'

'Well, it is safe enough here.' He puffed on his pipe. 'It is away from the byre, and it looks well enough to me.'

'I have some expertise in these matters. From my father, who was a keen plantsman. What if it should wither from disease – or the roots become waterlogged? It should be protected. It is too precious to risk in this way.'

'"What if" never served anybody well. Thou art

40

making speculation without cause. It is here now. I see no reason to interfere with it. It is safer in God's hands than in the hands of any herbalist.'

God's hands. Alice felt the familiar dull ache of grief. She still struggled with the cruelty of God's hand. 'But...' She opened her mouth but the words were stuck. She swallowed hard; something seemed to be clotting her throat.

He showed no sign he had seen her discomfort. His brown eyes regarded her steadily, his hands hung loosely at his sides.

'Let us leave it here where it chose to grow. It looks fine in its own natural setting.' He smiled. 'I hear thou art a painter. Perhaps thou wishest to sketch it before the flower fades?'

Alice kept her thoughts to herself. Only the slight quiver at the corner of her lips betrayed her emotion. Wheeler appeared to be oblivious to it.

'Yes,' she said. 'Thank you. I will return tomorrow, by your leave.'

She walked stiffly up the path.

'Come, Ella. We will return to the house.'

Was it her imagination, or had the girl been smirking?

'Yes, madam.' Ella's face returned to its usual dour expression.

When she revisited the wood the next day, Wheeler stubbornly resisted all her attempts to make him relinquish the orchid to her. Apparently he had heard rumour that a Widow Poulter, the cunning woman from Preston, had been seen in the village and was treating a boy for toothache. He suspected she would want to dig out the plant for her remedies and so he had forbidden anyone

41

to enter the wood. He was of the opinion that Widow Poulter, though perhaps not exactly a witch, moved in very undesirable circles.

Oh, it was such a beauty! She gauged it with her outstretched thumb, one eye half closed. Her thoughts returned to the task in hand, the drawing of the intricate twisting sepals. It felt good to have the orchid here in the light where she could use the lens and the calipers to check her accuracy.

She worried, though, that it might die when she tried to split the rootstock. Orchids were complex. Their seeds so small, they were difficult to capture or sow. They needed a fungus for them to germinate – a strange alliance between the light and shadow. This was her little secret, plant lore passed down to her from her father, and she was itching to make use of it. And no one, especially not a rough-hand Quaker like Wheeler, was going to prevent her.

Chapter 3

Richard Wheeler dropped the few remaining leeks into the sacks and stacked the empty baskets inside each other. He stood up and straightened his back, before bending to tie the ears of the bag. It had been a good day. The sun was out, the autumn wind had held off and the market had been busy. His stall was popular, for he would not haggle but had set a fixed price for each item.

Word was out that whoever came to his stall, whether they be master or stableboy, the price was always the same. Takings were up. He caught the eye of the old soap-seller on the next stall and gave him a broad smile.

'Trade has been brisk for thee,' he said, nodding at the half-empty table. 'We could do with a few more days like today.'

'Aye, it's picked up. Folk are coming out more.'

They fell silent, remembering. When Parliament ruled, the market had been a dull one, with the alehouses all but closed for gambling and all types of merriment quashed. Now there was uneasy peace, the king was back and business was improving. Times had been hard, particularly for the likes of the soap-seller – goods such as soap were purchased only if there was enough money left over after the family was clothed and fed.

'Well, I daresay I'll be here next week,' he said. He nodded to Richard and returned to sorting the little faggots of scented lavender and myrtle, the bottles of rosewater and the yellow blocks of sweet-smelling soap.

Richard watched for a moment as the old man bent stiffly over his panniers. The scent of flowers reminded him of the lady's slipper. He was disturbed by the recent turn of events. Alice Ibbetson had taken it, he was sure. Yet if he were to openly accuse her it could lead her to the pillory, and he baulked at being responsible for putting any woman, particularly a woman of breeding such as she, through such a cruel indignity. But she had lied brazenly to his face and a part of him wished her come-uppance; he felt like shaking her and telling her to come to her senses.

Surely she did not think him so lacking in intelligence that he could not see the nose in front of his face? It was possible – since he had changed his silks for homespun, people assumed he was an unlettered tomfool, and this riled him more than he cared to admit. He sighed, turning the conundrum over in his mind.

The market was getting quieter now; the bustle and heave had become dribs and drab, and the light would soon be gone. The sky was turning to ochre, and the manure in the pens began to steam in the chill autumn air. The drovers moved their livestock away down the road, calling out *hoy, hoy!*, and flicking their hazel switches over lazy rumps.

Returning his thoughts to the task, he rubbed his hands on his apron and prepared to lay the leftover gooseberries in nests of straw before loading the crates. He was glad to be going home. Standing at the stall made him restless. Almost everything was on the wagon except the fruit – he always left that until last in case it should bruise.

'Fetch me two of those bottles. My lady will need sweetening, since I am so long away.'

The voice was loud and irritable. Richard stiffened and instinctively reached for his sword, forgetting momentarily that it was no longer there. He knew that voice. Still staying low, he raised his head from the punnets of gooseberries to look at the speaker. He scanned him quickly, almost unconsciously, observing him from the feet up: broad-tongued shoes with silver filigree buckles, long legs in blue silken hose, fine woven breeches,

44

blue damask embroidered coat and matching waistcoat. Above it, a long, pale face with a thin mousy moustache. He was right, it was Geoffrey Fisk.

What was he doing here? He swallowed hard. A tightness squeezed his chest and throat. He looked down at his own thick grey worsted breeches and then back to Geoffrey's fine attire. He could almost feel the goosedown texture of the soft-coloured silks and brocade on his own skin, so well did he know them. He longed sometimes to feel the slip of silk stockings instead of the itch of the woollen ones he was now wearing. More than anything else, he felt naked without sword or musket. Keeping himself low, he reminded himself that giving up his sword and his fine things had been a free choice.

He watched Geoffrey covertly – his expression of bored impatience, the way he slapped his thigh with his riding crop, his face half turned away from the market stalls, looking over to where the horses were tethered. He saw him chivvy a lad and repeat the instruction.

The lad ran over, calling, 'Two bottles of rose-water, for the gentleman.'

The soap-maker placed two bottles in the lad's basket. 'Two farthings, if it please you.'

Geoffrey interrupted, imperiously. 'There will be no payment. We will take it as tithe.'

'With respect, sir, I have already paid my dues.'

Richard ducked well out of sight and watched as Geoffrey raised his eyebrows and slowly approached the stall himself. 'Are you so insolent that you will argue with me?' He leaned towards

45

the soap-seller, one gloved hand resting on the table. 'I think you have not paid quite enough. Pass me your purse.'

The soap-seller backed away, his eyes darting side to side, as if looking for a place to run. 'If I have offended, Sir Geoffrey, then beg pardon,' he said hastily, bowing low, his hat in his hand. 'There will be no charge for the rosewater.'

'I said, hand over your purse.' Geoffrey's voice echoed in the sudden quiet. He signalled to the lad with his gloved hand.

The old man did not move. He looked rooted to the spot. His eyes watered and his hands stayed glued to his hat, kneading the felt brim with his fingers.

A riding crop came down heavily on the trestle like a musket shot. It swept everything onto the cobbles in a great clatter so that people turned round to stare at the commotion. The bottles and phials shattered and liquid dribbled away in scented rivulets, exploding an odour of lavender and roses. Flowers fell in the dust to be crushed underfoot by the passing handcarts and wagons. The old man fumbled as he untied the purse from his belt.

Richard saw the gnarled fingers hand over a leather pouch fat with the day's takings. It was unfair. He knew he should challenge Geoffrey. But he also knew that should he confront him he would risk a penalty himself. And he had worked hard over months for his purse this day, in all weathers – harder physical work than he had ever done in his life before. He had no desire to cross Geoffrey again; that chapter of his life was closed now, no point in reopening old wounds.

The old soap-seller looked grey and tired. His back slumped as he felt in the dirt for the lumps of soap, anything he was able to salvage. Crestfallen, he filled his poke with the broken bottles and dusty bundles. Uneasy, Richard watched him load the mule. A sickness gnawed in his belly. I am a fine friend, he thought, a spineless maggot who lets an old man be bullied and robbed in broad daylight. Somehow the incident had diminished him, made him shrink inside himself.

Geoffrey climbed onto the mounting block and onto his horse, the twisted whalebone riding crop in his hand. He did not even glance at the old man as he jogged past. His two servants followed behind his big bay mare with the loaded packhorses. He jostled past the people and livestock, flicking the cattle with his crop if they got in his way.

'Stop.' Richard felt a voice come out of his throat as if it belonged to someone else. Somehow he had stepped into the path of Geoffrey's horse. The horse startled and let out a whinny, trying to side step.

'What do you think you're doing? Get out of my way.'

Richard stood his ground. He lifted his head and took a deep breath.

'Thou hast treated the soap merchant ill. It is not seemly to treat people in such a way.' There, it was out. He had said it plain.

'And who are you to tell me how a gentleman behaves?' Geoffrey's tone was one of mild annoyance. He looked Richard up and down; a suggestion of a well-disguised sneer on his lips, before it gave way to the shock of recognition. Geoffrey's horse, sensing something amiss, tossed its head.

Richard realized he would have to carry this through, now that he had begun. 'The man deserves proper payment for his goods.'

'You,' Geoffrey snapped, and Richard found himself addressed like a servant. 'Richard Wheeler. I see now who you are. Remove your hat when you address me.'

'I shall take off my hat only if thou removest thine.'

By now a curious crowd of tradesmen and stallholders had gathered round, anxious to be a part of whatever little drama was unfolding in the corner of the square. There were several short intakes of breath when Richard refused to take off his hat.

'Do you dare to insult me?' said Geoffrey. 'I said, remove your hat.'

'All men are equal. I defer to no one, and no one defers to me. Give the soap-seller fair payment.' It felt good to be doing something. To feel his character expand to fit the clothes. He repeated, 'When thou removest thy hat, then I shall remove mine.'

He heard a few murmurs of agreement from the crowd. They had seen so many changes of rule in the last few years that they were ready to be on whichever side was winning.

Geoffrey's cheeks grew blotchy and his lips tightened. Richard saw the knuckles stand out white against the reins and round the leather handle of the crop. Geoffrey raised his arm in a sudden movement.

The crop flashed through the air. Richard's hat was off and onto the ground before he had time to move. The crowd gasped as it rolled away under the wheels of a cart. The shock of it made Richard take a step back.

'That's better. Now, get out of my way.'

Richard swayed, and a trickle of blood trailed from his ear and onto his neck, but he carried on with new resolve as if nothing had happened.

'My hat may be gone, but my purpose is not. Give the man back his purse.'

More agreement from the crowd. The people pressed closer in, to see what would happen next. By now the two men were surrounded. Richard saw Geoffrey take in the growing number of people. During the exchange his servants, sensing trouble, had sidled away. Geoffrey was left alone, outnumbered by a hostile crowd, who had taken the side of the underdog.

He panicked and tried to kick his horse on through the throng, but the people closed around him like a wall, and his horse was skittish and would not obey. It clattered and skid on the slippery cobbles, eyes rolling white with fear.

In a fury, seeing he was trapped, Geoffrey lashed out at anyone within reach. There was a murmur, then a hubbub of outrage. Those at the back of the mob started to pick up animal droppings, handfuls of rotting vegetables and stones. Those nearest to him clawed and dragged at his legs trying to unseat him, and others grasped at the reins, restraining his horse.

The horse danced on the spot, tossing its head, its neck white with a lather of sweat, hooves churning. With one last vicious swipe of his crop, Geoffrey knocked over a woman who was clinging to the stirrup. He kicked his terrified horse into a gallop. A group of youths set off in pursuit until, outrun, they contented themselves with a rain of stones, which fell clattering like hail onto the cobbles.

Richard watched him go, still standing in the same spot as if he had been planted there. The world seemed to be moving very slowly around him, creaking back into place. Slowly he walked over to retrieve his hat. His head ached and his mouth felt dry as tinder. He looked around for his friend the soap merchant, and at first could not see him.

The marketplace was littered with debris. A mother comforted a frightened child in amongst the stones and vegetable peelings that had been thrown in the disturbance. The old man dabbed a linen cloth on the cheek of the woman who had been knocked aside. He looked up reproachfully as Richard approached.

'This is your doing.'

Richard looked at the cut on the woman's cheek.

'No,' he said quietly. 'That cut was not from my whip, though maybe I was the cause of his anger.' He sat down next to them and addressed his friend. 'I did not mean for this to happen. I only wanted to see justice done.'

'There will be more trouble from this, I warrant,' the old man said. 'We are marked out now as troublemakers. I could have afforded the purse. But I cannot afford Sir Geoffrey as an enemy.'

'They will single us out,' whispered the woman.

'He is like this with the sheriff.' She pressed her two index fingers together, side by side. Then she held the dampened cloth against her cheek and rocked as if to comfort herself.

'I am sorry for this. If I have caused thee hurt, then it was not intended. I wished only to see him pay his dues like the rest of us.' The woman withdrew the pad again for Richard to see the cut. 'Ah, it is not too deep. The bleeding seems to have stopped and, God willing, there will be no scar.'

The old man sighed. 'You're a strange one. I don't understand what made you do what you did, stand there with your hat on, brazen as you like—' a smile started to form at the corner of his lips – 'but his face was a picture.' He screwed up his mouth in disapproval and pulled a face like milk gone sour, his nose up in the air.

The expression was unmistakably Geoffrey's, and the woman tried and failed to suppress a giggle. The release of tension was infectious, and before long all three were consumed by mirth. The cut cheek was forgotten and they laughed till their sides ached, but their hilarity masked a deep disquiet; Richard knew the incident would not be easily forgotten. And if he knew Geoffrey, he would not brook this affront to his dignity; it was certain he would want to exact payment in kind for his loss of self-esteem. Richard hoped their paths would not cross again. They were strewn with enough blood.

Chapter 4

It was almost dark by the time Geoffrey arrived home, dishevelled and angry. After riding up the long driveway to his estate, he had the lads turn out the new horse to grass straightaway. He would never ride the brute again. As he returned from the stableyard the household were flanking the steps between the great stone urns to greet him after his long voyage, but he was in no mood to stop and exchange pleasantries. He strode up the curved flight of stone steps, handed his gloves and crop to the manservant and took himself straight to his chambers. A stiff drink would both steady his nerves and ease the heat and irritation that crawled on the inside of his clothes. Riding was more and more painful, but he was reluctant to take the coach like an old man yet. Not only that, but the voyage from the Americas had been rough; they had been nine weeks at sea, and he was still trying to find his land legs.

He summoned Patterson, had him light the candles, then sent him to make a tepid bath, a luxury he had not enjoyed during his time abroad. At the side table, he poured himself a large glass of Madeira. He settled down in the cushioned chair by the window, rubbed his forehead with his fingers and ran the day's events through his mind.

How disconcerting to come across Richard Wheeler in those circumstances – no topcoat, like a farmhand, and his hair straggling unkempt over his collar. Last time he had seen him he had been in the colours of the Puritan army, surrounded by a fawning rabble, and he had never expected to see him again.

He had been caught off guard. It seemed Richard had become even more dangerously unhinged than before. Even when they had been friends, something about him had always made Geoffrey feel a little inferior, like a stone that rankles in your shoe. He pushed the thought of him away; the memory of him made him want to retch. A few moments later his manservant reappeared.

'What is it, Patterson?'

'Your wife awaits you in the drawing room, sir.'

'Tell her I will be along presently.' Was the stupid woman unable to wait? He had barely set foot in the house and already she was demanding his attention. Geoffrey sighed and circled his fingers on his temples. Emilia caused him nothing but irritation. Over the years it had become insufferable – to set eyes on her filled him with an urge to strike her silly face, to see the heat of blood rise to her waxen powdered cheeks. She was so dull, and uncomely, and insipid. Like a child, she was only interested in the gifts he had brought her, and unable to participate in intelligent discourse.

She had never, even through the troubles, asked him anything about the reason for the uprisings, even with the sound of musket-fire echoing down the chimney and Cromwell nearly camped on their back doorstep. She paid no attention to his scientific pursuits, except to make veiled complaints about the expense of the equipment. Nor had she shown the slightest concern for his ships or land in the Low Countries or New England, or his idea for developing the quay at Lancaster. Not that he expected her to know anything about such things – after all, she was a woman – but he did expect her to show some regard for his affairs to denote her affection.

When he had married her she was young, and passably pretty, and he had been attracted by her larger than average dowry and her father's lucrative mines and connections in the world of finance. He had hoped for companionship and even affection. In this he had been sadly disappointed. Despite the fact that he no longer found Emilia remotely attractive, it still irked him that he had not developed a particularly intimate relationship with his wife. Things had begun to slide downhill almost from the beginning. His affliction, which was an embarrassment, had seen to that. He had always been reluctant to show his scaling skin in the bedroom.

He recalled with distaste the hurried fumblings in the pitch black of the stuffy bedchamber, and Emilia's scrabbling fingers, which had only served to make things worse. Once a few months of marriage had passed and Emilia was with child, he had begun to seek the company of other women as soon as he was in town. He could pay for the gentle touch he needed, and they would not be finicky about his appearance, as long as his purse was ample. He downed the Madeira in one, then poured another amber stream from the decanter and emptied it down his throat before reluctantly making for the drawing room.

Emilia was standing before the broad stone fireplace, wearing the latest fallback-styled gown from France – not that it made her any more attractive. Geoffrey looked at her heavily powdered complexion and wispy blonde hair with distaste.

'It is good to have you home, husband, we have been waiting all day,' she said coquettishly.

He regarded his wife's jutting collarbones, goosepimpled shoulders and flat stomacher. His thoughts momentarily strayed to the ample bosom of his last fancy, but he pulled himself up short, it would do him no good to think of her. His breeches chafed and, although it was a fine cambric, his shirt itched.

'I would have been here sooner, but for an unfortunate incident in the market place, when I stopped to buy you some rose-water.'

'That is sweet of you.' She rushed over to him in a rustle of dun-coloured taffeta and lace. 'Where is it? Fetch it for me, Lizzie.'

He signalled to the maidservant who proffered the two bottles tied with silk ribbons. She took up the bottles but soon lost interest, as if they were of no account, and waved the servant away. Geoffrey recalled the trouble it had cost him to procure them, of his narrow escape from the baying crowd. At that moment he felt a surge of hatred for Emilia. But he buried it. He was a master of self-control. Besides, he was used to hiding things. He would not be bringing her any more trinkets from his voyages.

She moved to take him by the elbow. He discreetly shook her off.

'What else did you purchase whilst you were away?'

He answered his wife with a fixed expression. 'Patterson has left all the gifts in your dressing room.'

'Then I shall go there directly.' She gave him another teasing look. 'Is it some goldpoint lace? Or more of those marchpane delicacies? Or something else?'

She held up her cold dry cheek to be kissed. Seeing that the servants were watching, Geoffrey brushed his lips against it with the barest touch. Her face lit up and she tapped him playfully on the arm with her fan. He flinched inwardly. She should know by now that her feigned coyness stuck in his craw. He watched her rustle away, but then she paused by the double doors, patting her fan on her hand.

'I forgot to tell you, the Rawlinsons are coming for supper. Robert wants to talk to you expressly about some difficulties he is having on his estate.'

'Then you will be supping with them alone. I am not in mind to deal with his petty squabbles. I have just spent more than a month attempting to keep the peace on my estates in New England. I am not going to spend my evenings at home doing the same.'

'But, Geoffrey,' she wheedled, 'they know you are at home. There's talk of another insurrection, and I am afraid.' Her lower lip quivered. 'I fear that the king may call Stephen to arms.'

Geoffrey sighed. This was a calculated move on Emilia's part to get her own way; she knew perfectly well that mention of their son would ensure his attention. He had wanted more sons, but could not bring himself to go near his wife again. Nevertheless, an insurrection did sound serious. Rawlinson owned vast swathes of the uplands and many local farms, and besides that he was the county Justice of the Peace. So if anyone knew what was happening in the county, it was Rawlinson.

Geoffrey let go of the idea of a soothing bath, a few more drinks and an early night between cool sheets.

'Very well. What time are they coming?'

'The card said seven o'clock.'

'But that is within the hour!'

'Do not fret. Lizzie will bring them in here for some sweetmeats, and I will send Patterson up to tell you when supper is served.' Seeming to sense his increased annoyance, she gave him a curt little nod and retreated to her private chambers.

Supper was the usual affair. Geoffrey was glad to be carving at his own table again. The food in New England was plentiful but not to his taste – too many green vegetables that gave him wind. He had longed for a good piece of roast beef or pheasant, and proper ale brewed the English way.

Emilia had found the gifts and was enthusing to Jane Rawlinson about the silver snuff boxes and a pair of fine lace gloves that Geoffrey had brought back from the port of London, where they had made a brief trade stop.

Jane Rawlinson was a stout, matronly woman who had no interest in fripperies such as lace gloves and snuff boxes. She was sitting upright on the mahogany dining chair with the napkin set squarely on her lap. Geoffrey saw her cast her eyes around the room as if searching for something to disapprove of. But the room was elegantly furnished, a fire blazed in the carved stone hearth and candle sconces bearing droplets of glass cast a flickering glow.

Geoffrey had hung the recent paintings of himself – one on horseback, and the other standing outside the house with his brindled greyhounds – either side of the fireplace. Jane tried not to look impressed, but he caught her leaning towards them for a closer look. The dining table was laid out with a good amount of clean white linen, silver cutlery and pewter trenchers. Unable to find fault with her surroundings, she turned to her hostess and began to ask questions. She asked how Emilia ran her household, how many gardeners, cooks, handymen and so forth Emilia employed, and what all their exact duties might be. Apparently Jane's own household was run with precision and an authoritarian hand.

Of course, Emilia soon found herself floundering, probably because she was quite unable to confess to Jane Rawlinson that she had not the faintest notion what her servants did. Geoffrey knew that while he was away the hired hands were often left to their own devices, whilst Emilia tinkled the spinet and, now that it was permitted again, planned her 'little entertainments'. Besides, he suspected that his wife was actually a touch afraid of her housekeeper. And this was a fact she certainly would not reveal to Jane Rawlinson. Geoffrey watched his wife twirl her thin blonde hair and toy with the cutlery, whilst Jane told her how she should keep her servants on their toes. He let her stew in it. It might make her a bit more useful.

He returned his attention to Robert, who was slurping his way through his second tankard of ale. Robert continued to talk.

'So you see, Geoffrey, I am determined to quash these troublemakers before they get out of hand.' He bit off a large chunk of beef and chewed, wiping his dripping mouth on his napkin. 'There has been a broil in the church, with a woman getting up and calling the curate an infidel. A woman!'

The two ladies looked up.

'She raised a fine old commotion. Apparently she said there was no such thing as the Devil except in the hearts of those who abuse the poor.' He nodded round the table to make sure everyone was listening. 'She said the church was taking grain from their mouths. Some good folk stood up to defend the church but they were set upon by her supporters and flung down. Then they carried the curate out saying they had no need of him, and threw him into the ditch.'

'When did this happen?' said Geoffrey.

'On Sunday last, but I have arrested the woman.'

'Was she one of those women from Lingfell Hall? One of Fox's followers?' asked Emilia.

'Yes. Felicia Darby. She claims she was not intending to create a disturbance, merely to point people to God.' He snorted. 'Since then I have had any number of them knock on my door and

59

demand her release. I told them all the same thing – that she was inciting a riot and would be detained until further notice.'

Jane leaned forward in her seat. 'It seems to me she was not only courting trouble, but wedding it.' She made a clacking sound through her teeth. 'To dare to imply that the curate be a devil – and in a church. It is hardly going to convince the congregation of one's moral rectitude.' She leaned towards Emilia and let out a laugh like a horse. Emilia sat back in her chair and raised her napkin to her mouth.

'One of those that came to my door was that man who recently took the house by Helk's Wood,' said Robert. 'I believe you know him, Geoffrey. Didn't he used to be one of your acquaintances? And the gossip in my stableyard is that he threw rotting mangels at you in the marketplace today.' Robert gave Geoffrey a grin and helped himself to more bread.

Geoffrey was annoyed to think that news of the incident in the marketplace had travelled so fast. The ladies were agog. Jane put down her knife and gave her husband her full attention.

'Mangels?' Jane looked incredulous.

'No, not mangels, I mean to say, he didn't throw anything,' said Geoffrey, 'that's to say ... somebody did, but it wasn't Richard Wheeler.'

Robert's mouth twitched in amusement and Geoffrey wished he could push his fork into the simpering face.

'What is this?' Emilia's high voice brought all attention to her. 'Why did you not mention it before?'

'I did mention it,' Geoffrey said. He glared at her. 'Before dinner. It appears, as usual, you were not listening.'

'Let us retire, Jane. I am sure we do not want to listen to such dull men's business.'

They scraped their chairs back and stood. Emilia dropped her napkin deliberately onto her half-empty plate, where it sank into the gravy. Then she picked up her skirts and flounced out. Jane raised her eyebrows and flashed Robert a look that clearly said such disagreements would never happen in their household, then she followed Emilia and shut the double doors behind her with a click.

Geoffrey had hoped the embarrassing afternoon would soon be forgotten and not become the subject of servants' gossip. But no, it seemed he was already a laughing stock at his own table. It was humiliating. Added to that, Emilia had then ruined a perfectly convivial evening. His earlier anger hardened into stony resolve.

'Wheeler's behaviour is tantamount to treason,' he said. 'He refused to do me that honour, and as I am the king's representative in these parts, it could be regarded as an insult to the king. Besides which, he was telling people to withhold their taxes.'

'We must be careful,' said Robert, 'circumspect.' He talked as he chewed. 'If we accuse him openly of treason then it will stir up more dissent. We would end up with another rebellion on our hands. We should re-call the county committee to discuss strategies for how best to deal with them.'

'But the county committee has not met in years.

Cromwell's damn fool parliament disbanded all our local committees.'

'Then we will need to reform. The more muscle we have behind us, the easier it will be to stamp out the dissenters.'

He paused to shovel a pile of mashed turnip into his mouth, and leaned over to scoop more from Jane's half-finished plate. 'There is a whole nest of them up at the Hall. I have no idea what possessed Dorothy Swainson to open her house to these ranters and ravers. It would never have happened in the days of the old king,' he said.

'How will we ever have any sort of stability if we let these pockets of civil disorder continue? You know what they say – one bad apple could brown them all,' Geoffrey said. 'No, these dissenters need to be put back in their place. Cromwell gave them too much free rein to get above themselves. There was no discipline in his army. Did you hear there was looting over at Kendall's house?'

Robert shook his head.

'And although the king is back, our good men have been routed; their lands cut up and dispersed. It's a complete scandal.' Geoffrey paced the room, tankard in hand. 'Have we even enough loyal men left for a new committee?'

'You will join us yourself?'

Geoffrey nodded his assent.

'Then we have Fairfax, Kendall and Hetherington. They are all staunch royalists and churchgoers and can be relied upon.' Robert leaned back in his chair and stretched his stomach, clasping his fingers over his barrel-like paunch.

'What about Lord Esham?' asked Geoffrey. 'I

know he is a good day's ride from here, but we need six.'

'I am not sure he is trustworthy. I heard he had cast his lot in with the Puritans – that leather-seller Barebones and his bunch of uncouth ruffians. But if there is no one else then he will have to suffice. We can carry his vote if necessary.'

'Well, times have changed. We must do what we can with who we have. With a properly formed committee we might be able to detain Wheeler's rabble through the magistrate, and make sure the charges stick.' An image of Richard Wheeler's ridiculous brown hat came back to him. 'But tell me this, have we the power to confiscate Wheeler's land should we decide tithes are due?'

Robert shook his head, pressing his lips together. 'Not without good reason. I'm not sure we could prove without a doubt that he has withheld his dues. But the committee can be, how shall I put it, enthusiastic, about ensuring tithes are paid.' He gave Geoffrey a smile. 'But you say he is hand in glove with Lady Swainson?' Robert rubbed his cheek, considering, before saying, 'Dorothy Swainson is not without in-fluence. She is from one of the oldest families in Westmorland, and has her staunch supporters. It is one thing to hold one of them a few days – it would be quite another to confiscate their land or charge them with treason.'

'I see what you mean,' Geoffrey said. 'Let us meet as soon as is convenient then. The sooner we quash this revolt and things return to the way they were, the better.'

Geoffrey was glad when he could summon the Rawlinsons' carriage and was free to retire to his chambers. The long-awaited bath was ready for him, and he was glad to peel off his uncomfortable stiff breeches and long shirt. Patterson had left two jugs of hot water on the tallboy and a brown parcel marked with a postal seal from Preston. He had also discreetly put out a decanter of port and a glass on a silver tray. Often Patterson seemed to know exactly what Geoffrey required even before he asked for it. Patterson's family had served the Fisks for four generations, despite their changing fortunes. Geoffrey gratefully poured himself a large measure of port into the glass and drank. Then he turned to the parcel with curiosity.

He untied the jute string and opened out the paper. It contained a deal-wood box, with a small flat porcelain jar packaged in straw, and a note accompanying it. This was written in an unsteady round hand and gave a barely intelligible list of ingredients, along with instructions to apply the tincture every day. He remembered that he had sent for this from a herbalist and so-called cunning woman he had heard of from the Master Mariner before leaving on his voyage, a Widow Poulter. A potion she provided had cured the Master's gout, and immediately Geoffrey sent word to her from the dockside, explaining his skin condition and asking if she knew of anything that might ease it. She must have sent the salve by the king's post for it to have arrived so quickly.

He looked at the note again – he must look up the ingredients in *Gargrave's Herbal*. She asked for a payment of a half-shilling, and that he should have one of his servants deliver the coinage by hand. Evidently she did not wish to chance the post with such a large sum.

He glanced down at his body. It had been the same since childhood, red and itching, with inflamed patches of skin he always wanted to scratch. Fortunately his face and neck were usually clear, but the backs of his hands were often pocked with scabs the size of a penny. When these patches appeared he had become adept at hiding them under gloves. He never took off his shirt, for his chest was scarred and scaly like reptile skin, and he was fortunate in that the fashion was for high necks and lace cravats.

He looked down at himself with loathing, and lowered his long limbs into the wooden hipbath. The water was silky against his skin. He exhaled audibly and sank into the warm water. He felt comfortable for the first time in two months.

With care, he poured more hot water from the jug. The steam filled his nostrils and his limbs seemed to melt into the water. His mind drifted back to a time when he was about three years old. He was lying in a wooden cot, whimpering for his mother. He could see the turned wooden rails magnified on the walls into thick black hourglasses by the light from the window. His skin was red and sore but he couldn't resist the urge to scratch. He scratched until his nails were thick with blood.

His mother had wept at the sight and talked to him in her soothing voice. He heard again the noise of her wringing out a cloth. He saw in his mind's eye her white hands on the muslin, cold as a fall of snow. Afterwards she had given him little cotton gloves to stop him from wounding himself, and when he was too fretful to sleep she had put Madeira in his milksops and stroked his burning forehead with her smooth fingers.

Only his mother had understood exactly how much pain the condition gave him. When he was a child she had cared for his scaly body herself, despite his father's insistence she hire a wet nurse, for his father had been wary of his sickly son. His mother knew all too well that Geoffrey would be taunted, that they would laugh at him. People didn't understand, they would shun him and make his life wretched if they knew, and she was prepared to trust no one else with her only son. Over his childhood years she had impressed upon him the need to keep his skin hidden and protected, and she had tried many unguents, poultices and potions. All to no avail.

It was this that had led to his interest in herbs and plants, and lately in science. He was half hoping that one day he would find a salve or a secret, a pill or a potion that would heal his condition. In the meantime, he busied himself with his trade and scientific interests, for the more occupied he was, the less the disease bothered him.

He loved his study, the carved oak panelling, the paraphernalia of stone mortars, iron pestles, distilling glasses and crucibles. On his desk, he cared not that his confusion of papers was stained with powdered mineral matter, sediment from dripping sieves and numerous tell-tale wine-glass rings. Alcohol in large quantities had been the only thing so far to alleviate the torture of the continual itching. Over the years he thought he had resigned himself to the condition, but there were some days when he was driven mad on all sides.

He poured more warm water from the jug and gently soaped himself all over. After his bath, he opened the little jar and applied some of the tincture. It was pale green and slimy, and smelt of seaweed. The balm did feel remarkably soothing. Perhaps this cunning woman really was as knowledgeable as the master said. A small hope budded, a momentary lightness of heart, before it withered under his scrutiny. He would wait until he saw an improvement before sending money. There were too many charlatans about, and he had supped his fill of quacks and their promises.

As soon as he had sorted out the estate orders, he would call on Mistress Ibbetson. There had been a dispatch from her to say she had found a rare wild flower – an orchid. She would have the orchid waiting for him. It was rare but, he suspected, not very showy. He weighed up the potential profits in his mind. She had said it was possible to cross-breed orchids, the way farmers cross-bred cattle. In that case she would be able to cross it with the flame-red orchid he had bought from the Portuguese, and then he would have a unique and showy plant suitable for temperate conditions. The Portuguese orchid was magnificent; landowners would pay handsomely – it would be a sensation.

He needed the botanical skills of Mistress Ibbetson. She was an excellent gardener, he knew, but it would be inconvenient dealing with a woman in business. And it would have to be soon; flowers don't last forever. She must be persuaded somehow to show him the breeding technique, then he would have no need of her.

Chapter 5

Alice did not often get to Kendal town, to her regret. Hiring a hackney was expensive, and could only be done once in a while. But today she had a number of errands to run that could not be trusted to anyone else. She had Thomas's letters to deliver to the post and was to collect some other documents from the notary. It was chilly, and she was wearing a closed bonnet and a black woollen cape, but she was anxious not to be away from her work or the lady's slipper for too long, so she made haste down the narrow streets, clutching the bundle of letters in her cold hands.

The town was thronging. Today was the meat market, and there were many horses and carriages from neighbouring villages, anxious to secure salt beef and bacon for the coming winter. She side-stepped a man carrying a shoulder of mutton, and headed down the cobbled hill towards the notary's office.

On the counter in front of the ironmonger's board, a bright copper kettle caught her eye and she paused to look at it, idly contemplating the other items – flat irons, crimpers, goffers, and tongs, scoops and ladles. She picked up a pretty doorknocker embossed with a rose and held it up into the light to see the pattern. As she did so, she caught sight of a familiar figure in a brown felt hat, just rounding the corner. He was striding purposefully up the hill, his head bent down into the wind, a bulging canvas bag slung over his shoulder.

She bolted inside the shop, the doorknocker still in her hand, and turned her back to the door, feigning interest in the hanging scuttles, brushes and pokers. The shopkeeper followed her inside.

'Yes, mistress?'

She kept one eye fixed on the road outside as she held out the doorknocker and asked, 'Have you more of these?'

'More?' He looked at her as if he did not understand.

Of course, people usually only needed one doorknocker. She saw Wheeler's tall figure flash past the open awning.

'Well, yes, I do have more, mistress. How many would you like?'

Distracted, she said, 'No thank you. Nothing at all. Good day.' And she put the doorknocker down on the table, leaving the shopkeeper staring down at it, nonplussed.

Scanning left and right as she came out of the dingy interior of the shop, she saw Wheeler's broad back wending uphill between the other pedestrians. She crossed the road, for she did not want a battle of wits with him again if she could avoid it, and made her way quickly to where the overhanging buildings provided a shadow. She set off walking in the opposite direction.

She stopped briefly at the hosier's, where she

69

had ordered some new stockings in knitted silk. The weave was very fine, practically transparent. She put her hand inside one of them and admired the white silk look of her skin through the fabric, and the almost invisible seam with its tiny fairy-like stitches. They were costly, but Thomas had never been close-fisted and she always had tokens in her purse, despite hints from acquaintances that his money-lending business was teetering.

She had a few minutes' very pleasant conversation with the hosier, who told her about Geoffrey's wife, Emilia, and her latest order for long hose with tiny beads sewn up the back, and lace garters. Naturally these would be unsuitable for a woman in mourning, such as herself, but she enjoyed hearing about them before she swung out of the door, the thin wrapped parcel under her arm. She was still smiling as she launched herself up the street and straight into the solid chest of Richard Wheeler.

Agitated, she stepped back.

'Mistress Ibbetson, I beg pardon.'

'Mr Wheeler.' She assessed the width of the path to see if she could make her excuses and leave, but he was blocking her way. She was sure it was deliberate. Curse the man.

'Thou art not at thy easel today, then?'

'No. No, I had some business in town.' She lifted the letters into his view.

He looked casually away, tapping his boot on the ground. 'The rare orchid that was taken from my wood. There has still been no word of it.' He returned his gaze to her face, which by now had grown hot under her bonnet. 'But if it were to be replaced, returned to its natural growing place, then I assure thee, that would be the end of the matter.'

She steeled herself. 'I have said before, I know nothing of it. Excuse me.'

'Besides, it has a sentimental value to me. I desire its return most fervently.'

'Then I sincerely hope you will find it, but I say again, it has nothing to do with me.'

Again she made to pass him, but he would not let her by. His face was stormy now, his eyebrows lowered. His voice came out loud and harsh. One of his hands was balled into a fist. He looked as though he might grab hold of her. Astonished, she backed away.

'Mistress Ibbetson. I do not like to be taken for a fool. I tell the truth and I would seek the same courtesy from thee. What wouldst thou have me do? Shake thee? Send for the constable?'

'You must do as you think fit.' She turned on her heel and left him standing in the street behind her. She did not look back, just hied away as fast as she could. When she had put a good distance between them, she stopped to catch her breath, leaning against the warm stone wall of the bakehouse.

She was appalled at herself. She knew she had somehow crossed a line, that there would be no going back now. Her heart throbbed at her throat. Patently, there could be no more polite conversations with him. What had got into her? Partly she knew it was stubbornness. But he got under her skin somehow, with his refusal to see her point of view. And to think she had thought him pleasant, a man with a kind heart.

71

A few months ago she had stood behind him in a queue at the miller's when a lad had come in for a bushel of corn. The miller had upped the price by a third for the lad from the price it had been for Kendall's steward, and Wheeler had stepped forward.

'Everything has a fair price,' she overheard him say. 'And if it is a fair enough price for the steward, then it is a fair enough price for the lad.'

It had made her smile, the lad's face open-mouthed with glee at his 'fair price' bushel of corn as he ran out of the shop, and she had caught Wheeler's eye. He had returned a broad grin. Although not acquainted, this shared incident had meant they used to nod to each other or exchange greetings if they crossed paths. But all that was finished now. She would have to be more vigilant in the future to keep out of his bounds – and she certainly had no intention of following his suggestion that she should covertly return the lady's slipper. Her first loyalty must be to securing the future of the orchid.

She rushed through her errands in a state of agitation, anxious to take her carriage home and stand guard over the lady's slipper. He had said it had some sentimental value for him. She wondered what this could be – after all, a few weeks ago he did not even know of its existence. It was surely a ploy to persuade her to give it up, and that, she had sworn not to do. She worried he might ride home before her and find it hidden in the summerhouse. He would not know how to tend it, did not understand about its fragility, its rarity. But she had sent word to Geoffrey about it; he shared her love of plants and would understand the exciting nature of her discovery. Geoffrey was full of enthusiasm for collecting and for science, but not very well versed in plant lore. He had always deferred to her superior knowledge – he at least understood how much her father's skill meant to her.

Chapter 6

The room was already full when Richard arrived. About twenty people, men and women, all dressed in muted colours, greys, browns, dull tweeds. They were sitting or standing in small groups in the panelled room that had once been a library but was now furnished simply with benches set in a circle. A chandelier was suspended over a central table, casting light onto a Bible, a rolled parchment and inkstand with quill. There was a faint smell of beeswax and lavender-oil polish. Richard breathed in the familiar aroma.

'Ah, Richard!' Dorothy Swainson approached him with a smile. 'It's good to see thee.' She talked as she led him over to two other men, a farmer in rough tweed breeches and a leather waistcoat, and Isaac Fuller, the town clerk. 'We were just talking about Felicia.'

'Is she still being held?' Richard asked.

'Aye, she is,' the farmer said. 'We've tried to plead for them to let her go, but the magistrate is determined to hold her until the quarter session

– and that's another three weeks away.'

'It does not bear thinking about,' Dorothy said. 'She's to be charged with inciting a riot, and anyone less likely I cannot imagine.' Isaac nodded in agreement.

'What happened?'

'I was there, and it was not Felicia, but some of the congregation that got carried away.' The clerk shook his head. 'The curate was preaching that the Devil is amongst us. The same old sermon – you know the one – that the Devil comes in many guises and lurks inside the most innocent exterior. And that we should all look out for him.' He raised his eyes to the invisible heavens. 'He was stirring up the crowd – setting up the old atmosphere of fear and mistrust.'

'Was that what made Felicia angry?' Richard looked to Dorothy.

'Not exactly. The shipping tax has already been levied this week, and the grain tax. The curate was after the salt tax,' Dorothy said. 'Felicia thinks these taxes on the working people are unjust. She stood up and calmly said that the only devil as far as she could see was in the hearts of those who would take money from people who could ill afford it.'

Richard nodded his head vigorously, to show his allegiance with Felicia's stand.

'Anyway, once she had pleaded her case, other rowdier members of the congregation got up too and started shouting her down, and some more people got up to support Felicia, and then the youths started calling the curate names, and you know what happened next.'

'Was no one else arrested?' asked the farmer.

'There was all sorts of confusion. Someone rode for Constable Woolley and his men, and they arrived in a great huff to arrest the troublemakers. When I spoke with her afterwards Felicia said that Lord Kendall, who was sitting in the reserved stalls at the front, apparently testified that it was all her doing. He has always been ready to condemn us – he thinks women have no place in religious ministry.'

She turned to Richard. 'What must it be like for her in that cold damp cell? We are sending people every day to petition the magistrate, and to take her food and blankets and anything else we can think of that might make her comfortable.'

She paused a moment to look around the room at the assembled people, and then, brushing down her skirts, said, 'It looks as if we are all gathered.' She clapped her hands and addressed everyone warmly. 'Friends, welcome to the Hall. If you would like to prepare yourselves, we will start this evening's meeting.'

Despite the evening chill, some people went to hang their coats on the hooks next to the door before filing into the two rows of oak benches. There was never a fire lit here, lest the warmth should set folk sleeping. There was a rustling of cloth against smooth wood, then boots scuffing the floorboards, as everyone sat down, followed by the usual few coughs and sighs as everyone settled in their places. The candle flames swayed in the movement of the air, then steadied, casting long shadows under their feet.

Richard glanced at Dorothy. Her broad forehead

was relaxed, her lips slightly parted. Her hair, once chestnut, but now greying at the temples, was tucked under a plain linen coif. In her lap her hands lay unmoving on her dark grey skirt, one palm resting on the other. He sat upright and still, glancing around the room, taking in the open faces and lowered eyes. The moon was just visible floating like a half-pearl outside the long casement window. In the dim light the silence deepened until it was broken only by the ebb and flow of breath. Richard felt an excitement as a fullness entered the room. A strange sense of potency. He forced his body to be still, waiting for the inner voice to move him, listening to the subtle sound in his ears, a nearly inaudible hum behind his breath.

There was a slight noise to his left and Dorothy stood. Her cheeks were flushed as she spoke, her hands animated. 'I feel moved to say to you that perhaps what has happened to our friend Felicia could contain a greater message. That maybe we should seek to change ourselves first, before looking to change others. That we should look deep within at our own shortcomings, and in seeing them allow the Spirit to work in us.'

There were nods and expressions of agreement around the room. No one spoke. They sat silently considering Dorothy's words and letting their meaning sink in. Often it was like this, that only one, or maybe two people felt moved to speak, and then only a few short words. Richard mulled over his own shortcomings. He wondered if he had been too hasty calling so early at Alice Ibbetson's house yesterday, and practically accusing her of stealing the orchid from his wood.

76

He had been fired up by indignation, and should have waited until a more respectable hour. It had been awkward, and may have antagonized her into her stubborn behaviour in town today. But he was quite sure she had taken the flower – he had seen pink paint water in the jar and felt sure she must have been painting the orchid when he called, not that other, most uninspiring green plant. He had been of a mind to search her house there and then. But that would have been tantamount to saying she had stolen it, and her husband was already bristling at his early intrusion, and he looked like a man who did not like surprises of any sort. He knew Mistress Ibbetson was supposed to be an authority on flowers, but it riled him to be treated as an idiot. When he had bumped into her today on Highgate she had been almost arrogant. He cast his mind back further to the empty hole, and the coppers; he frowned, they were obviously intended as an insult.

Someone had been trespassing in his wood last night, despite the fact that Isaac had helped him keep watch on the orchid. There was talk in the village that Old Margaret, the cunning woman, was about, and asking after it. She would be interested in its use for medicine, and he certainly did not want to be party to any sort of witchcraft or sorcery. Dorothy would never forgive him. He was determined to make sure Alice Ibbetson returned the flower to its rightful place, and that it stayed out of Widow Poulter's hands. It was his duty before God to restore the orchid and deal fairly with the person who had stolen it, and he would do this to the best of his ability. After all, he had fought for the common man to have his own patch of land, to be able to keep his roots, not to be pushed from place to place on some wealthier man's whim.

Not a day went by when he did not remember the men who had died fighting for a piece of this black soil that lodged in his fingernails each day as he dug his vegetable plot. This rare orchid, with its blood red petals, sprung from that same earth, also deserved to stay where it belonged. No good comes of it, if you interfere with the natural order. He sincerely hoped Alice would return it, as he had suggested.

His thoughts slid back to Alice as if on skates. Her hands had been trembling when he visited her, and he knew she was hiding something. He had seen it in her eyes. He had quite liked the feeling of seeing her flustered. It made her more attractive, more feminine. Was he imagining it, or had she looked a little in disarray? Little tendrils of her copper hair had escaped from her cap. She had blushed scarlet when he said he liked her paintings, and it was becoming to her to have a little colour in her cheeks. When he had seen her before, she always looked so pale and sad. And she had very beautiful hands. He went over the image of her hands smoothing her apron in his mind and a slight sweat broke out on his forehead, the room seemed to have grown warm. He imagined Alice's hands painting the waxy petals of the orchid. Between his legs, his breeches began to stiffen and bulge.

Suddenly he realized he had been caught up in a train of his own thoughts and he dragged his mind back to his place before God, and the silence in the room. Dorothy was right. There was a battle to be fought, and it was with his own mind. He fought to gain control of himself. He gathered his thoughts, and returned his mind to the company of the good people around him.

After a time he managed to settle back into the companionable quiet. When about an hour had passed and the candles had burnt low, Dorothy leaned over to the person next to her and shook hands. This little ritual was repeated round the room with people reaching out to each other to smile and clasp each other's hands.

Isaac Fuller, the clerk Richard had been talking to earlier, stood up by the table in the centre. 'I have one or two items of business for us to attend to, Friends.' He looked genially round the room. The people craned forward to listen. Richard shuffled. He hoped the business would not be too long.

'Firstly, this petition, which is going to the king.' He held up a piece of parchment.

'Many other groups, Friends like ourselves, have already signed it, and it will go forth from our meeting to other groups. It is our testimony against strife and war. We have all seen to our cost what war between people brings. The paper here is for you all to bear witness to this with your signatures. Those who can't write may make a mark and I will scribe his name alongside.'

He held up the quill and beckoned. 'Make sure thou canst stand by thy word. It will be no shame on thee if thou art unable to sign. But I hope that most of us will.'

Already there were men and women standing in the queue. At the mention of the war Richard's thoughts lurched back to his command in the Roundhead Army. He had a sense of drowning, as if the pictures were filling his lungs, choking him. Fragmented images of galloping horses and mutilated men lying in pools of their own blood swelled in his mind, but strangely distant, as if he was seeing them whilst floating under water. He glimpsed again a white ringlet of hair still attached to its bloodied roots, and saw before him a soldier's wild laughing mouth, the strings of saliva between his teeth – broken pictures that made his heart pound and his body turn cold. He saw Geoffrey's eyes, full of horror and disgust, and he saw himself, as if from above, turning away in shame. Richard remembered, and shakily lurched to his feet. One by one they went to the table and signed. When it was his turn, Richard picked up the quill and read the words on the parchment.

'We, the Society of Friends of Netherbarrow, do hereby testify that we are against all war and strife. We declare that we will not lend our support to any armed force, and that we will not take up arms or weapons against another for any cause whatsoever. We will seek to bring peace and truth to our dealings with others. We seek that all people might be brought into love and unity with God and with each other. On this Day of our Lord the 3rd September 1660. We state that our word is our truth, with the help of God. Amen.'

He dipped the nib in the stoneware inkpot and rested it a moment on the edge of the pot to drain the excess ink. He took a moment to bring his attention to the act of signing. Resting his left hand on the parchment to hold it flat, he added his name carefully and deliberately. The nib made a scraping sound as he formed the curled capitals 'R' and 'W' of his name.

As he stood up he moved a little too quickly and his sleeve trailed across the parchment. He glanced down and saw that his name was smudged. He picked up the blotter next to the paper and pressed it down, but his signature still looked ragged below the other neat names. He felt a pang of disappointment; he had spoiled the parchment. He was angry with himself – he should have taken more care. He sat back down heavily on the bench.

Outside the window a drift of cloud eclipsed the moon. An owl screeched in the darkness. The farmer next to Richard, sensing some unknown disturbance in Richard's demeanour, patted him on the shoulder in reassurance.

When Richard's mind quietened, he found Isaac saying that George Fox was shortly to be released from Lancaster Gaol, and was to speak on the hill above Lancaster town in three days' time. A 'threshing meeting' was what they called it, where the good grain would be separated from the chaff. Anyone who wished to hear him speak should make their way there. There was great excitement in the company and much talking whilst people arranged to convene and travel together. Richard offered some of the farmhands and the cobbler a ride on his wagon. It looked like it would be a grand day out, with a big crowd of people. The women were already discussing foodstuffs for a

81

shared repast, and neighbours they might invite, who might possibly be 'convinced' at the assembly.

Richard had never heard Fox speak. He was supposed to be a man of great charisma, inspired but not a fanatic. Dorothy had been convinced at one of his meetings. Richard had great respect and admiration for Dorothy, who always seemed to be able to see past her own concerns and into a larger view. She was kind, no matter to whom she spoke. All people were equal to Dorothy, rags or royalty. To Richard she seemed the model of self-control and common sense.

Richard had met Dorothy by accident when he was garrisoned with Cromwell's men on her land. After one of the early skirmishes with the king's army, he had brought one of the injured young men up to the Hall because it was obvious the soldier was going to die from his wounds. Richard had heard that Lady Swainson was a religious woman, that she was a Puritan, and hoped she would be able to do something with the dying man. The young man was screaming in pain from a wound to the stomach, and was obviously terrified. He was disturbing everyone else, and it seemed politic to take him away from the other young men who were raucous with drink and jubilant at the latest victory. The Puritan ethic of abstinence rarely held when there was something to celebrate. He and a friend had carried the soldier still screaming between them.

Richard had been surprised that Lady Swainson received them without fuss, almost as if she had been expecting them. She received them in the drawing room and had them lay the young man out on the tapestry day bed, despite the fact that the wound was still pouring blood. She calmed the man with her soft voice, talked matter-of-factly to him, telling him that yes, he was about to die, but to be at peace. She did not use any religious language, but spoke plainly. She asked about his family, and how he remembered them, and how he would like to be remembered himself. He quietened, as if he had drunk a draught, though indeed he had not, and began to talk. Richard asked if he should fetch anything. Dorothy turned briefly to him and said, 'There is no time. But let us pay him the honour of our full attention for his last moments with us. Listen well.'

And she bent over him and listened while he talked about his parents and his home, and how much he would miss them, and of a grievance he should have settled with his mother but for which there had been no time before he enlisted.

Dorothy Swainson did not speak, she just nodded every once in a while, her brown eyes resting all the time on his face, his hand clasped in hers. Richard and his friend listened too. The young man's voice grew fainter and more broken, until he seemed too tired to speak. When he was still they sat for a long time, just looking peaceably at this man who was so recently alive. And there had been something different in this man's death than any other death Richard had experienced. It was nothing he could put a label to, but rather an atmosphere, a quality of light in the room he would always remember.

After the last unspeakable battle and the atrocities perpetrated in the name of faith, he had remembered that night like a beacon, and finding no enduring peace he had sent word to Dorothy Swainson asking if he might be admitted to the meetings. He was so warmly welcomed that he had purchased nearby Helk Cottage and its little plot of land so he could be close to the meetings at the Hall. He sold his estate, and all his fine possessions, placing the capital at the disposal of his new-found brethren for their alms work. His life had begun anew. People called such folk the Quakers, and laughed that they trembled before God. But Richard preferred the term 'Society of Friends', for that was how they seemed to him, in nature as well as in name.

Chapter 7

Alice ate her soup and bread alone in the dining room. Thomas was never in for lunch. The empty chair and the cushion where Flora used to sit stared back at her. The house echoed as she moved in it now, the rooms grown too large and silent. Alice pictured Flora opposite, eating slowly, spooning the food into her mouth with concentration, in her little white lace cap and pintucked apron, her peg doll laid beside her plate. Flora would have loved her painting of the orchid. The watercolour was finished. It had turned out well – working quickly had given the picture a fresh and lively quality.

She had hidden the picture face to the wall

behind the others in the summerhouse. The orchid itself she had hidden in an old beehive amongst the ones in the orchard. Wearing her protective veil and gloves she had planted the pot directly into the ground, underneath an empty hive. That way the wooden walls protected it from view, and also from herbivorous animals such as deer or rabbits. The bees were used to her coming and going to collect the honey and ignored her presence. She had left the roof of the hive open so the plant could have sunlight and air. At night, or if Wheeler came back, she could slot the sloping roof back on again. It was a good hiding place. People would not approach other people's hives for fear of setting a swarm.

After her meal she returned to the summerhouse to finish the commission for Geoffrey's client, Earl Shipley. She was enjoying the challenge of painting solely in tones of green. She hoped one day, with practice, to be as great a painter as the French woman, Louisa Moillon, whose paintings of fruit and flowers were much in demand and fetched high prices. Geoffrey owned a small panel by her, and it had a quality of stillness she much admired and wanted to emulate. When Alice had shown early talent for painting, her mother had hoped she would paint miniatures and had taken her to see a number of exquisite portraits by Nicholas Hilliard. But except for her sketches of Flora, she found painting people tiresome, and the miniature too constrained. Instead she loved to paint her father's plant specimens, the flowing beauty of natural forms.

She set out the fern on the table and began to

layer in more shadows in the centre of the plant. This time of year there would be an early sunset and she was anxious to make the most of the precious daylight hours – the changing light often meant a piece had to be put aside when the weather was too dull.

She was soon happily engrossed in the lacy texture of the leaves, until the light changed again, and she leaned back in her chair to look out of the window for the passing cloud. The sky was clear. Maybe she was imagining the change in light. But then she caught a glimpse of something brown – a dark shape, something moving through the greenish glass of the window. She went closer to look out. A face loomed up in front of her, peering in from the outside. She gave a cry of surprise and stepped back. The face continued to stare at her through the glass. Alice recovered her composure and went to the door. Warily, she opened it a crack.

'Yes, what is it you want?'

'Mistress Ibbetson?'

'Yes,' Alice said, repeating, 'what do you want?' The woman was shabbily dressed, her cloak was old and mended, and her collar and cuffs rubbed and grey. Obviously a servant. Two shrewd brown eyes in a round moon face looked out from under the hood.

'I am Margaret Poulter.' She paused, looking at Alice inquisitively. 'Margaret Poulter,' she said again, smiling a grey-toothed smile, 'the herbalist.' She shuffled in and dropped a heavy brown leather bag on the flagstones.

She wasn't behaving at all like a servant, how odd. The name took a few moments to register.

Alice's mouth went dry, and her stomach turned to liquid as the facts clicked sickeningly into place. This was Margaret the herbalist, the one Wheeler had told her about, who was thought to be something of a witch. This nondescript woman with her grey hair sticking out like a hedgehog was Margaret Poulter. Alice wiped her hands nervously on her skirts. She was not what Alice had imagined at all.

Unsure how to respond, she merely nodded, but her mind was racing. If Margaret Poulter was a witch then it would be best to try to keep calm and not antagonize her. The woman was looking with interest at the portraits of Flora. 'By, what a bonny lass,' she said.

'Can I help you?' Alice did not like the old woman looking so close up.

She did not seem to hear, but moved to bend over the fern on the table.

'This seems a good healthy specimen.' Margaret plucked off a leaf and held it to her nose. Alice refrained from saying anything, she did not dare, but hoped she wouldn't do it again as the picture of it was as yet unfinished.

'Mash the leaves, and it is good on open wounds, in particular if you mix it with woundwort. It will stem the bleeding.' She flung off her cloak and laid it over the back of a chair.

Alice realized with dismay that she was intending to stay some time.

'Now then, where is this wild orchid of yours?'

She thought quickly.

'Come with me and I'll show you.' She led the way out of the summerhouse with the old woman

87

hurrying a pace behind – over towards the orchard, past the beehives and out of the garden gate. Hearing Margaret's uneven footsteps still behind her, she turned past the box trees and into the lane next to the house. Here she stopped and knelt over the verge, pointing out a small, insignificant-looking plant with rows of minuscule lilac flowers.

Margaret narrowed her eyes. 'Not that orchid, you crafty woman, not the common spotted orchid. Did you think to pull the wool over my eyes? You might fool Wheeler, but I have more wit than Wheeler any day.' She grabbed Alice's wrist.

Alice tried to pull away but finding the woman surprisingly strong she said, 'Let me go! I don't know who you are or what you want. I have shown you the only orchid I know of in these parts.'

Margaret hung on with claw-like hands and brought her wrinkled face close up to Alice's. 'Come now, Mistress Ibbetson, you know that is not true. We could be friends.' She smiled lopsidedly. 'We both have a mind to see the flower grow wild for all to enjoy. Show it to an old lady, now.'

Alice twisted her wrist trying to free it.

'Leave me be. I don't know what you're talking about.'

'Oh, but you do.' Margaret sniffed. 'I just want to see it, is all. I have waited fifty years for a glimpse of it. I'm sorry if I startled you. My mother and grandmother before her both spoke of it, its scarlet ribbons and pretty little petal like a shoe.'

Alice finally managed to wriggle free. As she did so she caught sight of a movement at the upstairs window of the house. She was just in time to see Ella move back behind the curtain. That was all she needed, to look a fool in front of Ella. The girl was already getting above herself. But this was really too much, to be manhandled by this old woman

She turned on Margaret. 'Get off my property.' Then in a lower, more controlled voice, said, 'You have offended me. Please leave, and do not return.'

Like the weather, Margaret's demeanour had changed again. She regarded Alice steadily. She planted her hands on her hips. 'I'll be leaving when I'm good and ready. My cloak and bag are in your garden, so if you've finished your bit of play-acting, we'll go and get them. Then you can show me the flower.'

Alice realized she was not going to get rid of the woman so easily. Feigning a haughtiness she did not feel, she marched back to the summerhouse. Margaret hobbled rapidly alongside, seemingly ignoring Alice's ill-humour, talking all the while under her breath. 'That's henbane, and there's cuckoo pint, over there with the white hood, that's good for coughs, and here's knotgrass, for shining up your pewter, and the hawthorn – look at those berries, must be going to be a hard winter.'

Alice shut her ears to the old woman's mutterings. Witch or no witch, she thought, she would not let the old woman make her look a fool before her servants. Back at the summerhouse, she picked up Margaret's cloak, bundled it together and thrust it out towards her. Heat rose to Alice's face, and almost in tears with embarrassment, she

89

said, 'If you do not leave right this minute, I will send Ella for the constable.'

Margaret reached for her cloak. 'Hold off, hold off. I'm going. Don't upset yourself, you've had your share of sadness, I can see that.' Her eyes were soft.

Alice wavered, feeling a lump come to her throat. But then she saw Margaret's eyes take on a steely glint. 'I'll be back, though, before the flower fades, when you change your mind. And I know you will. My mother told me your orchid has healing properties. Nerveroot, she used to call it. Said it was a visionary plant. Makes you see things – people from the other side. I'd like to take a look at it, just once. When you're ready, I'll be back.'

Alice didn't reply. She just lifted up the bag and heaved it clumsily onto the path. She was surprised at how angry she felt, and at how heavy the bag was. It seemed to be full of glass bottles, which chinked as it landed.

'In the meantime,' Margaret said, 'you must mind the orchid well. And be careful. I saw three ravens on my path this morning. Three ravens is an ill wind.' She pulled the brown hood over her unruly grey hair and stepped forward. As if it was a secret, she whispered, 'I'm staying at the Anchor, if you find anything ails you.' Alice wasn't sure if this was a threat or an offer of assistance. She drew away, but Margaret was already picking up her bag, and the squat figure in the threadbare brown cloak was soon out of sight round the garden gate.

Alice sat down on the window seat. First Wheeler, and now this. How could Margaret Poulter have possibly known that she had taken the orchid? Was she an acquaintance of Wheeler's? That did not seem plausible, given that he was one of the strange sect of ranters from the Hall – and he had been hiding its existence precisely from people like Margaret. Had she got wind of it from Geoffrey? Again, Sir Geoffrey Fisk was hardly likely to befriend someone of the class of Margaret Poulter, still less tell her of the orchid.

She paced the summerhouse, trying to unravel the conversation in her mind. Margaret Poulter seemed to know altogether too much, and, even more disturbingly, she seemed to be warning her of something. Despite the fact the sun had broken through, Alice shook her shoulders, ridding herself of some invisible pestilence. She was uneasy. The flower was causing her more strife than she had bargained for. What if Thomas were to return home and find that beggarwoman Margaret uninvited in the garden? It would be difficult to explain away. Perhaps a walk would help her clear her mind and make sense of it all.

She locked the summerhouse with the little bronze key she kept hanging with her pomander, from a ribbon on her belt. She paused by the door to slip the pattens over her shoes. She had left them, as she always did, outside the door, so she would not tread mud into her painting room. And as she slipped her feet inside, she remembered her shoes.

They were still in the sack of turnips where she had left them two nights ago. So much had happened since that they had fallen completely out of mind. Best dispose of them before Thomas should ask awkward questions about why she had ruined such an expensive pair. She hurried into the house and into the kitchen. Betty Tansy, the cook, was there rolling out pastry for an apple pie.

Cook bobbed, and said, 'Good afternoon, mistress. Apple pie for supper. We've far too many apples this year. Ella's going to wrap them and put them in the loft to keep through winter.'

Alice nodded. 'I've a mind to take some for the harvest festival. If you'll give me a basket, I'll take some from the sack in the pantry.'

'I'll get some out for you, mistress, we've plenty.' Cook was already brushing off her floury hands and coming round the table.

'No need.' Alice lifted one palm to stay her. 'You carry on with the pies. Pastry spoils if it is left too long.'

'Yes, mistress.' Cook returned to her rolling pin.

Alice picked up a wicker basket from underneath the long table and went into the cool dark of the pantry. Hastily she filled the basket with apples from the windfall bag. Then she felt inside the turnip sack for the shoes. She could conceal them under the apples to get them out of the kitchen. Her hands searched round inside the sack, feeling only the gnarled heads of turnips. She opened the sack wide and put both hands inside. They must be here somewhere, she thought.

'Looking for something, mistress?'

Alice turned round. Ella was slouching in the doorway, a sly smile on her face.

Chapter 8

'Good morning, Richard,' Benjamin said.

The two young ploughmen, Joseph Taylor and his brother Benjamin, were early. Richard had them wait in the house whilst he finished washing at the pump outside the kitchen door.

He ushered them into the cottage and bade them sit. He saw them eyeing the neat piles of books and papers on the table, the wheel-backed chair by the window with its feather cushion, the pipe rack and its collection of wooden and clay pipes on the mantel.

The young men stood uncomfortably, obviously unwilling to sit down. Despite his changed life the farm lads still insisted on deferring to him as if he were a gentleman. They probably thought he had a servant, for the carved oak cupboard used for keeping the winter supply of flatbreads was polished to a high sheen, but Richard enjoyed polishing – he liked to keep busy, keep his house tidy, and his Sunday boots clean and lined up next to the door.

After washing he put on his work boots and picked up a tied cloth bundle from the table.

'Bread and cheese – enough for us all.'

The boys grinned shyly. When Richard was ready they put the horse in the traces and drove up to Lingfell Hall. The wagon always caused a bit of a stir as there were few in the country. Most still travelled on horseback, the lanes and tracks too narrow or rough for a cart's cumbersome wheels. Joseph and Benjamin were delighted to be in the cart with Richard driving up front. It was breezy and the horse was fresh, pulling smoothly up the hill, hooves clopping in the puddles, tail swishing.

At the Hall there was a ramshackle crowd – some on horseback, some on donkeys, some with packhorses and goods in case there was time for trade after the meeting. Dorothy stood in the yard, handing out nettle beer and making sure everyone had a place in the assorted carts and traps that were already queuing down the drive. People were leaning out and calling to their friends. Blankets were settled over knees, and hats tied down more firmly, ready for the journey to Lancaster.

George Fox had been released from prison yesterday, and the rumour was that he was to talk on the hill above Lancaster town. No building would be big enough to house the throng, and anyway Fox did not believe in churches – he called them 'steeple-houses', claiming that God could not be confined to a building, and that churches were no more special than any other house.

The cavalcade set off, all the motley conveyances following one after the other down the narrow gritstone lanes. Fortunately the weather was fine but dull and the rain held off – no one wanted a drenching on such a long journey. In places the road was rough or boggy and horses had to be led round potholes lest the carts overturn.

With so many of them, it was a four-hour journey to Lancaster. After the small grey wood and clay houses of the village, Lancaster seemed imposing. As they crossed the packbridge over the River Loyne, they saw tall warehouses on the quay, a masted merchant ship and barges loading bales of cloth alongside. Stone houses squatted at the bottom of the town with the twin landmarks of St Mary's Church and the ramparts of the castle above. Skirting the town, they came at last to Gant's Field. Lancaster had been an impressive sight, but not as impressive as the field full of horses and traps, and the sight of hundreds of other Friends, moving up the hill, all dressed in muted colours like autumn leaves. From a distance it looked like the whole hill was alive, its skin rippling like a horse's flank.

Richard and his companions got down from the wagon, leaving it at a tethering post, and joined the upward-moving crowd.

A woman next to him smiled. 'Where are you from?'

'Lingfell Hall,' he said. 'There's a good few of us have come together.'

'I'm all the way from Sedbergh,' she said. 'My name's Hannah, and this is my husband, Jack.'

Jack smiled. 'I hope there won't be any trouble today. Such a big crowd is bound to attract attention.'

'Surely not,' said Hannah. 'Though what happens is in the hands of the Lord.'

Richard kept silent. Sometimes he doubted that everything was the Lord's doing, and that people had no responsibility themselves for their foolishness. These doubts disturbed him, lest they be heretical, so he kept them to himself.

They were all a little breathless from the climb, so conversation naturally slowed as they reached the top. There, they had a fine view of the surrounding landscape – the town in the distance, with the wide silver river flowing out towards the bay, and the fields with their dots of sheep and cattle. More and more people approached up the hill. On the top an open trap had been dragged up to act as a sort of makeshift platform. The crowds settled down on blankets or sacks on the ground. Quite a few seekers had carried pails or baskets which were used upturned as seats, and others carried planks of wood for benches to keep their backsides off the wet ground. Richard and Jack stood behind, letting the ladies pass through to the front. At last some people got up onto the platform, and Richard was surprised when a woman addressed the assembled crowd.

'Friends!' she called out. The crowd fell silent, listening. 'It is good to see so many of you make the journey here, and I know you have come to hear George Fox speak. But he asks that we wait on the word of God as usual. He asks that we fall silent and listen, and if moved by the power of the Spirit, any one of you is welcome to come up here and witness.'

She glanced to the man standing off to the side of the platform, and he nodded his agreement.

'That's him,' Jack said, 'that's George Fox.'

Hannah turned to look back at Richard. 'They let him out of gaol, but he wants to clear his name, so he is taking himself to London to be tried. Fancy that! Of course he is innocent of all their trumped-up charges.' She pointed over to the side of the wagon. 'Those others with him are accompanying him on the journey, God be praised.' Hannah turned back to the platform.

Richard looked at George Fox with interest. He appeared quite ordinary, a tired middle-aged man in a shapeless grey topcoat and scuffed boots. Richard had expected to see someone with a bit more presence, perhaps with something arresting in the eyes or a bit of an air about him. This man was a disappointment. Still, he closed his eyes a moment, hearing the small sounds of the rustling of the ladies' skirts and whipping of the ribbons on their bonnets. In the distance a horse neighed. After a few minutes Richard opened his eyes, taking in the stillness of the crowd, now twelve deep, many with their faces turned up towards the sky, some with their palms raised, their faces trusting and expectant as if waiting for rain.

He marvelled – they were for all the world like living statues. Each person was so much an individual and not merely part of the crowd, like the man next to him still wearing his farrier's apron, his cap clasped to his chest, his ruddy face perspiring slightly. That woman in front – her shoulders were rising and falling with her breath, her hands closed into tight fists of concentration. There were hundreds here, all of them silent and respectful, waiting. Without warning, a peace descended on him, heavy and deep as January snow.

Something inside him cracked, and he felt a fizzing sensation at his temples. Heat flooded over his face and his legs seemed to turn to goosefeathers. He found himself repeating in his head the words, 'I am here, I am here.' He wasn't sure if he was addressing God, or George Fox, or the crowd in general. Or whether it was God's words addressing him. He just kept repeating the words, 'I am here.'

When it was finished, the crowd were still standing waiting. Richard swallowed hard, in the thrall of an unknown emotion, fearing he might blubber like a child. So he remained silent, standing red-faced and wondering. The men had their hats in their hands – it looked strange to see so many men hatless, he thought. Something had happened to him, of that he was absolutely sure. A shaking affected his knees. He looked around again at the other faces, still waiting as before, and watched in a daze as George Fox got up to speak.

In that moment George Fox looked out over the crowd, and it seemed to Richard that he looked directly at him. He remained motionless, drinking in George Fox's words. Afterwards it was as if he had been listening from the centre of his chest, and not from his ears at all. He heard the words and he knew that George Fox spoke the truth. Strangely, though, he couldn't seem to fathom exactly what had been said, only that Fox had said that apostles of Jesus exist today, here in this crowd – that the spirit in those men, so many lifetimes ago, is the identical spirit that lives here, now, in these men.

He wondered if any of the apostles had felt like this, and if they had, whether they understood it. Then a spasm of fear fell over him. He didn't want to be an apostle. He had thought the Quakers a solid, kindly people, mild-mannered and fair in business. But strange feelings and sensations were welling up in him and he did not know what would happen next, for he was in the grip of something, possibly in the grip of God, and was both elated and terrified.

When George Fox stood down and the crowd erupted in a spontaneous cheer, Richard cheered along with them. Hannah turned to him, an ecstatic look on her face, then she ripped her hat from her head and began to push her way through the crowd to the platform.

'The Spirit is on her,' cried one man, almost lifting her through the crowd.

'Make way, make way!' said others as she forged her way through. Finally she was hoisted onto the platform where she spoke loudly and fervently, an outpouring of tumbled words. It was a strange language the likes of which Richard had never heard before – it wasn't Latin or Greek, or French, or like anything he had ever heard. To him it sounded like nonsense words, but Hannah continued the torrent of strange syllables, 'Rorshamo, atzimol gulam shivolim, paarth hosamalkum...'

Jack looked pleased and proud. 'She has the gift of speaking in tongues,' he said.

On the platform Hannah's head was thrown back, her blonde hair blowing in horsetail strands over her face and mouth. Under her half-closed lids, her eyes slid from side to side. She clutched her shawl with her fingers, and swayed as if caught on a rolling ship. The crowd watched quietly, barely moving, until her speech seemed to be reaching a crescendo, her lips white with spittle. Near the platform some of the crowd started to join in with cries of 'Praise the Lord!' Finally, with a strangled half-cry she collapsed backwards, where she was caught in the arms of two gentlemen of Fox's party, who fanned her face and helped her bodily off the platform. Jack and Richard hurried forward through the crowd to assist her. When they arrived she was sitting shakily on an upturned bucket, being given a flask of water. Close up her face was pink, the scars from a childhood pox standing out white against her cheeks.

'I saw an angel,' she said breathlessly to the little crowd that had gathered around her. 'He had armour and a lance and was all aflame! Look at me, I am trembling.'

The old woman bending over her patted her hand. 'Hush, dear, don't thee fret. Thou hast been a vessel for the Spirit. Let us give thanks to the Lord for sending us this sign.' She sank to her knees on the grass to pray, as did Jack. Richard followed their example. He gave his thanks, but was not sure whether he was praying for Hannah or himself. They stayed there, heads bowed, whilst Hannah continued to tremble and pray under her breath.

When Richard finished, his attention was taken with Fox talking with two of the men who had caught Hannah when she fell. He knew he was staring but could not help himself. One of the men with Fox gestured over to Hannah, and Fox looked over to them. Catching sight of Richard's eyes fixed upon him, Fox smiled at him. Richard hurriedly lowered his head. The smile was a simple friendly act. There was no hint that anything unusual had happened. Richard was confused. He ran his hand around his neck, feeling the clammy skin and the ragged pulse of the blood beating in his veins.

He stood up and stretched his legs. He walked about, feeling his boots sink into the soft mud. He felt better then, his knees stopped shaking and the breeze against his face was fresh and chill. Fox and his party made their way down the hill. Hannah and Jack were still at the centre of a small crowd, while Hannah described her vision again.

Richard looked around for the others from the Hall, and saw that some traders had set up at the edge of the field and the crowd was gathering there. Now that Fox had finished speaking and was on his way, a market was springing up, with wares from all over Lancashire. He knew the trade would be brisk, as Quakers were renowned for their fair dealings and level measures – a bushel was a bushel, and a peck a peck, no matter who was buying. Richard set off towards the huddle, wishing he had thought to bring some of his goods, but glad too that he was unencumbered by his trade for at least one day.

He found his fellow travellers and they ate together, supplementing the bread and cheese with a lamb pie they bought from a wandering pieman, and some greengages from someone's pocket. As he was eating he saw a familiar figure approaching. It was Dorothy. They all stood up and Richard brushed the crumbs from his coat.

'Well, Richard!' She rubbed her gloved hands together. 'He was splendid! It is the first time thou hast heard him speak, is it not?'

Richard nodded.

'Didst thou like the way he spoke? Did it move thee?'

Richard found himself unable to answer this question directly. He needed more time to think, to make sense of it all in his head.

'There was a young woman near me speaking in tongues,' he said, by way of a diversion. 'I've never seen anything like that before.'

'I saw. It was certainly extraordinary. But when George Fox speaks, thou canst be sure the presence of the Lord is with us, and when people feel the touch of the Lord for themselves, then sometimes surprising things can happen.'

She was looking at him as if to weigh him up, so that he felt himself turn away to the two young men behind him.

'Did you enjoy the meeting?' he asked them. They started to reply, but Dorothy ignored them and placed her hand on Richard's shoulder, turning him so she could look into his face.

'Richard. I am so glad for thee. Thou hast been touched! I see it in thy face.' Then, seeing that he was looking at the ground, 'Thou canst not deny me the evidence of my own eyes?'

Richard turned away from her, embarrassed. 'Thou art mistaken,' he said gruffly, and strode away down the hill. He could feel Dorothy's eyes follow him, but did not look back.

He said not a word on the journey home but wondered if he were losing his senses or whether it really had been the Lord speaking to him. If it was, then there must be some reason for it. Perhaps there was some work for him to do in the Lord's name – some vocation or quest. This thought troubled him, that he might be called upon to act in God's name, and yet, as a Christian, hadn't he thought he was doing that all along? He knew he had lied to Dorothy, denying his true feelings, and the thought of it rankled like a burr.

His hands were tense as he drove the horses on through the dark lanes, on the coastal path towards the village. A horn blasted its warning to sailors out at sea, for the mist was rolling in and a sea fret hung over the fields and hedges. He pondered the odd utterances of the girl from Sedbergh, Hannah, turning over the peculiar phrases in his mind. By all accounts she had seen a holy vision, and she had been trembling and crying out. But it was so unlike what he had experienced – the peace and the clarity of the moment when he felt the heat rise in him and a presence round his temples blowing like a wind. He told himself that what happened that day was between him and God. So there was only one way to begin to understand it.

It was dark by the time he got home. He lit some tallow candles and took out his plain ebony cross from the dresser drawer and put it on the mantel. Without even taking the time to light a fire, he knelt on the rag rug and bowed his head to pray the Lord's Prayer. 'Our Father, who art in heaven...' Then he continued, 'Thou seest me, thy servant, Richard Wheeler. Today I felt thy peace with me, and maybe thou hast work for me to do. If thou wilt, send me a sign by which I might know thee, and advise me what I should undertake in thy name.' Here he paused, aware of his own voice echoing oddly in the empty room.

He continued to kneel in silence for some while, but everything remained as it was. The cold ashes in the grate, the spitting of the wicks on the candles and the slight draught from under the door. He began to feel a little foolish. What had he expected, he asked himself, a bolt from above? He stood up, wishing he could have a bottle of ale. But it was something the Quakers did not hold with, and though he missed it, he had seen enough drunks to understand their reasoning. Instead, he picked up a pipe and stuffed it with tobacco. This too was forbidden. But he had never seen anyone staggering under the influence of tobacco, so he often allowed himself a pipe in private in the evening.

He had hoped for a simple, peaceful life, but today more than ever he longed for the life he had before, one with fewer questions. He thought back to the time when servants did his bidding, he slept in his fine feather bed and he could enjoy a day of hunting followed by a game of cards with a bet on the side. What's more, he could have been married by now, with children running in the hall, but of course it had been naive to hope that Frances would ever have stood for this life.

He must get outside, do something. He flung on his coat and walked out, down the path to the wood, breathing in the damp smell of the undergrowth. He lit his pipe and sucked hard, savouring the sweet woody smoke in his mouth and lungs. Immediately he felt more relaxed. He looked over to the clearing where the lady's slipper orchid had been growing, before it was uprooted from its place. The woods were dark, despite the new moon, and the air damp. Fog hung in skeins over the ground making the path disappear, as if the earth itself were shifting. A movement caught his eye – a white fluttering in the trees. A white dove was hovering over the clearing. Its wings were outstretched, beating silently as if it was momentarily frozen in space. The image etched itself into Richard's mind like a white-hot brand. A white dove – the sign of the Holy Spirit.

Chapter 9

Margaret Poulter had lied to Alice. She was not exactly lodging at the Anchor. She could not afford to pay for a room. But the landlord turned a blind eye to the fact that she slept in the hayloft above the stables, and tolerated her peculiar comings and goings in exchange for remedies for his children. He had five children, all of whom suffered from one malady or another – mostly coughs and lice, from what Margaret could see.

After Margaret left Alice in Netherbarrow, she took her time returning to the inn. This was her gathering time, like her mother and her grandmother before her. The world was one big apothecary's shop to Margaret, and the source of a good living. She was stocking up, for in times of good health and plentiful harvests like these she was often poor and hungry, whereas at times of war or plague, or when harvests were thin, her draughts and remedies were needed. Then Margaret grew fat and comfortable whilst others suffered famine and disease.

Daylight hours were for scouting along the hedgerows looking for anything useful, and watching out for signs or omens or shifts in the weather. The underlying web on which the world was hung might be moving or shifting. This was her way – to find out how the land lay – and she did this quite literally, through her senses, sniffing, poking, tasting and fingering with her nut-brown hands. Wherever she went she collected small observations in the same way as she collected the ticks that stuck to her skirts.

Today, she walked a circuitous route which took in the coast, where she gathered seaweed, and the moors above Long Scar, now black with bilberries. She filled a small sack with these, working methodically up the hillside. She moved quickly, for she was as fit as a terrier and as hardy as a native pony. Younger people had trouble keeping up with her scurrying gait, despite her age and the heavy bags she carried.

She followed the trading route down into Silverdale village, past Silverdale well, where the fresh water bubbled up out of the ground only a stone's throw from the sea. The well had been walled with limestone and made into a great square pond for drinking water. Further down there was a place for the livestock, and further down still a place for washing and bathing before it trickled away down a dyke into the beck. At the well she submerged her flagons under the surface. The water gurgled in through the necks. In Preston the water was hard, but here it was soft as a horse's muzzle.

By the livestock pond, hooves had churned the

106

ground to a slippery paste and bruised marsh marigolds clung to the bank, half in and out of the water. Spotting the purple-flowered spikes of wound-wort, she snapped off some stems and tied them together with string she fished from her bag. She knotted another string around the bundle and hung it over her shoulder. The plants too were different from her native Preston. There were herbs to be had here that were rare in her locality, so passing some yarrow she paused to snip off some of the leaves under the ruff of whitish-grey flowers. When she had left this morning the landlord's youngest son was having another nosebleed, and one of these stalks, with its green feathery tufts, would stop the blood right enough if he pushed it up his nose.

She paused in her tracks, thinking of Mistress Ibbetson, and the lady's slipper, for Margaret was keenly aware that she had reached her autumn years and had not been blessed with a daughter whom she might instruct in the craft. She had been secretly keeping watch on Mistress Ibbetson since the last waning quarter-moon; her fame for painting beautiful life-like pictures of flowers had reached even as far as Preston, and Margaret's sharp ears.

She might do, Margaret thought. But these gifts could not be given lightly, no, she must be sure and certain Alice Ibbetson was the one, and judging by the look of her, even if she was, she would need some coaxing, and she would have much to learn. Margaret sighed at the sheer size of the task, and absentmindedly plucked some elderberries from an overhanging bush and stowed them away. But Alice Ibbetson had a love of plants, and no mistaking it. She had never seen such bonny work, it fair took your breath away.

Margaret had been irritated when Alice refused to show her the lady's slipper. Last week she kept a watch on her house, to gather a better picture of her character. When she saw the candles snuffed out downstairs she was about to go home, but had heard the sound of the latch. Surprised a lady should be out unaccompanied so late, Margaret followed Alice Ibbetson down the lane at a safe distance, skirting behind the trees. She could not see what she was up to – it was too dark, and she feared she would be flushed out from her hiding place. But she had heard rumours in the tavern about a rare slipper orchid and guessed this was what she was after. Good girl, thought Margaret, pleased that her excitement matched her own.

She was not so pleased to see her dig out the orchid and take it home. Margaret knew well the orchid liked a certain sort of soil and would not take kindly to being uprooted without so much as a by-your-leave. She had hardly given Margaret much of a welcome either, when she called. But never mind, she would come round in the end, her love of plants was written all over her. Might as well have sap in her veins, thought Margaret.

Margaret arrived back at her lodgings after dark. She had smelt the woodsmoke from a good half-mile away, and now went into the tavern in search of a warm fire, some cider, and maybe some hotpot, if she could sweet-talk the landlord. The bar was full and stank of sweat and beer, but it was warm and steamy. Smoke from the fire hung thick in the rafters under the thatched roof. The windows were stained yellow from tobacco.

Striking a bargain for a dinner, she promised the landlord she would look at his sons in the morning, and was given a plate of greyish meat and kale steaming in a greasy liquid that should have been gravy. Holding the platter in both hands, Margaret eased her bottom into a corner next to two women who were gossiping about a local landowner. Dunking her bread, Margaret ate steadily, letting herself be entertained by the tales of the women at her table.

'Well, he has some *disfigurement*–' the red-haired woman pointed between her legs and dropped her voice to a hoarse whisper – 'down there.'

Her friend's watery eyes were round like a magpie's. 'What sort of disfigurement? Is it the pox, or what? Is it shaped like a parsnip?' She bent her finger into a hook and guffawed, spluttering through the gaps in her teeth.

'I don't know. But my sister's wedded to his manservant's brother,' the red-haired woman went on in a conspiratorial voice, 'and he says, it's withering away and His Lordship has all sorts of slimy poultices to try to stop the rot.'

'That's disgusting. Small wonder she looks down someone else's breeches for her pleasure. Still – he should be able to keep control over his own wife. He don't sound like much of a man to me.'

'Ah, but Lady Emilia's as sly as a fox. She had a goodly portion, you know. Her pa made a stack with his mines up at Keswick. She's no better than the rest of us, but she's got her head screwed on tight.'

Her companion raised her eyebrows, and leaned in to hear more.

'He had the title, and she wanted it – Lord, how much she wanted it! She schemed for years to catch him in marriage. Her pa just about broke himself to give her a big fat dowry. That's what keeps the Hall, and all his fancy servants.' The red-haired woman nodded her head up and down, with her lips pursed.

'She'll be taking a big risk, then, having some other man. She'd lose all that.' A pause. 'And if she gets caught she could be hanged!' She chortled with evident delight at this idea.

'Nah, Audrey, there's been no hangings for that, not since the king came back. Anyways, they're all at it – king included. Nah, flogging and gaol's more likely.'

'Who is it, then, that she's romping with?'

'Nobody knows.'

'Pfff.' Audrey rolled her eyes in contempt and folded her arms, as if to dismiss it.

'Ah, but secret letters come back and forth through her maidservant, Lizzie Pickering. Patterson's seen them, all lovey-dovey. They're not signed, though, or owt.'

'Pah. Sounds like a lot of daft gossip to me.' Then more brightly, 'But if there's to be a public cuckolding, I'm ready to join ye. It's years since we had such sport. Village is ready for a bit of fun and games. It's been right miserable, these past years, with that old nob Cromwell.'

Margaret slurped the last few mouthfuls of stew and wiped the platter with the bread. She latched onto the names that had been mentioned. It paid to be informed, in her experience. Lady Emilia was the wife of Sir Geoffrey Fisk, the gentleman to whom she had sent the potion for scaly skin. His wife's infidelities could have a bearing on the problem. As for the potion, she had taken pains to get it right, for something in his letter made her feel a bleakness about him, a black void like an empty house.

She remembered mixing the sheep grease with chamomile and borage, and adding some chickweed to reduce the itching, along with three different types of kelp. She always took more care with the gentlemen's remedies, for that was where the money was – yet she had not received payment for her pains, though she had expressly asked for a delivery boy to be sent straight away. You couldn't trust the king's post. As she was in the vicinity, she would call on the gentleman as if to enquire after his health, and then collect her payment in person. Most gentlemen would pay up sooner than have you hanging round on their doorsteps, she'd found. If he was indeed of the choleric temperament, as she suspected, perhaps she could persuade him to buy some figwort tea whilst she was about it.

It was a shame, she thought, that Mistress Ibbetson was a typical melancholic, for her face had darkened, the black bile risen to the surface when they spoke. But sooner or later Mistress Ibbetson would show her the orchid, for she was soft and tender underneath that cold shell. It was only a matter of time, and a little more persuasion.

Margaret placed her spoon on the table, ruminating. She would not be surprised if the lady found the orchid brought her more than she bargained for. There was an odd scent about it, as if it was half in this world and half in some other darker world. A scent that was nothing to do with the flower.

She wiped her gravy from her mouth with her sleeve. She was prepared to wait; all things have their season.

Chapter 10

Ella took the shoes out from under her mattress to look at them. She often did this; she liked to feel the cool smooth silk against her cheek, to run her fingertips over the slightly raised nap of the embroidery. The blowsy roses and the curled sprays of leaves lay flat against the yellow sateen, and Ella traced their texture, amazed that anyone could sew such lifelike flowers. They glowed against the rough calico of her bedsheet and the greyish wool blanket. She couldn't bring them out often, for she shared the bed with her sister, Sadie, and if she saw them she might tell her pa, and he'd use it as an excuse to leather her. He might make her give them back, or worse, sell them, and she would never see them again. She pondered over the dark red stains too, what they could mean.

It was cold in the room. The draughts were less since she had stuffed the cracks in the wall with paper and rags, but the chill seemed to seep up from the ground. There had never been a fire in this room and her breath sank in a white cloud in front of her. The bed smelt of soot from the smoke that crept through the dividing wall when the fire was lit in the hearth next door, and the same smoke had stained the ceiling beams black.

It tainted her, the soot; turned her skin and clothes grey, rubbed smuts onto everything, tell-tale black marks. It filled her with a rage she could not understand, a rage that made her pinch and slap her little sister in the night till she cried out. But when she looked at the shoes it reminded her that somewhere inside her the fine lady was still waiting, that she had been born into this house by some sort of error and her rightful place was somewhere else, somewhere a girl would wear yellow embroidered slippers. She looked at them and imagined what it would be like to slide her toes into the cream silk lining, in front of a crackling fire. To feel a heavy petticoat swing slowly round her ankles and know that she smelt sweet and clean from bathing in water boiled on the fire. There would be servants to do her bidding, but she would treat them with respect and call them by name, and say 'if you please' and 'thank you kindly' when they bowed and scraped before her.

She could have been wed by now, but she didn't want to marry a labourer who would expect her to drudge for him just as she drudged now, but with not a penny to show for it. And the local lads knew it. No, she was going to make the most of herself. She wasn't going to squander her looks on some clod of a man with no prospects and no money. Her plump figure and her even white teeth could buy more than that.

Master Thomas and Mistress Alice – now, there was a thing. Lately she had seen him looking at her when she bent over to clean the grate. She had pushed her rounded backside even further into the air when she noticed his eyes lingering on her. Since her sister died the mistress had been pale and thin, wearing her dark clothes and weeping when she thought no one could see. She disappeared for hours each day into the summerhouse, and came back red-eyed with paint-spattered hands. Her face was distant, as if she were never quite there in the room but somewhere a long way away.

Ella glanced down at the curving line of her breasts, and placed her hands to feel the narrow span of her waist. She stood up and admired herself; tied her apron a little tighter to emphasize her shape, took out a small pot from her pocket and reddened her lips. No wonder Master Thomas was looking at her. He deserved more of an armful than that miserable wife of his, of that she was certain – a real woman was what he needed, one full of heat and life. You could not say it was a bewitching, could you, if the idea was already in his head? A little encouragement, that was all it was. Yes, she would give him a little encouragement.

Alice and Thomas were still at breakfast when Ella came in to tell them Sir Geoffrey Fisk was at the door.

'Excuse me, Thomas,' Alice said. 'He has come to collect the watercolours for Earl Shipley.' She stood up and left her half-eaten bread and ham on her plate.

'Are you taking him out to the summerhouse?'

'Yes.'

'Then I'll finish my breakfast, and come and pay my respects to him before I leave.'

Alice went out into the hall and took her shawl from the peg. Ella was waiting by the open door and bobbed her head half-heartedly as she passed.

'Good morrow, Alice. It is a beautiful morning,' said Geoffrey, indicating that she should walk in front of him down the path.

'Yes, the light is very good.' She turned the bronze key in the lock.

'And this unusual orchid – it is still in flower?'

'When your servant brought me the message you were coming today, I brought it out from its hiding place, so you could view it. I must keep it hidden because–'

But he was already ahead of her, at the table. 'Is this it?'

Alice nodded. Geoffrey blew out through his teeth.

'It is not as handsome as I imagined.' He frowned as he took out a magnifying lens on a red silk cord from his waistcoat pocket.

Alice sprang to the flower's defence. 'It is fading a little, but I think it quite beautiful. Look at the shape and colour of those twisted petals.'

'Hmm.' Geoffrey peered though the magnifying glass. 'This pouch-like petal is certainly an oddity. But it's nothing like as fine as the one I purchased from a Portuguese trader in the Americas – such a beautiful scarlet and orange spotted specimen. Great big showy petals. Patterson is on his way with it. Wait till you see it – the bloom is ravishing. We all went quite mad vying with each other to purchase it.'

'Indeed?'

'Yes, it cost me a good deal. But it will be worth it, for I will take it to Hampton Court – I know that if the Portuguese bloom were to be in gardens here, it would cause quite a stir. Head gardeners would flock to buy. Nothing so fantastical is available in England.'

Alice walked over and looked at the lady's slipper. She could not imagine anything more beautiful.

'Have you examined your little plant in detail?'

'Yes, I have measured it and made a study in paint. Of course I have had to keep its whereabouts a secret. You see, the landowner was quite unable to see reason. He refused to let me purchase the plant at any price, so in the end I had to take it without his knowledge.'

Geoffrey dropped the lens from his eye and stood up. 'How rash.' He looked surprised, but his voice held a touch of admiration.

Alice blushed. 'Yes. There was no alternative. The orchid would have perished in Wheeler's hands. It would have suffered the same fate as the others – taken by a cunning woman or witch, and the roots mashed and squandered to serve a vain woman's complexion.'

Geoffrey seemed confused by Alice's conversation. 'Are you telling me that this was on Wheeler's land? Richard Wheeler? Of Helk Cottage?'

'Yes.'

She was surprised to see Geoffrey almost laugh,

but then he suppressed it.

'Well, well.'

'He was here yesterday, but he has not seen the plant, and he has no idea I have it.' She mentally crossed her fingers at this half-truth.

'Well done.' His eyes glinted with amusement. 'You quite surprise me with your daring.'

'It is only what any plant-lover would have done. I am glad to have it here in a safe place. Flora would have loved to see it, you see, it was her favourite...'

She paused, as Geoffrey was not listening. His servant, Patterson, had appeared at the door with a large wooden carrying-crate.

Geoffrey put the crate on the table and dismissed Patterson. He lifted a hessian sack from the crate and peeled it back to reveal an exotic orchid, flame-red against the waxy green leaves. Despite herself, Alice's eyes widened. She had never seen anything like it. Five red petals like billowing taffeta, splashed with orange, round a scarlet hood. Inside the hood, a long red tongue hung lasciviously. A stiff greenish-yellow protrusion stood proud above the hairy lip of the flower.

She moved closer, fascinated. Side by side, the flowers could not have been more different. The small creamy-yellow lady's slipper orchid with its delicate claret-coloured markings was overshadowed by the glaring Portuguese flower.

She glimpsed Geoffrey eyeing her reaction. He said nothing; he let the plant work its magic. She was absorbed for only a moment before turning away in embarrassment for she would have liked to cover the flower with a cloth – it seemed altogether too naked. The flower was showy, thought Alice; it seemed as if it flaunted itself too much – it was popish somehow. She could no more picture it in her garden than she could picture herself turning Catholic. She wiped her moist brow with her sleeve. The summerhouse was warm today.

She picked up the magnifying lens and brought it up to the centre of the red flower and was immediately transported into another world. The artist in her followed each part, the curving yellow column with its hairs bristling at the pink-tinged base, the halo of petals flaring like a sunset. Unusually there was no dust, but clusters of orange grit formed into flat discs or pellets. She placed the lens back on the table, as if it were too hot to handle. The red orchid was an impostor, Alice thought – an impostor in outrageous fancy dress. She did not want to use any of the precious yellow powder from her pretty little orchid to make more monstrosities like this.

'Showy, is it not?' said Geoffrey.

'Bold enough. What would you have me do with it?'

'I want gardeners all over England to have borders full of these. I have promised the first few to Hampton Court. But they need a hot climate to flourish. You said you have the skills to breed this one with your English orchid, make it more robust – and that is what I want you to do.'

'It is by no means certain that I can produce a tougher variety. The lady's slipper is a delicate plant. My father's work with plants was experimental. He was not a plantsman by profession,

118

merely a gentleman enthusiast. There were failures as well as successes.'

'You vex me. I will suffer no refusal. I do not understand why you are so reluctant.'

'I am surprised the plant is in such good condition, given the sea voyage,' she said, trying to turn the conversation away from her own recalcitrance.

'Oh, this one is the best of the specimens. We traded hundreds of plants, maybe thousands, but not many survived. Lack of fresh water, you see. Most plants cannot tolerate the seawater. I had the containers in the hold checked regularly, and my men threw them overboard if they looked to be rotting or diseased.'

Alice was shocked by this admission of waste, but it was not her place to query Geoffrey's business. He carried on, 'There are only two or three more of this type. Johnson, the gardener, has care of the others at the manor in case this one should fail. We are going to try growing them in the sheltered part of the garden under glass.'

She saw that Geoffrey had turned his back to her to study the lady's slipper in the light of the summerhouse window. Suppressing the urge to take the plant away from his avaricious eyes, Alice moved to the stack of paintings to fetch the watercolours of the ferns for Earl Shipley's dining room. The light was good today, the colours shone out, and the effect of the three paintings together was very pleasing. They had been framed simply by the joiner in polished oak frames. She had enjoyed the commission, and she knew they looked well. Now she laid them out on the table for Geoffrey's pleasure.

'Here are the paintings for Earl Shipley.'

Geoffrey bent over the lens, engrossed in his examination of the lady's slipper, and did not even look up. Instead he said, 'So you have no idea why this particular plant is so rare, or why there are so few?'

'I cannot be sure, Geoffrey, but I think perhaps because it is reputed to be medicinal; it was dug out over generations for its roots, and now there are few remaining. I never thought to see one, except in a book. You know that it is supposed to be a cure for nervous disorders?'

Geoffrey stood up. Alice continued, 'Yes, the spots on the inside of the flower draw out spots in the afflicted person. It is good for hives on the skin. In *Gargrave's Herbal* the description says it is also beneficial in any sort of restlessness or mania, fevers or other symptoms of overheating.'

'How extraordinary. A cure-all, by the sounds of it. How is it prepared?'

'The book says that the roots should be mashed and strained, that the juices can be drunk as a potion and the pulp spread over the skin. The flowers themselves can be boiled and made into an infusion. It can even be used to treat poor souls who are insensible or mad with the fever – the potion may be administered through a goose quill via the mouth.'

He went back over to the pot. 'Let me see these roots, then, Mistress Ibbetson.'

'It is not wise to disturb the roots again, Geoffrey. I have already moved it from the place it grew, though naturally I tried not to touch the lower part of the plant but dug it out carefully leaving the earth around it intact. After all, it could be the only one. We must take the utmost care not to do anything to weaken the root system. Now is its most vulnerable time – for it is setting seed and will need all its strength.'

'I am sure that we will not harm it, Mistress Ibbetson. I would like to examine the roots.' He took hold of the pot and gripped the plant by the stem.

'Be careful of the flower, Geoffrey!' Alice lurched forward to grasp his arm. Geoffrey spun round and gave her an irate look. Then he moved to the other side of the table and emptied out the little pot of earth, vigorously shaking the roots free of dirt. Alice breathed in sharply.

Geoffrey seemed unaware of the fragility of the stems, and of the dirt on the table. He started to feel the thick, waxy roots, pulling them this way and that, prodding them with his red scaly fingers. Then he scraped at them with his fingernail, until a white scar appeared. He sniffed at the substance, wrinkling up his nose, before rolling it between finger and thumb and touching it cautiously with his tongue. Alice was outraged. She followed him round the table and hovered at his elbow.

'Let us put it back now, Geoffrey.'

'All in good time.' Geoffrey ignored her, making a small movement with his hand as if to brush her away. With a quick snap he broke away a portion of the root, wrapped it in his kerchief and put it in his pocket.

She felt a rage boil up inside her and the urge to slap the self-satisfied smile from his face. With

121

tight lips she pushed the pot towards him.

'I' faith, Geoffrey – I hope you have not damaged the root.'

'Nonsense, woman. It was just a small sample.' He put the plant into her outstretched hand.

Alice glared at him. She scooped the earth back into the pot and carefully tucked it around the roots.

Geoffrey's eyes glittered. 'I can take it back to the manor and do some experiments with it, to see if it really is a cure-all. If it is, there could be much profit in it. But it will need to be tested first in exacting conditions.' He seemed to have forgotten all about the crimson flower, and was oblivious to Alice's stony stare. He wagged a finger at her. 'What you will do is produce as many of these lady's slipper plants as you can, as soon as possible.' He paced around the room. 'How long will it take until the new plants grow enough to yield flowers?'

'My father always said it is very slow growing,' she replied, 'and may not flower for five or even ten years.' She relished giving him this information, for she knew it was not what Geoffrey wanted to hear.

'Ten years? I will be an old man by then. You never mentioned this before. Can it be done more quickly?'

Alice felt strangely satisfied. She paused as if weighing it in her mind. 'It is complex. These orchids cannot be cultivated easily. It requires a specialist knowledge of their habits. But perhaps in the right conditions–' she paused for emphasis – 'and looked after in the proper way, something might be done.'

'It must be done, Mistress Ibbetson.' His mouth had taken on a stubborn cast. 'You promised me you would let me have more of these lady's slipper plants.'

Alice moved away from his looming presence.

'Beg pardon, Geoffrey, I promised no such thing. I merely said I thought it was possible.'

'You said you had the skills from your father to breed orchids. I am willing to pay you for those skills.'

'Do you think I am to be bought, Geoffrey?' Alice's voice was quiet. 'I undertook to show you the orchid in the spirit of friendship, because you have always been interested in plants as I am. No contract between us was made. I showed you the orchid as a favour, but now I shall grow it on as I see fit.'

He frowned. She felt her cheeks redden. 'Just because my circumstances are somewhat reduced, it does not mean you may treat me as a servant to do your bidding.'

'I am relying on you, Mistress Ibbetson.' He smiled slightly, and then trailed his fingers in the dirt on the table. 'Though what my good friend, Justice Rawlinson, would make of me associating with a common thief, I do not know.'

It took a moment before she realized this was intended as a veiled threat. She should not have told him she had stolen the orchid, it had given him leverage over her – she knew too late she had made a mistake. Awkwardly, she gathered up the three watercolours and held them out to him.

'Your commission, Sir Geoffrey.'

He turned away from her. 'I do not remember commissioning anything.'

'But you expressly asked me...'

'Did I? I forget.'

He picked up his soft leather gloves with one hand and slapped them on his palm, pointedly ignoring Earl Shipley's paintings. 'You will keep me informed of your progress with the orchid. It could be a valuable commodity. But payment will naturally depend on how many plants it yields. You may concentrate on that, until we know if it is efficacious.'

She masked her anger with a toss of her hair, but he continued, coming up close to her. 'Perhaps in the future you would be wise to stay on the right side of the law and conduct yourself with a little more restraint. After all, you would not want the thief's brand on your pretty little thumb.'

After he had gone, she was so hot with anger she filled a cup from the water butt and let the draught of icy liquid cool her throat. When she returned she stared down at the three paintings on the table. She had spent many hours working on them, and now Geoffrey was denying he had even commissioned her to paint them. How on earth would she tell Thomas? There was no doubt that the money would be missed. Thomas's health grew worse – he was breathless now even climbing the stairs to bed, but although she had heard he was a little slipshod at work, she knew he would never admit to her that his money-lending business was not going well. She could tell by his smiling reaction to her small offerings that her commissions were needed more and more.

She took the paintings off the table, blowing some specks of dirt from them, and stacked them away. Thomas seemed distant with her recently – he had snapped at her at breakfast, so his business must be worrying him. They had conversed as usual, but he had appeared to be preoccupied and restless, not his usual placid self. After Ella had brought in his mail he looked positively ill and seemed to be perspiring. She did not know how he would take it when she broke the news to him that Geoffrey had withdrawn his patronage.

The remains of her anger still fluttered in her chest and would give her no peace. She had always been cordial with Geoffrey; she had thought he admired her work and held her in some esteem. What a gull she was. She had been deluding herself. Things seemed out of kilter with her since she had brought home the orchid. Her shoes still had not been found; someone in the kitchen must know what had happened to them but said nothing of it. She could not imagine it to be April, the scullery maid, she was far too timid. Cook was honest as the day, always had been. No, Ella was the most likely, but what would she want with a pair of ruined shoes that were too tiny for her bulging toes? It was a mystery that had caused her a gnawing unease.

She looked at the flower. It looked pure and innocent, almost shy, next to the larger more showy plant. Yet it was surrounded by this strife. She let her eyes trace its delicate outline until her anger at Geoffrey's attitude was replaced by cold determination.

After Ella had shown Sir Geoffrey to the summer-house she hurried back, for Master had not yet left for the counting house and was still at the table with the news sheet and his folios of figures. Today was Friday, and Cook had gone to the fishmonger. Cook always had a good gossip with the other women and wouldn't be back just yet. Ella was going to make the most of this opportunity. She took a dish towel from the kitchen and tied it tightly round her bare ribs, under her bust. This pushed her breasts up like two mounds. Then she unbuttoned her chemise a little more and pushed it down low so the fabric just covered her nipples. She had recently taken to rouging her nipples with some of the madder 'borrowed' from Mistress's paintbox. She picked up an empty tray and went into the dining room.

Thomas was sitting at the far end of the long oak table and looked up from his papers as she came in. She saw him take in the bare flesh in one unwitting glance. She sauntered to the near end of the table, taking her time, and bent low opposite him to pick up Alice's platter and put it on the tray. She could feel his eyes on her, but he didn't speak. She moved even more languorously towards him to fetch his plate. She glanced out of the window, to see if the mistress might be returning, but there was no one there.

She moved behind his chair and then leaned over close to him to put the tray down on the table, turning slightly so that her breasts jutted up right in front of his eyes. As she paused there, she felt his hand slide around her bottom and his fingers squeeze tight into her flesh. At the same time his other hand reached for the inside of her blouse. She swung easily over so that she was almost sitting on his lap facing him, with her thigh between his legs. His breeches bulged under her thigh, and she rubbed slowly up and down.

His face was expressionless, but his breathing was shallow through his open mouth and his hands were kneading her flesh rhythmically in time with her movements. She saw his tongue slide from side to side to moisten his lips. When she felt his breath quicken, she pulled herself away suddenly and, taking hold of his platter, whisked the tray from the table. Without looking back she went out through the door to the kitchen. He was easy, that one. She'd have him soft as butter in no time.

Chapter 11

After he returned from the Ibbetsons', Geoffrey paced the drawing room still wearing his coat and fallback leather boots, unable to settle. He chastised himself, for he had handled Alice Ibbetson badly. He knew he had been a little high-handed with her. Keeping her goodwill would make for smoother business if he wanted to have her help in producing more of these interesting orchids. But women made him impatient. He could not assume obedience as he could with the servants, and he found dealings with the weaker sex hard.

Next time, he would try to make more of an

effort. He pulled his handkerchief from his pocket and unwrapped the piece of root, turning it over in his hands. The odd leathery smell assailed his nostrils again. What an unexpected boon that the plant might be a remedy.

He bounded up the stairs to his chambers and rifled through his mahogany cupboards to fetch out the equipment for grinding, slaking and sieving the root. If the plant was really as potent as Mistress Ibbetson seemed to think, then he was going to be the first to test its properties, judiciously of course, and the first to take full financial advantage. The method of preserving it would be crucial. He set immediately to dissecting the root. He did not dare hope that the plant may have some salving effect on his skin, no, he doggedly put that thought to the back of his mind. The root was quite unexceptional in appearance – it could have been any dandelion, or other common species.

Taking care not to waste any of the sample, he grated and pressed some of the root with rapeseed oil, and pickled a portion in alcohol. Some of it he ground finely in a mortar and set to bake dry in a billy tin. He worked with speed, for he knew his experimentations would be cut short by the evening meeting with the newly re-established Westmorland Committee.

Although he knew it was his duty to try to stamp out the trouble with the Quakers up at the Hall, he wished he did not have to go out again to the Rawlinsons'. He was engrossed in his blending of the plant with the different carrier oils, and in mixing differing strengths of the resulting elixir, and he

128

wanted to write up the preparations he had produced. When the hall clock chimed five o'clock, he reluctantly curtailed his activities, but not without first sampling a small amount of the ground-up root.

Alice Ibbetson had said it drew blemishes out of the skin, so he mixed a little less than an eighth of an ounce in a glass phial with a measure of brandy. To make sure it was all in suspension and none left in the glass, he swirled the brown liquid around before swallowing it. Despite its foul smell, it tasted bland – only the brandy burnt on his tongue, its afterglow hot in his throat.

He was even more irritated when he went down for dinner to find that Emilia had organized some sort of entertainment and dancing for the weekend without consulting him. She wanted to give him some of the invitation cards to deliver when he went to the committee. When he remonstrated with her, and said that he was not prepared to feed the entire county from his coffers, she fell into a sulk.

'But, Geoffrey, dearest, we are quite the poor relation! What will people think of us if we dine in their houses and sup their wine and never return a single favour?'

'Emilia, you tire me with the constant comings and goings in this house. I come home for rest, and it is never quiet. Quite apart from the expense of such lavish arrangements – what did you say? Seven musicians *and* some players?' He sighed and shook his head. 'Why can't you be content with a simple dinner and a little agreeable conversation, like other men's wives?'

Emilia pouted and pulled at her hair. 'I like a little gaiety in the house. We were so long without it, during the king's absence.' She turned to face him. 'And Lord knows, you are miserable enough. Other people's wives don't have to put up with a husband whose face is as long as a horse!'

'You must watch your lip, wife.'

His tone was icy. Realizing she had overstepped the mark and would need to make him an apology, she bustled over to him, a contrite look on her face.

'I beg pardon, Geoffrey. I am not fully myself today.' She raised her eyes under her eyelashes in appeal. 'I am concerned about Stephen, and it is making me ill-tempered and sharp.'

'Hmm.' Geoffrey was not convinced. He had endured several such incidences of rudeness from his wife recently, and was inclined to punish her. But then his head had begun to throb; it must be the strain of the day. It hurt too much for him to be troubled asserting his authority. Next time, he told himself.

'I should not have spoken to you in that way, please forgive me. I am upset because a letter came this morning from Stephen – there are rumours of the death pox in London. He is as yet undecided whether to leave his lodgings and return home. Of course I shall send to him to tell him he must come home.'

'Where is this letter?'

'I have left it on the stand in the hall, so that you may look it over before I pen a reply.'

'Stephen must remove himself immediately. If he were to breathe in the infection, then it would be too late for him to come home and he would have to take his chances.'

'You would deny him his home?'

'If he were to breathe in the death, yes. I have a responsibility to my estate and my business, and to the County of Westmorland.'

'You would turn away our son?'

When there was no reply, Emilia pressed her lips together and walked over to take a pile of cards from the side table.

'Here are the cards, for your friends on the committee.'

The cards were in his hand before he registered it.

She turned on her heels and went out through the doors into the dining room. Geoffrey watched her stiff back as she walked away – it was un-bending, like a plank, as if she was holding onto herself too tightly.

Geoffrey looked down at the square cards writ-ten in Emilia's distinctive ornate hand. All the capitals were frilled and curled like a woman's hair. Emilia had no taste, he thought. He slipped them into his pocket and sighed, resigned to deliver them as requested, for with annoyance he realized Emilia had managed to get her own way again.

After dinner Geoffrey rode out to Justice Robert Rawlinson's house. It was a wet and windy night and he needed his surcoat and heavy leather gloves for the reins were slippery in this weather. He enjoyed the feeling of the rain on his face, even if his eyes stung, and he usually liked the sound of

131

the steady rhythm of hoofbeats as a background to his thoughts. Today, though, the jolting trot only served to worsen the pain that had begun behind his eyes. Fortunately the house was not too distant. It was an edifice a little like Robert himself, squat and heavy, built of stone in the latest style with great chimneys on the outside walls reaching past the slated roof. It also had two separate withdrawing rooms away from the main hall. It was to one of these that he was shown when he arrived.

The group of men that made up the newly reformed Westmorland Committee were already assembled in a fug of smoke, seated near a fire that was almost bursting out of its grate. A servant drew the curtain across the door where Geoffrey had been admitted, and he realized with distress that the room was already very warm. He looked around for the coolest place to sit, and took the chair furthest from the fire. Heated rooms made his skin itch and made it difficult to concentrate. At home, his rooms were always cool – Emilia called them draughty and said her hands were turned blue because of it, but then she would wear those flimsy dresses with no shawl or gloves.

The men introduced themselves to each other, whilst a servant dispensed Madeira wine. The conversation was informal but the atmosphere one of watchful assessment, each of the men weighing the character and outward appearance of the others. Geoffrey knew them all except Lord Esham. Ralph, Lord Hetherington, he had known for years through the county hunt. They had been friends since they were boys. Ralph had been the younger by five years, but was always first in the field on his big grey mare, even as a boy. Now a small, wiry man with sinewy arms, he was renowned for galloping up next to the Master, or sometimes acting as Whipper-in. He did not look strong, but Geoffrey had seen him pull a horse up out of a bog single-handed, and then shoot it dead with a musket when he realized its legs were broken.

'Geoffrey! Good Lord above, you look soaked!' said Ralph. 'Come and sit here near the fire.' He tapped the seat next to him.

Geoffrey smiled. 'I'll just help myself to some of that excellent wine first.' He refilled his glass with a generous measure from the cask, then sat down again in his chosen chair away from the fire.

The men were conversing about the king's plans for a new observatory, which was going to be built at great expense. Sir John Fairfax, a large stooped old gentleman who looked as if his spine had been bent out of shape over an anvil, had apparently seen the drawings and pronounced it to be an architectural blight. And too far away from the centre of the city, he said, to be of any use to the gentlemen of Oxford, who, after all, would be its patrons.

Lord Kendall said it was an utter waste of money when it could be spent on more research into the circulation of the blood, or how the organs of the body work. Look close to home first, was his view, before looking at the sky. Geoffrey remembered that when they had been students Lord Kendall had been involved with experiments in anatomy. Kendall was always sickening for something and

133

was quite obsessed with his own health. His dour face and greyish skin belied what seemed to be a rock-like constitution. Geoffrey had always avoided him at Oxford because his conversations about his imaginary ailments, when his own were a constant bane, made him want to throttle him.

Lord Esham remained silent through the conversation about the king's proposed building plans. Geoffrey looked him over with interest – this was the man who was reputed to have had some dealings with the Rump Parliament. Dressed entirely in black, Esham sat back in his chair, hooded eyes observing quietly. His hands looked soft and flabby – white, with perfectly shaped nails – and something about the way they lay so still on the arms of the chair reminded Geoffrey of a corpse. Wearing black was usually associated with Cromwellian sympathies – it looked odd in this room with the blazing fire and the others with their fine embroidered waistcoats and fancy hose in damson or fawn or shades of green. Esham's black made him feel as if they were all slightly overdressed. When Esham finally spoke, his voice was low and smooth.

'Shall we proceed to business, gentlemen?' His voice undercut the conversation.

Whilst they took stools at the refectory table, Robert spoke first. 'Gentlemen, you remember Henry Swainson, of Lingfell Hall.'

The men nodded, and Fairfax said, 'He was a good man. I was shocked when I heard how he died – Clitheroe Castle, cut down from his horse by a common foot soldier. It was a ghastly ending for such a fine man, less than he deserved.'

'Yes, and he served this committee well over the years. I shall miss his presence at these meetings. But his widow by all accounts has lost her senses and joined the dissenters against the king,' Robert said.

'I had heard as much,' said Ralph. 'Some of my tenants have taken up with her ideas and are refusing to pay their tithes. They will not worship in the churches and I fear are gathering people together with a view to some sort of unholy rebellion.'

'Lord Kendall had to get the army to suppress an incident in the church only last week and it was Felicia Darby who started the trouble.'

'It upset me mightily,' Lord Kendall said. 'It brought on the most prodigious stomach ache which lasted for days.'

'Dorothy Swainson and Felicia Darby keep company together–'

'Like man and wife?' Fairfax interrupted with a snigger, and there was a round of laughter before Robert continued.

'And between them, they own most of the land west of the river. Now that there are no men in their households to keep them in order they are able to have free rein with their Quaker foolishness.'

Fairfax added, 'According to their Mister George Fox, each person has his own God within. It's immanence gone mad! It is the worst sort of blasphemy. Can you imagine where that idea would lead us? Every kitchen maid and ale woman could get into the pulpit and impart to us her wisdom.' There was more laughter from the group.

'Isaac Fuller, the town clerk, is part of their

faction, though, and Richard Wheeler, so they're not all servants and farmhands,' Ralph said.

Here was a moment's silence.

'I think Wheeler is dangerous,' Geoffrey said. 'I knew him personally before he turned traitor and became one of Cromwell's men.'

Lord Esham, who had been listening intently, leaned forward.

'Is this the Richard Wheeler who went north with Lilburn, and led Cromwell's men to victory at Cartington Castle?'

'Yes, the same. But now he is up to something. He sold up his estate, and bought a small farm near the Hall. He is a well-known anti-royalist. He has joined Lady Swainson and Lady Darby in this Quaker group. Lingfell Hall has turned into a place of safety for any ranter, raver or revolutionary who wants to turn away from the church. I think Wheeler is gathering a force together again to overthrow the king. The number of meetings has increased, and now half the village goes up to the Hall for their so-called worship. Only last week Wheeler was in Kendal marketplace stirring up dissent. I was set upon by a mob and barely escaped a lynching.'

Lord Esham looked thoughtful. 'So what do we suggest should be done?'

'Well,' said Robert Rawlinson, 'we could gather a list of the names of these Quakers and find a way to divide or split the group. That way Wheeler will have no one to lead in his planned rebellion. Lady Darby is already in jail, but we can't hold her much longer without a proper charge. Let us hope her new lodgings will make her see sense.

But be warned, she sent an appeal to the king last week, and her husband was well known at court before his death. The king has shown leniency since his return from France and she may never reach the assizes.'

'The opinion of his majesty is that he would like to return to a settled kingdom. There are to be no harsh retributions against parliamentarian sympathizers. Cromwell failed. We are to put it behind us.'

At Lord Esham's words the group fell silent.

'Surely something must be done or history may well repeat itself. And I, for one, do not want another war,' said Fairfax.

'The only thing we can do is to administer the law as it stands and make sure we allow no room for error with these Quakers. The king does not want persecutions. He is sensitive to his position in terms of his popularity with the people. If tithes are not paid, then arrest the debtor and take goods in kind. This can be sanctioned within the law. And—' Lord Esham paused and looked round at the others with a thin-lipped smile – 'we can always pay somebody to infiltrate these Quakers, befriend Wheeler and find out what is really going on.'

'Like a spy?' Fairfax appeared slow to comprehend.

'That could be dangerous. Whoever undertakes it would need to be able to convince Dorothy Swainson that he shared her religious zeal. In short, someone who can play the part. And they must be absolutely trustworthy,' Geoffrey said.

'I have usually found generous payment the

best way to ensure loyalty,' Esham said.

'I cannot think of anyone who is not already known to Lady Swainson or Isaac Fuller. They would become suspicious if one of us were to suddenly turn Quaker,' said Ralph.

'On the contrary. That is exactly what they expect at their conventicles,' Lord Esham said drily.

'Yes,' said Geoffrey. 'I have a feeling that Wheeler is playing the same game. His sudden conversion, hot on Cromwell's death, seems a little suspicious to me. I think he is using these people for his own ends.'

'The whole phenomenon is like a circus already, from the reports I have heard. It is the Devil's work – claiming to be touched by the hand of God, and falling over and trembling and so forth,' said Kendall.

Esham's mouth twitched at the corners. 'We'll leave the Devil out of this discussion for the moment, shall we?'

'I agree with Lord Esham,' Ralph said. 'One more person claiming to be won over would not surprise them at all, they are so stupidly convinced of their own wayward ideas.'

'But who?' Geoffrey stood up and walked over to the window. The heat of the room was making him restless, even though the itching seemed to have abated.

'Are any of us prepared to do it?'

There was an uncomfortable silence.

'I thought not.' Lord Esham sat back in his chair.

'None of us wish to be associated with such a rabble.' Kendall was adamant. 'I, for one, am not strong enough in health.'

'And we all have our reputations to consider,' Fairfax said. 'There would be considerable risk – there were whippings and brandings when the king last took against them. And quite right too – the county needs to be rid of these heretics.'

'Well, without proper evidence we cannot proceed against them,' Esham said.

'It could be a long business,' said Ralph. 'The spy must be prepared to sustain the act, for it may take time to win their trust before we find out the nature of Wheeler's interests.'

'It will need thinking about. If we were to approach the wrong person with the task it could warn the Quakers off and our work would be finished before it has begun,' Fairfax said.

'Let us think further on it and talk again at the next meeting. We have to deal with the Enclosures Act and the arrangements for the forthcoming assizes before we depart, and it is already late.' Robert indicated the agenda on the paper in front of him.

With reluctance it was agreed to postpone further discussion until the next meeting. Geoffrey struggled to maintain his attention through the other items; his head felt thick, like sheep's wool, his eyes bleary. He could not focus on the parchments in front of him, the letters jumped about like fleas.

As he got ready to depart and felt in his pocket for his riding gloves, he came across the cards Emilia had given him earlier. Now a little damp, the corners furred and the ink curlicues smudged, they came out with his gloves and landed at his feet on the hall flagstones, in full view of the departing gentlemen. Ralph bent over to pick them up for him, reading them as he did so. He would have to proffer the invitations now.

'Lady Fisk asked me to remind you of our dinner next Saturday evening, at my home. The cards are here.'

'Ah yes,' said Robert, 'Jane has told me about this. We are looking forward to it. She tells me there is to be dancing – not that I do much of that these days.'

'Do you think there will be time for the gentlemen to play a round or two of cards, Geoffrey?' Fairfax was a gambler.

'Perhaps.' Geoffrey knew no one would want to play against Fairfax – they would be sure to lose. 'Emilia has planned the entertainment, so I really couldn't say what her plans are.'

'I believe she mentioned a play – an allegorical drama, she said. It sounds as though it will be quite an event.' Ralph reached out a gloved hand for his card.

Geoffrey handed the last card to Lord Esham. 'I know it is a long ride out for you, but we would be delighted if you and your wife would join us.'

'I must unfortunately decline your invitation. We are already otherwise engaged. Please thank your lady wife for the card, and send her my apologies.'

Geoffrey could not help feeling somewhat relieved. Lord Esham set his teeth on edge, he had a knack of looking straight through you. Geoffrey's head throbbed fit to burst, so he made perfunctory farewells and, trying not to look unseemly in his haste, stepped outside into the welcome cool of the rain.

Chapter 12

Alice stood as soon as she heard horses approaching – for since stealing the orchid a tension had lodged around her shoulders and she was alert to any background sound. A serving lad had been over that morning to tell her that Geoffrey would call today to see her transfer the yellow dust in the orchid. Geoffrey had visited every day, suffocating her with his questions and his leaning presence. He had grown more persistent and she feared he would want to take her little plant, so she hovered over it whenever he appeared, like a mother hen with its chick. She wiped her brow with her sleeve. The afternoon light through the windows of the summerhouse was hot on her black wool dress.

She heard someone leave a trap at the mounting block, the shuffle of horses' hooves and a rap at the house door. Ella's slouching footsteps followed, accompanied by men's boots on the path. So she was ready when Geoffrey's tall figure pushed open the door without so much as a knock. His groom lurked just outside the door.

'Good morrow, Mistress Ibbetson.' Geoffrey smiled at her, but she could see now it was more from habit than warmth.

'Won't you come in, Geoffrey.' Alice felt herself withdraw, as if to put a wall between them, but observed the usual pleasantries; it would not do to give Ella cause for talk.

Geoffrey dismissed his manservant. Ella, apparently eager to engage him in gossip, followed him up the path leaving Alice alone with Geoffrey. Alice had to run out to call Ella back so that she might order refreshments. She also set her to bring hot water steeped with coals from the kitchen fire, and to fetch over some warming pans.

Geoffrey sat himself on a tall stool by the table, as if to observe the proceedings with a proprietorial air. Alice did not speak. She would do as he asked, yes, but she would not be genial. She expressed her rebellion against his attempts to browbeat her by her detached, efficient manner. There was a tense silence until Ella staggered back with the pan of hot water, and a further chilly emptiness until she appeared again with the tray of cordial and sweetbreads.

'You may go,' said Alice, a little tardily, for Ella was already slinking away, 'and if anyone should call, I am not at home. We are not to be disturbed. Do you understand?'

'Yes, madam.' Ella ducked her head. 'Will you be lunching as usual?'

'Lay out a cold repast in the dining room. I will eat it when my work here is done. My husband is at home today for a meeting this afternoon.' She looked coolly at Geoffrey who was helping himself to the small lemon cakes and sugared figs from the tray. She saw him pick out something from his teeth. 'Sir Geoffrey will not be staying.'

'And, girl – tell the groom to attend to the horses and clean the trap whilst I am busy,' said Geoffrey, between mouthfuls of cake.

'Yes, sir.'

Alice had resolved to humour Geoffrey. She had been thinking about the likely scenes if she was found to be a thief. Like the rest of the village, she had seen Sissy Robinson dragged in her shift to the pillory and left there to be pelted and spat at before being whipped to the gaol. The uprisings in what they all called the 'days of shaking' had left a strange atmosphere in the air; there was a skin of normality over the village, but underneath an unease still seethed, like an unknown creature in a deep pond. A knot of fear had tightened in Alice's stomach and would not let go. She felt its squeeze all the time now, like a slowly twisting tourniquet.

She moved her paintboxes and jars from the table and stood them on the washstand. Methodically, she set out the equipment she would need: the magnifying lens, a selection of fine squirrel-hair brushes and a large earthenware pot. She dropped the pot into the boiling water and left it to soak for a while. She also dropped in a pair of iron bodkins she used for embroidery. From a barrel of earth near the door, she used the trowel to fill a flat wooden tray with a few inches of dark soil. This she laid over the warming pans on the flagstone floor, turning the soil over and stirring it.

'What are you doing that for?'

'I am warming the soil. Although it is warm today, there was a sharpness in the air last night. You want your orchids to survive, do you not?'

After a while she put on gloves and used a pair of iron fire tongs to bring the pot out of the boiling water, before filling it with earth from the warming box.

'And you have boiled the pot to make sure it is clean, and free of any pestilence – is that right?'

She nodded. Geoffrey continued to watch her, shuffling restlessly on his stool. His knee jiggled up and down, she heard the rhythm of his silk breeches rustling. He was never still, she thought – always impatient, always restless. The lady's slipper orchid was hidden out of the servants' view under the table. Ignoring his fidgeting, she bent to bring it out and calmly set the flower down on the table.

'Hang me if that's not a fine sight.'

Alice gritted her teeth. A week ago he had told her it was miserable-looking and not as fine as that other popish flower, but that was before he had decided it was of medicinal interest.

'So what happens now?' Geoffrey said.

Alice answered briskly. 'First I will repot the lady's slipper in the warmed earth; this will give it the best possible chance to set seed, once the dust is put in place.'

She felt his eyes resting on her as she transerred the orchid into the large pot and put the warm earth around it, tamping it down with her fingers. When she had finished she took off her gloves, filled a small jug from the boiling pan and took it to the basin at the corner washstand. Using hot water and a piece of lavender soap she washed her hands thoroughly and dried them on the linen cloth hung above the basin.

'Well,' she said, 'I will take a moment to examine it to see how complex it might be to transfer the yellow dust from one part to the other. Only if I think it can be done without damage to the plant will I go ahead.'

She must have been looking some time because Geoffrey appeared over her shoulder wanting to peer into the lens. She handed him the glass without a word. She must be careful when transferring the dust not to damage the flower with the needle and to keep everything clean. Her orchid must remain unsullied, pure. She was relieved that Geoffrey, although a plant enthusiast and so-called scientist, had scant knowledge of seeding or growing plants. He would certainly have wanted to do this for himself had he known what to do, and she wanted to keep this process to herself. She thought of her father, whose knowledge of the plant kingdom had been almost legendary, and hoped he might be looking down on her kindly.

Using the tongs that were resting in the boiling water, she withdrew one of the needles with difficulty. She waved it in the air to dry it.

'It is essential that you do not move whilst I do this,' she said, looking directly at him for the first time. 'The least breeze could cause me to lose some of the precious dust which will set the seed in the plant. Please keep absolutely still and do not speak.'

Geoffrey leaned forward breathing heavily, trying to see what she was doing. She felt his breath on her neck, but she was careful to shield the plant with her body. Looking through the glass she opened the delicate pouch of the lady's slipper orchid and, using the tip of the bodkin,

145

gently lifted out a single cluster of yellow dust. This she carried to the centre of the petals and placed in a small well in the central column, brushing it inside with a squirrel-hair brush to mimic the insect's path. She did this tenderly, as if brushing a child's hair.

She repeated this process once more before replacing the needle on the table and stepping away, wiping her hands on her apron.

'Is that it?'

'Yes. It is done.'

'How will we know if it has worked?'

'That was only the first part of the process. When the seeds have started to form, the petals will fade and drop and the top of the plant swell. When the seed pod has ripened I can catch the seed and sow it. This too is a difficult process. Orchid seeds are very tiny, like particles of ground pepper, and it will need special dry conditions if they are not to rot.'

'But there will be plants if it all goes to plan?'

'Yes, Geoffrey.' Alice was resigned. 'There will be plants. But not for some time.'

'How many?'

'I can't answer that. You know as well as I that though there may be hundreds of seeds, only very few will germinate.'

She did not mention her father's secret, that they needed to be sown alongside a fungus if they were to thrive. Instead she said, 'I have to warn you, the new plant may not be as showy as the parent plant.'

'I am not so concerned about the look of the thing. Good strong roots, though, Mistress Ibbet-

146

son. Make sure they have good strong roots.'

'As I have said before, it will take time. Nature can be led, but not forced. Much like people.' Her eyes met his. He looked away.

'There will be a profit in it for you if you produce more than a dozen of the plants.' He wandered around the room, scanning the walls, obviously looking for something. 'And where are Lord Shipley's paintings? I will take those with me now. You will be reimbursed for your time with the paintings when the plants are large enough for me to grow on.'

'But that could be years...'

'I am sure you will find a way to hurry the process along, Mistress Ibbetson.' He smiled, but it did not reach his eyes. He gave a grunt as he spotted the framed ferns, stooping to pick them up. The room had become damp. Alice noticed the windows were steamed up. Droplets of moisture were running down them, leaving transparent trails like sweat.

'My manservant will return in one month to see how the orchid is doing,' he said. 'If there should be a problem, let me know immediately. And if it takes too long, I will send for another expert to assist you.'

Alice did not deign to acknowledge his last remark. She would never let another botanist near the little orchid. She wiped her hands on a cloth, unlocked the door and rang for Ella to see him out.

Ella was a while appearing, and when she arrived she was flustered and red in the face. Her apron was all greasy and her hair had escaped in rat's tails from her bonnet. She looked slovenly. Even through her annoyance, Alice was momentarily ashamed that one of her servants should look so unkempt. She resolved to have a word with her later. Geoffrey gave Alice a slight bow, but she gave him only a terse nod in return before going back inside the summerhouse.

Alice took up the watering can. She dribbled a little water into the black earth around the lady's slipper. Once the seeds were sown, she would be able to return the stolen orchid many-fold, and plant the new plants in other places too. She would follow in her father's footsteps. And she had her heart set on a lady's slipper to stand over Flora's grave, Flora had loved it so.

Alice packed away her equipment and washed her hands. There was nothing to do now but wait and let nature take its course. She had done all she could. The flowers would wither and the seed pods come – and then she would harvest and sow the seeds. After that she could divide the rootstock and nurture the seedlings until they could be replanted. She carefully carried the lady's slipper back to its hiding place in the orchard, ducking under the low-hanging branches with one hand shielding the top of the plant.

Thank goodness Geoffrey seemed to have forgotten all about his monstrous flame-red orchid. She had made her mind up, she would never give him a single lady's slipper. He would maul it and dissect it, and use it for his strange experiments in physic. Perhaps she could pretend the plants had failed to thrive. But he was a powerful man, not someone whom it was wise to anger. If he found out she had deceived him, her life could become extremely uncomfortable. There were rumours that when he was crossed he would send his men to plunder all your household goods in tithes. Previously she had dismissed these rumours as idle hearsay, but now she read them as a caution, she must watch her step. It was evidently better to have Geoffrey as a friend than an enemy.

As she put the lid back on the beehive, she remembered how Margaret, the herbalist, had told her to be careful. This warning had stuck in her mind like a knife. Perhaps it was this awkwardness with Geoffrey to which Margaret had referred.

Then again, perhaps Margaret was warning her to be careful of Richard Wheeler. She still did not know what to make of him. He knew she had the orchid, she was sure of it, yet he had not called the constable or asked Thomas to search the house. It was almost like a pact between them, an unspoken understanding.

She paused and looked out over the landscape, the trees interspersed with the slate rooftops, the squat square tower of the church. She thought again of him arriving at the door so unexpectedly. His old-fashioned manner of speech could have been quaint, but it only made him appear formal and distant. She could tell from the way he walked that he was a man used to action, but that this was somehow pent up under his unruffled exterior, like a wild horse in traces. She remembered the intense look in his eyes. Alice felt herself blush for no reason.

Whilst Alice was entertaining Geoffrey, Ella led

the manservant to the kitchen, where they sat down with Cook to hear the latest gossip about Sir Geoffrey and his wife, the Lady Emilia. The groom had heard all about Lady Emilia's secret affair and the letters that went back and forth, but Lizzie, Emilia's maid, was refusing to tell them anything. According to the groom, she was too frightened of losing her position. They were agog to hear more, but the bell was tinkling from the summerhouse, and Ella reluctantly went to answer it.

She had chuckled when Alice had summoned her to fetch refreshments and said that she had not to be disturbed. Thomas was still at home and was in the parlour, going over some papers. She told the manservant Sir Geoffrey's message, and he went off to clean the trap and see to the horses. When she made up a tray for Mistress and her guest, she made up another tray for Thomas. Cook was busy with the meal preparations, and a huge pile of gooseberries she was topping and tailing.

'I'm off to polish the cutlery in the dining room and clean the windows,' said Ella. 'I'll take this up for Master on the way.'

'Well, don't be long. I need some help with this bottling.' Cook gestured at the full baskets under the table. She grabbed angrily at the gooseberries, ripping off the tops and tails as if it was their fault, and throwing them into the pan where they rebounded like gunshot. 'And Mistress has pinched the boiling pan. How am I supposed to melt the wax to seal the bottles? I don't know how she expects me to do all this, and start tomorrow's breadcakes.'

'Well, there's a lot needs polishing too. I'll be as quick as I can.'

Cook raised her eyebrows in question. She knew Ella's usual manner of working, which was never exactly brisk, so she resigned herself to a long wait. Ella put the basket of polishing cloths over her arm and picked up the tray. She went straight to the parlour and shut the door behind her.

Thomas looked up from his scattering of papers and smiled, putting them aside. Ella sauntered over and put down the tray on the table. His hand reached round her waist and pulled her towards him.

'Now then, Master Thomas, whilst Mistress is busy I've brought you a few tasty morsels...' She looked at him with a coquettish smile.

'You are quite a tasty little morsel yourself,' he said, enjoying the banter, and stood up, starting to lift her skirts to feel the bare flesh of her legs.

She reached round to the tray and picked up one of the figs.

'Better have a taste then,' she said, putting it between her white teeth and turning back to face him, leaning towards his mouth. He bit into it and soon their lips were touching and their tongues probing, and the pulp and seeds were pressed between their mouths. Thomas licked her chin greedily before thrusting his tongue into her mouth again and pulling her hard against him. She clung on, grinding her hips against his as he licked and sucked her neck and the top of her breasts.

She stepped away a little and pulled the laced shoulder of her bodice down, lifting out one of her breasts, rolling the nipple between her finger and

151

thumb until it stood proud. 'Another fig, Master?'

'Ella.' He said her name and fastened his lips over the offered nipple, as if he would take her whole breast into his mouth. He started to lick it the way a dog laps water, the noise of it loud in the quiet parlour. Ella was becoming aroused, despite herself. She pushed herself towards him and took hold of the hair at the back of his head, feeling for his crotch with her other hand. He freed her other breast whilst she unbuttoned his breeches, and then took him in her hand, pumping up and down. He groaned and pulled her skirts higher until his hand felt the wet crack between her legs.

She steered him over to lean against the wall. From that position she could see Sir Geoffrey's groom out of the window, currycombing the horses.

'Sir Geoffrey's manservant,' she said hoarsely, 'he's just outside the window in the lane.'

The idea seemed to excite Thomas even more. He pushed her over towards the window, pulling her bodice off her shoulders, both hands rubbing her bare breasts, his jutting penis thrusting at her back.

'No, Thomas, he'll see us.'

'Then let him.'

She squirmed away, turning him so his back was to the window, and pushing him so he sat down hard onto the carved oak linen-chest.

'Wait there,' she said, holding him with her eyes as she went over to the table.

In the centre of the table were set the salt cellar and a small pewter dish with a lid. Ella took the lid off the dish and put in her fingers, bringing out a knob of yellow butter. Thomas watched her, with his breeches open. She knelt down in front of him with the butter and smeared it over him until it melted into a yellow grease. Cupping her hands over it she slowly slid them up and down. Thomas lay back with his head against the window, moaning as she worked the hot butter between her hands.

'What do you think the manservant would say now, if he could see you through the window? You with your cock all buttery, eh?'

Thomas groaned and his eyes closed.

'Should I lick it off now? Lick it clean?'

A faint but insistent tinkling noise was just audible over Thomas's moans.

'Mistress's bell.' She rubbed her greasy hands on her apron and hitched her bodice back over her breasts.

'Ella?'

But she was already halfway out of the door, tucking her hair into her cap.

Chapter 13

There was a fluttering in the blackberries and Richard saw that a starling had its leg caught in the nets he used to protect the fruit. The bird was thrashing and beating its wings in distress. He took a knife from his pocket and swiftly cut the thread, watching the bird fly in a haphazard arc to the garden wall. There, it preened itself, before hopping to take a mud bath in his newly dug trench. Smiling, he re-tied the thread with his earth-stained fingers.

As usual he was out early digging in the vegetable garden. As he plunged the spade into the ground, he admired the bed where he had been sowing the winter spinach and planting turnips for their green sprouting heads, a welcome sight in winter when the ground was hard. The sun frayed behind a veil of early morning mist, pale lemon-coloured above the horizon; the air was damp and chill. Along the wall next to the cottage he could see the fruiting raspberries – today he must harvest them, ready for market tomorrow. And he must remember to hang new wasp traps, and to bury the tips of the blackberry shoots to form more plants.

It was a lonely life, this. He missed the camaraderie of the barracks. The friendship at the Hall was of a different kind, less free and easy, more controlled. He always felt a little as if he was not quite up to the mark, his Quaker brethren seemed so upright and noble.

He paused for a moment over his spade, the sweat standing in beads from his brow, looking around. Nature's bounty. His little piece of ground, filled with the fruits of his own hard work. He wiped his hands up and down briskly against his leather jerkin and sliced the spade again through the damp soil. He thought of the rumours that some of the villagers were to be dragged off their land for the new enclosures. As long as a man had a plot of land, then he was rich enough and need never starve. He wondered if a time would come when all men would be free to own their own land, and none would be bound to another man's service.

He hefted the spade again and stood on the edge of it with his boot. It did not give, so he paused again and looked around. He felt a presence grow about him, like the swelling of music – a tune that was strange yet familiar. Even the clods of earth seemed to be part of this music, to have their own note distinct from all the others. It made him yearn for something lost. Perhaps this feeling was what made things grow, made them burst out from the seed to burgeon up and out, to flower and fruit, and then when their longing had gone, to wither and die.

He applied his full weight to the spade and finished the trench for the winter spinach. Afterwards he stood up the spade and pummelled his back with both hands. Then he wheeled the wooden barrow of rubbish to the midden. Earlier he had been down to the wood and stood in the spot where the orchid had been growing, the place where he had seen the white dove. Had he imagined it? He had stood perplexed over the hole in the earth, trying to fathom its meaning. Maybe it was a sign. Perhaps God was telling him he should fight for people to stay on their land. In his mind's eye he saw again the bird's white outstretched wings. At the same time, an image of Alice Ibbetson's face came to him. He saw her rapt expression when she had first seen the little flower. Her face all lit up as if from within.

She was lying, though, and it made him feel

sad. He would speak with her again. It was a slippery downhill slope, lying and deceit; a trap waiting to spring. She was a good woman, a sensitive woman. No one could paint nature the way she did and be entirely without a soul. He would save her from herself if he could. Maybe this was what God wanted of him, to bring her back to a life of honesty and truth. He pictured her face, contrite.

Picking up his spade, he went back to the house. The vegetables would have to wait. They were releasing Felicia today, and he was going to ride to Lancaster with the others from the Hall, to meet her and accompany her home.

It was nearly a month since the unfortunate incident in the church, and Felicia had been in gaol all that time. It was important to be there when she was released, to show support. And he wanted to prove to Dorothy that he was fully committed to their cause.

The little group stood expectantly at the gates of the gaol. Noon, they had said.

The sun was high in the sky, but despite this it had become cold, a wind was coming from the north and blew sharp round their ankles. The women gathered their shawls tight round their shoulders and blew on their hands; the men stamped, stepping from foot to foot. They could hear noises from behind the big wooden door but couldn't see anything. Dorothy saw Richard approach and held out her gloved hand to greet him.

'I thought to find thee here,' she said, smiling. 'No sign yet?'

Dorothy shook her head. There was a muffled clang from behind the door and the people shuffled forward. Huge, strong as the oak that made it and studded with iron nails, the door towered over them. Within it was a smaller, man-sized door with no handle, just a small square peephole. It was next to this door that the group of Quakers were waiting. Richard looked fondly at the unassuming group in their greys and browns. He noticed Jack and Hannah amongst the group, from the conventicle with George Fox, and nodded to them.

'It's past noon,' said Isaac, the town clerk. 'They said noon.'

No one answered him; they were used to waiting for authority. There was nothing they could do but be patient. They stood close together near the tumbling-down outer walls. The Earl of Derby had ordered the demolition of the walls during the war – until of course he realized he was actually destroying the county gaol, whereupon he stopped.

Richard looked around him. He could see that the city looked prosperous and busy again. There were new houses now, with big windows and double entrance doors. Even after the civil war had finished, the earl and the king's men had been so irked the castle had been surrendered to the parliamentarians that they laid siege to it. When it proved impregnable, he had turned on the town and set fire to it – more than two hundred people had lost their lives.

The war had continued to claim lives, even when it was long over, thought Richard. He turned to his companions, broken from his thoughts by the

157

sound of Isaac's voice.

'Thou wilt take her back to the Hall?' Isaac looked to Dorothy.

'Yes, she will need a hot meal, and a chance to bathe and recover herself. I will send for her sister in a few days to fetch her home. My carriage waits at the bottom of the hill.'

Richard blew on his hands and rubbed them together; they were cold. He wished he could have a pipe, it would have warmed his hands, and he found standing still with nothing to do burdensome.

'I know,' Hannah said. 'Let's sing.' No one looked very enthusiastic, but Hannah raised her voice and started to sing.

'Ho! Threshers of God's harvest,
Why stand with idle blade...'

Her voice rang out loud and unwavering, echoing in the streets around her. Jack's firm tenor joined her, and then one by one the rest of the assembly, getting louder as their confidence increased.

'Trust in thy whetted sickle,
And gather up the grain,
The day is fast approaching,
And soon will come again,
The Master calls for reapers
And shall he call in vain?
Shall souls lie there ungather'd
And waste upon the plain?'

158

By the time they had reached the end of the verse they were all singing, even Dorothy, whose voice was surprisingly deep and melodious. Richard did not know the hymn, but he picked up the tune and joined in. Their voices carried through the stonework of the walls, and from within more voices could be heard, as if in answer. Dorothy turned to Hannah, and smiled through her singing. The Quakers inside the gaol had heard them and were joining in. By the time they reached the last verse the sound was loud enough to gather a crowd from the surrounding streets. People came to see what the noise was, and stood pointing and jesting at the group outside the gatehouse door.

'Be faithful to thy purpose
In service of the Lord,
And then a life of friendship
Shall be thy just reward!'

As the verse finished there was a spontaneous cheer from the little group of Friends, followed by boos and laughter from the onlookers. In the jail the hymn ended not with cheering but with a strange silence. Then muffled sobbing, followed by wailing and rattling and banging against bars. Shouts went up from inside the gaol, the sound of angry voices and heavy running feet. The small door creaked open and two men emerged. The older man, obviously an official, spoke.

'Get away from these doors before I have you arrested.'

Richard went to approach the men to talk with them. The man gesticulated with his hand as if to

159

push him away.

'I am warning you. Remove yourselves forthwith or I will send for the constable.'

The young lad standing behind him nodded his curly head up and down, safe on his side of the law.

'We're not budging. We'll stand here all day if we have to,' Jack shouted. 'Mistress Darby is to be set free today and we'll wait here till she walks out of that gate.'

'Then you'll have a very long wait. Felicia Darby died this morning. Now move away.'

'What? What did he say?' They turned to one another in confusion. The officer and the young lad slipped back behind the door and it started to creak shut.

'Wait!' Dorothy said.

Richard jumped forward and pressed his body between the door and the stone wall. 'In God's name, tell us what happened to her.'

'She died of a fever,' the man said shortly.

'Lord have mercy. We must see her,' Dorothy said. 'Let me see her.' She seemed suddenly smaller, wearier.

'Bubb, go to the gov'nor, see if the body still lies there. If it does, ask if we can sign it over.'

'Yes, sir.' The young man scurried back through the wooden door, followed by the officer, who shut it behind him with a dull thud.

Dorothy wept silently. Richard and Isaac moved to support her. She leaned on Isaac's arm, one sleeve pressed against her eyes. Inside the gaol the moaning continued.

'Give us another tune!' shouted someone from

the crowd.

Jack turned to the still-watching onlookers.

'Our friend is dead,' he announced. The crowd hushed. 'Falsely imprisoned, for bearing witness to the love of God. They say she died of a fever. May she rest in peace.'

'Good riddance! One less Sabbath breaker,' a woman shouted from the back of the crowd.

'They should put 'em all in there,' said another.

'For murdering a tune!' a young lad called out. A ripple of laughter went round the crowd. They turned to each other, spreading the news, enjoying the entertainment. They were about to move away, thinking it was all over, when the older man's deep voice came from behind the door.

'Do you want charge of the body?'

Dorothy and Richard exchanged glances.

'Yes,' said Richard.

'Then wait.'

The crowd of watchers stayed where they were, surrounding the subdued Quakers. Some of their group were weeping; Dorothy was outwardly composed, but Richard could see her cheeks were hot and her neck was red. Richard moved to her side in case she should faint.

A coal-haired man near the front of the crowd rubbed his hands together and said, 'When the body comes out, look for the iron marks round the wrists and ankles. The more they struggle, the blacker they be.' He nodded over his shoulder to those behind him. 'You'll see.'

Richard hoped Dorothy had not heard this and wondered how he could protect her from the sight. He remembered how she had dealt with his

161

friend's death all those years ago in the war. He was a soldier, he was used to such sights. He hoped her strength would not fail her now.

When the door opened again Richard and Isaac moved forward. The officer came out, followed by the curly-haired lad and a burly gaoler with a pock-marked nose, sweating under the weight. They manhandled Felicia through the doorway as if she were a bundle of laundry and let her slump heavily onto the pavement outside. With a brief glance Richard took in the motionless form – the bruises on her face, the cut lip where the blood had dried black. The body was Felicia, but not as they had known her; the features seemed bland, ordinary, gave no hint of her extraordinary verve and intelligence. Richard's face tightened. The older man stepped right over Felicia to hand Richard a paper.

'Sign here.' He sniffed, and made to give Richard a quill.

Richard ignored the quill and looked the man square in the face.

'Lay her out properly,' he said. His voice would brook no argument. 'She was a decent woman, and a good friend. She deserves thy respect.'

'She don't care now 'bout respect. She's gone.' The burly man prodded at the motionless body with his boot. Richard lurched towards him and grabbed his collar.

'I said, lay her out properly. Then I'll sign.'

The man's cheeks turned reddish purple as he jerked to free his throat.

'Don't thee fret, Richard.' Dorothy's hand was soft on his arm. 'Come away now. They are right.

Her spirit has passed out of her. She cannot hear us now.' Richard opened his mouth to speak but was stayed by a stronger pressure on his arm. 'But it is not seemly to haggle over her in the street. Sign'st thou the paper and let us take her home to the Hall where she belongs.'

Richard let his grip loosen and the man pulled away.

'The paper, Richard.' Dorothy was firm.

He wrenched the quill from the gaoler's hand and scribbled his name, thrusting the paper back at him. He felt Dorothy's eyes on him, on his hot face, and was ashamed. He had let her down. He saw Isaac gently straighten out Felicia's body. Dorothy moved to her head and held it between her hands. Felicia's face was serene in death, smooth as plaster; it made Dorothy's pink face seem even more vibrant and alive.

Richard swallowed hard, took control of himself and stripped off his coat. 'Thou must take off thy coat too, Isaac. We can use them as a makeshift sling, to take her down to the carriage. 'Tis too narrow to bring it up.'

Isaac took off his coat and they lay them out flat on the ground. Jack and another man helped them lift Felicia's body onto the coats. Then the four men lifted the sleeves, making a sling, and carried her sombrely down the hill. The band of Quakers followed, bare-headed for once, and walking slowly, as a mark of respect, followed by the rest of the spectators trying to get a look at the body. Everyone crowded round the carriage as Felicia was laid inside on the back seat. Dorothy looked to Richard. She spoke matter-of-factly.

'There is nothing more to be done. Isaac will accompany us home, where we will make all the necessary arrangements.'

Richard winced. She did not need him, he was being dismissed.

She turned to the little group of Friends. 'Best for you all to go to your homes now. We will honour Felicia's life at the evening meeting.' Climbing stiffly onto the front seat with Isaac, she signalled the driver to set the horses going.

Richard turned away and heard the clopping of the horses' hooves as the carriage moved off. He walked back up the street and sat down on a piece of the tumbledown wall to gather his thoughts. His boot traced a pattern over the damp cobbles. He had almost lost control of his temper and got into a brawl. He thought of Dorothy's notion of the 'watchman'. He was supposed to be alert at all times, looking out for moments like these, when evil could creep in unbidden. Richard knew his watchman had been asleep and he felt ashamed. He had let Dorothy down at a time when she needed his support. He raised his head and looked down the street. From his vantage point he could see the people begin to disperse, now there was nothing more to see.

'Friends!' Jack's voice rose, strident above the chatter of the crowd. Never one to miss an opportunity, there he was, standing on a mounting block, his face shining with zeal. His wife Hannah was on the lower step, looking up to him with her brown eyes wide. Some people turned back to stare at them. Richard was uneasy; surely he wasn't going to witness to God now?

He heard Jack launch into speech. 'I spit in the face of death! Why? Because there is no death in God's kingdom.'

'Then why was that woman stiff as a besom?' called the lad from the crowd, sniggering to his companions.

'Whilst she was alive, Christ lived in her, and now he lives in each of us, if we hearken to our inner voice.' Richard saw Hannah climb another step up on the mounting block. She was warming to his theme and wanted to have her say.

'Cast away the lessons of priests and parsons,' she said. 'There is no church and no God, but He who lives in each of you at this very moment!'

'Heresy. The woman is speaking heresy. She said there was no God.' A man pushed towards the mounting block and aimed a gobbet of spit at Hannah's face. Richard sprang to his feet and started to run down the street. The mood of the gathered people had shifted without warning; a tide was on the turn. Now it was sullen, the dissent spreading like a bruise.

Richard saw that Jack was still talking, oblivious to the change in the crowd. He saw one of the men pick up a spade from a shop doorway.

'Jack!' he called out. But Jack did not hear him.

'I strip myself of all outside trappings, of all that perishes, of goods, profession, clothes. Yea, even the church itself, for there is no God except Him that lives in me.' Jack paused, for dramatic effect. 'Henceforth I shall go in the streets unclothed, as a sign that I give up all material goods.' Richard was nearly at the bottom of the hill. He saw Jack strip away his woollen waistcoat as the crowd watched, half horrified, half fascinated.

'God does not live in your steeple-houses,' Hannah cried, 'but in the human heart!'

'Let this be a sign.' Jack threw off his shirt and bared his torso. His thin chest was white against the red sandstone of the prison walls.

'Get him!'

The hoarse cry from the back was answered by the crowd surging forward like a pack of terriers, their hands grabbing for him, eyes wild, mouths wide open in snarls of abuse.

Richard saw Jack's look of astonishment before the crowd swept forward and Jack disappeared under a mass of shouting men. Richard tried to push his way through the crowd, but their blood was up and they had their quarry in their sights. With dread Richard saw that one man was armed with a spade, another with a broken bottle. On the other side of the street he caught sight of Hannah. She scrabbled to pull the people away but she was thrown to one side.

'Stop,' she sobbed. 'In pity's name, stop!'

A man grabbed her by the hair and punched her in the mouth. She staggered before she slumped to the ground. 'That'll stop your mewling, you little heathen.' Richard tried to break out of the crush of bodies to get to Hannah but he was being carried along.

Richard could not see Jack or hear his voice. He had no idea where he was but kept trying to push his way into the centre of the crowd. His sword hand felt empty and useless. With teeth gritted in frustration he forced his way to the centre, where he could see glimpses of Jack's white chest.

Already it was cut and bruised and oozing blood. Richard muscled through and tried to shield him with his back. A glancing blow from the spade caught Richard between the shoulder blades and he keeled over in pain.

In the confusion he had not heard the sound of running boots, but then an explosion and the smell of shot made the crowd panic and start to fall away. The constable and his men surrounded them. Smoke hung in wisps where the gun had been fired. Richard continued to shield Jack with his shoulders. Those in the act of beating them turned their heads to see what was happening.

'Stand up,' the voice commanded. Richard stood up and faced the approaching men. Jack lay at his feet, bubbles of blood forming round his mouth. From the corner of his eye Richard watched the people on the outskirts of the crowd scuttle away like insects, back to their holes.

'Stay where you are.'

The rest of the crowd stopped in their tracks and stood still. Jack was moaning and could not stand. His face was unrecognizable, his shoulders and chest a mass of cuts and bruises, one arm lying at an odd angle as if somehow disconnected from his body.

'Was this man causing a disturbance?' The constable pointed to Jack.

'No,' Richard said. 'He was preaching, and they set upon him.'

'You,' said the constable, turning his ferret-like face to a man in the crowd, 'what do you say?'

The man spat onto the ground. 'Aye. He's only himself to blame. Blasphemous bugger. Started

167

strippin' off his shirt, tellin' us that he's got Christ inside of him.'

'Deserved all he got,' the coal-haired man said.

'Aye.' Richard heard murmurs of righteous assent ripple through the crowd.

'Does that make it right that he should be flayed within an inch of his life and his wife punched to the ground?' Richard raised his voice.

'You keep quiet,' the constable said. He pointed to Jack. 'Put the irons on him and fetch his wife alongside, there will be no more rabble-rousing this day. We'll detain them at his majesty's pleasure.'

'But someone should attend to his wounds.'

'Do you wish to join them, sir?' There was laughter from the crowd. A pause. Richard flushed.

'Yes. If that is the only way that someone will attend them, then yes, arrest me. I will go with them gladly.'

'He's moon mad,' said a woman near the front, wagging her finger next to her temple.

'Step away, sir,' the constable said. 'The prison is not an apothecary's house, nor an inn for your pleasure.'

Richard stayed where he was, bending over Jack, who was writhing on the ground, and talked gently to him. 'Jack. 'Tis I, Richard. I'm here.' He was at a loss what to do; Jack was badly beaten, his wounds needed washing and dressing. His hair was dark and matted with blood. Jack tried to speak but blood was filling his mouth and no words would come.

'Chain him.'

Richard was forced to watch the constable's

men put irons on Jack's wrists. Two of the men took hold of Richard by the arms and roughly dragged him to one side, holding him firm. He heard Jack groan as the limp arm was wrenched up and roughly bound to the other by iron chains. It hung uselessly, like a leather washcloth. Hannah was dragged alongside him, half conscious, one side of her face a mess of blood, her blouse stained with streaks of it, but she was too groggy to protest.

'Let me go with them, I can vouch for them, and they are personal friends of Lady Swainson,' Richard said, standing in their path.

'That cuts not a shilling's difference with me. Now get out of the way. Or I'll order the men to shoot.'

The men raised their muskets. Richard spoke quickly to Jack. 'We will not rest till thou art released,' he said.

'Like Felicia,' laughed Hannah bitterly through broken teeth, 'to be buried.'

'Dearest Friend, it will not come to that.'

They hoisted Jack roughly onto a cart and the constable shackled Hannah to the bars of the tailgate, and they were goaded back towards the castle. Richard felt faint and sick. He followed as the horrible procession filed up the hill towards the gaol, the crowd's taunts in his ears. Good God in His mercy. What would he tell Dorothy?

'Let me look at you.' Emilia stood on the stone steps, and grasped Stephen by both arms, smiling down at him.

'My dear Mother, you haven't changed at all.

169

You look in fine health.' Stephen pulled away and bent to kiss her on the back of the hand.

'And you, my son, how are you? I take it you are well?'

He smiled back at her, with an expression of delight. 'I am glad to be here. The Westmorland air is so much purer. London is full of foul odours and lung-retching smoke. No wonder people are stricken – the pestilence is carried in the air, I am sure of it.'

Emilia frowned, patting him on the arm.

'And people will burn that stenching sea-coal,' he went on. 'It makes me cough. I was glad to see your stack of timber by the stables.'

'Come on into the house. Your father has re-decorated all the chambers with green leather and gilt, a pot-headed idea he had from the houses in Antwerp. Come and see how brazen it looks.'

'Where is Father?'

'He is out at a meeting with the stewards. He is hardly ever at home, and when he is, he goes to his chambers and puddles his senses with wine. He seems even worse these days. He's taken up with some new salve he is making. Spends hours locked in his chambers. Some days he seems hardly sensible.' She shook her head.

'The stewards seem to want to do nothing else but fester in meetings all day long. It sounds like a pretty dull life to me. Father should get more of a grip on them.'

'Have a care, Stephen. Show a little respect to your father.'

'Let us go in then, I will greet him later–' he winked at his mother from under lopsided blond hair – 'before he partakes of the wine. Have Patterson tell him I am here, and will be sleeping in the red chamber.'

'Yes, Stephen. It is so good to have you home. You have thickened out, and I can see you'd have a fine beard coming, were it not for the barber.'

'Oh, Mother, do not be impertinent – you make me sound like a child.' He rubbed his chin, feeling the fine blond stubble. Then he grinned at her. 'Come along, you had better show me these famous wall-hangings.'

They went inside arm in arm.

Geoffrey was in a good mood. He could scarcely believe it, but the itching had abated, thanks to the new infusion, and it was good to see his son. Stephen looked older and seemed more confident than when he had last seen him. He showed him the new drawing room, where he made much of their new gilded leather panels, the latest elegant design from the Low Countries. When they got to his chambers, Geoffrey was delighted to find that Stephen sat politely and seemed to listen well as he recounted the day's events. London must have done him some good. He was glad, for it would not do for him to emulate Emilia's coarse habits and way of speaking. Geoffrey explained how he had agreed to move the boundary hedges and had been reassured of a bigger income for the New Year, but that the decision was not popular.

'Will the changes provoke strife then, sir?'

'Some of the tenants will no doubt stir up a dust storm, as they will be losing a proportion of their land to the new divisions. But then they are always griping about something – at least now

171

they will have something of consequence to complain about.'

'Mother tells me there's been a deal of trouble of late with our tenants.'

Geoffrey outlined the incident in the church and Felicia's subsequent arrest. 'I have heard today that she died in gaol, of a fever. It sparked off another disturbance – a lynching in Lancaster Town, with two more arrested. And what is even more disquieting is that, according to the servants, Richard Wheeler was there.'

'His name sounds familiar – who is he?'

'You are too young to remember him. You were four years old when he left Westmorland. He is a man who was once a good friend of the family but has turned traitor. He is not worth my breath. But he was one of Cromwell's men and is hatching another rebellion against the Crown, of that I am certain.'

Geoffrey told Stephen about the Westmorland Committee, and of Lord Esham's suggestion that someone should infiltrate the meetings at Lingfell Hall.

When he told Stephen they had been unable to find anyone suitable, Stephen stood up. 'But, sir, did you not think of me?' His face was eager, like a pup on the scent of a fox. 'I am the ideal man for the task,' he said, caught up in the romance of the idea. 'I am loyal and discreet, and even if it does sound boastful, I am quite an actor.'

'No,' Geoffrey said, taken aback. 'Quite unthinkable. Not until whores drink holy water.'

'But, sir, why not? Am I not to be trusted?'

Geoffrey shook his head in annoyance. His son

172

was more naive than he thought. 'Of course I trust you, it is that nest of adders at the Hall I do not trust. I have seen what Richard Wheeler and his Puritan friends are capable of. It is too great a risk to put my own son there.'

'But I thought the Quakers were peaceable – fools perhaps, heretics even, but not dangerous, surely?'

'Do not underestimate them.' Geoffrey shook his head. 'This is a serious matter. You do not know what you are dealing with. Wheeler's regiment seized Cartington Castle, his men tortured and raped on his orders, he is a cold and heartless man. And as for Lady Swainson, she used to be for the king before the war. Then she turned traitor. She has been often to court, yet now she sups with farm labourers and scullions. Why would she be harbouring these crop-eared Roundheads, and why has there been rioting and scuffles on the street involving her friends?' He shook his head again. 'No, they are amassing, and we do not know what they intend to do. Wheeler has Lady Swainson in his thrall and who knows what might happen? I say again, you are too young, and the risks too great.'

'Let me meet your committee. They shall decide if I am too young. Kings have ruled countries at a more tender age. Let the committee decide.'

Geoffrey had always found it hard to resist his son. Although Stephen drove him to distraction, for he had always been weak and easily influenced, some might say soft, Geoffrey had always held out a hope that somewhere inside him a boy like himself was buried and would one day emerge.

Perhaps this would be the making of him.

He sighed. 'Very well. You may put your case to the committee. But you must stand or fall on your own merits, no word from me. And if they fail to hire you, then you understand – this conversation must go no further.'

His father's agreement in his grasp, Stephen replied, 'Of course, sir. Yes, sir.' Then, smiling broadly, 'Snug's the word.'

'And, Stephen,' Geoffrey looked pensively out of the window to where Emilia was just sauntering in from the garden with a nosegay of flowers, 'say nothing of this matter to your mother, she knows nothing of men's affairs.'

Chapter 14

Something was wrong – very wrong. Alice stood in the orchard, holding the lid of the beehive in her hands. The orchid's leaves were starting to curl over, the edges tinged with yellow; the flower head drooped limply from its stalk. She put down the lid and, oblivious to the possibility of being stung, removed her hat and veil. She lifted the pot from its little well in the ground and brought it up to her eyes. There was no sign of slugs or snails or any other insect – the hive kept them out, but nevertheless the lady's slipper was wilting, and she didn't know why.

The weather was mild; there had been no frost that night, and the other flowerbeds were bloom-

174

ing as usual. The little knot garden of herbs in the corner was buzzing with bees, and the white autumn lilies stood upright and tall in the corner. She looked again at the wilting flower. Perhaps it needed more light, or more warmth. She hurried over to the summerhouse, where she stood the pot out of view in a place where the sunlight cast yellow diamonds on the floor.

Throughout the day she kept returning to look at the lady's slipper to see if it was reviving. She could not leave it alone. She tested the soil for moisture, she turned it to face the light, put a little cane next to the stalk to support the drooping flower, fed it shakily with diluted ground chamomile and black tea. By the evening it had still not recovered.

That night she tossed in her bed, not sleeping, her forehead rigid with tension. The responsibility of it weighed on her, the idea that it might die and Wheeler be right. She ate breakfast with her eyes red-rimmed and without bothering to wash her face or comb her hair. Thomas made a comment about it, and she slammed down her cup on the table and burst into tears, occasioning more sharp words.

By now the leaves of the little plant were starting to turn brown at the edges. She agonized over her decision to take it, wondered if she should have left it where it was. She pored over her father's leather-bound notebooks about plants and their conditions, riffling through one after another in a rising panic, turning the pages quickly, searching through his spindly handwriting for an answer. The orchid would not set seed in this condition, nor would it be safe to divide it.

Poor flower. It had placed its trust in her. She felt her own inadequacies as a gardener more keenly than ever before. She longed for her father's calm presence – he would have known what to do, what ailed it. The thought of him brought a lump to her throat. It had been a shock when he died, there had been no warning – it was as if the heart had suddenly gone out from him. Yet he had survived the fighting, even when Cromwell's men set fire to their house and they had to run into the darkness with nothing but the clothes on their backs. Her mother had been frantic when he had insisted on collecting his notebooks. 'They are my legacy,' he said calmly as the smoke filled the hallway and she tugged at his arm. Later, with an unerring instinct he had guided them across the countryside. 'Don't look back,' he kept saying, and the words had stuck with her all these years.

But he had not been the same man without his garden. It had always been his abiding passion. The life seemed to seep away from him. Although their new town house was adequate for their needs, the loss of their family home cast a shadow over them all. When Flora was christened, they were still in mourning for his death. Less than a month later her mother was gone too. Weakened by childbirth, she had succumbed to an infection of the lungs.

Alice bit her lip; she seemed to have been wearing black for half her life. 'Don't look back,' she thought, bitterly. She could not help but look back. She lifted up one of the flaccid leaves in desperation. and let it fall. She knelt down.

'Come now, little flower, be strong. Come now, I will look after you. Please don't die.'

When she spoke these words tears sprang to her eyes. She had said nearly the same words to Flora barely a year ago. She had watched helplessly, unable to prevent it, as the life ebbed away, as Flora's warm face grew pale as whey and her hands turned grey and icy on the coverlet.

She prayed harder, asking God for his forgiveness if she had offended by bringing the plant home, begging him to restore it to health. Perhaps he was going to punish her after all, for her lies. Perhaps Wheeler was right, and God was displeased with her. She prayed fervently, her knees pressed into the hard floorboards. She heard no answer to her prayers, nor any sign that anyone was listening, just as she had heard no answer as she bent to pray on the blue rag rug at the foot of Flora's bed.

The lady's slipper looked sickly, as if it too had given up on life. She had failed Flora, watched her slip away moment by moment. A sense of her own impotence overwhelmed her. There was no one to help her. She moved about the room like a linnet confined to a cage. Her hands tightened into fists.

'No,' she said. 'Don't you dare die.' The room echoed oddly with her voice. Flora's pink and white face stared down from the walls, smiling, her white teeth painted like a row of barleyseeds, but her eyes seemed to grow sadder. As Alice looked, the smile no longer looked sweet and natural but full of sorrow, as if her sister was watching her and grieving. Alice had a sudden

177

desire to take her on her lap and comfort her. But the image was only paint. She would never feel Flora's warm arms around her neck again.

'Damn you,' she sobbed. 'Damn you!' She picked up a pot of ferns and hurled it at the ground. 'Why did you have to die? It's all right for you, you are not left here all alone.'

The crashing noise was louder than her voice. Shuddering with tears, she took up another empty pot and threw it at the wall. It smashed down hard on the tiled floor, shattering. It felt good to make this much noise. She kicked her feet amid the debris of broken fern and clods of earth, a wild destructive wind inside her. Sobbing uncontrollably now, she swept her arms across the table, sending pigment jars crashing to the ground in puffs of saffron and pink and splinters of glass. Her breath came heavily but still she didn't stop.

She caught a glimpse of her hands, stained yellow, small cuts dribbling dark red blood, before she grabbed her paintbox and threw it with all her might across the room. It rebounded with a crack against the window before falling to the floor, its hinges broken and the porcelain jars in pieces. Still sobbing, she dragged the watercolours from the table, feeling glass crunching underfoot, and started to tear them into small pieces. Each one shredded with a satisfying ripping sound until they lay like ashes round her feet. She lifted up a vase of white lilies and turned to throw it at the door, but the door was open. Her hand hovered above her shoulder in mid-flight.

Margaret the herbalist was standing in the doorway.

'Get out,' screamed Alice.

Margaret stood her ground, looking steadily back at her.

Alice drew back her arm, threatening to throw the pot. 'I said, get out!'

She saw Margaret take in the state of the room. 'Bit of a mess you've made.'

The vase narrowly missed Margaret's head and flew out of the open doorway to smash on the flagstone path. Unarmed, Alice paused. She looked in astonishment round the room, at her sanctuary – at the broken bottles, at the floor strewn with earth and paint, at the lady's slipper orchid wilting in its pot amidst the debris. She felt the fire drain out of her, her legs buckle and give way, and she sank down to the floor, tears silently coursing down her cheeks.

'There, there.' A pair of strong arms grasped her round the shoulders. Alice did not push them away but held on with both hands, her fingers wound tight into the cloth of Margaret's cloak. She inhaled a smell of damp wool and grass, and another smell that could have been nutmeg. She let herself feel the warmth of the other woman until her breathing calmed. Her tears gradually subsided and she felt a peacefulness descend, a hollow in her chest. Alice leaned up against Margaret, who rocked her quietly, murmuring and clucking under her breath.

'Better get cleaned up, before your husband comes home,' Margaret said. 'Then we can have a look at what ails the orchid.'

'How did you know?' Alice drew away and wiped her face on her sleeve.

Margaret stood up and looked at it. 'Well, any-one can see it's not thriving. Get up now, and let's get started. Make haste.' Alice took a proffered kerchief, noticing it was none too clean, but stood up sheepishly and blew her nose. Her skirts were smeared with gold and green paint, her eyes must be red and puffy from crying. Margaret was already picking up pieces of plant pot and putting them in a log-basket by the door.

'Have you a broom?'

Alice fetched it from the corner.

'Get sweeping, then,' Margaret said. Alice swept. She did not know what to think; she surely should not let this woman just make herself at home. But she had been so kind. Alice did not know what had come over her to cry all over a stranger like that. She watched Margaret out of the corner of her eye, heard her humming tune-lessly as she worked, gathering up broken jars and strewing damp sawdust to pick up the dirt and mud as Alice wielded the broom. After a while Alice began to feel better. Her shoulders relaxed and she put her back into the task.

'Might as well give everything a good scrub-bing,' Margaret said, wringing out a cloth and passing it to her.

She wiped the walls and the windows and the tops of the cupboards. It was satisfying seeing the cloth pick up the grey dust, watching the pigments darken; good to wring it out in the water. Margaret found an old leather bottle and put a few sprigs of lavender in it from her bag. When they had fin-ished the room smelt sweet and clean. Everything was back in its place, the broken pots stacked neatly in the wooden wheelbarrow just outside the door, the lady's slipper orchid set on the scrubbed table. Margaret drank it in with her eyes, her breath coming out in a small whistle.

'What a beauty.'

Alice gestured to it. 'I thought I could save it, but it is dying and I do not know what's the matter. Except that I uprooted it from the place it belongs. Richard Wheeler said I was interfering in God's plan. Do you think that? That I am going against God?'

Margaret reached down into her bag. 'While I think, let's keep body and soul together.' She drew out a small hard-looking loaf, some grubby cheese and two dark plums. She divided these into two portions and bit through her plum. 'It's not possible to go against God, as God is everything,' she said matter-of-factly.

Suddenly Alice was hungry. But it would be considered quite unacceptable for her to be sitting here opposite this dishevelled old woman, eating plums. She pushed this thought away because the plum's sweet flesh beneath the bitter skin was delicious, and after it she finished all her bread and cheese, trying to eat politely despite the strange circumstances.

'I should think the plant is missing something in the soil.' Margaret indicated the orchid with an inclination of her head. 'Where it grew – does the Quaker keep cattle or sheep?'

'I do not believe so. No, there's probably only deer, and rabbits and badgers maybe.'

'Not droppings then.' She stood up, brushing off her clothes. 'We had better go back for a look

181

at where it grew.'

'I cannot. Wheeler already suspects me of stealing it, and if he saw us trespassing on his land he would have us arrested.'

'Can we get close to his land then?' Margaret asked, even though she knew the answer.

'Well, I suppose we can get into the field next to the wood without actually trespassing.'

'Get your cloak then, there's no time to be lost.'

The two women peered over the wall into the leafy depths of the wood, towards the place where Alice had removed the orchid from the ground. Margaret scrutinized the mesh of leaves and foliage. Then she threw her brown cloak back over her shoulders and bent down, digging into the ground with her rough fingers, scraping away at the rocks under the soil.

'Limestone,' she pronounced. Alice looked at her questioningly.

'It's limestone,' said Margaret. 'That's what your orchid is pining for. Here, help me get one of these loose stones out.'

She scratched in the dirt trying to loosen a piece of the chalky white stone. Alice was tentative, reluctant to dig in the dirt with her bare hands. 'Come on,' Margaret insisted, and Alice got down on her knees; she found herself bending to Margaret's will. They both worked away, scraping the ground, levering the stone, trying to prise it from its bed of hard-packed earth.

A sharp crack as a shot whirred past the top of the wall, glancing a blow to the keep stone which showered them with grit. The stone rocked in its housing and almost toppled off.

The two women slowly stood up, Margaret clutching the piece of limestone they had dug out of the earth in her hand. A tentative look over the wall showed Richard Wheeler striding towards them, armed with a smoking rifle. When he saw them, he stopped, a mortified look on his face, before running up.

'Good heavens, Mistress Ibbetson,' he said from his side of the wall, 'I could have killed thee. What on earth dost thou there?'

Alice recovered her composure. 'We were looking at some wildflowers.'

She saw Margaret slip the white stone into her bag, and saw also that Wheeler had seen it too. He frowned and looked at Margaret.

'I mistook thee for the deer that has been stripping the bark off my birch trees. I just saw something brown moving near the wall. The shots were meant to scare it off.'

'You must be more careful with your gun, Mr Wheeler,' Alice said. 'If one of us had stood up at that moment, we could have been killed.'

Wheeler looked at Margaret. 'It was the cloak, I thought it was the deer.'

Margaret had kept quiet until now, and Alice hoped Wheeler might think she was her servant, but now she spoke. 'No harm done, Mr Wheeler. As you can see, we are both unhurt.' From her tone it was obvious she was no servant.

Wheeler looked her up and down, then turned towards Alice. 'Thou hast not introduced us.'

Heat rose to Alice's face. 'This is my friend, Widow Poulter.'

'Isn't it a lovely day,' Margaret said.

Wheeler's face stiffened as he realized who she was. He took an involuntary step backwards, away from the wall, as if he had come across something distasteful. Alice's heart sank. If she was seen abroad with Margaret, he would surely think she was involved with some sort of devilry. The idea that he would not think well of her was disconcerting. He addressed her in a tight voice.

'I guess thou knowst thou art trespassing on Milner's land – that is none of my business, but if I were thee I would get on home before he sees thee. He may want to really take a shot at the pair of you. He does not take kindly to strangers on his land.'

'We will heed your advice.' She paused and looked to Margaret. 'We had finished our study anyway. But maybe you should think twice before you fire your gun from now on, Mr Wheeler. Come along, Margaret.'

Wheeler's face was stony. She knew she had slighted him.

She took hold of Margaret by the arm and almost carried her away, feeling Wheeler's eyes boring into her back as she went.

When they were back on the path to the village, she spoke. 'We were fortunate. Quite apart from the fact he nearly killed us, I am sure he has heard of you by reputation. Around here they think you are a sorceress, caught up in the ways of the Devil. I am surprised he did not find some reason to detain you.'

'And why would he, when I'm as innocent as a little lamb?' Her eyes twinkled with mischief.

'He's a good man, but rigid, too tightly bound in himself. He needs shaking up a little. But a shake-up is coming and no mistake. For the past few weeks I have woken shivering. Something is stirring the air.'

'You scare me, Margaret, with your sooth-saying. You told me to take care, and since then I have had nothing but trouble.'

Margaret made no answer, except to smile to herself. Back at the summerhouse Alice followed Margaret to the table.

'Now then, let's look at you,' said Margaret, add-ressing the orchid, peering at it with her wrinkled eyes.

She extricated the rootball from the pot and turned it to look at it.

'Did you do this?' It was an accusation. Alice blushed.

'No ... a friend took some of the root to make a remedy.'

'A friend, is it?' Margaret frowned, her disposi-tion changed in an instant.

'Yes. Well, no, not exactly. Geoffrey Fisk, my patron. I did not want him to touch it, but–'

Margaret gave her a sharp look and returned the plant to the pot. 'I have heard tell of him. There is some darkness about him. The use of this root needs care – it is not for troubled souls such as he. Even a small press of it in an infusion could agitate him, make him befuddled. He should look to a proper herbwoman.' She held up the plant. 'And look, it feels the loss of its limb.'

'I know,' said Alice, shame-faced. 'I will not let Geoffrey touch it again. I could not bear to let

185

him near it. Is that what ails it?'

Margaret tutted. 'I would not be surprised. That, and losing its home. An excess of grief, I'd say – that's melancholic.' She rummaged in her bag and took out a few little bundles wrapped in muslin and placed them on the table. Taking up the piece of limestone, she chipped off some flakes with a piece of flint and mixed them in with the soil. When this was done she unwrapped one of the bundles and grated a small amount of a gnarled beige root into the pot. Alice watched fascinated.

'What's that?' she asked.

'It's ginger root. Hot and choleric. Mark it well. Now fill the earth back in. Careful, now.' Margaret guided her hands impatiently.

Alice began to feel she was having a lesson, but somehow she did not mind. Margaret was obviously knowledgeable about plants.

'I'm going to say a few words, now the plant is more comfortable,' Margaret said.

Alice covertly watched Margaret's round face as she intoned, eyes closed:

'Nature Wilde, o nature deepe
who all the worldly mysteries keepe,
no more dampe of grief or rue,
let the flowre growe strong and true.'

Alice was discomfited to find herself witnessing some sort of spell. Her stomach gave a lurch. Confused, and afraid her very soul could be at risk, she repeated 'Lord have Mercy' over and over in her mind. It could be that she really was harbouring a

186

witch and could be in mortal danger. She clung doggedly to her short phrase as Margaret continued:

'In the web of the worlde I play my part,
Guide my fingres, guide my hearte,
Great Mother of all, helpmeet and friend,
In the beginninge, now, and at life's ende.'

But when Margaret opened her eyes and smiled – a lopsided smile which fattened her cheeks – Alice found she could not countenance her as evil.

'That should do the trick.' Margaret reached out and clasped her by the hand. 'And when the seeds come, leave them in the frost, make sure they get good and cold. And sow them when they are young and tender, still green. Don't dry them out, they take years that way, so my mother told me. But I'll be back long before then, what am I thinking about? I must hasten to Arnside now. I have a man with a toothache to see to.'

Alice squeezed her dry leathery hand. 'Thank you,' she said, 'you were very kind, this afternoon. You are welcome to call to the summerhouse any time, as long as you are...' Here Alice foundered.

'Discreet,' finished Margaret. 'Yes, dear, no one sees me come and go; that is one skill I most certainly have – to blend into the background. That's why the brown cloak.'

'Though have a care you are not mistaken for a deer!' She laughed at her own words. It was a long time since she had heard herself make any kind of jest. But Margaret simply waved her hand as she sped away.

Chapter 15

'Who's getting the wagon?' Ella asked.

'Farrier's bringing his dray,' one of the men said.

'And you're sure it's to be this Saturday?'

'Aye, there's to be a ball and a dinner,' the butcher said. 'There's been all sorts ordered – fancy stuff. Not just the meats off the estate, but – wait till ye hear this – a peacock and a suckling pig out of season.'

'I wouldn't mind being sat at that table,' Ella said, her mouth watering.

'There's to be a haunch of venison, and eight woodpigeon set aside, and the pastrycook's even making a flower garden out of candied fruit and marchpane.' Lizzie Pickering, Lady Emilia's maidservant, was wide-eyed.

'Oh that old windbag. I wouldn't eat anything she'd cooked,' Tom Cobbald said.

'Anyway, it will take more than a few oranges and honeyed plums to sweeten up Sir Geoffrey when he and his guests see what we've got in store,' Audrey said, pulling at the greasy strings of her bonnet. 'Get them out, Tom.'

With a flourish Tom produced a large pair of curving ram's horns from a sack. Ribald laughter ensued. Ridged into a full twist, the horns were the largest Ella had ever seen. The villagers stood back, sucking in their breath and making admiring noises.

They were gathered on the village green next to the pump, near the lines where people hung their clothes and sheets to dry. On summer evenings after market days, it was where people got together for a smoke or a chat or to see who was in the stocks, on the way home before the evening chores. There were several felled tree stumps, used as seats, but today the ram's horns were set down on one so everyone could see what a fine pair they were.

'Tom Cobbald! Wherever did you find a ram that size?' Ella said.

Tom smirked and looked pleased. 'You and Sarah from the mill can dress them,' he said. 'Tie some ribbons round and some strong ivy, and make a loop for nailing them. Make them fair and pretty.'

'The farrier's set on being Lady Emilia, he's after getting one of her gowns. Any chance, Lizzie?' Audrey said.

Lizzie shook her head and bit her lip. 'No, I daren't chance it, I'm risking my position already. If they thought I had anything to do with the cuckolding, I'd be cast out, sure as milk turns to butter.'

'Aw, go on, Lizzie, you could borrow an old gown. Surely there's one clout she wouldn't miss.'

'Not a one. She's that fussy and particular, and she often opens the closet just to look on her gowns.'

'How many has she got? What are they like?' Ella was curious to know all the details of Fisk Manor.

'Must be twenty or more – all satin and lace,

189

and embroidery, with pale silk petticoats with flying birds, and hems trimmed with gold point – all fastening at the back. I swear if I wasn't there to help her fasten them, she'd go about in just her chemise!'

'Hang me for a dog if she don't when she tiptoes off to her turkeycock. And I'm sure and certain he knows better how to undo her stays than to fasten them,' Audrey said.

'Mind you, she don't look that type. Bit bony, to my mind,' said Tom. 'Be like sleeping with my old mare – all ribcage and teeth.'

'She's not that bad,' Lizzie said. 'She's got a fair complexion.'

Tom did not look convinced.

'Reuben the farrier'll do a fine portrait of her airs and graces – he looks less like a horse than she does,' Ella said.

Lizzie twisted her apron strings between her fingers. 'Are you sure this is a good idea?' It was as if Lizzie had not spoken – nobody bothered to respond.

'Who's to play Sir Geoffrey?' Ella asked.

Tom put his finger on his top lip in imitation of Geoffrey's curling moustache, and gave a low bow, twirling his fingers as he went. Everyone laughed.

'He's had a lump of flax sewn into a hat, with some extra for a moustache,' giggled Audrey, 'and he's to redden his face, and scowl and scratch his ears!'

'Let him have a flagon of ale, but scribed with "Madeira", and be half falling off the wagon,' Ella said.

'Be careful,' said Lizzie, 'don't go too far; he

190

might do for us all, he has a right evil temper.'

'Yes,' Audrey said, 'he hit my cousin with his riding crop last week at market, and nearly trampled her boy on his horse. She's got a red mark on her cheek to prove it.'

'He never,' Ella said.

'He did. So he's got it coming.'

'The miller's grinding lads have said they'll play the lovers, and be as lewd as you like.'

'Sarah and me are making tie-on codpieces, big as your forearm, out of stuffed straw,' Ella said.

'That'll be some sight to make your eyes pop,' Audrey said. 'Word's spread already – some people's mouths run on wheels. I reckon there'll be a fine turnout to see our procession when they hear our drums and cymbals.'

'Better keep quiet when we get near the manor, though, and put out your torches, or Sir Geoffrey might get wind of it before you can nail up the horns,' said Lizzie. 'Or worse, he might catch you at it, and then we'd all be done for.'

'Nah, he can't do much with all the lot of us. Make sure you're wearing a vizard, Ella, to hide your face, and a long cloak to hide your gown. Miller'll give you some sacks to make a cape if you've no cloak,' Tom said.

Lizzie laughed nervously. 'I'd best go, before Mistress misses me. There's such a lot to do for the dinner, and Mistress'll be wanting her lace collars pinked and pressed.'

'Meet us here next week then. We want to know what their faces were like when they clapped eyes on it. And we'll tell what sport we had,' Audrey said.

'Aye. But I fear it will be trouble. Sir Geoffrey's in with Rawlinson, the magistrate,' said Lizzie.

'Oh, get some backbone, girl,' Tom said. 'It's only a bit of fun. Nothing bad'll happen.'

Lizzie continued to twist her apron strings round her fingers. 'I'll be off then,' she said.

Tom called out, 'Soon as you can after the day's work on Friday – we want to get the wagon ready and decorated before sunset if we can, and the nights are beginning to draw in.'

'We'll be in the taproom at the Hare and Hounds,' Audrey said.

'I can't wait till Saturday!' Ella's face was glowing. 'Ibbetson's cook and all her family are turning out to see us. See you all at the inn yard.'

The group began to disperse.

Lizzie picked up her basket and set off disconsolately to the manor. What would happen if her master or mistress were to hear about it? She would be thrown out, and her with no family or other place to go. It didn't bear thinking about. She must keep her head down and have no more to do with that Ella. She was trouble. It was written on her face, plain as a pikestaff.

Thomas was delighted when the invitation arrived from Fisk Manor for the Grand Dinner. He waved the gold embossed card at Alice over the dining table, his face beaming with satisfaction. He saw it as an indication of his high standing in the county that he should have been invited, and a welcome opportunity to talk business with the squires, giving him the excuse he needed to sell them his financial services. It had been a few years since anyone had dared to throw such a luxurious party, and rumour had it that it was to be a sumptuous affair. He was perplexed that Alice did not share his enthusiasm.

'I would rather not attend,' Alice said. 'I feel it is still too soon to be enjoying myself. Forgive me, dear, but I am not ready to put away my mourning just yet.'

She could not tell him that she had offended Sir Geoffrey, and that there would be no more lucrative commissions; nor could she tell him that she was too worried about the lady's slipper to be concerned with ostentatious dinners at the manor.

Thomas threw down his napkin. 'For God's sake, woman. Are you going to closet yourself in that damp summerhouse for the rest of your life?' He ran his hands through his thinning brown hair. 'Moping won't bring Flora back. It's been a year; it's time to pick up the pieces and move on.' And then, with soft entreaty, 'She would not have wanted this ... to see you so–' he searched for the words – 'so faded and dull.'

Alice shrank further away from him. His words had stung her heart.

He approached her as if to take her by the arm, but like the tail of a bee-sting, the words could not easily be withdrawn and she moved sharply away from him towards the window, presenting him with a view of her tense shoulders in their hard black worsted. So he thought her unattractive, did he?

'I have told you, I am not ready for Sir Geoffrey's wasteful frivolities. And by the sounds of it, you will be glad – since I am so dull.'

There was a palpable silence as he took in the bite of her words.

'Very well. If that is how you feel, I will attend without you. I will tell Sir Geoffrey and the Lady Emilia that you are indisposed.'

She heard his footsteps and the creak of the floorboards as he left the room, and then the door bang shut in the hall.

She gazed out of the window unmoving. A fine drizzle clouded the glass except for a few clear rivulets through which she could see the full weight of autumn – sycamore leaves strewn on the grass like twists of brown paper, the ash tree's yellowing fringes swaying over dripping U-shaped branches.

Was she so faded and dull? She stared at a raindrop sliding down the glass outside. She supposed she was. She thought back to their old family home in Cartmel, the glossy cherrywood table with its fine white linen and lace runner, with the fat bowl of roses and wildflowers dropping their scatter of petals over the polished surface. In her mind's eye, she saw her hand reach out to run a finger across the wood, saw the dab of flower-dust on her fingertips; her fine crocheted lace cuff above a hand wearing a cluster of amethyst and ruby rings. She heard again the faint swish of her orange-scented pomander against her damask skirts, saw the lavender-coloured silk, felt the stiffness of the linen embroidered skirt-panel with its intertwined moss-stitch leaves and chubby silken birds. But that was before the days of shaking.

Another bead of water formed a transparent runnel down the windowpane. Alice looked down at her feet in their dull black bootees, and the dark folds of her lustreless woollen skirts.

Thomas was right, she was a different woman now. It was as if she had got lost somewhere, but she did not know how to get herself back – she was even making friends with an old beggar-woman. She could no longer imagine herself as a woman who could wear satins and jewellery, and touch a glass stopper from a perfume bottle behind her ears. The world was a cruel place; she mourned for her loss of faith in the fairness of the world as much as for the loss of her childhood home. There was so much to mourn. And the death of Flora had drained the last of her joy.

Her thoughts turned to her husband. Though she and Thomas had never been more than cordial, there had always been a deep tolerance between them. Thomas had taken her in marriage when nobody else would – for what other man would want a woman who had a child already? Though Flora was her sister, she had been in every respect like her own child. Thomas had loved Flora. Oft-times Alice suspected that without Flora, Thomas would never have married her, for he had always treated Alice like a friend rather than a wife.

Now, though, she sensed something was out of kilter between them. He had weathered Flora's death, but she herself had found it hard to put thoughts of her aside. It was as if she and Thomas were ghosts from different times but floating in the same house, they almost passed through each other as they came and went. Thomas no longer placed his arm in hers when they went out, no

195

longer put his hand on the small of her back to guide her across the street; his eyes evaded hers when they met, and any easy companionship had gone. They led separate lives, held together only by the thin veneer of appearances. There was something different about Thomas; he even evaded her company now.

She would not go to Fisk Manor. Let Thomas go alone. She could not face Geoffrey, who would want to take her aside and enquire, God forbid, after the health of the lady's slipper and when the seedlings would be ready. The thought of it made her weary.

She sighed and leaned on the windowsill. The glass showed a dark reflection drizzled with beads of rain. Her eyes stared back, grey, like troubled pools. She lifted a stray bronze-coloured curl and almost tucked it in her cap. She had been pretty once, her fiery hair an emblem of her energy and enthusiasm, her lust for life. Where had all that energy gone? She felt the soft warm texture of her hair and, having second thoughts, pulled out more curls until the glass showed a warm glow around her pallid face. She pinched her cheeks until a tinge of red bloomed there, pulled herself up straighter, pushed back her shoulders.

Thomas was right. It was time to put the mourning behind her.

Chapter 16

Richard walked briskly up to the Ibbetsons' front door and knocked. He had thought long and hard about this visit, and had asked God for guidance. He must apologize to her for the accident with the rifle. Horrified, he had disposed of it immediately afterwards into the river. He could have killed her. The incident seemed like a prompt from above. He had sworn to give up firearms, but had thought a little innocent target practice would not matter. Now he knew better.

He knocked again. He hoped he would be able to convince her to hear him out. He was worried for Alice – she was playing a dangerous game, fraternizing with that cunning woman from Preston. Widow Poulter was a keeper of the dark arts, so he had heard, and when he had asked Dorothy about it, mentioning no names of course, she had said it was his duty to warn Alice not to stray onto the dark path.

He could not but think there had been some divine purpose in how he had come to be in Netherbarrow, to worship at the Hall. There had been the sign of the Holy Spirit in his woods. He still could not decide if he had imagined the wonder of it – whether it was really something quite ordinary, just a turtle-dove lost from some-one's dovecote. But the memory made his spine tingle. And he could not separate the image of the orchid from the picture of Alice, her white skin, the red of her lips. Something about the orchid spoke to his heart, an unmistakable yearning. He wanted to bring the orchid home.

Ella the maid answered the door. He wondered briefly why the Ibbetsons kept her on. Thomas Ibbetson had not fared too badly in the war, he knew. His modest house had remained, whereas he had heard that Alice's family home had been sacked and burnt to the ground by the New Model Army. Since the war, many were living in reduced circumstances. But their maid looked unkempt, and her bodice was too low – he noticed with annoyance how his eyes automatically dropped to the white flesh of her bosom. She was not even particularly pleasant or efficient. She mumbled, and kept him waiting in the hall.

He looked around him at the dark panelled walls hung with more of Alice's luminous flower paintings. It was of course grander than his own cottage, but he could see it was nowhere near as grand as the house he had given away, or the house the Longleys had seen burnt to the ground. A tenderness arose in him, thinking of how Alice must have felt seeing her family's possessions reduced to rubble and ashes.

He hoped that Thomas would be out at the counting house and that Alice would be willing to receive him. There was no reason why she should, yet he felt he had to try. She was a fair-minded person underneath her protestations – his instinct told him that. Surely she would let common sense prevail.

When he turned back from looking at the walls,

she was standing quietly waiting.

'Good afternoon, Mr Wheeler.'

She looked different, somehow, softer. She was wearing a dark green velvet bodice over a matching fine wool skirt. It was very becoming. He noticed her trim waist and slim arms, and her white throat rising out of the dark emerald neckline.

'May I speak with thee a few moments?'

'What do you want?' Her eyes were wary.

'Perhaps it would be more comfortable if we were to sit,' he said.

'I would prefer to remain standing. Whatever you wish to say, I can hear it perfectly well here in the hall.'

Nonplussed, he realized his attempts to make some sort of peace were already failing. His eyes took in the fact that she was no longer in mourning, that her hair was a deep russet, like beech leaves on the turn. She saw his stare and prompted him.

'Well?'

He found himself taking off his hat, for his old notions of gentlemanly conduct were ingrained despite his new Quaker lifestyle.

'I wanted to apologize about the incident with the gun.'

She was waving away his apology. 'There is no need–'

'And to talk with thee about the lady's slipper.'

There was a silence.

'To be blunt, I think thou hast taken it. Since it has been lost to me, I have been...' He struggled to find the right words. 'I mean, I have made a covenant with God, and I think … that is, I have had a sign, God wills its safe return.' This was damnably difficult to explain; she would think he had lost his senses. He started again with something simpler.

'I have prayed, and I believe…' Again he petered out, unable to find words she might be able to understand. 'Thou must return the orchid to me,' he blurted.

Alice looked at him strangely, and started to shake her head. He blundered on.

'Thou canst not, in all conscience, pretend to me thou hast no knowledge of it.' He felt too large, standing in the hallway, towering over Alice in his workaday boots and scratchy tweeds. Alice backed away from him towards the dining room.

'I have told you already, Mr Wheeler,' she said unflinching, though her cheeks were red, 'I know nothing of it, now please leave.'

He advanced towards her, staying her retreat with his hand on her shoulder. She winced. He looked down into her grey shifting eyes.

'Tell me the truth,' he said. 'For I would not have thee fall from the grace of God.'

She squirmed away and her hands came up to her chest as if to protect herself, and at that moment Richard saw himself as she must see him, as overbearing and threatening.

'Ella,' she called loudly for the maid.

'The truth, Mistress Ibbetson,' he insisted. He was powerless to stop himself. Her back was against a door, presumably to the dining room; her eyes would not meet his.

Ella appeared from the shadowy back stairs.

'Show Mr Wheeler out.' Her voice wavered a little.

Ella held open the door and a draught of cold air buffeted in. Richard jammed his hat back on his head, holding it with one hand against the wind. He heard himself say, 'Thou must make thy peace with God then, as best thou can, Mistress Ibbetson, for I shall give thee none till the truth is out. And as God is just, thy reward will surely come.'

He turned to go, but her brittle voice carried after him.

'How dare you. How dare you come here and accuse me, and preach at me in this way. You are not a priest, Mr Wheeler, just a farmer.' She looked scathingly at his boots, her eyes blazing. 'I don't need a farmer to plead my case with God.'

He turned on his heel and strode out, in a silence as thick as soup. Ella watched him go with a slight smile, before closing the door very gently so the latch was barely audible over the tick of the clock. Alice stood stock still in the hallway, the colour flaring in her face, her chest rising and falling with her breath.

Chapter 17

'Come quick,' Ella called out to Cook as the noise of the drum cut through the night air. *Rat-a-tat-tat, rat-a-tat-tat. Brrrrm, rat-a-tat-tat.* They rushed out into the lane, hatless, to get the first glimpse of the cavalcade as it wended its way to the alehouse.

Behind them Master Thomas, already dressed for the dinner at the manor in his best silk breeches and wig, stood at the half-open front door, trying to see what all the commotion was about. When he saw the noisy rabble coming down the lane, preceded by a group of giggling girls carrying jack-o-lanterns, he hurried indoors. But Ella saw his shadow at the window, all the same, watching her.

She smiled to herself, remembering his breath on her throat and breasts. He did not want to get involved with their fun, he thought it beneath him, to associate publicly with the likes of her; like them all, he was two-faced as a coin – but he was that much in thrall to her she might yet persuade him to set her up somewhere in her own place. Of course he was as nosy as the next person to find out what all the hubbub was, and well he might be, as he was up to the self-same cuckolding game. He followed her like a dog after a bitch on heat, the minute Mistress's back was turned. And she had been out somewhere this afternoon, sketching or gathering flowers – and still not back, even though it was getting dark.

Ella had been hard pressed to keep Thomas at arm's length today. She'd dodged and ducked, and nipped out the back door out of his way when she heard him coming. Without the presence of his wife nearby, Thomas's passion was wont to get the better of him. Ella wanted to keep him dangling until he'd agreed to purchase her a new gown, at least. And keep him away she must, for she was not going to miss the cuckolding for anything. He'd wait. The heat was on him like a fire.

The procession drew up alongside, where they could see the ram's horns strapped to the front roll-bar of the cart, and the fake Sir Geoffrey in his flax wig, with a withered carrot tied on as a codpiece, sitting on an upturned barrel. And there was the parody of Lady Emilia, with a pair of painted bolsters for breasts, the nipples round and red like two strawberries. Behind her two young men, the miller's boys, strapped with tumescent straw codpieces, feigned lewd gestures as they attempted to mount her from behind.

'Look at her hair.' Ella pointed at the Lady Emilia, who was wearing a white cap with sawdust shavings ringlets, and a straggle of blonde horse-hair. Beneath it, the face of the blacksmith leered lasciviously through rouged lips, his cheeks scarlet over white leading.

'Go on, boys,' yelled Cook, 'give her what she deserves!'

The boys waved their codpieces in the air, and the crimson-lipped Lady Emilia bent over, plumping up her bolster breasts with spade-like hands. The false Sir Geoffrey stood up stagger-ing, miming drunkenness with a flagon in each hand, winking at Ella and signalling and beck-oning with his arms.

Ella and Betty the Cook fell in behind the procession, Betty picking up her skirts and doing an ungainly polka. Betty walked with a limp – her legs were uneven from a childhood ailment. Ella dawdled along behind, waving to people who came to their doors.

'What's up?'

'It's a cuckolding,' shouted Ella.

'Who?'

'We're off to Fisk Manor. Old Scratcher. The horns are for his door.'

The answer proved popular and more people joined the throng – people who had given more than their due in tithe, others who were being forced to move because of the new boundaries. A good number were there to spite Sir Geoffrey, but many more followed along just for the fun of the spectacle. Nights were drawing in and it was dull in their poky parlours, they were ready for some free entertainment – particularly at someone else's expense.

When the procession reached the tavern, they stopped for an hour or more, filling themselves with ale-soaked bravado and picking up a large contingent, virtually emptying the place. Ella hoped some of those carousing at the back would have the sense to shut their mouths when they got to the driveway of Fisk Manor or their plot would be foiled. They rattled through the village singing the foulest folk song they knew that featured a wife and her lover being discovered by an angry husband.

In his cottage Richard Wheeler heard the noise but did not go out to look. To him, the voices sounded the worse for ale, and he was determined to concentrate, reading a printing of the work of Jacob Boehme lent to him some months ago by Dorothy, before Jack and Hannah were arrested. He was curious, though, at the sound of the drum and the strident voices, and stood up, looking out of the window into the dark, glad to have an excuse to leave the impenetrable tract. But then he remonstrated with himself, telling himself the noise outside was a disturbance he could do without.

He wondered if Alice Ibbetson had been disturbed by the noise. He sat down again, sighed and turned the page, leaning on the table with his shirt sleeves rolled above his elbows, puffing on his forbidden pipe. The fire in the grate streaked the walls with a rosy warmth, the candles burnt bright. Richard returned to devouring each page, looking for something – searching for his own experience, for a description of what went on in him at the meeting with George Fox – weighing each word, cutting out the noise of the revelry outside.

But it was no use. The sound of the drum made him restless. He picked up his Sunday boots and began to polish them, rubbing vigorously until they gleamed.

Amongst the servants, the tale of the events at Fisk Manor that night were retold for years afterwards, the dinner growing more mouth-watering with every telling. There were of course the roast meats – the crispy beef, succulent venison, and the famous whole suckling pig, decorated with sprigs of rosemary and thyme, its mouth skewered open with a row of sugared plums on a stick. The telling always included the peacock, carried in on a silver salver, its tail displaying exotic iridescent green eyes, and it never failed to include the almond paste flower garden with lifelike roses and leaves from green eglantine.

Emilia's maidservant Lizzie enjoyed all the bustle and excitement of the preparations, and in her chambers Lady Emilia was at her most vivacious, in a crimson gown that gave a glow to her face. She looked more alive than Lizzie had ever seen her. As she fastened her into armfuls of slippery silk, Lizzie saw that Lady Emilia was trembling.

'Oh, Lizzie,' she said, 'I have missed the gaiety of entertaining these past few years.'

Lizzie nodded her head, her mouth full of hairpins.

'Do I look beautiful?' Lady Emilia asked.

'You look as fine as I have ever seen you,' Lizzie said, pressing Emilia's curls into submission. 'That colour suits you well.'

Lady Emilia clasped Lizzie by the hand. 'It is important that I look at my very best tonight,' she said with an urgent look in her eyes.

Lizzie knew full well what that meant – he would be here, amongst the guests, Ralph Hetherington, Lady Emilia's paramour. Lizzie felt uncomfortable.

'I am sure Sir Geoffrey will think you a credit to him.' Lizzie staunchly disregarded Lady Emilia's puppy-dog eyes and turned away to reach for a hairbrush from the table behind.

Over dinner Lady Emilia sat next to Justice Rawlinson, who seemed unaware of the fact that she drank several glasses of wine far too quickly and was in a state of palpable excitement. He showed far more interest in the food than in Lady Emilia anyway. Sir Geoffrey was seated to her other side, but he ignored her and sat glowering over his meal, rubbing his forehead and wiping his neck with a napkin.

When dinner was over, the dancing began. Virginals, lute, tambour, horns – the music was full and rich, a fluid river of sound, swirling round the stone walls and out through the open windows into the gardens. The dancers tapped their red heels and the sound rang out on the stone flags. Lizzie could not remember ever having seen such finery. In the light from the sconces, the women glowed like jewels in their beautiful silk and taffeta gowns, their necks twinkling with gold and diamonds, feathers and ribbons in their topknots.

Lizzie wore her best navy outfit with clean starched apron and stiff white cap, holding a tray of little savoury parcels filled with duck and peas. But she felt like a sparrow amongst golden pheasants. She stood next to the big stone fireplace and watched as the dancers whirled past, their rustling gowns setting the candles in the chandelier a-flicker, feeling the draught as they swooped curtseys to the men dressed up in their periwigs and fine silver-buckled shoes.

She saw Sir Geoffrey sitting off to one side, ramrod-stiff as usual, away from the fire on an upright chair, with a large glass of Madeira on the side table at his elbow. Next to Sir Geoffrey on the other side of the table sat Lady Jane Rawlinson, dressed in a very unbecoming mauve silk, which was almost the same colour as her face and looked so heavy it would probably stand up without her. She was trying to engage Sir Geoffrey in conversation but he was watching the dancers, keeping his eye on young Stephen, who was dancing wildly and recklessly and already looked quite the worse for ale.

Lizzie fervently hoped Sir Geoffrey would retire to his chambers before the villagers arrived with the cuckold's horns. She was getting more and more nervous as the evening drew on and there had still been no sign of them.

Sir Ralph Hetherington approached Lizzie and took a couple of the savoury morsels from her tray. Lizzie bobbed a curtsey. Over his shoulder she could see Lady Emilia glance at his back before turning back to her dancing partner, the bent old Sir Kendall, who was out of step with everyone else. She saw Emilia throw Sir Ralph a look under her arched eyebrows as she dipped and swayed by, and saw his answering smile.

Lady Emilia looked vibrant, almost girlish. Her husband, on the contrary, seemed to be growing more morose by the minute; he had given up all pretence of listening to Lady Jane Rawlinson and stared resolutely at his feet. So he didn't notice that Sir Ralph and Lady Emilia had become dancing partners. Nor did he notice when they slipped away through the doors into the darkness of the garden.

Lizzie saw them go with foreboding. The game would soon be up. There was trouble brewing and no mistake. If her lady was discovered, then what would become of her, her maid? Lizzie chewed her lip, her stomach rolled over like sour milk in a butter-churn.

Unable to bear the suspense much longer, she took the platter down the back stairs to the kitchen, where there was much hustle and bustle as the dishes of sweetmeats were being served up and glasses were being washed and dried. Lizzie watched Cook pull out some dainty jambals from the oven, but their sweet buttery smell made her belly heave. She could not stay there either, so restless had she become, so she loaded a jug of sack-posset and some more drinking cups on a tray and went back up the stairs. As she emerged into the hall, she saw the party already assembled and seated for the play that Lady Emilia had been at such pains to organize.

To Lizzie's vast relief, both Lady Emilia and Sir Ralph Hetherington were back in the room, although Lady Emilia's cheeks were red as apples and her eyes glittered with an unusual wildness. Lizzie noticed that the back of Sir Ralph's breeches were damp with dew and pursed her lips in disapproval. Though she was apt to disapprove of anything Sir Ralph did, simply because he was rich, and careless, and because, like Sir Geoffrey, he treated servants with a detachment that told her they were chattels and not people.

The play began with a fox-like man pretending to be dying and worshipping his stock of gold. Lady Emilia glanced towards Sir Geoffrey. As the play progressed Sir Ralph smiled over to Lady Emilia as if with some amusement. It became clear to the watching Lizzie that they were sharing some kind of private joke at her master's expense.

For the first time Lizzie wondered what it might be like to be Sir Geoffrey. A strange, unlikeable man, he often spent days alone in his study. The servants were not allowed to touch the bottles and leather pipes and bladders full of odd liquids, so the study was covered in a thick layer of dust. When he was at home, it never seemed as if he was really present. But every now and then he would stalk the house, fly into a rage and lash out. On those days, staff knew to stay below stairs if they did not want a flogging, or to be dismissed with no papers. And there were the disturbing rumours that he was deformed or disfigured in some way; Lizzie shuddered – he was ugly enough without that. She supposed he could have been handsome once, but his complexion was pitted and scarred, and his face was all furrows from frowning.

He looked to be sweating now, his cheeks glistened and he rubbed at his temples and the nape of his neck as if trying to erase invisible smears of dirt. He did not seem to be taking in the play at all. He was in his own world, a world that seemed to be somewhere near his feet, one he viewed through bleary bloodshot eyes. Lizzie saw him scratch at the back of his knees, then take a small bottle from his breeches and up-end it, trickling the contents into his mouth.

In a seat by the window, Emilia's pointed profile turned once more to look across the room to where Sir Ralph lounged on a wool-work cushioned chair, leaning back with one leg crossed over the other, engrossed in the players' loud foppish voices. Lizzie's stomach gave another lurch as she caught sight of Stephen, the young master, staring at his mother with a look of worried attention.

Whilst the revellers at the manor were dining on suckling pig, and clapping at the extraordinary feats of housewifery that had produced a march-pane garden, Margaret walked briskly through the leafy lanes, her wooden clogs making a tap-tapping noise on the cold-hardened ground. She leaned forward as she walked as if following her nose, her movements purposeful and direct, her brown worsted cloak flapping. Her eyes were used to darkness – she was often out and about at night gathering herbs that were best plucked by moonlight, and oft-times she was called out for a birthing in the dim hours between dusk and dawn. Tonight she was on an errand for herself. The harvests were plentiful and the people healthy, so her purse was growing thin, like a dog with worms. She remembered the salve she had sent to Sir Geoffrey Fisk, and today she would collect payment. For she had waited and waited and no errand boy had come.

The cream was efficacious, she knew it. So Margaret reckoned a personal call would bring her a more speedy payment. No gentleman wanted an old crone settling on his doorstep, particularly if he happened to have guests, so he would pay up if only to be rid of her. Margaret was a little tired, for she was not as young as she once was; her bones were starting to creak a little and her fingers were becoming twisted like hawthorn branches. But to give in to infirmity was not Margaret's way – she'd a will of stone and ignored her body's weak protests, hurrying on, her hood shadowing her face, bony fingers hooked around her travelling bag.

She opened a five-barred gate and strode into a field full of bullocks – she would take a short cut, for in the distance she could dimly perceive the high walls and turreted chimneys of Fisk Manor. The yellow squares of lit windows, floating in the dark, were a good compass. She set them in her sights, pushing past the warm damp flanks of the curious beasts who surrounded her – like all other animals, they recognized some sort of kinship with her and sought to make acquaintance. As she got nearer to the manor, she fancied she could hear music. Then again, these days she was becoming a little deaf and perhaps it was only her imagination.

Above her the sky was dark and swirling with clouds, like the tidal flux of the ocean. There were no stars visible behind the impenetrable moving mass, the air was heavy and damp. There was no birdsong, no night-time hoots of owls, no cry of a fox. It was eerily silent, as if the wild creatures had retreated into their holes and lairs and were watching with sly eyes. Margaret slowed, straining her ears. Perhaps she was deafer than she had thought, for the world seemed hushed. The blue-black clouds tilted and rolled silently overhead. Into her mind came the image of a procession, an odd group of masked people following a silent carriage. They were shuffling forward, their faces covered, as if groping blindly in the dark – like mummers, puppets caught in an age-old drama over which they had no control. The vision disappeared as quickly as it had come, but Margaret knew not to disregard these signs. It was a funeral cortege, that much was clear. Sir Geoffrey Fisk had better be careful. Death was stalking him through the lanes.

The motley troupe from the village wound its way past the end of Richard's lane, around the bottom of Helk's Wood, past the village green and headed south, out onto the main mail track, away from the lights of the village. Alice heard the noise from where she was stooped in a hedge, cutting ivy. She had been out far longer than she intended and had wandered far from home, collecting wild flowers to make studies for her flower diary.

She had relished getting out and about into the countryside to make notes on what was still flowering. She had been cooped up too long indoors. To her great delight, the lady's slipper had revived, Margaret's remedy had worked, and she could relax a little whilst she waited for the seeds to come. She hoped Margaret might call again to see how well it had done. She looked forward to learning more from her about plant physic. On the way back from her walk she had been attracted by this ivy, the first she had seen in flower that year, its round star-globes of milky green barely silhouetted against the sky in the darkness.

The sound of drums and clapping of cymbals could be heard in the distance. As it got closer, she stood up from the hedge in astonishment. The noise was tremendous, like an army on the march, a bobbing cavalcade of lanterns coming towards her and the trundling noise of cartwheels over the flinty ground.

Afraid, she stepped back a little into the hedge.

'Ho, mistress!' called a voice.

Alice did not reply, taking in the cart hung with bells and horns, the grotesque cavorting figures

213

dancing weirdly in the darkness like a scene from a masque. It looked like some sort of outlandish fertility rite, something against which it would be wise to shield one's eyes.

She turned back to the hedge, intending to ignore them and let them pass by. She took her knife from her basket and bent low beside the ditch, pretending to cut some more ivy.

'Don't ye want to join us, mistress?'

The voice right behind her made her jump. She startled and stood up. She heard laughter and muffled whispers. She was sure it was Cook's voice. But she couldn't see anyone's features, they wore hoods or cowls pulled down or vizards covering their faces. In the dusky gloom, these cackling masked creatures appeared ghoulish and threatening – she became acutely aware that she was alone, unchaperoned. Alice hastily picked up her basket and pruning knife and, feeling slightly foolish, set off in haste towards the safety of home. The laughter followed her as she hurried by.

In the procession, the merriment continued until they were close to the drive to Fisk Manor, which was marked by two stone balls on stone pillars. At the gates they hushed, anyone who giggled or laughed was silenced with a hand over the mouth. The farrier bent over and tied sacking round the horses' hooves to muffle the sound of the iron shoes, and all lanterns and torches were extinguished.

'Not a sound now,' Audrey said. 'We will wait close by and send these two to the door.' She pointed to the fake Sir Geoffrey and Lady Emilia.

'Once the horns are up, then we can all make as much noise as we like, but only at a safe distance.'

'They could set the dogs on us,' the farrier whispered hoarsely, 'so be ready to run like hares.'

'Get the old ones up onto the wagon then,' Ella said.

A few of the older people were hoisted up onto the cart before the procession pulled through the gates; the rowdy crowd was subdued to the rustling of cloth, shuffling of shoes and creak of wheels. Whispers were quickly silenced by shushes.

Inside Fisk Manor, Sir Geoffrey looked gloomily into space. He hated the pretentious sound of the players' voices, their exaggerated mannerisms, their way of trying to draw the audience into their charade with their winks and asides. He wished it were over, but when he had enquired into the length of the play he had been told it was three acts, some several hours. And all at his expense. Emilia let money trickle through her hands like water, he thought. It was what came of having over-indulgent parents.

Money was tighter these days. His newfound interests in the plants and healing herbs of New England had meant his voyages were less lucrative than they had been when his ships were filled with spices and exotic foodstuffs. Storms at sea meant wasted cargos, and the new decorations at home had cost him dear. Still, he wasn't to be outdone by Robert Rawlinson at Brockhurst Manor.

He took another draught of wine. It tasted bitter. Recently all his wine had tasted dry as

215

aloes. Unless his palate had been changed by his time abroad, his wine merchant would be getting better instructions. Since taking the nerveroot the torment of the itching had stopped. It was like a miracle to be free of it after all these years. He would not have been able to stand such company else.

He carried a phial of it with him all the time now, and if the tetters started again he knew to take his physic. But his eyes were unaccountably dry and his head throbbed as if it would burst. He rubbed at his temples with his fingers, surprised to find he was damp with sweat, but his face felt numb as if it did not belong to him. He would just get some air; the wine must be off. As he stood, he found himself clutching the arms of the chair. His hands seemed to have turned into claws, the room swam around him. The walls took on unusual curves as if falling inwards, the players' faces slid out of kilter like melted wax.

He slumped back into his chair but a wave of nausea propelled him out of it and he keeled towards the doorway. The room was curdling around him, the walls like soft cheese, the doorway swaying before his eyes. He saw the darkness of the hall and staggered towards it, away from the harsh sparkle and heat of the dripping chandeliers, to where the night air would be cool and he could retch unobserved. As he got to the doorway Jane Rawlinson was just passing through, her purple-hued face lurid in the shadows. She smiled and her face seemed to turn into a snout like a snarling fox's mask, the lips curled strangely out of shape into two ballooning wads of flesh. He pushed past

216

her roughly, ignoring her indignant look. Her eyes were glass marbles in the pouchy sockets of flesh.

He stumbled to the door and tried to tug it open but it seemed to be stuck, and he thought he heard voices on the other side. He pulled harder and it flew open into the hall with a clang and a rattle. A grotesquely painted woman's face stared back at him, her hair hanging lank as a horse's tail. Geoffrey saw over her shoulder that dark figures were running in the darkness, scattering in all directions the way rabbits run from a blunderbuss.

A wisp of colour caught his eye. Geoffrey glanced up. He saw there was something pinned to the door. He made out a pair of ram's horns, begarlanded and hung with bells, ribbons and old man's beard. By this time the woman was halfway down the steps. Geoffrey roared and made a grab for her but he was too late, she squirmed out of his reach. Geoffrey reached for his hunting knife from the cabinet in the hall.

At the same time, Margaret saw the lights ahead and brightly dressed figures moving like gaudy smears past the windows. Her sharp nose smelt food, too, something roasting, potatoes and the pungent tang of rosemary. As she approached the steps to the big front door, she was almost knocked aside by a man fleeing down the steps as if his life depended on it. He was wearing fancy dress, a flaxen wig and what appeared to be a false moustache. She ignored him and continued to make her way up the steps. As she got halfway up she saw that the door was open, and in the light from inside the hall she could see another figure, a man dressed in a gown, made up as a woman. Margaret paused. Momentarily confused, she sensed some other commotion behind her and turned to look. There were people running down the drive, cowled ghostly figures scattering in all directions.

As she turned back to the door the man in the gown shot past her, holding up his skirts and leaping down the steps two at a time, just as a tall gentleman cannoned into her, something glinting silver in his hand. He made a noise, a cross between a snarl of rage and a cry of pain. Margaret instinctively turned to run, but he was on top of her before she knew it.

'Thought to get away with it, did you?' A sharp pain in her ribs. 'Who put you up to this?' His face was close to hers, his eyes wild and his breath thick with wine, foul-smelling and rancid. Another sharp pain in her side. Everything seemed to be happening very slowly. The world exploded round her, the pain exquisite, unbearable. Almost immediately everything shimmered into a new kind of light – as if washed out, colours drained of their hues. At first Margaret struggled to get loose and run away, but something in her had already given up. Her cracked fingernails ceased to scrape at the buttons of his waistcoat, and now it was she who was leaning on him, her legs buckling, and he was backing off, trying to get away from her. The tables had turned in an instant. He pushed at her with bloodied hands, but she let her weight fall towards him, her body heavy, warm.

'You can't get away from me,' she said, 'you'll

never get away from me – I will never let you go. You will see me in every old woman you meet.' The words seemed to spill out of her mouth without her bidding, as if her mouth and mind were already disconnected. She tightened her grip on her old leather bag; whatever happened, she would never be parted from it.

'Leave go,' the man groaned, pushing her so she reeled down the steps.

From inside the house there was applause and calls of bravo. Somewhere down the drive out of sight there was a huge cheer, as if the crowd had somehow managed to assemble there as well. Margaret heard the applause and the cheering, though it was faint through her ears. It seemed somehow appropriate. She wondered if everyone heard cheering before they saw the white light.

Her other hand tried to pull her cloak about her but her arm felt weak, like a feather. She allowed her body to fall, like a plum drops from a tree, rolling over and over in the dust until she lay still at the bottom of the steps. Her bag was still over her arm, its hard leathery corner pressed against her shoulder where she fell. She looked up into the swelling depths of the sky, her face calm. So it was her, not the gentleman, after all. She had seen the signs but not realized it was her own name they were calling. She smiled at the glorious irony of the world. Her knowledge and skill – it all died with her. She was the last of her line. A huge sadness engulfed her. Was this all it was? These few years, and over so quickly? She held more tightly to the leather handle, although she knew she would soon have to let go.

'Alice Ibbetson.' She felt as if she shouted the words, but they were faint whispers from her mouth. 'Pass my bag on to her.'

She was surprised to hear the final rattle she had heard so often before – but this time she heard it anew, and it sounded different from her own throat. Her cloak lay round her on the gravel like a brown pool. In a few moments her chest sank, like the settling of silk, and she was completely still.

Geoffrey stared without comprehension at the heap of rags at the bottom of the steps. She had tried to speak at the last, but he had not caught her words. There was an uncanny silence now that her breath had stopped. He did not understand how this woman came to be lying there. He had meant to cut down the horns from the door with his knife. Now, suddenly, there was a body of an old woman, and his hands were wet and sticky with congealing blood. It was as if he was caught in a chain of events that were nothing to do with him. He licked his lips; they were bitter as wormwood. He was dimly aware of more applause and laughter from the open windows. The start of Act Two. Garnering his wits, he ran down to the motionless heap. There was blood seeping into her cloak in a thick slippery stain.

Realizing she could not lie there in full view of all his guests, he wrapped the cloak round her and prised the heavy bag out of her white hand. He dragged the body across the stony drive out of view of the house to the stables. Her head bumped against the rough ground, her lips seemed to move

220

as if speaking, her eyes rolled open, staring. He saw her hair, shining white in the darkness, a fine floss like sheep's wool. He recoiled, and stopped to drag the hood down over her face.

He thrust his hands in the water trough at the stables and brought them out of the icy water dripping. He rubbed at them in a sort of trance. It was so dark it was difficult to see if he had washed them clean. He saddled his horse with fumbling fingers. He could barely see the holes in the girthstrap, his head throbbed and the leather traces on the sled shimmered and waved before his eyes. He turned aside and his guts heaved. A stream of hot vomit shot from his lips. He hung over the steaming patch of liquid, the sting of sweat running into his eyes. Still fighting nausea, he bundled the body and the leather bag on the sled and attached the traces. The bag was almost heavier than the woman and crunched as if full of broken glass. The horse trampled and side-stepped but Geoffrey mounted and kicked it on into an almost silent canter along the grass beside the drive.

There was no sign of anyone now – as rats do, they had bolted back to their holes. At the end of the drive he emptied the sled unceremoniously into a ditch, pushing the body under the hedge-row. Even in the dark he could see the sled was stained with blood. A sense of unreality hung over him, a weariness. Now he would have to clean the sled. Back at the stables he swilled it over with straw and water from the trough. His head ached still, his teeth were clenched. He watched his hands sliding the straw back and

221

forth across the wood as if they were not his own. He lugged the sled back to its storage position and swept the bloodstained straw under the dung heap in the corner of the yard.

As he did so, his thoughts raced. He could make no sense of it. Cuckold's horns on his door. The old woman had it coming. He would not stand by and be humiliated in front of his guests. She should not have been on his land. A trespasser. It was an accident. It wasn't murder, it was protecting his property.

Geoffrey scuffed the gravelled chippings over the small tell-tale stain at the bottom of the steps with his red-heeled shoe. The shoe-buckle glinted eerily in the light from the house windows and he found himself thinking it was fortunate that his heels were red and would not show the blood. How did he come to be scraping blood from his driveway with his dancing shoe? He looked up at the house. The noises from inside had ceased and the air was still.

Realizing the play must have finished, Geoffrey turned back towards the big oak door. The horns were still there. Geoffrey loped across and using the bloodstained knife began to cut them down. As he did so there was a flurry of activity in the hall and Robert Rawlinson and his wife appeared, dressed in their outdoor cloaks and mufflers. Geoffrey hastily pocketed the bloodstained knife.

'Geoffrey. There you are. Can you arrange for our carriage to be brought...' Robert paused, sensing that Geoffrey was not listening. He peered at Geoffrey's ashen face, at his sweaty forehead and bloodshot eyes. 'Good God, man, you look most unwell.'

He called out behind him into the vestibule. 'Someone fetch Patterson, his lordship is unwell.' Robert tried to steer Geoffrey towards a chair.

Acutely aware there might be blood on his clothes and that his eyes must hold evidence of his guilt should he look at anybody, Geoffrey thrust Robert away and wordlessly rushed past him and up the stairs.

Robert's eyes followed him reproachfully.

'The worse for drink, I'd say,' said Jane, in a whisper that was designed to be heard.

As they bustled through the front door they caught sight of the horns, still hanging there.

'Well, I'll be damned,' Robert said. 'No wonder he was so upset.'

'Do you think there's truth in it?' Jane indicated the horns by touching the coloured ribbons hanging down the door.

'Well, who would have guessed it? I've always thought Emilia a bit of a cold fish, and Geoffrey's never exactly been known for his "amour" either. But someone knows something, and the sign's up for all to see.'

'Do you think anyone else has seen it?' Jane said.

'I doubt it, dear, we're the first to depart.'

'We could take the horns down then, before the others see them.'

'Well, it's not my house and I wouldn't know what to do with them – it's his servants' job to do that sort of thing.'

'Of course, dear, you're right.' They smiled at each other in understanding. 'Much better to let the servants do it.' And they strolled down the steps, arm in arm, leaving the door open and the horns there for all to see.

Geoffrey lit all the candles in his chamber so that the room blazed with an unusual fierceness and the thick scent of beeswax and tallow assailed his nostrils. He felt safer in the light – he needed to somehow shine a light into the corners of his mind, to clarify the dark and confusion. It was as if he had forgotten something important but did not know what. He undressed himself with shaking hands and put himself into a robe. He bundled his other clothes into a trunk at the back of the closet, the knife still in the pocket. He shoved the trunk into the dark recess, noticing as he did so that his hands were peculiarly white and bloodless.

Patterson arrived, having heard he was indisposed. Geoffrey dismissed him and sent him to remove the hideous object from the front door forthwith and get rid of it. Geoffrey pressed his temples. The blood had brought back images of the war, and the memories had somehow entwined themselves with the night's events. He had killed a woman and felt the life ebb out of her. Killing men in war was quite a different thing. Women were defenceless, untrained, unready for conflict or acts of heroism. Especially old women. He thought of his mother, remembered how her body lay limply in his arms, heard the hoofbeats of Wheeler's men galloping away.

Geoffrey continued to wash his hands and meticulously soaped and rubbed his clothes and boots until all evidence of the night's proceedings was gone. Thankfully, the woman's thick cloak had absorbed the stains and protected his clothing. Geoffrey could not help but wonder who she was, whose mother, and who might be waiting at home for someone who would never return. The knife had slid into her belly, so softly, with barely a sound, like gutting a fish – easy, slippery, over in a moment with the minimum of fuss. That moment would never leave him, she said. He felt cursed. He sensed the noose already tightening around his neck.

He paced the room, tugging distractedly at the hem of his clean shirt, his fingers unable to be still. His life seemed to be falling into pieces around him. He was unwell. True, his skin had improved, but now some other dreadful malady assailed him. The world would suddenly slip out of focus, he would see things that weren't there. He could be losing his wits. He seemed to think a woman was dead, and somehow he had done it. It could not be true. He remembered scrubbing the sled and groaned. His stomach gave a great lurch.

As if he had not trouble enough already. He had lost control of his finances, his estate was full of dissenters and his wife was cuckolding him behind his back. And now there was this.

With a start he recalled the memory of Emilia dancing. He had been gulled by his wife. What was more, he was a laughing stock, and people must know – be sniggering behind his back. Bile rose in his throat. He would make her pay. Emilia would not get away with this, the two-faced trollop. He put his head in his hands. The thought incensed him. Who was the man? He racked his brains. The whore. It could have been any of them.

'Hetherington,' he said aloud. The bastard. To think he had let it happen behind his back without so much as an inkling of suspicion. He must be losing his powers of discernment – he had always thought he had the measure of Emilia, that he understood her stupid petty needs. As far as he could see, her only desire was for frills and fineries. And he had supplied her, like the dutiful husband he was, with all she requested; he had been a good provider.

But even this he knew was a lie. She had brought her money and bought him – bought him in return for a title and a ticket to the higher strata of society. He had been bought, and now he had been duped. He shirked from looking deep in himself, for he knew they had never felt any real connection, that he had somehow missed the way of making a meaningful relationship with her, but it still came to him as a shock that she would dare to do this to him. She had betrayed him, opened her legs for that scoundrel Hetherington before coming home to eat dinner and hide her lust behind that limp and simpering façade.

The blazing lights of his room dazzled him, made his eyes water. He blew each taper out with a controlled and deliberate breath and lay down on his bed in the hot clammy darkness behind his locked door. When the knocking came he ignored it and rolled over, clutching the crumpled feather pillow to his face, feeling the room lurch and keel as if he was still aboard his schooner. When he retched again, he thought he was leaning over the rails with the black ocean below, but the vomit splashed with a clap over the wooden floorboards and seeped sour and yellow into the edge of the turkey rug.

Tomorrow, by God, he would deal with Emilia.

Chapter 18

In the village, word was soon out that old Widow Poulter had disappeared. The landlord of the Anchor was irate because she had left without paying him, and his son was still suffering with a rash of boils she had promised to poultice that morning. The general opinion was that she had sneaked off in the night, probably back to Preston, and folk thought no more about it, other than to think the worse of her, as people are wont to do.

It was one of the milk lads who found the body. When he was out on his round, he'd stopped the dray to have a smoke. When he went to relieve himself in a hedge he'd seen her lying there. He'd thought her drunk, until he tumbled her over and saw the deep red wounds gaping through her bodice, her white-filmed eyes rolled back in her head. He'd run back to the dray, all of a bother, pipe still smouldering in his lips, and set off to fetch his brother. Between them they manhandled her onto the back of the cart and took her to the constable's.

The milk lad lost no time in announcing it to all and sundry in the village, and so the speculation began. Some said Margaret was a great healer, almost a saint, and others that she was an evil charlatan involved in certain skulduggery, who deserved everything that had happened to her. Nonetheless, everyone was concerned that there might be a cut-throat in their midst, and it soon became the favourite occupation of the day to guess the identity of the perpetrator of the crime. At Ella and Sadie Appleby's house, the news was delivered by the neighbour, who'd heard it from the milking lad at Trout Farm. Ella had answered the door reluctantly, in her shift, for she had been late abed after a night of carousing in the alehouse after the great success of the cuckolding. But Ella was soon excited by the scandal of Margaret's passing and interrogated the neighbour for juicy parts of the story she could savour and pass on as the centre of attention. She hurried to dress and get to the Ibbetsons' with her tale before anyone else got there first.

She dressed provocatively, for now it was a habit; her low-cut blouse would attract Thomas's attention, like a pig to swill. And he was on the verge of buying her a new gown, she knew it. Just a little more persuasion and he would be in the draper's, ordering her something fancy. She took a peek at the shoes under her mattress. She did this every day, partly to reassure herself they were still there and had not been stolen by her sister or her father, and partly because they embodied for her all her ideas about gentility and beauty. To walk on the muddy ground in such peach-soft, smooth, light slippers, with their delicate sprigs of floral embroidery, must surely mean you had arrived – you were a lady of refinement. Shoes spoke a lot about folk, she thought. You could tell what sort of a person you were dealing with straight away by what was on their feet. Thomas's fine brown calf-leather boots were a mile away from her father's down-at-heel clog-boots with his grimy toes pushing through cracks in the leather.

The shoes held a fascination she could not have explained. Partly it was just the texture, the almost sexual smoothness of the satin, its coolness, the slight sheen of the surface. Partly it was the colour, a rich butter colour that spoke of the fat of the land, that conjured the foods she would never eat at home and had to connive and wheedle to get whilst at work. She stared again at the dark stain disfiguring one of the cream stitched roses, rubbing her finger over it before pushing the shoes back into their hiding place.

She smoothed down her apron, twirled her brown hair into a semblance of a ringlet at the front and straightened her cap.

When she got to the Ibbetsons' she was aggrieved to find that the news had already reached the kitchen – Cook's husband had been to the farm and heard it direct from the farm boys. Petulantly at first, but then with growing enthusiasm, she joined the gossip about who could have been responsible.

'Slit right across the belly, she was. Must have been a carving knife or a hunting knife.'

'I'm not surprised,' said Ella. 'She had a right temper on her. I saw her last week, right here on our front path, shouting at the mistress.'

Cook put down her mixing bowl, and the young scullery maid, April, put down the laundry that was steeping in the stone sink and set her posher to one side, and they gathered around, wiping their hands down their sides.

'Really?' April said.

'You're right,' Cook said. 'I saw them too, from the upstairs window.' She indicated the floor above with her eyes. 'I'd gone up to collect the tea tray from Master's room and I saw them there – Mistress Alice and that old woman – the one that's been killed – they were shouting and carrying on.'

'You don't say.' The scullery maid's eyes widened.

'Yes,' Cook said. 'She had a hold of Mistress Alice by the arm and was cursing and swearing. I've never seen Mistress look so angry.'

'She was screaming like a she-cat, and spitting,' Ella said, 'and I heard Mistress say, "Get out and never come back, you old witch!"'

Cook looked doubtful. 'I didn't hear her say that.'

'Well, you're getting on a bit. I heard her clear as anything. Mistress was red in the guts and yelling like you've never heard. I tell you, if looks could kill...'

'You don't think, I mean, surely you don't think...' April said.

'No, don't be a lummock,' Cook said, glaring at her.

Ella turned away from the conversation. Her hands absentmindedly picked up the scrubbing board and she started to rub away at one of the master's shirts. A seed had been planted in her mind and was slowly germinating. She scrubbed gently at first, with a slight smile on her face. Her hands worked mechanically, lathering the soap back and forth on the white cotton fabric. Her eyes stared unseeing out of the steamy window. Then the scrubbing became faster and more fevered and the water splashed and frothed around her elbows until Cook said, 'Leave off that collar now, Ella, you'll wear it out.'

Ella came to, as if with a jolt. She dropped the shirt back in the sink. Cook and the scullery maid were staring at her as if she had lost her senses.

'I'm taking the morning off.' Ella unfastened her apron and threw it over the back of a chair.

'But you only just got here–' April began to speak at the same time as Cook.

'But what about Mistress Alice? What am I to tell her?'

'Tell her what you like.' Ella paused by the door. A shadow flitted across her face as if something else had just occurred to her. 'I've changed my mind,' she said. 'I won't be coming back at all.'

'Not in time to help with the dinner either?'

'No, not at all. I'm not coming back here, not to this house, not whilst she's in it. It's evil, and I will be well out of it.' With that, she turned on her heel and swept out of the room, leaving Cook and the scullery maid staring at her retreating back in astonishment.

'What did she mean?' asked April, timidly.

'I've no idea,' snapped Cook. 'Something she's cooked up in her head, I shouldn't wonder. She always was a bit fanciful.'

'What did she mean, that the house is evil?'

'I don't know. All I know is, there will be one less hand today and there's all this to do.' Cook held out her arms in a gesture of frustration towards the heap of sodden clothes in the sink before pushing her hair back under her cap and saying, 'Shape up now, girl. You get on with that lot, whilst I run over to Jennings's – I'll see if their Lottie's free to give us a hand.'

April looked despondently at the clammy pile of dripping cloth and the washboard. She knew it would be harder without Ella to help wring the sheets and hang them out. Ella was strong, whereas April was always considered a weakling – like a weeping willow, she seemed to buckle if she was asked to carry too much weight. And Ella had told April stories whilst they worked. Cook said they were tall tales and that Ella was a tittle-tattle and it was all scum and lies, but April always enjoyed hearing them all the same. Seeing her still standing gazing at the sink, Cook flashed her a warning look and April scurried over to it, rolling her damp sleeves further up her skinny arms.

Ten minutes later Cook was back, with young Lottie Jennings in tow.

'There's trouble brewing,' she said. 'Lottie's pa saw Ella outside the constable's. He reckoned she must have done something real bad.'

'Do you think Mistress has found out about her pinching stuff?' April looked back over her shoulder.

Cook's chin retreated back into her neck and she looked blankly at April for a moment before her chin jutted forwards again and she said, 'What's this?' She approached April with her eyes narrowed.

Realizing from Cook's reaction that it had been a mistake to open her mouth and hastily retracting, April quivered. 'If she pinched stuff, I mean to say, she wouldn't, but if she did...' She tailed off lamely, red in the face.

'Do you think I don't know what goes on in my own kitchen?' Cook shouted. 'Lottie, stop gawping and help April with the wringing.'

Out of the corners of their eyes, over the twisting of the sheets above the sink, Lottie and April watched Cook go straight to the pantry. Moments later they witnessed her bring out several half-full jars of jam and line them up silently on the table. Neither of them spoke. They dared not. Cook's face was clabbered, as though she had just swallowed a ball of camphor.

Chapter 19

Stephen Fisk set off early to the Quakers for the morning meeting. To his father's annoyance, the committee had agreed Stephen should be the one to find out what was afoot at Lingfell Hall. His father's instructions from the night before were etched into his mind: that he must trust no one, keep his ears and eyes open, and try to win Wheeler's confidence. He must speak as little as possible lest he give himself away.

In preparation he had managed to speak incognito with the town clerk, claiming to have been convinced at one of Fox's so-called 'threshing meetings'. The thrill of being in disguise was even greater when no suspicions had been aroused and

Isaac had agreed to introduce him at the meeting. Stephen had said that his name was Sam Fielding. It had amused him to keep the same initials for his alias, as if it gave him more veracity. He had let it be known he was a mercer from Burton-in-Lonsdale, and indeed he had spent several days reading all he could about the mercer's trade. With his father's collusion he had taken one of his worst nags, a plain bay with a white blaze, the most unremarkable beast, as his mount. It was slow-going on such a horse, but it gave him time on the way to the meeting to go over his imaginary life story in his head.

He was in truth not just a little nervous, but terrified. He wished he had never volunteered. His father had warned him that the meetings were a cover for the king's enemies to plan their treasonous activities, and Stephen knew if he were identified as Sir Geoffrey's son he might not leave Lingfell Hall alive. He remembered someone jesting with him in Oxford that the Quakers themselves were an unruly bunch of madmen who refused to submit to common law. They did not seem quite so amusing now. His hands were sweating slightly, rubbing the saddle soap from the reins until his palms were stained brown.

His horse picked its way along the stony lane, seemingly in no hurry to reach its destination, which was exactly how Stephen himself felt about the task ahead. Dressed in dun-coloured tweed breeches and a matching plain wool topcoat, he felt like a gamekeeper, and for this reason he had sneaked out before breaking his fast lest he should meet his mother – she would certainly have something to say about his odd attire.

He ran over his tale in his head, but did not have long to practise it before it was required. Hoofbeats behind him made him turn in his saddle, and a lone rider on a big Cleveland bay horse cantered up alongside.

'Going to the Hall?'

'Aye.'

'For the morning meeting?'

'Aye.'

The man swivelled in his saddle to get a better look at Stephen. 'Then we can ride together. Thy face is unfamiliar, wilt thou introduce thyself?'

'Sam Fielding. From Burton-in-Lonsdale. I've not been to the Hall before.'

'Well, there's always a fine welcome – especially to young faces. Hast thou ridden from Burton this morning?'

'Aye.' It sounded an odd word to Stephen, but the other man seemed to notice nothing amiss.

'That's a fair old ride. We'll make sure thy horse is well watered when we get there.'

Stephen just nodded. He knew engaging in small talk would be difficult. He could not get used to the old-fashioned speech, and he feared his schooling might give him away. So he rode on. The other man also rode quietly, as if it was expected, pausing only now and then to point to the vivid yellow linden leaves on a solitary tree, and to a red fox as it ran along a furrow in the field alongside. Stephen let the other man go ahead, watching his horse's rump sway from side to side. He pondered over last night's dinner and wished he had not had so much wine. His father had upset his mother again by drinking too much, retiring early and leaving her to deal with all the servants and the guests. Patterson had been required to sort him out as usual. Stephen sighed and gathered up his reins in his damp palms. Why couldn't his parents be civil to one another?

So consumed was he by these thoughts that he was taken by surprise when they drew up and he saw the gables of the house and the cobbled yard with several horses tied there. A fresh bout of nerves made his stomach flutter. He dismounted and followed the other man's lead, tying his horse alongside his.

'Come along then, Sam,' the man said. 'We'll go and make thee known to Dorothy.'

Stephen followed him, his neck hot, palms sweating, through a darkened passageway where there seemed to be any number of dirty sheepdogs lying around – the owners presumably in the meeting room, and probably equally dirty, he thought. Everyone turned round to stare as the pair entered, but his new acquaintance shepherded him forward towards a tall woman in a grey dress.

'Dorothy, this is Sam Fielding, from Burton-in-Lonsdale. He's the young man Isaac was telling me about – from the conventicle last month.'

'Good morning, Sam. I am very pleased you have come to our meeting. But tell me, are there no others like thee who could meet together in Burton? It is a long way to ride.'

'There are but a few of us, ma'am,' said Stephen, and then smiling, despite his dry mouth, 'I had heard tell of the spirit at meetings here. I

236

wanted to come and see it for myself.'

Dorothy smiled back. He had made the right impression. 'Welcome then. I daresay Richard will show thee where to hang thy coat.'

'Thank you.' He was alert at the sound of that name. And there was something odd in the woman's tone of voice when she said it, a sort of disdain. She had not introduced them, but this could be Richard Wheeler, the man his father told him had killed his grandmother. The hairs prickled on the back of his neck. He had no time to move away as Richard grasped his arm and pointed to a row of iron coat hooks and benches at the side of the room. 'Over there.' And then, as an afterthought, 'Sorry, I never said, I'm Richard Wheeler.'

So it was him. Stephen hung up his coat, feeling vulnerable in his shirt-sleeves and vest. He followed the others and sat down in the circle of benches. During the meeting he watched Richard covertly. He was a tall straight man, broad-shouldered and swarthy from outside labour. He had a high forehead and expressive eyebrows which were furrowed as if in some invisible conversation with himself. His hands were strong and capable. He was a bigger man than Stephen, and more powerful. Stephen baulked at the idea that he could be his enemy; his instincts told him he would bear the worst of it should it come to a fight.

During the meeting nobody spoke, people were silent and sat still. No one had asked him any awkward questions or wanted to know his background.

It was twenty minutes before anything hap-

237

pened. A woman got up and talked of a husband and wife who had been jailed and beaten for preaching on the street. He noticed that Richard looked uncomfortable during this, biting his lip and frowning at his boots, and that he kept looking over to Dorothy to see her reaction. It was interesting, observing people, like an experiment he might perform during his studies at school. Dorothy ignored Richard's glances.

After that there was more sitting in silence, which Stephen found extremely dull. Eventually, Isaac, the town clerk, whom Stephen had already met, stood and announced they would discuss the group's business affairs, and everyone shuffled on their seats and looked at him expectantly. More tedious talk followed, of giving alms to beggars in the district, of visiting the sick, and the two that were in gaol after a lynching.

Then the meeting was called to a close and they were offered some refreshment. The older ladies of the gathering busied themselves bringing round little oatcakes and cups of barley water, whilst the men stood in groups conversing. Stephen kept close to Richard, his ears open. Now surely, the real business would begin.

'Hast thou heard – our brethren in Sedbergh have refused to give up tithe this harvest?' said one old man.

'Yes,' said another. 'They have set a guard on the tithebarn, and are refusing to give up any portion.'

'The church will not let them get away with it, they'll send troops in if they have to.'

Stephen's ears pricked up at the mention of soldiers.

'We should stand with them, then. The church is a false edifice,' said the first man. 'No man needs a church to be with God.'

'Aye,' said Richard. 'I'm done with lining the pockets of priests and parsons, whilst those in real need still go hungry.'

'Shall we moot it at the next meeting?'

'We can try,' said the first man, 'but there are a fair few in gaol already. Last time we tried with-holding our dues, Fisk's rough-hands came and turned over our barns.'

Stephen froze on the spot, feeling a crimson glow spread across his temples. His father's name already.

'What thinkst thou, Sam?' asked Richard.

Stephen did not reply; he was still taking in the information that his father's men were fighting with the Quakers over tithes. The second time his name was called, he recognized it with a start.

'Yes, Sam, how is it over Burton way?' They all looked expectantly at him for a reply.

'Oh, I think we, I mean... I think we will prob-ably pay our dues as usual,' he finished lamely. Richard stared at him without saying anything.

'Though, of course, we are with you on prin-ciple,' he added, floundering but trying to sense the lie of the land. He hoped he sounded suitably committed.

'So, Sam, if we should rally enough support, thou wouldst join us in opposing this unholy law?' pressed Richard.

'Of course,' he replied. Had Richard spotted something suspicious about him? Was that why he was questioning him? Stephen felt uncomfortable

239

and looked down at his feet, newly shod in solid leather work boots. His father had told him to rough the toecaps with a grinding stone, and he had done so. When he looked up, Richard was still looking at him, as if his clothes were of great interest. Stephen swallowed and tried to look nonchalant. Richard's eyes travelled over Stephen's tweed suit, over the horn buttons, his unpressed cuffs, the yellow cotton cravat at his neck. Prepared to brazen it out if necessary, Stephen drew himself up to his full height. But Richard turned to the other two, and clapped his hands together.

'Well then, we are all agreed. I will raise it to the vote at the next meeting.'

'I must be on my way,' said Stephen, eager to leave the group and reorder his thoughts.

'Yes, yes,' said one of the men. 'It is a good distance, if thou art to be back in time for a day's trade.'

Stephen bowed slightly as he had seen the others do, and withdrew to the coat hooks where his overcoat was hanging with the rest. So the group was going to organize a rebellion and refuse to pay tithes, were they? His father would have something to say about that. And it was indeed the dissembler Richard Wheeler who was instigating the idea and persuading the others to vote on it. Stephen took down his damp coat, which smelt of greasy wool, and threw it round his shoulders. As he did up the frogged fastening he felt a firm hand descend on his shoulder and, startled, spun round to find himself looking directly into Richard's face.

'Now then, Sam, I will accompany thee down

the hill,' said Richard.

'Oh no, I can ride on alone,' said Stephen, fear gnawing in his guts. What if Richard had seen the resemblance to his father and was going to take him somewhere to dispatch him? Stephen had no desire to be alone with Richard.

'It is no trouble, and I have a mind for thy company,' said Richard, insisting.

'Very well,' said Stephen warily, 'if thou art sure it will not inconvenience thee.' He spoke slowly, struggling with the archaic-sounding form of address.

Richard was smiling at him now, but Stephen's mind was racing, planning how he might escape should he be attacked on the route to the main highway. Richard steered him out of the hall with a hand at his back.

'You have not fooled me, young man, though you might have fooled the others.'

Stephen's stomach lurched but he tried to remain calm, letting himself be guided out to the yard.

'What do you mean?' Richard had not used 'thou', but 'you', and Stephen likewise had fallen into the trap and used the more modern expression. He had no idea what Richard Wheeler had in mind, but he hurried to the horses, his armpits clammy, his heart hammering against his ribs. He would get mounted first, so at least he would stand a chance of escape.

'Thy clothes. This is the first time thou hast dressed this way, I can tell.'

Stephen swung himself into the saddle and cast his eyes rapidly over Richard's silhouette – no

241

sword or musket.

'What of it?' He decided to try a bluff. 'Cannot a man have new clothes without that all the world derides him for it?'

Richard was mounted now and drew his horse alongside. 'Thou art used to finer stuff than this.' He prodded at Stephen's breeches with his whip hand.

'Maybe.' Stephen was almost out of the yard now and within sight of open fields. He got ready to kick his horse on, moving himself ahead. Richard urged his horse into a trot so his stirrup-iron clashed with Stephen's and the horse's damp belly brushed against his thigh as he came up beside him again.

'Like thee, Sam, I am a recent convert, and a former gentleman. It takes one to know one, I suppose.' Richard turned his head and smiled. 'I still cannot abide these rough cotton shirts, and find plain speech more difficult to master than any fancy Latin.'

Stephen was taken aback to realize that Richard was being friendly, that he had understood his clothes to be an emblem of the power of his convictions, not a ploy to disguise the fact he was his father's son.

Stephen nodded, trying to sort out a proper response. Richard continued to speak with an air of someone about to bestow a confidence.

'I have been a Quaker since the war, but still find the simplicity of the life hard. I feel for thee, for I see how discomfited thou art in those clothes.' He looked at him and laughed. 'And I applaud thee, for I know how hard it must have

242

been to give away the fine life you had before.'

Stephen gave a noncommittal shrug.

'Tell me,' said Richard. 'Where are thy family? Perhaps I know of them?'

Nothing had prepared Stephen for this unexpected turn of events. Pictures of his parents flashed behind his eyes as he struggled to find an acceptable answer. With a stroke of inspiration he answered, 'My family was killed by the king's men in the war.'

Richard was silent but shook his head in sympathy. Stephen did not dare to speak. He had lost track of his invention, Sam Fielding, and had constructed no imaginary life for a parliamentarian son of a dead nobleman.

With a flash of inspiration he said, 'Tell me about these people that are in gaol, Hannah and Jack Fleetwood.' If he was crafty, he might be able to steer the conversation and get some information out of Richard about the plot against the king.

Richard outlined some events surrounding the Fleetwoods' arrest, after which he said, 'I still feel badly, Sam. I should have done something to stop it getting that far. Turn the crowd somehow.'

'But what couldst thou have done? Thou hast vowed not to take up arms.'

Stephen was fascinated by this idea of a pledge of peace. He could not imagine making such a vow. What if they were to be set upon by highway robbers on the return journey? He would certainly lift his fists then. He had thought it extraordinary that the Quakers carried neither sword nor musket. Why, even ladies held a little dagger concealed about their person when they were abroad.

In London, Stephen had worn his fine sword with a swagger; it had been lovingly crafted and he was itching for a chance to use it against some scoundrel, to show off his thrust and parry. He had a fine pair of muskets too, but somehow a gun seemed less manly than a sword, and there had been many a frightening accident with the powder.

A pair of crows flapped by, making their raucous call. They watched them fly by and out towards the estuary.

'Dorothy has not spoken with me properly since the day Jack and Hannah were arrested.' Richard was rueful. 'I think she blames me for it, because I stood by and let it happen, and am not imprisoned for my faith along with them.'

'Surely she cannot be that uncharitable?'

'She tolerates me, yes. She is never ill-mannered, just distant.'

Stephen made a sympathetic grunt. 'Hast thou tried to speak plain with her on this matter?'

'Well, no. I see what thou art saying, Sam. It does no good to let wounds fester.'

They rode on. Stephen's shoulders relaxed; he had not been discovered. The horses clopped down the wet track, both men sunk in their own thoughts. Stephen knew that Sam's history had become more convoluted and that he must master its intricacies if he were to carry on going to meetings at the Hall.

Richard seemed to be mulling over their conversation silently, until at length he said, 'I will speak with her the morrow. Thanks to thee, friend – thou hast seen clearly what I could not.'

Richard gave him a smile of such openness and warmth that Stephen immediately felt ill at ease. He had to remind himself that this man was planning to withhold from the church its rightful levies, that Richard was in dispute with his father and was a traitor to the king, and worse, that he had murdered Stephen's kin in cold blood.

Stephen nodded stiffly in return. He was resolved to tell his father what he had heard. He would do his duty by the committee; he could not afford to be swayed by this semblance of friendship. Richard was his enemy, and he must be on his mettle, remember his responsibilities. The safety of the whole country could depend on it.

After they parted, Stephen kicked his lumbering horse into a gallop, doubling back from the Burton road to the track to Fisk Manor. It was best to keep out of the village in case people began to talk and he was recognized. He enjoyed the sensation of the wind racing past his ears. Even after only a few hours he was glad to lose the constraints of being Sam Fielding.

When he arrived home there was a carriage waiting outside the door, full of portmanteaux and travelling baskets.

Lizzie Pickering was standing blubbing at the bottom of the stairs, her eyes red-rimmed and her scrawny fingers chewing over a sodden napkin. When she saw him go by to the stables she looked up at him with an imploring expression. He put the nag in the stall then hurried in through the back door where there seemed to be more confusion, with furniture out of place and the noise of

245

feet coming and going in the corridor above.

A writing desk was half blocking the doorway to the dining room and there was a big bundle of something cluttering up the passageway to the study. It looked like the drapes from his mother's bed. He wound his way round these obstacles until he could get to the stairs, and mounted them two at a time. On the upstairs corridor he managed to catch hold of Patterson as he pushed a wheeled bassinet full of lace petticoats past.

'What's going on?'

'It's not for me to say, sir.'

'Don't be ridiculous. Tell me unless you want to join Lizzie on the front step.'

Patterson looked shiftily from side to side.

'Lady Emilia, sir. She's...'

'Stop mumbling. What about my mother? Is she ill?'

'She's been given an hour, sir. To get out and never come back.'

Stephen could not take in the words.

'Who says this? Is this a joke?' Although he knew whatever was happening was no laughing matter, he wanted it to be. The house had a different air already; it looked uncared for, a random collection of meaningless possessions.

'Where is my father?'

Patterson shook his head. 'Out, sir.' Then, seeing more information was required: 'He went out at ten of the clock, and will be back at eleven. Mistress has one hour to gather what she can of her personal possessions. What will go in the carriage and the handcart. If she's still here when he returns he'll have her clapped in gaol.'

'Is she still here?'

'In there, sir.' Stephen was already squeezing past towards his mother's chamber. When he flung open the door he could see Patterson had been right. The drapes had been stripped from the bed; the overmantel tapestry of the wild hart had gone, leaving a sooty stain around a light mark. The looking glass and delicate scent bottles, boxes of jewels and silver candlesticks were gone from her dresser. His mother was under the window, bent over an open trunk, already overfull, trying to stuff in more combs and lace caps and gloves. Her face was white, and she was still in her nightgown.

She looked up when she heard him enter. He approached her with his arms outstretched as if to embrace her, but she stayed him with her eyes. 'Do not say anything,' she said, stony-faced. 'There is no time. Help me.'

Stephen looked on helplessly. 'How?' There was no answer. 'What am I to do?'

His mother did not even turn, but carried on pressing the lid on the trunk. He could see the small muscles working in her neck. 'Look for some plate – gold or silver, anything to hand. The servants have been told not to let me near it, but they'll obey you.'

'But...'

'Quickly, now, there is little time.' As she said it, as though to punctuate it, all the clocks began to chime the quarter. He had not realized they owned so many clocks, nor that all their chimes were so different.

Seeing his hesitation, she entreated him. 'Go! Please, Stephen, it may be all I have to stay me for the years ahead.'

He stumbled out of the room and down the corridor, passing the servants scurrying with their heads down, carrying armfuls of vermilion silk, a washstand with several basins balanced one on the other, a tray full of glasses and jugs. Stephen ignored them and headed for the dining room. Patterson was at the door as if guarding it. He seemed to know what Stephen had come for.

'She's not to have the plate. Master was quite adamant on that, sir.'

'Get out of my way, Patterson. Master is not here. You will take my orders. Open that cupboard.'

'No, sir. Master said not to.'

'Give me the key.'

Patterson remained stolidly where he was, unmoving.

'If you do not immediately give me the key, I will knock you flat, do you hear?'

'You are not to have the key.' Patterson looked Stephen brazenly in the eye, before Stephen's fist came out and he reeled backwards into the room. Stephen pressed his advantage and wrestled him to the floor.

'You bastard,' Patterson said thickly, the words out before he could stem them. He tried to stand but Stephen had him in a headlock. Stephen dragged the metal key-ring from Patterson's pocket with his free hand. He thrust Patterson's head to the floor and it made contact with a thud. Stephen struggled towards the cupboard, but Patterson punched him from the floor, landing a blow to his ribs that made him bite his lip.

He crawled away and stood up, frantically groping to fit the key to the lock. He tried one key but it did not turn, and had another almost in the lock when he felt hands pulling at his knees, trying to unbalance him. He kicked out backwards, intent on the lock, felt his boot make contact with something soft, and heard a groan. The key turned sweetly and the polished oak doors swung open.

Stephen hauled goblets and platters off the shelves, stacking them in his arms, going for the thickest gold ones first. When his arms were almost full he dragged the silver-chased punch-bowl off the shelf, the ladle banging and scraping round the inside.

As he made for the door, Patterson was staggering upright, barring his way, one eye nearly shut and bleeding. Stephen could feel the rage emanating from him like steam from a bull. He had no choice but to bludgeon his way past. He clasped tight to his booty and cannoned forward. Sheer momentum knocked Patterson sideways and Stephen was out, straight down to the waiting carriage.

As he did so, he turned to see his mother hurtling pell-mell down the steps, her bare ankles shockingly pale in the daylight, her arms full of table linen. The thought crossed his mind that table linen was useless with no table to set it on, and surely there must be other more useful goods in the house. For the first time he had some insight into his mother's mind. To her, table linen must be very important. Her servants were already man-handling the trunks onto the handcart and tying it

249

by its shafts to the back of the carriage. His mother grasped him by the shoulders and looked up at him.

'God bless you. I will find a way to get word to you.' She pushed her wispy hair out of her eyes. 'Where I am, I mean.' And she climbed into the carriage, which was already beginning to move off. 'And get out of those ridiculous clothes,' she called.

'Wait, I'll come with you,' he shouted, but the stablehand cracked the whip and the horses swept into motion, the carriage dragging after it the handcart, which jerked over the ruts in the drive so that one of the trunks, the one his mother had been at such pains to close, flew off and landed on the drive with a thud, scattering combs, reticules, lace gloves and frilled caps in its wake.

Stephen rushed forward to pick them up, and as he did so he was surprised how light all these items were. Is this all a woman's life is, he thought, these little pieces of lace? He stooped to bring a goosedown powder-puff to his nose and inhaled the familiar dry odour of his mother's cheek, a smell that seemed to take him back in time, back to learning his first letters, back to his first grazed knee. He breathed deeper, and a pang of nostalgia that was both a sweetness and a pain gnawed in his chest, a loss that was for something he had perhaps never had, but was now gone forever. A faint dust was settling on the dirt carriageway. Stephen watched it drop from the air, the odour of powder strong in his nostrils. He was standing thus when he heard the clocks chime the hour, and the sound of his father's horse on the drive.

Chapter 20

Alice was one of the last to hear of Margaret's death. She had hidden herself away in the summerhouse, for she and Thomas were more at odds than ever, like mismatched horses in double harness. She busied herself with her nature study pursuits and her paints, and hoped this particular bout of bad weather would pass.

The lady's slipper flower had bloomed and faded, the petals had dropped away to reveal a green swelling. She had been observing the plant closely for any further signs of distress, and to watch with fascination the seed pod come, now that the flower had gone. She was anxious to collect the minuscule dots of new life from the precious plant and to treat and sow them. In her mind she saw a field full of nodding orchids, their delicate buttercream bowls lit up by the morning sun. She hummed a little tune as she got out the blotting paper and tweezers.

Once divested of flower and seed, the orchid would be hardly noticed amongst her other specimens, she thought. The leaves looked like wild garlic, and unless you knew the plant intimately, it would be hard to distinguish one from the other. Richard Wheeler had called at the house, bold as brass, still asking about it, and the visit had been very disconcerting. She had been unwittingly rude to him in her fervour to keep him from the lady's slipper. It had left her feeling unsettled, as if someone had stirred up the bottom of a clear pond and the silt and scum were rising to the surface. His dogged persistence in the matter had surprised her.

He wanted her to return it to him because of a covenant with God; that was what he had said. What did he mean? She did not quite know what to make of it. His eyes had an intense quality about them that had not been there before, and it was unnerving. She squirmed inside. He was not going to leave her in peace until the plant was restored to its original position. He had asked her to examine her conscience, and fearful at the pricking of it she had prayed last night extra long, asking for forgiveness for this deception and for the lies she had told him.

She understood herself enough to know that she had been moved by the flower's beauty, and a certain covetousness lay at the heart of her decision to take it, as well as her more noble ideals of preserving it for future generations. She had so much wanted to save something, to take control somehow. God probably saw that too. Despite the prayers she had the sense she was becoming a stranger to herself.

After Thomas's harsh words, she had abandoned the mourning clothes for colours, yet still hues with a degree of restraint. Perhaps this might help her feel more herself, help her regain the old lost Alice. As she first put on the soft green dress instead of the sober black she had to bite back tears, for the black had been a daily concrete reminder of Flora, a homage each day as she dressed, and she feared forgetting her, becoming rootless, unfaithful to her family's memory.

She was fully aware that her new mode of dress had made people notice her and treat her differently. Richard Wheeler had looked at her almost with admiration – he had removed his hat, something she had never seen him do before in her presence. When he did so, she saw with surprise that his hair was thick and wavy, the colour of polished oak. She had wanted to touch it, feel its texture, and for the first time she realized he was an attractive man. She wondered why he had not married, but surmised that his peculiar faith must consume all his time.

When he had approached her in the hallway, almost as if he would force her to do his bidding, she felt the nearness of him, and her body had trembled not only with fear but with some other more strange feeling. She sensed he was doing what he thought proper; she knew him to be righteous, and it was she who was the deceiver. He had been terribly earnest, and overcome by an emotion she could not fathom. She felt unclean next to him, as if her faults were on display – it was as if his mere presence was like a lantern, showing up the dirt under the furniture.

She was musing on this when April, the scullery maid, rapped timidly on the door.

Alice put the orchid out of sight.

'Excuse, mistress, but Cook said to come tell you that Ella's upped and left.'

'What? Given notice?'

'No, mistress. She just walked out. Said she weren't coming back.'

Alice put down her gardening mittens and took off her apron. 'Tell Cook I will come.' She sighed, irritated that her sowing of the delicate seeds was interrupted by a domestic crisis. She locked up the summerhouse and hurried over to the house, where further questioning revealed that Ella had indeed gone, and that Lottie Jennings had temporarily taken her place.

This was a nuisance. Good maidservants were hard to find. Ella had never been ideal, she was inclined to be lippy, her appearance slovenly, but Alice felt herself to be tolerant and she had ignored Ella's shortcomings as long as she was left undisturbed in her painting. No real reason had been given for Ella's sudden departure. Both Cook and April seemed baffled by the whole business.

Certainly Ella would be given no reference, and Cook had made insinuations that there had been some pilfering in the kitchen behind her back. Alice's thoughts turned to her missing shoes. It was probably Ella who was responsible. But why would she want a pair of shoes that were far too small?

She dreaded telling Thomas they were short-staffed again. He had been curt with her that morning when she had told him the commission money from Earl Shipley's paintings was subject to a little delay. She had made an excuse about Earl Shipley being suddenly called to go to France, but Thomas had reprimanded her that she had not secured payment from him earlier. Apparently the Grand Dinner at the Fisks' had not yielded him the lucrative business contacts he had hoped to make, and worse, he had been forced to sit through a play that was interminably dull. Geoffrey Fisk had been drunk and had not introduced him to anyone, and he had lost a quantity of cash to a man called Fairfax at cards. None of this had improved his temper.

Alice was anxious to return to her gardening so she cut short Cook's obvious intention to give her all the details of Ella's departure and simply reassured her that a new maid would be sought with as much expedition as possible. She arranged to see her after dinner to discuss it. She must persuade Thomas to offer higher wages if they did not want such unreliable staff.

She managed to sow the seeds of the lady's slipper in the afternoon, following Margaret's advice to sow them early, but also making sure they were returned to the same soil, within which lay the invisible black fungus. This was the hidden food without which the new seedlings would fail to thrive.

The process was delicate and all-consuming. She hardly dared breathe, and darkness snaked into the summerhouse when she was still transferring the seed. Although the room was furnished with wall sconces and a good few candelabra so she could work at night, such tiny specks of seed were difficult to see in the wavering light. According to her father, the small seeds would be very slow to germinate, and it would be a while before she would be able to gauge her success.

The little pots looked just like pots of bare earth, the seeds all but invisible. They were quite unremarkable, so she left them on an open shelf where she could watch their progress. She wondered whether Margaret was right and they should be put out into the frost, but she was too frightened to do this, they looked so fragile. Her thoughts often turned to Margaret. She had not returned yet to visit her, and Alice was a little sad, for she had liked Margaret, and wanted someone else to share in the excitement of the process.

Afterwards she planted three larger pots of foxglove seeds. These would show much earlier, brought on by the warmth of the summerhouse, and would make a splendid early display by the front gate in years to come. She stood these on the top shelf, alongside the original lady's slipper plant, unremarkable now without its flower head.

When this was done, she went to the house and, heeding the difficult conversation to come, made a special effort with her dress, a dark blue fine wool, with velvet trim and small rosettes of dark blue satin ribbon on the bodice. Her bare shoulders she half concealed with a fine muslin kerchief, and she teased her hair into loose tendrils either side of her ears.

She hoped the attention to her dress and a suitably demure manner might smooth the way whilst she discussed domestic affairs, never a popular topic with Thomas, over dinner. When she heard his horse on the road outside, she called April to bring warmed wine to the dining room. The weather had been windy and the tide had come up through the estuary; Thomas had had to make a lengthy detour through ill-kept tracks, and from his demeanour she saw with a sinking heart that he was already not in the best of spirits.

Once he was settled in his favourite chair at the head of the table, with a drink in front of him, she led him gently into conversation, asking him about his day and listening to him talk of the price of Lindsey wool and the coiners' guild and so forth, until the meal was served. Obviously Cook had been unable to find much help in the kitchen, for here was yesterday's fowl pie, a little burnt around the edges, with no gravy and only a few parsnips at the side.

Thomas looked at his plate and wrinkled his nose. Alice was about to tell him about Ella, when he put down his knife and said, 'There's been a murder in the village, over near Fisk's place. The milk lad found the body in a ditch. I thought we were done with killings now. It seems we still cannot go safely abroad. She was stabbed to death, poor old soul.'

'How terrible,' said Alice. 'Who is it? Is it someone we know?'

'No. Some old woman from Preston way. She had lodgings above the Anchor Inn.'

The colour drained from Alice's face.

'Did they tell you her name? What did she look like?'

'Widow Proctor? Poultice? Something or other. No, I can't remember. Why?'

Alice swallowed. 'No reason. I just thought I might recognize the name. What's happened to her?'

'I've already said.' Thomas picked up his knife again and stuck it into the rock-like pastry. 'She was stabbed to death and left lying in a ditch, wrapped up in her own cloak, and before you enquire, nobody knows who is responsible.'

The saliva dried in Alice's mouth; she held tightly onto her napkin. It had to be her. Margaret was staying at the Anchor. There was no one else it could be. Alice continued to chew but she found she could not swallow. Her stomach was sinking into a gaping hole and she felt she would gag.

'It's not acceptable, is it,' said Thomas, shoving away his plate and knocking his goblet of wine so that it slopped onto the table. He mopped at it ineffectually with his napkin. 'I can't eat it either. I will tell Cook she must do better or look for another position.'

'Do not be angry with Cook. It is not her fault.' Alice's voice sounded small and far away; she tried to carry on as if she was unconcerned about Thomas's news, but her mind was racing through questions and answers. She continued to speak. 'It is because Ella has left us.'

'Left us? What do you mean, left us?'

'She just walked out, told Cook she was never coming back.'

'And you did not try to stop her or find out why?'

'Well, no, I...' She tailed off, astonished by a sudden commotion as Thomas pushed his chair back and leapt to his feet.

'You stupid hare-brained woman! You just let her go, as if it's of no consequence?' Alice had never seen Thomas move so fast. She was taken aback by his overreaction. He was still shouting, his mouth was crooked with anger. She did not understand why he was in such a temper. Alice stood too, tears were coming and she needed to

258

get away from his angry face.

He threw his wet napkin down on the table. 'Just because she's a maid you think she can be dispensed with, like an old coat, thrown off whenever you fancy, do you?' The spittle flew out from his mouth.

'But it had nothing to do with me. The first I heard of it–' She could not reason what had upset him so, but he cut her off sharp.

'You make me sick, do you hear? You've never given me a thought since Flora died. I might as well have not have existed. You are not a wife in any common sense of the word. You just fill the house with your gloom; you stink of it, and it makes everyone else miserable. Ella was warm-hearted and kind, and you always treated her like a piece of dirt under your feet.'

Alice was too stunned to speak. Tears coursed down her cheeks but she could not have told anyone what she was crying for. Like a ship battered by a storm and thrown off course, she had no idea what wind had hit her, nor any idea where it would lead.

Had she treated Ella like that? She did not think so. Surely her husband could not be talking about the Ella she knew. She began to speak.

'Cook says she stole things from the kitchen–'

Thomas did not let her finish. His pudgy face had broken out in beads of sweat, red veins stood out in his forehead. 'So that was your excuse to get rid of her, was it? And how is her family going to manage without her money coming in? You are a selfish, thoughtless woman, and...'

It dawned on Alice in one hot rush of shame that

259

her husband was talking as if Ella were the wife, and Alice the servant. The truth of the situation between her husband and her maidservant hung there between them in the room. Her eyes widened as she realized what had been going on underneath her nose, for – well, for how long? In the same instant, Thomas saw the look dawn upon her face and cast his eyes down to the floor.

'You put us to shame, Thomas.' Her voice almost choked on the words.

A loud knocking at the door. They both turned towards it but keeping their eyes locked, as fighting foxes circle one another. Of course with Ella gone there was no one to answer the door, so after the second bout of knocking Thomas opened it himself. The constable was on the doorstep, standing in the rain, with some of the king's garrison behind him.

Thomas looked at him impatiently. 'Yes, Woolley, what is it?'

'Is your wife at home?'

'She is. What is the matter? Is it my aunt? Has somebody died?'

'In a manner of speaking. It's your wife. We have come to take her in.'

Alice, hearing her name mentioned and alert that something concerning her must be afoot, pressed the cool backs of her hands to her eyes, for they were still hot and stinging, and tried to regain some composure. She moved to stand behind Thomas. The king's men pushed in through the door in one swift movement and took hold of her roughly by both arms. Surprised, Alice struggled and cried out, but one of them put his hand over her mouth and tugged back her head, so that her words were corked at her lips.

'Leave go of her,' she heard Thomas say. 'At least do us the courtesy of telling us what on earth this is all about.'

'We are arresting her. We're told she knows something about the murder of one Mistress Poulter.'

'Now just wait a minute.' Thomas was indignant. 'There's been a mistake. My wife does not know this woman. I have just conversed with her about it. And she cannot possibly have had anything to do with any murder. She's been at home all morning with me.'

'The woman was killed last night, and we already know from other witnesses that you were at the Fisks' having dinner. But where was your wife, sir? Answer me that.'

Thomas looked to her in confusion. Alice struggled and tried to speak but was silenced by the sweaty palm over her mouth and nose. It was so tight that she could not open her mouth.

'At home, I suppose, where else would she be?'

'Not according to some,' said the constable. 'And there's talk of witchcraft. She will be held until further notice.'

Alice redoubled her efforts, squirming her cheek against the rough hand that smelt of horse and metal and kicking out at the men's ankles. 'Tomcat,' one of them said, as her pointed leather boot caught him on the shin. Helpless, she felt herself lifted by her arms over the threshold and dragged into the dark towards a waiting carriage.

It made no sense. Nothing was making any

sense. How could Margaret be dead? Alice's feet and gown were trailing in the mud, her heels made a scraping sound, the rancid armpit of a soldier was pressed against her throat. Above her in the sky she caught a glimpse of a sickle moon before it was swallowed by cloud.

In the doorway of her house, the stout silhouette of her husband was sharp against the gold glow of the hall sconces – the man she thought she knew, up until five minutes ago, the man she had lived with for five years, who never said boo to a goose, who had suddenly turned, boiled up like scalded milk. When she managed to momentarily free her mouth from the soldier's hand she called out to him, 'Thomas,' but the silhouette did not even quiver; it remained a black outline, unmoving, a flat likeness of her husband, cut from stiff black paper.

Pinioned to the seat of the carriage by the two soldiers, she watched helplessly it moved off, seeing its lanterns reflected in the summerhouse windows as they passed. A moment of sheer panic assailed her – the lady's slipper seedlings, who would tend and water them? Thomas would not know to do it. Her hand felt for the bronze key to the summerhouse on its length of ribbon and her fingers closed round it, gripping it tightly, fingernails cutting into her palm. But it must be a mistake. Thomas would sort out the misunderstanding. From the back window, she screwed her head round to see if he followed on his horse, but she could see and hear nothing, only the lights of the village fading to pinpricks, and the view from the windows sinking into the hood of the night.

Chapter 21

Stephen was not surprised to see that his father was drunk. Geoffrey dismounted clumsily in the driveway, ignored Stephen completely and zigzagged up the steps, having abandoned his horse with its reins flapping, where it wandered off and had to be rounded up and caught by four of the lads. Stephen followed him as he shoved his way past the sundry items lying in the hallway that his mother had discarded or dropped as she fled. Geoffrey blundered into his chambers and slammed the door, and Stephen knew better than to go after him.

He was nervous about talking with his father. His mother had always been the arbiter between them, and it was only recently that Geoffrey had begun to treat Stephen like a man and coach him in the necessary duties of estate management. Stephen was desperate to know if there was any chance his mother might be allowed to return. He did not know where she would go, could not imagine her anywhere else but in her cushioned armchair, sewing before the fire, or combing her soft yellow hair before the looking glass in her chamber. Who would replace the flowers fading in the vases? Who would play the open-lidded spinet now ominously silent in the withdrawing room?

Also, despite visiting the Quaker meeting at Lingfell Hall, and being on tenterhooks in case he should be unmasked by the traitor Wheeler, he had been unable to uncover any evidence for a plot against the king. When eventually his father summoned him to his quarters, he was shocked at his father's appearance. Stephen thought he himself had been hit hard by his mother's departure, but his father looked like a ship without a wind. His breeches were muddy and crumpled, his waistcoat was stained with food and his cravat dangled unevenly over his chest.

Stephen noticed a Bible open on the table, which was unusual, because his father hardly even paid it lip service and it was always put away immediately after morning prayers. His face was sunk into his neck, but his skin looked unusually smooth and grey as ash. His moustache was unkempt over dry, cracked lips. He was clutching a tankard – his father never drank ale, only wine and port, and the hand that held the handle had skinned knuckles and fingernails full of dirt.

'Father?' Geoffrey waved his son to a chair. 'Is my mother–' Geoffrey cut off the question.

'Are you stupid? I said she was not to have it. The plate will go straight to that scoundrel Hetherington's bookmaker. Your mother is gone for good. Don't dare to mention her again, Stephen.'

The look in Geoffrey's eyes made Stephen's innards turn to water. In this mood he knew better than to cross him, he could read anger simmering under the surface. Stephen lit a small clay pipe to calm himself, and savoured the smoke a moment before daring to speak.

'I have been to Lingfell Hall,' said Stephen awkwardly, 'and met with Wheeler.' His father's eyes refocused themselves with difficulty.

'I have found out that they are planning a rebellion against the tithe laws and are going to set a guard on the barns to stop your men collecting.'

'The devil they will. What else?'

'Naught else, sir. They are mostly rough men, and homely women, sir, they do not seem like an army to me.'

'And you know what an army looks like?' came the cutting reply.

Stephen bit his lip. 'Sir, there was no mention of anything concerning the king, or his troops–'

'The fact that they do not mention an insurrection does not mean they do not have it in mind. What is Wheeler doing up there?'

'He is one of their brethren, praying and so forth. There is no sign he intends anything else. He says he has given up his house and intends to live a simpler life.'

'You expect me to believe that? That a wolf has become a lapdog overnight?'

'He told me he finds the life hard.'

'Gone soft, has he?' A bitter laugh. 'What more?'

'I have told you, sir, nothing more. That is all there is to tell. They are planning to withhold their dues.'

'And you did not delve deeper? Has he flummoxed you too? I thought you had more wit than that.'

Stephen coloured at his father's harsh tone and looked at his carefully roughened boots.

'I cannot tell that to Lord Esham and the committee,' said Geoffrey, 'that you have been taken in by them, my own son. I am already a laughing stock – thanks to Ralph Hetherington. And now there will be this – look, there goes the cuckold Fisk, and his idiot son, who could not see a rebellion when it was dangling like a nosebag in front of him.'

'I will go back, sir,' said Stephen hastily. 'I think I can win Wheeler's confidence. I will go back to the Hall tomorrow, and try to find out the real reason he is there.'

'My good name depends on it. But be careful. It sounds like you are blinded by the trees and cannot see the wood. Use your eyes, boy. And do not let him catch you off guard under any circumstances. He can be...' His voice trailed away as if he had momentarily lost sight of the conversation and had seen something over by the bookcase. Suddenly he snapped back. 'Now leave me be, and if you should see Patterson, send him here, I have an errand for him.'

Stephen found himself summarily dismissed, and wandered into the gloomy drawing room. The dust was already gathering on the polished mantel. There were still half-packed trunks in the hall. His mother would not be returning. Her absence would make the time hang even more heavily on his hands. His father had not seen fit to give him any further duties or to suggest they ride out together to check the grounds and the new building work on the boundaries. The fires remained unlit, and there was a blank space on the wall where a portrait of his grandfather used to hang. Next to the chair was a side table with an embroidery hoop. He picked up the cotton cloth, feeling the silky threads under his fingers where the half-finished butterfly had begun to emerge under his mother's nimble fingers. He unfastened it gently from the hoop and, folding it neatly into four, put it in the front pocket of his satchel.

As he left the room he saw Patterson heading for the back stairs. He ignored him, skulking back behind the door, for he had no desire to face him again, to look upon the recrimination of his black eye, nor did he have any desire to deliver his father's request.

Over the following week, Stephen continued to dress in his rough tweeds and ride up to the Hall for the morning meeting. He kept his gloves on, for his knuckles were bruised by his encounter with Patterson and he knew this would certainly give him away if it were to be noticed. Quakers did not hold with fighting for any reason.

When he rode up the valley, more often than not he would hear familiar hoofbeats behind and Richard Wheeler would draw up beside him, smiling under his brown felt hat. To his surprise, Stephen began to enjoy his new, fabricated personality. Sam, the mythical Quaker version of himself, was quiet and thoughtful, hardly ever spoke, listened instead of giving an opinion. It was restful to be like this, not to be giving servants orders, or be concerned with keeping up appearances, or having to keep track of his father's ideas of who was beholden to whom.

He told himself his silence was to avoid giving himself away, so that he could find out about the plot against the king. But he warmed to his new quiet self. As the days wore on and he had seen no suspicious talk, nor had Richard Wheeler given any indication he was anything other than a misguided man whose faith was sadly at odds with his own, Stephen was inclined to believe that his father was wrong and there was no plot against the king.

More than that, he began to enjoy his visits, particularly the discourses on their journeys to and from the Hall. Richard Wheeler treated him as an adult, asked for and valued his opinion. Richard confided in him the circumstances of his conversion by George Fox, and although it sounded strange to Stephen's mind, perhaps even heretical, there was no doubting Richard's sincerity. So strongly was Richard possessed by the spirit and love of God, and so strong was his sense of purpose, that Stephen began to feel a little envious. Richard was so certain in his conviction, and Stephen began to feel his life impoverished, dry and empty in comparison. He wondered how it might feel to have a vocation, to be needed, to do things purposefully instead of just being in the sway of events.

On one of their return journeys they stopped to shelter under a tree whilst the looming clouds shed their rain. Stephen, under the guise of Sam, asked Richard whether he thought, as did his father, that all women were of feeble virtue. Richard wiped the rain off his hands and onto his jerkin, and said, 'No. That is surely untrue. I'm sure we are all of equal virtue. Look at Dorothy. She is certainly not weak, nor Hannah Fleetwood, who's enduring prison conditions that'd break many men, for her faith. It is a question of whom or what thou usest thy whole strength to serve, irrespective of whether thou art a man or a woman.'

Out of Richard's mouth, it sounded a noble ideal, to serve with one's whole strength. Stephen felt as if he was not serving anything, or anyone. But he nodded as if to agree. Since his mother had left, he had received no word from her, despite her promise. Stephen looked down the valley at the sheeting rain. He was unsure whether to return to London or to go and seek out his mother. He had heard rumours his mother and Ralph Hetherington had taken ship for Ireland.

'Let us hope this clears soon, it is a long stretch to Burton,' said Richard, shaking the water off his hat and replacing it again over his springy hair.

Stephen had forgotten he was supposed to live in Burton. He wondered what sort of a house he was supposed to inhabit there. It would be a cheerier place than Fisk Manor, that was for sure. For his home had remained exactly as it had been when his mother left. His father had dismissed all the indoor servants except the kitchen staff, so the house was cold as a crypt. Grey dust blew out of the grates into the rooms; candles burnt down and were not replaced in the chandeliers. Whenever he got home Stephen looked for his father to tell him his news, but more often than not found him slumped in bleary-eyed stupor, or heard him prowling the corridors at night walking up and down – back and forth, back and forth, in his hard-soled outdoor boots. By night Stephen could hear him moaning as if in pain.

None of this could he tell Richard. Fortunately

for Stephen, his counterpart Sam was a good listener, and Richard was used to Sam's taciturn demeanour.

'Shall we risk it?' Stephen said, looking up at the brightening sky.

Richard nodded and gathered up his reins. 'On Sundays I go over to the gaol at Lancaster to take provisions for Hannah and Jack. Meat and bread, warm blankets and so forth. 'Tis a long ride. I wonder, wouldst thou join me for a meal, and then ride out with me?'

Stephen was taken aback and did not know how to answer. If his father knew he was to dine sociably with the man who had killed his grandmother, he would never forgive him. On the other hand, perhaps his father would see it as a way for Stephen to worm his way further into Richard's favour to uncover the anti-royalist plot. Stephen hesitated, trying to weigh it all in his mind.

'No need to be embarrassed, Sam. It would be a pleasure to have thy company.'

Stephen looked at Richard's expectant face, his straight back, his rain-soaked shoulders broad and relaxed. This man had once been a good friend of his father, too, before the war, and it made him wonder. Stephen was curious on his own account to know more about Richard Wheeler. He did not seem to be the ruthless man his father had described.

'I would like that very much.'

'It is settled then.'

The two men rode on down the track, the muddy rainwater gushing past the horses' hooves in honey-coloured streams. Stephen did not know how he was to broach the fact with his father that he was mistaken about the Quakers. His father would not want to be told there was no anti-royalist plot, nor would he want to confess this fact to the committee. It would not be a pleasant conversation, and Stephen had a feeling that somehow he would be to blame. His father never admitted fault if there was someone else who would carry it.

After the men went their separate ways, Stephen did not hurry home. He had no desire to answer his father's questions. His answers would displease him, and Stephen did not want to see the thin veil of disappointment fall over his father's face, closely followed by the inevitable virulent temper. His father was more and more distracted and morose, sunk within himself. Sometimes he looked past him, as if seeing invisible demons over Stephen's shoulder. Also, Stephen did not want to be subject to the surly ministrations of Patterson and the other servants. Since the incident of the plate, Patterson glared upon him as if he were the Devil himself.

He chewed his lip. There was no telling how Richard might react should he find out he was not Sam Fielding, Quaker convert, but Stephen Fisk, spy. He was an impostor at the Hall, but he was also an impostor at home; he began to think there was no Stephen Fisk, just a name, and underneath, a whirlpool of swirling contradictions. When the heavens opened again, Stephen did not push his horse forward into a trot but loitered next to the woods, rain dripping off his nose and down his neck, staring deep in thought at the blurred

271

roofline of Fisk Manor, which rose grey and dismal through the sheeting rain.

'Fetch me my horse!' Geoffrey was impatient. He had been confined in the house long enough. He had woken with a hangover fit to shear sheep but he knew he could not let himself stay in his midden any longer. Since the death of the old woman and Emilia's departure he had avoided facing anyone. While Emilia was packing he had been seized by a terror that he might have left some sign behind on the old woman's body, so he had galloped out to the ditch to see if he could find a way to bury or conceal it completely.

When he got to the spot where he had dumped it he was astonished to find it gone, and in alarm he had scoured under the hedges for the best part of an hour, but there was no sign of it. With a sense of foreboding he had promptly gone to the Wagon and Horses and consoled himself with a measure of ale. If his name were to be linked with the murder, even if he were to claim it was in self-defence, it would be disaster. He knew that all prisoners' houses and lands were forfeit to the Crown. The thought of forfeiting his land filled him with fear. So he had ridden home and had stayed indoors since, trying to reason out his excuses.

He knew he must make an appearance before any questions were asked. As for Emilia, he was damned if he would let his wife's antics embarrass him. He would have to face the world sooner or later. He must act as if all was well with him, as if he was in complete control. As if he gave not a jot for Emilia, and knew nothing of

272

any murder. He must see someone reliable in the village who would then testify that all was well with him. He would ride over and see how Mistress Ibbetson was faring with his orchids.

He hoped she would have got over her recalcitrance about their business arrangement. With women, it was best to give firm guidance. He thought guiltily of Emilia; he should have kept her on a tighter rein, he could see that now. But Mistress Ibbetson would fall in with his wishes because that lazy goat of a husband had no business head on him, anyone could see that. Mistress Ibbetson would make a few extra pounds through his scheme, and he would have the prestige of being a pioneer in the use of this medicinal plant. For there was no doubt it worked. Like a miracle, his skin was softer, the itching had stopped. Even now, he could scarcely believe it.

When he got to the Ibbetsons' he tethered his horse as usual by the mounting block and rapped the brass knocker sharply against the door. When nobody answered he sauntered round the back and went down the path to the summerhouse. When he pushed the door it did not give, so he tried harder to force it open. When it remained obstinately shut, he banged on it with his fist. Still no answer. He peered in through the windows, but it was dark in the interior and he could not see anything, except the dim faces of the portraits of Alice's sister, looking out with their spectral eyes.

Irritated, Geoffrey marched back to the front door and hammered loudly. He was about to turn away in frustration when the door opened a crack, and a thin-faced girl opened it warily.

'You took your time. Tell your mistress I am here.'

'She's not in, sir.'

'When will she be back?'

'Don't know, sir. Could be weeks.'

'Weeks? Where has she gone? She was doing some business with me – she cannot just go off when she feels like it. Where is your master? I would speak with him.'

'Out at the counting house.'

'What's your name, girl?'

'April, sir. If that's all, sir.' She made as if to shut the door but Geoffrey slipped his foot into it.

'When she gets back, give her my card.' He held it out, and the girl relented and opened the door a little.

'Told you, sir, she might not be back – she's in gaol. I don't know when...' Then, seeing his expression, which clearly said he did not believe a word of it: 'They say she's killed someone, and there's witchery in it too.'

Geoffrey looked at her a moment in confusion before he realized she was serious. He said, 'That is ridiculous. I will go and tell them so. Her interest in herbs is artistic, not medicinal. She cannot have killed anybody.'

But even as he was saying the words he could sense the girl's discomfort was genuine and that something untoward had certainly happened. The girl was hovering half in and half out of the doorway, looking uncomfortably at Geoffrey's polished boot which was still holding the door ajar. She looked up at him and whispered, 'They say she did. Stabbed her, and left the poor old woman in a ditch, they say.'

Geoffrey took a step backwards. As he did, the door gently shut in front of his stupefied face.

Chapter 22

Alice heard the noise of large doors opening and the slow scrape of wood against flagstones. It was pitch black outside and she could see no lights through the barred window of the wagon. They had decided to transport her at night from the local cell to the gaol at Lancaster. When they had told her she was to be kept at Lancaster until the trial, it had filled her with cold terror, for Lancaster's thick forbidding walls had housed many a prisoner, now dead for their transgressions. It was known to everyone as the Hanging Gaol. From the cells they said you could hear the snap of the rope and the last strangled cry as the executioner pulled away the platform to leave the bare feet dangling in thin air.

The wheels of the carriage sounded loud and the horseshoes echoed oddly as if they were passing through a cavern. It must be the prison yard, because she could hear groans and shouting from all sides. They bundled her out of the carriage, her hands tied together with a length of fuse from an army musket. She shivered, for she had not regained warmth in her bones since they took her to the town gaol in the rain. Her good blue dress had been soaked through and had never properly dried. It smelt musty and sour now, like a sack of damp grain that had been left in a cellar. Her hands were bloodless and numb with cold. Her teeth chattered together so much that her jaw ached.

The soldiers shoved her forward. A fat gaoler with feet bursting out of his shoes nodded to them as if expecting them and went ahead with an iron ring like a bucket handle, clanking with keys. She caught a glimpse of the night sky, twinkling with an array of bright stars, but it was as if she had tumbled to the bottom of a well; dark masonry surrounded her; there were wet cobbles underfoot, slippery as river stones. They stumbled in through a smaller iron door which clanged shut behind them, then a wall sconce revealed a flickering passageway with stone steps leading down in a spiral. The walls and stairs were running with a thick green slime of damp, and behind the stench of mould and sewers, the tang of human urine stung the back of her nostrils.

As they reached the bottom of the stairs it was ominously silent. A sharp left turn and they were confronted by another narrow door, which the gaoler opened with much clanging and rattling of the lock and chains. When it was open she was pushed forward with a sharp slap in the small of her back into the putrid-smelling blackness. She fell forward and landed heavily on her hands and knees, where she felt a damp earth and flint floor, with a few wisps of straw. Almost immediately she scrambled to her feet again and wiped her hands on her skirts, something she had taken to doing frequently, as if the cleanliness of her hands would somehow convince people of her innocence.

She took some steps forward with her arms outstretched until she reached a wall. It was a cell of about eight feet compass. Turning her back to the wall again, she slowly slithered down the damp stones and wrapped her skirts around herself, awkwardly, as her wrists were still bound together and this hampered her movements. She had heard the gaol was infested with rats. If she could tuck the heavy fabric of her skirt in around her ankles it would keep them warm and guard them against vermin.

She listened. Faint echoes of retreating boots passed above. A rustle, as if something was moving. She pulled at her skirts and shrank back against the wall but the noise stopped abruptly. Listening more intently she thought she could hear breathing, and held her own breath to listen more closely. What if there were someone else in the cell with her?

She called out, 'Who's there?' but there was no answer, and when she could hear no more sounds, she let her chin drop down onto her chest to try to sleep. It was a fitful sleep, broken by confused dreams and by the pain in her stomach, which was hollow and churning with hunger. The night passed slowly, her bones ached, the only warmth her breath – blown onto her bruised wrists.

At sunrise the gaol creaked into life like a giant machine. Noises of scrabbling, hammering, rattling. Distant shouts and screams, more carriages coming and going and boots on cobblestones. Groans of misery, strange caterwauling and the noise of spoons scraping on wooden plates. Her cell was still dark for there was no window to the world, just the door, with a foot-square barred window that could only be opened from outside.

Eventually this little aperture opened and a lump of hard bread landed at her feet. Mercifully the hatch was left half-open so a glimmer of greyish-green light pooled in the centre of the dark. Alice stooped to pick up the bread between her outstretched fingers, but stopped short, staring.

She had been right, there was someone else in the cell. But the body was motionless, like a heap of old sacks thrown in the corner. Merciful heavens, had she been here all night with a corpse? It could have been there for weeks. Terrified of what she might see, she crept towards the ragged bundle.

It was a woman, unmoving, barely alive. Her face was white, quite pretty under the grime, but too thin. As Alice looked the woman gave a shuddering sigh and turned over. Alice recoiled. The whole right side of her face was mangled and swollen and disfigured by bruises. Her eye was closed and her cheekbone shapeless with a deep suppurating cut. Nausea made Alice bring her hands to her mouth. Her stomach was empty, she retched, but no bile came. Repulsed, she tried to move away without disturbing the woman, back to the other side of the cell. The woman heard her and agitated, tried to move further into the corner, moaning.

Alice realized she must be afraid and spoke quickly to reassure her. 'My name is Alice. Alice Ibbetson, from Netherbarrow.'

No response.

'They have thrown us some bread.'

Alice was going to break it and pass her some, but then became aware that she probably would not be able to eat it, when one side of her mouth was swollen so. She did not want to go near her, for the sight of the wound made her feel queasy, but she picked up the hard lump and seeing a pail of water began to soften the bread in the water and roll it between her fingers. The water was icy cold, and probably stagnant, but the woman would starve to death without sustenance.

As Alice approached, the bread held awkwardly between her bound hands, the woman cowered further into the dark recess of the cell.

'Do not be afraid. I cannot hurt you. See – my hands are tied.'

The woman's eyes looked up at Alice from her disfigured face, questioning, but she did not speak.

Alice squeezed the excess moisture from the bread and held it gently to the woman's lips. 'You must eat. It is soft, I have wetted it. Please try to eat.'

After a little coaxing the woman's lips began to move and Alice fed her as she painfully swallowed bit by bit, until the damp morsel of grey dough was all gone. Alice did not look at the woman's face, she dare not, it made her sick to do so, but she focused on watching her mouth opening for the next piece as though she was feeding a help-less baby bird. She had meant to save half the bread, but the woman's mouth kept opening and she could not bring herself to stop.

When the woman's eyes began to close in sleep,

Alice settled back in the opposite corner of the cell. Her mind raced round the knot of questions that kept repeating in her head. Why had Thomas not come yet? Even at the town gaol, she had had no visitors since her arrest. She wondered if Geoffrey knew. Perhaps they were meeting together to clear up the misunderstanding. They must be doing all they could to get her out, she thought. Thomas would come. Probably today.

She pushed away the sobering memories of Thomas's angry words before the constable came, and his guilty look, which was tantamount to a confession. What a fool she had been not to notice what was happening right under her nose. She gathered her skirts more tightly round her ankles. Ella Appleby. She would never have believed he could be so taken in.

Restless, she stood again and walked the few paces to the door. She listened, but there were no sounds except the sounds of someone bleating like a lost sheep somewhere further down the corridor. She moved back and forth, fretting over the fate of the lady's slippers. They would be unable to survive a drought and it was already four nights since she had been taken. Why had she not left the flower where it was? Since she had taken it, her life seemed to have become out of balance, like a badly loaded cart teetering on the brink of toppling over.

She was amazed anyone could seriously think she would murder an old lady like Margaret. She was surprised to admit to herself that someone of Margaret's bizarre appearance was her friend. But they had shared a love of plants that could not have been faked. She had felt an odd kinship with her, something beneath words and outside appearances.

She thought back to when Margaret helped her restore the ailing plant, and to her encounter with Wheeler when he nearly killed her with his gun. Wheeler. His eyes had been burning with a strange fire when he had appeared at her house; she had thought it made him attractive then. A good man, honourable and godly. What a mooncalf she was! She had not realized he was such a zealot. She clenched her fists and hammered them against the wall, angry with herself for her own gullibility.

It must be he who was responsible for her arrest. There was no other answer. There was nobody else who had seen her and Margaret together. Nobody else with whom she had a disagreement. He must have used Margaret's death as an excuse to put her out of the way whilst he retrieved the orchid. She imagined him going to Thomas and demanding the orchid back, and Thomas letting him take it, not understanding. As these thoughts came, she grew taut with frustration. Picking up a handful of the damp and mouldy straw she began to shred it between her fingers, picturing Wheeler searching her summerhouse in his big brown boots. She hated him.

'What's the matter? What day is it?' The woman groaned in the corner.

Alice turned at the sound of the voice. ''Tis Friday,' she said. A pause. 'How long have you been kept in here?'

'It is hard to say. Every day is the same.' Her voice was feeble and hoarse. Alice knelt next to the woman and took her hand. She squeezed it, compassion tightening about her heart.

Against the reality of another's suffering, her fixation with the lady's slipper faded into a phantom, instantly forgotten. She took a cup of water and brought it to the woman's lips.

Later, for the first time, she gained insight into her own obsession. She had been besotted in her determination to procure the plant and keep it for herself. She had sought to have a measure of control over nature, a task she recognized now would always be doomed to failure. Nature could not be bound so tightly as she would have it.

So in her blindness she had lied to Wheeler and been oblivious to her husband's infidelities. With dread she wondered if Wheeler too was so possessed by the lady's slipper that he would see her hang rather than give it up.

After three more days, Alice was losing hope that Thomas or Geoffrey would come to her aid. Her companion in the cell was clinging onto her skimpy thread of life despite injuries that included a broken shoulder as well as the blows to her head and face.

After a while the woman had thanked Alice for the bread, and Alice had managed to find out her name was Hannah. It was not clear what crime she had committed, but Hannah's constant entreaty was to find out what had happened to her husband, Jack.

Alice could do nothing to help her though, for she had only seen the fat greasy face of the gaoler since her arrival, and when she had enjoined him to speak with her, he had merely closed off their wooden window with a slam so hard it rebounded to its half-open position again.

'Wait!' she had cried through the gap, but received no reply. Alice did her best to wash and clean Hannah's wounds, despite her tied hands, using the none-too-clean hem of her dress and stagnant water from the pail. Alice had tried and failed to undo the fuse that was knotted so tight it cut into the flesh of her wrists.

'Help me, Hannah,' she said.

Hannah's white fingers were hardly able to grasp, and Alice's were stiff and numb, unable to reach the knot which had tightened as it dried.

'The pail,' whispered Hannah. 'Like the bread.'

'Oh yes, Hannah,' said Alice gratefully, 'let's try.'

She dipped her hands in the pail to soften the cord in the water. There was a thin layer of ice over the surface, which, strangely, burnt her hands like fire, but she soaked it well.

'It's working. Help me now.'

Fraction by fraction they loosened it between them, Hannah picking away with her thin fingers, until at last it fell away and Alice was able to rub her grooved wrists and bring some feeling to her hands. To have the proper use of them after all this time was such a relief that Alice's spirits lifted and she started to work for their survival.

'Come on, sit up.' She lifted Hannah into a propped-up sitting position and, tearing off a strip of petticoat, used it to make a sling for her shoulder.

From then on, she tried to keep them both as clean as she could, given the lack of utensils and

283

the condition of their water. No more bread came, though she hit the door and cried out for hunger.

In the day she walked and walked in circles to keep warm, and clapped her hands together to bring the blood to them. She rubbed her rosy fingers over Hannah's skeletal joints, thin as twigs of silver-birch. At night they huddled together for warmth, Hannah's grisly head lolling on Alice's shoulder whilst Alice prayed, sang, told the stories she used to tell Flora of rescuing knights and journeys to far-away lands – anything to keep the flame of hope alive.

On the sixth day the door of the cell swung open and the gaoler's flabby figure appeared with two more lackeys. Alice stood up, blinking in the unaccustomed light, and from habit brushed herself down.

'Trial's this day next week,' said the gaoler, addressing Alice, 'and the hanging's the day after. Not much time between them, so I reckon you'll need the parson before then.'

'But I haven't done anything wrong. Please, won't you get word to my husband, Thomas Ibbetson of Netherbarrow...'

'No one's been to vouch for you, not a soul.' The gaoler rubbed his yellowed whiskers, a half-smile on his lips. 'So I'm telling you that the parson will come Monday to do what he can. And my advice to you is to repent and confess, and save your soul. Not a hare's chance of saving your body.'

Alice set her shoulders back in an attempt to keep her dignity, speaking in her most reasonable tone. 'There's been a misunderstanding. My friend Sir Geoffrey Fisk will reward you if you tell him I am here.'

'You must think I have chaff between the ears. Everyone's talking about you, looking forward to the trial.' He grinned. 'Word is, you poisoned your parents and your sister, and a good few others too. And not a one has said otherwise, not your husband, nor your high-ranking friend.'

She could not take this in. He must be saying these things from spite. But a cold mist of dread began to settle about her.

'And what about her?' She pointed to where Hannah lay, barely breathing in the corner.

'Trial for all the Quakers later that same day. Not much likelihood of a hanging, though, unless they decide on treason.' He looked rueful. 'Likely a longer sentence.' He looked at Hannah with contempt. 'They don't believe in parsons any-way–' he spat on the ground – 'so state of her soul's her own business.'

'Let me speak with the parson and see if he can find out what is the matter with my husband. He must be ill, or he would have come.'

'No one's been. And I can bet a coach and four no one will.'

With that he shifted his bulk from the doorway and the two lackeys followed, slamming the door back into its place and sliding the rough window shut, returning them to the murky half-light.

'Thou art a good woman.' Alice turned at the sound of the small hoarse voice. 'No matter what they say about thee, thou art kind.'

'Oh, Hannah.' She leaned towards her and, feeling the wasted arms fasten around her neck, wept for them both.

Chapter 23

At Constable Woolley's house there was scarcely room to sit. The magistrate, Robert Rawlinson, had appropriated the constable's official chair behind the desk and now Woolley stood awkwardly wedged between the table and the tiny window, with Geoffrey Fisk occupying the only other chair. The room was small and stuffy and smelt of sweat and beer. A flagon of ale was on the table, along with all the other paraphernalia of ledgers and writing implements. Behind the door was a row of wooden pegs with the instruments of the trade: cudgels, nooses, whips, a scold's bridle, along with miscellaneous items of ill-kempt saddlery. Hanging next to these, the keys to the town gaol. Robert Rawlinson leaned back in the chair and lit up a clay pipe, puffing out clouds of throat-stinging vapour.

Geoffrey managed to ascertain that Alice Ibbetson had been transferred to Lancaster to await trial, and that, astonishingly, she had been seen with a knife, bending over the body in the ditch on the night of the murder. How this had come about, he did not know, but he intended to fuel this particular fire. He swallowed – the bitter taste of the lady's slipper extract seemed to lodge in his mouth all the time now.

'I should have known better than to do business with Mistress Ibbetson,' he said, pressing home this fortuitous turn of events. 'She always was a little unpredictable. I thought there was something awry from the first, but never dreamt her capable of something like that. Murder. Well, well, well.'

'You would be surprised,' said Constable Woolley. 'I've seen the most delicate little hands, hardly fit to lift a needle, yet they have strangled grown men.' He made a wringing gesture with his hands. 'Appearances can be mightily deceiving.'

'It certainly seems odd that all her family survived the war yet succumbed to mystery ailments,' said Rawlinson, tamping on his pipe. 'And her husband has not been back to speak up for her. I had to ask him to call, and he still has not appeared. It is very peculiar. What do you know of the husband, Geoffrey?'

'Not very bright, I would say. He is a moneylender at the counting house in Kendal. But he seems to have a slack head for figures. And he is excessively idle and dull. It would not surprise me if he were unable to keep track of his wife's comings and goings.' Geoffrey paused. 'Probably he knew nothing of her doings. She keeps her powders and potions under lock and key in a summerhouse at the back of their property. She makes out that the place is for her paintings, but...' Geoffrey looked meaningfully at Rawlinson, who sat forward in his chair.

'Well, Constable, I think we should go and have a look at the Ibbetsons' summerhouse. If the husband will not give us a key, then we will break in. Perhaps we will find the knife or the poisons there.'

'I would like to be there when you do that,' said

Geoffrey. 'She had some of my property on loan – some plants, and a few paintings she was sketching on commission. She had quite a talent for likenesses. Mind you, I have always thought her more than a little odd. After the death of her sister, who literally wasted away into nothing, Alice Ibbetson seemed to be in mourning altogether too long for my mind, as if she was making sure we all knew she was grieving.'

'We will go to the house directly, after we have spoken with the servant girl,' said Rawlinson.

Ella sulked outside the constable's door, chewing on a piece of grass. She had been somewhat affronted to be asked to wait outside the door when Sir Geoffrey arrived at the constable's. She had been enjoying being the centre of attention and repeating the tale of how she had seen Alice bending over the body in a ditch whilst they were out gallivanting on the night in question. Of course she had not revealed what she and her friends were really up to, out near Fisk Manor, but said that they were celebrating a birthday and had taken to the lanes by wagon simply in order to get the party from one alehouse to the next. She had persuaded the other villagers to keep this diversion from the truth and not to mention the cuckolding, because they all knew it was to their advantage to keep their lips buttoned.

Several others on the wagon had seen Alice bending over something in the dark, had seen the glint of a knife, and she had convinced them that it must have been the old woman's body she was crouching over. Ella smiled to herself. What a

288

crowd of gulls they were – ready to grasp at any drama, so long as they could have a part in it.

She took the bloodstained shoes to the constable's house the day after, and with her best innocent face told how she had found them concealed in the turnip sack only that morning. So far, her luck had held. No one else had come forward with any alternative ideas about who might be responsible, and once the seed of suspicion had been sown, people began to remember long-gone quirks in Alice's behaviour, and to recall the time their cows refused to give milk after her visits, or that their babes cried or would not suckle when she was near. With each tale Ella's chest swelled and her shoulders squared, and she was able to bask in the balm of righteous indignation. To think, she had been in the same house as a murderess! Had taken up her morning chocolate, whilst all the time her mistress's hands were black with blood.

The constable had taken her at her word and been to see Audrey and Tom, and the miller's boys, and all of them had added weight to her story – they too had seen Alice Ibbetson bending over the body in the ditch, whilst her husband was dining at the Fisks'. By the evening Alice was in gaol, and the next day Ella was back in the Ibbetsons' house, seeing to Master Thomas's needs.

Ella had wasted no time in filling the other side of Thomas's bed. He was confident it was all a huge mistake, that they would find no evidence and let his wife go. Until then, he saw no harm in a few nights with Ella in his bed. She had not yet told him her tales of bewitching – that Alice was tainted by the Devil's hand, that she had poisoned her sister and parents before that, and that he would be next if he did not take care. This was a shame, because her tales were so well told, so juicy and thrilling, that she almost believed them for the truth herself.

The trial was coming up, and the constable had wanted Ella to go over it all again before Justice Rawlinson. So he had summoned her back. Now Sir Geoffrey had arrived, and he would certainly know what they had been up to on the night in question. But he would not be able to prove anything, unless she slipped up with her tale.

She pushed her hair behind her ears, stopped chewing on the hank of grass-stalk she had idly pulled up from the hedge and pressed her ear to the door.

'Speak up, for God's sake,' she whispered crossly.

She could smell the waft of tobacco from underneath but could only make out muffled talk through the thick planks.

Inside the constable's office, Woolley squeezed past the table to the door and opened it. Ella, the Ibbetsons' maid, was just outside. The three men exchanged glances; it was obvious she had had her ear at the door.

They summoned her into the room and bade her sit down on the only unoccupied chair before beginning their questions. Ella was surprised Sir Geoffrey did not immediately want to know what they were doing on that night out in the lanes, or about the horns on his front door. She was baffled. He never mentioned it at all. She could not make it out, he kept asking about Flora, Alice's sister, and how she died.

'And only Alice was allowed to nurse her, is that right?'

'Yes, sir, she did not hold with anyone else taking up her broth or feeding her the remedies.'

'What, even the physician?'

'She said she would nurse her herself.'

'Did you see what sort of remedy she gave the child?'

'Once, sir.' She scanned round the room at the three gentlemen, all hanging on her words, and began to expand her tale. 'It was a right evil-looking mixture, smelt something awful. I remember thinking, she would have a struggle to get the little one to drink it. She had to hold her nose to get it down.' The men looked at one another. Ella could see that she had given the right answer.

As the conversation progressed Ella was surprised to find that far from being Alice's friend and staunch supporter, Sir Geoffrey seemed to be actively looking for gossip that would point to her guilt. She could not fathom it out, but she was more than happy to supply him with as much damning evidence as he might require. Indeed, it seemed to her suddenly that they were playing a little game: he would feed her a question, to which she could supply an incriminating answer. All the while the constable and Justice Rawlinson looked on, frowning and tutting.

When Woolley brought out the shoes, Sir Geoffrey seemed very interested in them too. He turned them over and over in his hands, examining them through an eyeglass that dangled from his button, paying particular attention to the brownish stains.

'Are you sure these are Alice Ibbetson's?'

'Course. I saw them in her closet most every day. Ask anyone. Half the village has seen her wearing them. In the summer she even wore them to church.' Justice Rawlinson raised his eyebrows.

'Yes, sir. When the sister was ill, before she died. I thought them a bit fancy, myself. Didn't seem right respectful, especially given the little girl lying there so poorly.' She stole a sidelong glance at Sir Geoffrey and was rewarded with a slight smile.

In truth she had been reluctant to hand over the shoes, for she had become sore attached to them, but they were a small price to pay. She had set her sights on being housekeeper of her own house, mistress in deed if not in name, and then she could have any number of silken shoes so long as she kept Thomas sweet. She had seen a pair in the draper's – lilac, with sprays of rosebuds made from wound ribbon.

A few more questions were asked, about whether Alice was present at the deaths of her parents, to which Ella answered that she was, though in actual fact she had not been employed by the Ibbetsons back then and had no idea. All Ella knew was that yes was the right response.

She sensed Sir Geoffrey was satisfied with her answers, and before long she was dismissed without a single word about the cuckolding having been spoken, just a scribbled message for Master Ibbetson, telling him that as he had not responded to their messages, they would be calling. She was free to go, and what was more, far from being her enemy, Sir Geoffrey Fisk seemed to be her friend. Ella tossed her head back and flounced up the street, her arms swinging. She was not going to enquire too deeply where the sudden change of events had come from, for they suited her just fine. She would go home and await Justice Rawlinson and his party, who would be along presently to search the summerhouse.

Ella had come back under their roof less than two days after she had made such a fuss about leaving. Cook was flabbergasted. Ella just turned up as if nothing had happened and Master Thomas had re-engaged her on the spot. Lord knows why, thought Cook, she was always a slow worker, and all the while young Lottie Jennings was after a position – she would knock spots off that wastrel Ella. But Master was quite set on it, and had insisted that April make up a room in the eaves for Ella so she could live in as housekeeper.

Cook fetched a piece of mutton from the cold store at the back of the pantry and looked it over. It would do for the evening meal. She slapped the joint down on the table and began to trim off the fat. With Mistress away, Cook could see that there needed to be someone living in – to put a flint to the morning fires, make the lists for the week and see to the master's breakfast and so forth, but why not herself? She was the ideal choice, not that lazy Ella. Or even April – she was far more reliable and hard-working, if a little green around the gills. She looked over to where April was preparing the fire oven. A corn of resentment rattled in Cook's chest. What was it all coming to? She shook her head. She had served Master Thomas all these years, and yet now she was passed over for that flibbertigibbet, Ella.

It was as if she never existed.

What was more, Ella had hardly done a thing since she was re-engaged – today, for example, halfway through the afternoon Ella blithely announced she had to go back to the constable's and they had not seen her since.

It was a good hour later when Ella walked in. April was wide-eyed.

'You're back,' she said. She began to ply Ella with questions.

I'll have none of it, thought Cook. She cut April off short and sent her to lay the fires upstairs. She told Ella she did not need any help in the kitchen, and to go out to the yard to fetch some milk from the cow.

'Get it yourself. I'm not engaged for a milk-maid,' Ella had answered, and sauntered off, swishing her brand new skirts.

Cook pursed her lips. She did not like this sudden reversal of the pecking order. And she did not trust Ella. Nobody had yet explained the pilfering in the pantry, and when she had questioned Ella that morning she had denied it outright, saying, what of it, Mistress must have fancied a little jam with her bread. Cook was not convinced – in her experience, Mistress had always asked if she wanted anything extra. She had always been mindful of the hard times and could not abide wastefulness; she would never have unsealed a bottle if there was one already open.

It was all wrong somehow, Ella in charge and Mistress Alice in gaol. Cook had turned it over and over in her head, like a dog worrying at a bone, but she could not deny it – on the night of the cuckolding, she too had seen Mistress bending over in the ditch at the very spot where they said the body had been found. And she remembered that Mistress had been holding a knife – she had seen its tip glinting in her hand – but she would have sworn it was the little pruning knife she always carried, and you'd have a hard time murdering anyone with that, she thought.

Cook cut up the meat and put it into a crock for boiling. She wiped her hands down her sides, trying to weigh everything up in her mind. She had known Mistress Alice all these five years and never known her to be short with anyone. True, she was often a little distracted, caught up in her own little paradise world of gardens and painting, and not in this earthly place alongside everyone else, but she had a good heart. She wouldn't hurt a fly. And as for the rumours that she had poisoned her sister, well – Cook's face took on a worried frown – she had seen the depth of Alice's distress at Flora's passing, watched her gradually become paler, thinner, turn into a flimsy shadow of her former self. When she had said this to Ella the other day, her prompt response had been – guilt; Alice was worn to nothing by guilt, and Cook could not decide whether she was right. But for the life of her, Cook could not explain away the fact that she herself had seen Alice in a quarrel with the old woman not two weeks before.

Cook's eyes began to water; she missed Mistress's absent-minded requests for a little less butter on her bread, for a drinking glass to put a posy of the first daisies in, for a sneaky taste of the madeleines when they were fresh out of the oven. In town she had been astonished to hear accusations from the draper that Alice had hexed his shop when she went in to buy stockings and he had had nothing but bad luck since. And that the fact Audrey Cobbald's chickens would not lay was because Alice had looked at her strangely in church. She had protested loudly at these accusations but got nowhere. It was a runaway cart, and all the world and his wife were sprinting to leap onto it.

When she had first heard that Mistress had been arrested, she had thought it was surely a mistake. She had made up a churn of beef broth and took it up to Master Thomas so he could take it to Mistress when he went to the gaol. But it lay on the windowsill for three days, untouched, and on the fourth day, tight-lipped, she threw its rancid contents down the sink. After that she resolved to deliver provisions to the mistress herself. The poor woman had been abandoned even by her own husband. Cook's eyes took on a flinty determination; unswerving loyalty was something expected but rarely freely given by a servant, but it was deeply embedded in Cook's view of what was right and proper. Besides, she knew that without something to keep up the spirits, people rarely lasted long in gaol, and Cook's heart was soft, tender as the mutton stew bubbling over the fire.

Chapter 24

Geoffrey rode speedily home from the constable's and, within a few minutes of searching, found what he was after in the back of his closet. He drew out the hunting knife and weighed it in his palm. It made him feel faint to look on it. The scent of blood filled his nostrils. He could not bear to hold it for long, so he had hastily wrapped it in a cloth and now it nestled snug in his pigskin holdall in the back of the carriage. Rawlinson and the constable had gone to fetch levers and hatchets and the necessary equipment to open the door of the summerhouse, should Thomas not supply a key. Geoffrey was to meet them outside the church gate after the bell rang the quarter hour.

In fact he had to wait until the hour struck five before their conveyance arrived, and the light was already fast fading. Geoffrey was sweating, his head throbbing. Sometimes his eyes lost focus and everything swayed. He knew it must be something to do with the new potion but he did not want to accept this. He was finally rid of the torture of the itching skin and he pushed the other effects to the back of his mind.

I must calm myself, he thought. It would not do for Robert Rawlinson to become suspicious. When he saw them wave from the window of the carriage, he followed on behind and the clattering

297

drew people to their windows as they sped by. Ibbetson obviously had not received the message from his maidservant to expect them, for when they arrived there was nobody to greet them, only Ella.

'Where is your master?' asked Woolley.

'Still out at the counting house, sir.'

'It is a bad business, Geoffrey,' said Rawlinson. 'Who would have thought it?'

'Show us the way then, girl,' said Woolley.

Ella led the way down the narrow path towards the summerhouse, pushing away overhanging boughs of the last fading roses, their perfume sweet in the damp air. Geoffrey let the party go on ahead whilst he lagged behind, protecting his face from the springing foliage with his sleeve. The scullery maid, April, followed them all and had brought lamps down, for twilight was upon them. When April lit the lamps the garden receded into darkness, and the bright wicks only emphasized the inky windows of the summerhouse with the pictures of the dead girl floating behind, like drowned children in a pool.

'There's no key, then?' asked Woolley.

'Mistress took it with her. Never lets it out of her sight,' said Ella.

Geoffrey watched as Constable Woolley took an axe to the doorframe, but the wood bounced it back in his face. Redoubling his efforts he hacked at the place around the lock but it gave little. The wood was solid oak, dense and close-grained, but limed over, pale and luminous in the growing dark. The constable lifted his arm again and again, but it made little impression on the heavy wood. Sweat trickled over his unwigged bald pate and onto his forehead.

'You need more muscle,' said Ella.

'Get back to the house, girl, and do something useful,' said Geoffrey. He gave Rawlinson a meaningful look, indicating Ella with his eyes.

'Yes,' said Rawlinson, 'we shall need refreshment after this, and we will need to wait to explain our doings to Master Ibbetson. See to it there is something laid out for us in the dining room.'

Ella's mouth turned downwards and she looked mutinous. Rawlinson was engrossed in watching Woolley trying to lever off the lock. Ella dropped the lantern she was holding so that it guttered and went out, and stalked off up the path. April scurried after her leaving the three men alone.

Rawlinson shook his head, picked up the lantern and relit it, then carried it around the side of the building.

'It'll have to be the windows,' Rawlinson said from round the back.

'Are you sure?' Geoffrey said.

Woolley gave a curt nod to Rawlinson, and the sound of splintering wood and glass brought Geoffrey to squint round the side of the building to where Rawlinson had made short work of the window frame with a pickaxe handle. Now there was a hole in the delicate framing, large enough for them to enter.

Rawlinson went in first, forcing himself with difficulty through the gap. It amused Geoffrey to see him struggle to get his leg over the sill and hoist his large girth through such a narrow opening. Geoffrey and Woolley went next, over some

299

sort of sideboard or table where their boots knocked several phials and jars onto the ground. Geoffrey jumped down carrying his holdall under one arm.

'Careful,' Rawlinson said. 'We do not know what this stuff is in the dark, it could be something poisonous.'

'I think it is just paint,' Geoffrey said. 'There are wall sconces and a candelabra here. Hold on while I find a taper.'

'Ah, but painters use arsenic to make yellow, and all sorts of other poisons,' Woolley said.

Geoffrey seized the moment. He felt for the clasp of his bag and pressed the catch. The top gaped open and he slipped his hand inside. The antler handle of his hunting knife found his open fingers. He drew it out from the cloth and slid out one of the desk drawers behind him silently. When he had pushed the knife inside he leaned his back on it, then went over and lit up the first sconce, and the room flickered into light. Geoffrey returned to lean nonchalantly on the side table, the brass drawer handle digging into the small of his back. Constable Woolley lit all the side sconces and then all the lights on the central table.

The room was flooded with a warm vibrating light that picked out the gilt on the portraits. The globe-shaped stoppers of the bottles refracted pinpoints of light around the walls like a hundred bobbing eyes.

''Tis almost as bright as day,' Woolley said, wiping his forehead.

'She needed it bright for painting,' Geoffrey said, without thinking.

'Or for mixing up potions,' Woolley said.

'True,' Geoffrey said.

'All these minerals, and powders. It might take a while to determine which are paint and which might be poison. It is a clever idea to conceal the venoms this way,' Woolley said. 'There was a woman once concealed rat poison in her pantry. Looked just like flour.'

'Ah,' said Geoffrey. He spotted the trestle shelf with two rows of earthenware plant pots, which might contain the lady's slipper seedlings he was after. He would make absolutely sure his precious nerveroot did not finish up with Constable Woolley.

'These plants are mine,' he said. 'I had loaned them to Mistress Ibbetson so that she could draw them when they flowered. But if it is of no matter to you, I will take them back to the manor.'

'What sort of plants are they?' Rawlinson asked. 'Are they poisonous?'

'No, just a pretty little wild garlic I brought over from Spain,' Geoffrey lied. He chose one from the top shelf and held it out for them to look at. He was glad to see it looked like nothing at all, barely germinated, just a few negligible green sprouts. 'But they are of no account' – he waved his arm airily – 'I can leave them here if you wish...'

His words hung in the air.

'Take them, they are of no interest to us.' Rawlinson barely glanced up but examined the ground minerals and powders with great interest. 'All these powders must be looked at by a physician to see what they might be.'

'Shall I break the door, to make it easier to load

301

the carriage?' Woolley hardly waited for a reply. He thumped the door from the inside now, using a hammer with obvious relish, until the door finally gave way to his boot and fell outwards onto the path with a great crash.

Geoffrey stepped onto it and methodically carried all seven plant pots to his waiting carriage. The largest plant looked like it might be already dead, the leaves drooping and withered as brown paper, but he took it anyway, it was difficult to be sure in the dark. Perhaps the roots could still be used.

When he got back after his last journey to the carriage, Woolley had discovered the hunting knife, still stained with blood, and he and Rawlinson were staring down at it where it lay glinting on the table, illuminated by the light of the dripping candelabra.

Woolley was looking at it in satisfaction.

'Well. I do not need to tell you what this means,' Rawlinson said. He placed his hand on Geoffrey's shoulder. 'I am sorry, man.'

'She was right,' Woolley said. 'That maidservant was right all along. Who would have believed it? I always said these gentlewomen were the crafty ones.'

'Why would she have done such a thing?' Rawlinson said.

'Rivalry,' said Woolley. 'I have seen similar cases before. You see all sorts in my business. Things you'd rather not see, if you get my meaning. Margaret Poulter was a herbalist – some say a witch. Happen it was some sort of argument over territory.'

'To think she had tea with my wife only a few weeks ago,' Rawlinson shuddered. 'Jane will be deeply shocked. If Alice Ibbetson is involved in the dark arts, then who else? It makes me fear for us all.' His usual jovial face had a sombre cast about it now. 'I must have a word with the parson. We must be certain all of our number are in attendance at church. Help me load the carriage,' he said to Woolley. 'All the jars and bottles. Search the rest of the drawers and bring their contents too.'

'Who will talk to the husband?' Woolley looked to the others.

'I have not the stomach for it,' Rawlinson said.

'Sir Geoffrey, what about you?'

'I don't think it's my place. Surely you will do that.' He looked at Woolley, who was clearly reluctant.

'I'll send one of my men, later. What about your commission, Sir Geoffrey?' Woolley said, remembering why Geoffrey was with them. 'Can you see it?'

Geoffrey looked blank for a moment.

'The painting you have come to collect?'

'She appears not to have begun it. There are only these.' He indicated the portraits around the walls. 'I cannot see anyone paying for these now, can you? They might bring bad luck with them.' He looked around the room appraisingly. 'But she will not be needing them. I'll take them for the frames, if you like.'

'Go ahead. We are going to clear the place anyway.'

Geoffrey took a pocket-knife and slit the pictures from the most handsome frames, discarding the portraits to the ground. The room grew big and empty without their witnessing presence. Then he loaded the gilded frames into his carriage and drove away. He had done what he came to do; the plants were secure in his care, and Alice Ibbetson would not be returning for them. He was in the clear. Woolley would send someone to tell Thomas they had found the knife in her drawer.

In the summerhouse the rain lashed in through the broken windows. Moonlight reflected in fragments of broken glass. The floor was bespattered with pigment, which melted with the rain into dark pools of carmine, viridian and burnt sienna. The crumpled portraits on the ground blew into the corners, their eyes to the ground, their mouths smiling into the tiled floor. The wind picked up the beech leaves and whirled them in through the gaping doorframe. Nature had already begun to reclaim her territory.

Chapter 25

Thomas returned a little late from his work, for he had earlier felt unwell and had ridden slowly. He had been breathless, and had found himself faint and sweating as if he had taken a fever. He was beginning to feel guilty that he had left Alice to lie in gaol for so long. Angry with her for dismissing Ella behind his back, he thought to punish her with a night in the town gaol. It would teach her a lesson. The next morning he had gone to Kendal as usual; when he returned home Ella was waiting and he had been so hot for her he had taken her on the drawing-room floor. Afterwards, when she suggested a warm bed, he had simply fallen into it.

He had let the situation drag on. Partly it was laziness, partly it was that he thought it was surely a mistake and they would soon let her go. And meanwhile he could have a few days' uninterrupted pleasure with Ella. More than that though, it would be unpleasant to look at the whole business, and if there was one thing Thomas hated, it was unpleasantness.

When he arrived home it was to find Ella settled in front of the drawing-room fire in Alice's chair, idly turning over a pair of white kidskin gloves in her lap. She jumped up sharply as he entered, from habit more than because she felt herself to be in the wrong. Thomas's eyes took in her hands.

'What's that you have there?'

'A pair of gloves, Thomas.' She shook them by the wrists, the empty fingers dangling.

He was tetchy, because he felt out of sorts. 'They are Alice's gloves, are they not?'

'Yes, but she won't be needing them no more, will she. And it seems a shame they should go to waste.' She stroked the flaccid leather with her forefinger.

'What do you mean? I gave no permission for you to go into her closet. I forbid you to touch Alice's things.'

The sight of Ella holding Alice's gloves affronted him. Partly it was the look of the tiny gloves in Ella's solid square hands, partly it was his ingrained notion of Ella as Alice's maid, and there was something disconcerting about seeing someone else sitting in Alice's chair. Another glimmer of unease about the situation arose in him, a small sliver of conscience.

'Where's the harm?' Ella flung the gloves carelessly down on the chair. 'Anyways, I don't want them. I don't want to touch anything that witch has had on her skin. Wearing them would be like wearing a curse.'

Thomas was about to protest, but Ella was already sidling up to him. She planted a lingering kiss on his mouth.

'Let's forget them gloves, Master.' He liked it when she called him that. It made him feel powerful and in control. Slowly she felt down the length of his body until his hardness sprang up under her hands. He groaned and grabbed her by a thick handful of hair, tilting her face so he could look at her. She rubbed the hard place in his breeches.

'Ella,' he said, thoughts of Alice pushed to the back of his mind by the hand between his legs, 'you will be the death of me.'

'Not before I've jocked the life out of you.' She licked his ear, before leading him up the back stairs.

Thomas looked down at the top of Ella's head, at the parting of luxuriant brown hair, at her smooth peachy skin above her low-cut chemise, and felt the sensation of her hands roaming exquisitely over his buttocks and his legs. He felt better. And he placed Alice firmly out of his mind, as he had done since the day they took her away.

He rubbed his thumb over Ella's nipple and started to manoeuvre her skirts up over her thighs. When they were done, she leaned over towards his somnolent body and poked him hard in the back.

'Justice Rawlinson and Sir Geoffrey have been over with the constable. They were after searching the summerhouse.'

'What's that?' Thomas was half in slumber. 'I do not see why Sir Geoffrey needs to come. He is not part of the constabulary.' He spoke sleepily, not really hearing what Ella had said. Thomas had always felt ill-at-ease in Geoffrey's presence. Geoffrey was his superior and Thomas knew it, no matter how much Geoffrey shook his hand or exchanged jovialities.

'No, but he is Rawlinson's friend, so I couldn't do much to stop them,' Ella said. 'And Sir Geoffrey said he had left a picture with Mistress, some business arrangement they had.'

'What do they think to find, though? A few jars of paint and a lot of pictures, that's all. There's nothing there. It will all blow over.'

He thought about the wild accusations that had come to his door – like a cartwheel rolling downhill, the gossip was now unstoppable. And he had watched it gather momentum, bemused, like a spectator, as if it were none of his business. It had come as a mild surprise to him to find that Alice was absolutely dispensable, at least whilst he had Ella's ample flesh to slide into. He knew he ought to care, and that caused him disquiet, but somehow he could not get around to doing anything about it.

Ella sat up and leaned on one elbow, fixing him with her catlike eyes. 'You can't get away from the facts, Thomas – her father, mother, sister, all dead within seven years. That sounds like a curse to me. And she was the only one near them when they died.'

'Nonsense. Her mother died after childbirth.'

'The midwife says she's seen witches stop off the womb with their magic, then the babe won't come. They had to pull and pull to tear the babe out, that's why she died. You were living with a she-devil, Thomas, and you must pray to the Lord above that you have not been tainted by it all.'

Thomas considered the state of his soul for a moment, uncertain.

'Poppycock,' he said. He sat up grumpily, aware he would get no peace.

'Did not you tell me that your mother and your brother had always hated her?' Ella asked.

Thomas nodded. 'That's true, they did.'

Thomas thought back to when he had married Alice. His mother had been adamant that it was a totally unsuitable match because Alice brought no dowry, only the burden of her sister. After the mother's death, Flora and Alice were living with an uncle, who worked them to the bone like servants for no recompense. It was Flora who had attracted Thomas, not so much Alice. Thomas had business dealings with the uncle, who was a pawnbroker, and had come across the little one carrying great scuttles of coal from the cellar. He had taken a shine to her and brought her secret supplies of sweetmeats when he called. He was always rewarded with a beaming smile.

The uncle was sharp-tongued and Thomas did not like to think of the poor mite skivvying for some hard-hearted ogre of a man. He had hit upon the idea of 'rescuing' the Longley sisters by marrying Alice, an idea which appealed to his sense of himself as a hero, but the more he insisted on marrying her, the more resolved his mother had become that it was an unsuitable match and he should not. Thomas had dug in his heels – it became a pitch battle between them – but he was determined, and for the first and probably the last time, he had rebelled against his domineering mother and won.

His reminiscence was interrupted by Ella. 'Are you listening?' Ella was still talking of his mother.

'They could see evil for what it was, right in front of their noses,' continued Ella. 'She took you for a fat-witted fool, foisting herself and that child on you, no doubt thinking to get a hold of your fine little house and all your savings. It is just as well she was stopped.'

'Maybe you're right.' Thomas was irritated now, and tired of talk of Alice, which pricked him with guilt, so he humoured Ella.

'Anyways, they did go in the summerhouse,' said Ella mulishly. 'They found a knife hidden in a drawer. All covered in blood it was.'

'What?'

'And they made a right old mess, broke the windows and battered down the door, and took away all her jars as evidence. They waited a while, but when you did not come...'

Thomas was straight out of bed and pulling on his breeches as she spoke. Ella followed him to the doorstep, clutching the quilt around her. He hurried down the path, his bare feet stuffed into his work boots. At the bottom of the garden he stopped dead in his tracks. The gaping hole in the summerhouse, where the door used to be, was ragged like a missing tooth.

A minute later he blundered out of the broken doorframe, carrying a pile of torn canvases in his arms.

Ella saw his shadow stumbling up the path, crashing into bushes as he came. He was weeping, and he yelled something unintelligible at her before the front door slammed behind him. Ella was worried. She had never seen a man cry like that before. She waited outside a while, wondering how to bring him round. When she crept back inside, she heard him upstairs, talking to himself and walking back and forth in the mistress's closet. When she called him he did not answer but moaned like a mare in labour.

Chapter 26

Stephen had decided in the end to say nothing to his father about his impending visit to the gaol with Richard. His father had become involved in enquiries about the murder that seemed to be the talk of the whole village. Unfortunately it was one of his father's artist acquaintances, a wife from the village, who was responsible, and so his father had been frequently in discourse with Rawlinson and

Constable Woolley concerning the matter. At least that meant that he was out and about and not slumped at home. Earlier in the day, when he had spoken with his father, he had jumped out of his chair and held his hands up strangely in front of his face.

'Take her away,' he said.

Stephen had looked either side of him, in confusion, but could not see anyone.

'Who, Father?'

'The old woman. No. Nobody,' he had said then, rubbing at his face in an air of confusion.

Stephen had felt sorry for him. He must have been asleep, dreaming; he had been most unlike himself since the day he told his mother to go.

After bowing his farewells, Stephen left, impatient to get on the road. In a clean shirt, moleskin breeches and vest, his obligatory wide-brimmed hat stuffed into his saddlebag, he trotted along the dripping lanes to Richard's cottage, hoping to pass unnoticed. The only person he passed was Miller Hardacre, who was driving his laden cartload of grain back to the mill for grinding. The miller nodded over to him as he went by, but obviously did not recognize Stephen as Sir Geoffrey's son – or else there would have been much cap-doffing and tugging of forelocks instead. Fortunately few people knew yet of his return from London, thought Stephen, otherwise he would have been expected at church, and his face would soon have been the object of much idle scrutiny.

On the lane down to the cottage he prepared himself to become Sam Fielding once more. He found it easier and easier to take up the part.

Stephen Fisk, the wag, the gambler, the rake about town, seemed to be receding daily. Sam Fielding was growing inside of him, pushing out Stephen like an unwanted guest at a wedding.

He rode easily on his common horse, which was as comfortable as sitting in an old chair – true, it lacked speed, and certainly did not look anything to speak of, but he appreciated its docile ways, its reliability, how it made every journey leisurely. He had not noticed the fine views when he was galloping hither and thither on his thoroughbred, and the open spaces were a relief after the crowds and squalor of London.

When he arrived at the latch gate to Helk Cottage, he was surprised to see Richard step out to meet him puffing on a pipe. As usual, he seemed to be full of energy. Even his pipe-smoking looked purposeful.

'Pump's out back there, if thou wants a wash.'

'Thanks to thee. I will,' said Stephen, tethering his horse and slapping it affectionately on the neck. He went to the stand-pump and rubbed his face and neck under the freezing water, shaking himself dry like a dog.

'Come in and sit thee down. There's tobacco on the table and a clay stem too, help thyself. There is no one to see, and I reckon there is no harm in the odd pipe now and then.'

Stephen sat himself down at the table and filled the pipe. He did not tell Richard that he smoked every night after dinner at home. He looked around him with interest as he smoked, curious about this man who was such a mystery. It was all very clean and tidy, almost womanly. There was a shelf with a few dozen leather-bound books and other printed matter, news-sheets, pamphlets and chapbooks and the like, all neatly arranged in size order. It was clear Richard was interested in book-learning, and Stephen tried to read the titles without looking too obviously at them – three Bibles, *Holland's Atlas*, in several volumes, similar to one he had been shown at school but which had been much too valuable for him to be allowed to handle, *Culpeper's Herbal*, and even, he noted with some amusement, one titled *The Cook's Guide*. Not that Richard seemed to need much instruction, for over the fire hung an iron pot from which a savoury steam was bubbling.

Richard laid out two plates. 'It's rabbit stew. Here, have some bread.'

When the plates were filled, he sat himself down and turned to Stephen. 'Wilt thou say grace, Sam?'

Stephen reddened – his family's Latin remercies would be out of place here. He decided to keep it simple.

'For this bread and meat, we give thanks. Amen.'

Richard bowed his head, his hands holding his hat on his lap. After Stephen's words he smiled broadly and picked up his spoon.

They ate slowly, chewing steadily, the only sound the rattle of the spoons and the tearing of the bread. The stew was excellent, with waxy turnip and carrots and plentiful onions in the gravy. Stephen mopped his plate with his bread.

When they were done, Richard said, 'I see thou hast taken a fancy to my books. Take a closer look if thou wilt.'

'I was looking at the atlas. Art thou interested in sea travel then?'

'There are Quaker brethren all over the world now. Sadly, some of the courts see fit to dispose of us by transportation to the Caribbees or the Americas.' He stood and lifted a heavy tome from the shelf, opening it to display an ink drawing of the Caribbean territories. He pointed with a forefinger to a few small islands marooned in a huge ocean drawn in curly rivers of ink.

'Some of our people have been sold here for forced labour in the sugar fields. I have heard it is half desert and half paradise, but the land is good for growing things, they say. Better than the wet of Westmorland, I'll warrant.'

Stephen stared at the scatter of odd-shaped islands and shuddered. The idea of being shipped across the ocean into slavery, with no hope of return, was a hard price to pay for one's convictions. These Quakers must be made of stiffer stuff than he.

Richard opened another volume and flipped the pages. 'And here, New England.' He indicated a country at least ten times the size of England. 'At least here they are not bound men. We have not heard how our folk fared on the passage yet. There are rumours they will not be welcomed there any more than here. But thou canst see for thyself, it is a vast country. God willing, they will find a place to call their own.'

'Dost thou think the Fleetwoods will be sent overseas?'

'Jack and Hannah? I hope not – I am petitioning for their release, on the grounds they are no longer a threat to anyone.' He shook his head and his face darkened. 'The trial is to be next week, but we do not know if they will let us speak for them yet.' He paused, eyebrows furrowed, evidently considering their plight. 'But let us get on the road, they will be expecting our provisions today. I have petitioned each week to see them but so far have had no luck. But the least we can do is to make sure they keep up their strength and spirits. I have some ham, ewe's cheese, and some more loaves in the cold press.'

Stephen helped Richard load his horse's panniers with food and water, a large supply of candles and a Bible into which Richard slipped a small pamphlet. Seeing Stephen's curious gaze, he said, 'It is a copy of Boehme's tract. I thought Jack may need spiritual as well as bodily sustenance.'

'Are they both lettered, then?'

Richard's face fell. 'Of course. I am forgetting myself. Thou art right, Sam, probably not.' He was immediately crestfallen, uncertain whether or not to add this small gift to the rest.

'But perhaps there may be someone to read it for him, or maybe just the comfort of having it in his hands, that someone has thought fit to send it,' said Stephen.

Richard smiled. 'Happen thou art right. We will take it.'

They drew up outside the big gate and dismounted. To Stephen, it was the first time he had actually seen the gaol, and as expected it looked a stark, forbidding place. A tremor of fear licked at his bones. If he became too closely associated

315

with the Quakers, he could finish up inside these dark walls.

Richard strode over and banged purposefully on the small gate, and a window slid open. He stated his name.

'Richard Wheeler. I have provisions here for Jack and Hannah Fleetwood.'

The door opened on its heavy hinges and a curly-haired lad ushered them inside the court-yard.

'Wait here,' he said and went to fetch the head gaoler. Inside the yard nothing could be seen except slit windows, and the scaffold with the noose slung to one side, ready. Stephen eyed the trapdoor with equal measures of curiosity and squeamish dread.

'What you got?' A thick-set man in heavy boots lumbered over, then led the way to the platform where Richard unpacked his baskets for inspec-tion. 'No knives or ropes?' He licked his flabby lips and grinned at the lad, revealing brown teeth. 'We wouldn't be wanting to cheat the crowds of their entertainment next week, would we?' The lad sup-pressed a snigger, his knuckles pressed to his nose.

Stephen and Richard remained silent, as the gaoler picked over the provisions laid out on the planking. He flicked the lid from one of the bas-kets and put his face over the contents, inhaling deeply.

'What's this?'

'Some cured ham, and some cheese,' Richard said impatiently. 'And here's a shilling for thee if we can deliver it to them ourselves.'

The gaoler sniffed at the two freshly baked

loaves and did not even turn around. 'Each?' he said.

'No,' Richard said, 'a shilling's all we have.'

'Then you can see her, not him. Come back the morrow with another if you want to see him.' He held out his hand for the coin, which he rubbed on the stained front of his jerkin before putting it in his grubby purse.

'I'll take Jack Fleetwood's dinner down to him, while Bubb takes you to the women's quarters.'

Bubb said, 'But, sir, Jack Fleetwood—'

Stephen saw the gaoler issue Bubb a warning look, and he promptly held his tongue.

'What about Jack?' Stephen asked.

'Nothing,' the gaoler said, glaring at Bubb. 'Just that he's looking a lot better of late.' Bubb turned his back, so Stephen could not see his face. Stephen suspected he was laughing, but when he turned back he seemed to be coughing.

As Stephen looked across the yard he saw two of the prison guards open the gates and a sedan chair entered, carried by two sweating, liveried attendants.

'Here.' The gaoler held out his ring of keys with one of them protruding from the rest, and Bubb, now recovered from whatever ailed him, took it.

Stephen watched the gaoler make haste over to the sedan chair and bow low as the well-dressed occupant stepped out, avoiding a puddle and holding onto his be-feathered hat to avoid knocking it off. The gentleman took out his purse and proffered a coin on his gloved hand. The gaoler nodded and deposited it in a bag hung from his belt. 'Thank you, Paucett,' said the gentleman.

317

'Shall we proceed?'

'Yes, sir, follow me, sir,' said the gaoler, bobbing his head up and down. As usual, there was one rule here for the rich and quite another for everyone else. Stephen stared covertly at the man in the sedan chair in case he was a friend of his father's and might recognize him, before turning back to see what Richard was doing.

Richard hoped he had not made a mistake in bringing young Sam here to the gaol. He worried it might test his faith a little too much, to see his brethren thus brought down, and might deter him from his calling. But Sam seemed to Richard to be a stout-hearted lad, and wiser than most young folks. Richard knew that embracing the Quaker way was not easy, and he admired that in one so young. He gathered up the provisions and the Bible.

The young Bubb had been assigned to take them down, and at his whistle two more guards armed with swords appeared from the opposite side of the yard to accompany them down into the belly of the castle where the prisoners lodged.

'I hope you said your prayers before you came,' said Bubb, his eyes bright with salacious gossip, 'because there's a witch in there with her now.'

Richard caught Sam's eye as they cautiously descended into the gloom; Sam shook his head. 'That does not sound good,' he whispered.

'Yes, she slit someone open too, knifed them from here to here–' he drew a long line across his belly – 'so I can't let you in. But you can eye her through the door. Mind you, not too close, she might grab for you through the hatch.'

He opened a barred gate with the key and they stepped through into a stinking corridor, with doors ranged along either side. Even when Bubb lit a rush torch, it shed little light in the prevailing gloom. As they passed, a few prisoners came to the squat iron-studded doors and hammered and shouted pitifully for assistance from behind, but Bubb ignored them, at last sliding back a small square window in one of them to reveal a dark interior. Then he retreated back through the iron gate, and shouted, 'Ten minutes. That's all.'

Richard called softly from outside, 'Hannah.'

There was no answer, so he called again, 'Hannah.'

A weary woman's voice came back. 'Mistress Fleetwood cannot stand. She is too weak. What do you want of her?' The voice was familiar. Richard peered through the hatch into the dingy cell, but his eyes were unaccustomed to the darkness and he could not make out a single feature within.

'We have brought bread and comforts from her friends at the Hall,' he replied.

Richard heard muffled voices, and the faint sounds of someone's skirts moving around on the straw inside the cell, before a white face appeared out of the dingy background and he was looking into the witch's grey eyes. Alice Ibbetson's eyes.

The eyes flared in anger. 'You.' The words were like a slap. 'You dare to come here now, after incarcerating me here all this time?'

Richard took an involuntary step backwards, and felt Sam's hand on his back. He was shocked

319

to the core, as if someone had thrown a pail of icy water over him.

'Mistress Ibbetson, I had no idea.' He could not fathom it. His thoughts raced, trying to reason it out. He had seen her at home, just the week before. He took in her unkempt hair and the broken fingernails where her hands grasped the bars, the dark circles beneath her eyes. 'How has this come about?'

'Do not play games with me, Mr Wheeler. Is the wild orchid so important to you, you would see a woman hang?' He stared back at her in incomprehension. 'For a murder she did not commit?' she asked.

She turned away from the window and disappeared into the gloom. Sam, who must have witnessed this little scene and noticed his discomfiture, pressed his arm, asked him, 'Richard, what's to do?'

'It is Mistress Ibbetson, she says she may hang – and she seems to think I had something to do with her arrest.'

'Didst thou?'

Richard shook his head. 'No. I am astounded she should think such a thing.'

'Is Hannah in there with her?'

He nodded, and continued: 'There has been a miscarriage of justice. Alice Ibbetson is neither murderer nor witch. I would stake my life on it.' He looked at Sam. 'What shall I do? Shall I try to reason with her?'

'I do not know what's best. But perhaps try to talk to her again.'

Richard went back to the open hatch and called

through. 'Mistress Ibbetson. I do not understand how you came to be here, but I mean to find out. You must trust me.'

There was no answer from within. He tried again, 'Please. Hannah will attest that I am a man of my word.'

He heard Hannah's small voice, hoarse and barely audible. 'Trust him, Alice. He would not willingly do thee wrong.'

Silence.

And then, Hannah's voice once more. 'What hast thou to lose?'

He heard the rustle of straw as Alice approached the window again. Her eyes glistened with tears. 'Please, Mr Wheeler, just one thing. Hannah asks, is there any news of Jack?'

Richard told her what the gaoler had said, and she called out to Hannah, 'Hear that – he is looking better,' and the sound of crying within caused the unshed tears to run down Alice's face. She wiped them away, as if ashamed of them, with her cuff.

'Quick, Mistress Ibbetson,' said Richard. 'We have only ten minutes. Tell us anything that might help.'

Alice told the story of how she had been brought to the cell, and how not a living soul had been near since then, not even her husband. How they had only hard bread to eat, and stagnant water to drink, and that although she had tried to help Hannah, she was getting weaker and needed herbs and physic for her wounds.

He could not believe it. He had heard that someone had been arrested for the death of Margaret

Poulter the cunning woman, but that the blame should rest with Alice Ibbetson was inconceivable. He would visit Thomas Ibbetson forthwith. Perhaps then some help could be sought for Hannah, too.

The noise of the turnkey opening the gate alerted them to the men's imminent return. Remembering the provisions that Sam had in his hands, Richard pushed the fresh loaf through, and the cheese and ham, and pressing his palm against Alice's cold hand he said, 'Keep thy spirits up. We will fight for thy freedom as much as for our sister Hannah.'

Then he reached into his pocket and thrust the Bible with its hidden tract towards her. 'For Hannah,' he said, and fumbled for the candles, and a flint and stone. She hid them quickly in her bodice and smiled her thanks. In return she pushed a small bronze key on a blue ribbon into his hand just as the gaoler arrived. The turnkey muscled past them to peer in through the door to check all was well before slamming the peephole closed.

'But be thou quick, Richard.' Hannah's voice was faint from behind the blank door. 'The trial's Tuesday – there's talk of her hanging.'

'Time to go, gentlemen,' Bubb said, shoving Richard from behind.

'Mr Wheeler,' he heard Alice call as they were jostled away. 'Your orchid – it is in the summerhouse. The seedlings too – the middle shelf.'

'Have no fear, I will see to it,' he shouted back.

Richard went back up into the yard and remonstrated with the gaoler for not taking down the food and blankets he and his friends had brought in the previous weeks. The gaoler was unrepentant.

'There's no point in feeding them that are going to hang, or die anyways.'

Richard made a move towards him, his fists lifting involuntarily as though he would strike him, but then he regained control, let them fall away to his sides.

'I gives it first to those in most need,' said the gaoler, backing off, but Richard was sure by the size of his belly that he considered that to be himself. He doubted very much that any provisions would ever reach Jack.

There was little they could do, except to say they would return, with another two shillings for visiting rights, the next day.

They rode back along the coast road, following the estuary. The tide was out and the sands looked to be wide expanses of rippled cloth with sandpipers and gulls flapping like white papers against them.

On the way back, Richard told Stephen about his disagreement with Mistress Ibbetson over the orchid, and described to him the uncanny appearance of the white dove in his woods.

'You see, Sam, I read it for a sign, it made the hairs stand on the back of my neck. It is my belief that that is how God speaks with us, through signs and wonders – and the small voice inside that will not be stilled.'

'Few would dispute it,' said Stephen, as if to sound knowledgeable, 'but if she is a thief, and stole the orchid, what is to prevent her doing even worse? Thou art convinced of her innocence?' He was thinking of his father. Alice Ibbetson must be the woman with whom his father had recently been associated, and in their last conversation his father had been certain of her guilt. But he kept these thoughts to himself.

Richard replied, 'Quite sure. It is an instinct, something I have no words for. Besides, stealing a plant for study and killing another person in cold blood are by no means in the same order of things. I wonder why that scoundrel Fisk, her patron, has not vouched for her?'

Stephen was about to reply when he realized he would give himself away, so he shut his mouth again. After they had ridden a little further he felt safe to ask, 'Who is Fisk, then?' He hoped to find out more about Richard's opinion of his father.

'A local squire – owns most of the land here-abouts. We used to be close before the war, we played together as boys. My father knew his father well. My family had land in the Loyne valley, and Geoffrey and I were like brothers.'

'What happened? Are you still close?'

'No,' he replied curtly, and his face darkened. 'No, we no longer see eye to eye. There were irreconcilable differences. And we fought for different allegiances in the war. There was–' he seemed to struggle for the words – 'an incident. A tragic accident.' Stephen stiffened, he wondered if this was his grandmother's death he referred to. 'Afterwards, Geoffrey tried to cut me down, ambushed me in the dark. But I escaped with only this.' He peeled open his shirt to show a deep scar across the chest.

Stephen looked at the raised white seam of skin. His own father had done this. He was transfixed by the sight of the mark of his father's sword. He rallied himself to reply.

'He sounds like a dangerous man. And he is Mistress Ibbetson's patron?'

'So I hear.' Richard's words were clipped, he seemed angry. 'When he is sober enough. Though I cannot see that my appealing for his aid will help Alice's cause. He hates me with a vengeance.'

Stephen took all this in. He realized his father's appetite for drink had become common knowledge and he was ashamed his family should be the subject of general gossip. He was hurt by it, and his conflicting loyalties rose up to choke him. He flushed scarlet and said, 'Perhaps Fisk has changed. After all, if you were friends once, you could be again.' Even as he said this, he realized with a sinking feeling that this was impossible. Richard pulled up his horse sharply.

'No. It is far too late for that.' He looked at Stephen as if he were half-witted. 'You have no idea, have you? What we went through in the war.' His voice was loud and harsh. 'Brother fighting brother, men cut into ribbons before our eyes, crawling with their quartered bellies gushing. Women sliced open like pigs to slaughter, their bloodied petticoats flapping from the ramparts...' His chest heaved with emotion before he went on. 'I did things then which are beyond speaking of.'

Richard gathered himself with difficulty, regaining control of his crumpled face. 'I was a lad like you once, but made old overnight. We all were.'

Stephen noticed that Richard had forgotten the Quaker mode of address but he remained silent. He felt uncomfortable seeing Richard in distress but also realized with a pang of guilt that he knew nothing at all about his father's early life, that it had been a closed book to him. Unsure how to respond, Stephen cast his eyes down to the ground where the last leaves of autumn rustled around the horses' hooves.

Richard hauled hard on the reins and dug his heels into his horse's ribs so that it set off at a gallop, mane and tail flowing in the wind. He drove the horse on. Stephen's horse was in a hurry to follow after, but it was slower and heavier, and Richard's horse soon receded to the horizon. Stephen did not know whether to ride harder to catch him up or to let him go on alone. He slowed to a trot, for his horse was panting from the exertion and Richard had disappeared from view. Stephen rode disconsolately for another half mile before seeing that Richard had stopped and was waiting for him in the track.

After an awkward moment or two, Richard said softly, 'I spoke out of turn, Sam. Thou hast lost thy family in the troubles, and that must have been hard.'

Stephen looked up into the older man's concerned face.

'Forgive me if I spoke harshly,' Richard continued. 'It is right thou shouldst know nothing of the fighting life. It is past, and should be buried whilst we build a better world.'

He paused, looking away to the horizon where the sun was just beginning to set, casting a pink-tinged glow over the empty sands. 'That is why I became a Quaker – to live and let live, each man giving due respect to his brother, and to make a pledge never to lift a hand against another. But I will not say it has not been hard.' He gestured with his hand to his side. 'I am used to speaking with my sword. It is hard to fight the ills of the world with an empty hand.'

He shook his head, then kicked his horse on into a smart trot and Stephen's horse ambled after.

Richard waited again for Stephen's slower horse to catch up. 'I was wondering why thou chose the Quaker life, Sam. What was it for thee?'

Stephen was ready with his story and it slipped like grease from his tongue. 'I was at one of Fox's meetings and felt the calling. I have no family to consider, so I followed my heart.'

As he said this a part of him longed for it to be true. That he should be the man following his convictions, that he should be Sam Fielding, the devout Quaker.

'I admire thee, Sam,' said Richard. 'Thou art an example to the sons of my generation, and thou hast all thy life ahead of thee to witness for peace in thy faith.'

Richard Wheeler was no traitor, but a peacemaker. Stephen realized the days of this friendship were numbered. His task was finished; he had found out what his father wanted to know, and though his father might not like it, he had fulfilled his duty. But if he were to confess this, there would be no more reason to be Sam Fielding. The noose of deceit seemed to tighten about Stephen's neck.

327

He baulked at stopping his visits to the Hall. Dorothy had made him so welcome – there he was somebody, a person, not a ticket with his title and income scribed upon it. But sooner or later, word would out that he was the son of Sir Geoffrey Fisk. He squirmed in his saddle, his stomach churning. For the rest of the journey he maintained a miserable silence, Stephen Fisk, the liar, caught in the trap of his own making.

When the time came to go their separate ways, he gave Richard heartfelt thanks for the meal and agreed to meet him the next morning as usual. But even as he spoke, he wondered how long his creation Sam Fielding would pass undiscovered.

Chapter 27

Geoffrey looked out of his chamber window absentmindedly, a glass of claret in one hand. Nowadays, apart from his usual wine, the little phial of physic from the lady's slipper was the first thing he turned to in the morning, to take the edge off the inevitable itching. His head always swam with the first dose of the day. He let the wavering world out of the window come slowly into focus.

He went over to the window and took in the view: the long-horned cattle grazing in the distance, the double avenue of beech he had planted as the main driveway, the yew boundary hedge beyond. It swayed beneath his gaze as if under water. His eye roved over the intricately designed gardens, laid out in the Spanish courtyard style, but the patterns danced and undulated and would not stay still. The red apples, growing ripe already on the espaliers, looked as if they were drifting against the wall. He rubbed his forehead, pushed his knuckles into his eyes. When he opened them the world quavered before him. It was disconcerting. He left the window and sat, ruminating.

He had ceased to scratch. The tetters were much improved. The backs of his knees used to be cracked with it so he could not sit comfortably, and last week's meetings with Rawlinson and Woolley the Constable, would have been sheer torture had it not been for the new draught. He had admitted to himself now that the potion made him feel a little peculiar, but it was a small price to pay if the itch had stopped.

Worry made the itch worse too. Still, he could relax now. Someone else was to take the rap for the old woman's death. He breathed a long sigh of relief and drained his glass. It was a shock to discover that the woman he had dispatched was not one of his unruly tenants after all, but one Margaret Poulter, the crone from whom he had purchased the green salve. A quack, that much was certain, for the ointment had been useless, as he had thought. But he darkened at the thought of her. What if she was genuinely possessed of cunning powers? Her words returned to his mind. He tried to shrug them off but they stuck like sealing wax. 'I will never let you go,' she had said. Geoffrey shuddered. He had no doubt the old woman intended to hex him.

At least his estate was secure at last. There

would be no one knocking at his door, no one taking him off to the gaol in chains and seizing his house and goods. The estate was for Stephen, and his heirs after him. It had panicked him when the old woman's family had turned up in the village intent on avenging her death. When he saw the son at Constable Woolley's, and the ire in his face, he did not much fancy his chances should he find out who was responsible.

But now it was certain Mistress Ibbetson would swing for it. It was regrettable, of course, he had some pleasant remembrances of times in her company before she turned unruly against him. In any case, he reassured himself, he had had nothing to do with her arrest – that seemed to be the way the river was flowing anyway, so who could blame him if he eased its passage.

He contemplated Ella. That maid must have a grudge against Alice Ibbetson the size of a boulder, but it suited his purposes very well. Once or twice though, to his mind, Ella treated him in a manner that was over-familiar. He frowned. He must keep an eagle eye on her.

He went downstairs carefully, holding the banister rail, watching his step, for even the stairs seemed to shift like quagmire, not solid wood at all. He went into the stables where he had unloaded the plants the previous night. He hummed a little to himself. It was ingenious to think of fetching the knife over to the Ibbetsons' summerhouse. He remembered the tableau of Woolley and Rawlinson standing staring at the knife on Alice Ibbetson's table, and with a little snort laughed out loud.

Now that he saw the plants in the light, it was apparent only a few were worth keeping. None of them was labelled, to his annoyance. There were three pots filled with earth, but he poked around thoroughly in the soil with his finger and found no trace of any seed or root in these, so he discarded them to the midden, shaking out the earth and stacking the pots to the side of the door.

There were three larger pots of sprouting seedlings which he was sure were the new lady's slipper plants. They had been on the top shelf right next to the big plant, which he recognized. He rubbed his hands together, pleased with himself, and watered them, placing them on the windowsill. He would tend these carefully. Johnson the gardener could keep an eye on them in his glasshouse. Perhaps they would grow faster under glass. The big plant, the original lady's slipper, had drooping leaves, now dried out and hanging over the edge of the pot, the leaf edges wrinkled like brown paper.

He pulled it up from the soil to look at the roots. Yes, this was certainly the same plant from which he had secured a part – there was the broken place where he had taken his first sample. His interest aroused, he carried it up to his chambers. He would cut this one up and grind more of the necessary mash from these roots to make his medicinal tea. He calculated that by the time that supply ran out, there would be new plants on the way. It was all very satisfactory.

He spent a pleasant, busy afternoon soaking one of the roots from the big plant to make tea, mashing the foul urine-smelling pulp with a pestle, grinding it into a paste and soaking it in brandy. It would not keep, else. He weighed it carefully with his apothecary's weights, making it into small doses of twelve liquid grains each.

Fresh herbs were always more effective, so he decided to take another dose forthwith. When stowing the glass away in the cupboard, he came across the oily green mixture the cunning woman, Margaret Poulter, had sent. Shuddering, he picked up the lidded pot intending to throw, it out. As he did so, a dizziness overcame him. His hand unaccountably slipped and the bottom fell away from the lid and smashed on the floor, splattering a pale green slime over the floorboards. It startled him and his heart began pounding like a battle-drum in his chest. He looked aghast at the broken pieces. The old crone's words came back to him again.

He recalled the expression in her piercing brown eyes, as if she could see into the depths of his soul and found it black as tar. He saw again her white head banging against the path. Like a nightmare he was back there, holding the knife slippery with blood in his fingers. Again he felt the sensation of scrubbing his hands under the icy pump. He dropped the lid with a clatter and backed away, staring at the floor. The slime made a pattern on the floorboards. It appeared to be a skull with a gaping mouth. A quick glance behind him. He had an intimation that someone was with him in the room. It was an omen.

Geoffrey rang the bell. Patterson entered and bowed.

'I dropped a bottle by mistake. See to it, will you.'

Patterson looked at it. 'I'll send the kitchen-maid.'

'No. Do it now. Now I say. I want it out of my sight. And bury it outside the grounds.'

'Outside the grounds?' Patterson looked at him uncertainly, as if he was not sure he had heard correctly.

'You heard me. Now get on with it.' He threw Patterson a washcloth from the rail near the wash-stand, then took himself downstairs on shaky legs.

'Master Stephen is home, sir,' said Patterson as he passed with a dustpan containing the green-tinged washcloth. 'I have seen his bay mare coming up the drive.'

Geoffrey nodded, and instructed him to send Stephen to the withdrawing room. He took a snifter of wine, just to fortify him. By now he had calmed down and begun to reason with himself, dismissing the breaking of the jar as an accident. He felt a little better.

He heard Stephen arrive from the stables and Patterson's voice rudely imparting Geoffrey's in-structions to him. Why did Stephen not reprimand him, take him to task for his rudeness like the mas-ter's son should?

His son had always disappointed him a little. When he was born, he had hoped he would be tall like himself, but he had taken after Emilia, short and slight, with his fluffy yellow hair flopping over his face. Even in a wig, his bearing was less than imposing. In character too he was soft like Emilia. Too much hanging around her apron strings like a milksop. If he had had his son's perfect skin, then nothing would have held him back. He would have been at court by now, making something of himself, not running away from London like Stephen did at the first sign of pestilence. Still, this spying might be the making of him. He had seen him going out diligently every morning dressed in that appalling brown suit. Perhaps he would have found out what was really afoot at Lingfell Hall.

Stephen was dressed in the same grubby brown breeches when he arrived. 'You might at least have changed,' said Geoffrey irritably, from the fireplace. Of course the fire was not lit; it was a relief to him not to endure the raging heat his wife had seemed so fond of.

'Sorry, Father. I will change before dinner.'

'What news from the Quakers?'

'Last week I spent a day with Richard Wheeler. He has signed a pledge for peace with the rest of the Quakers. It has gone to the king, with his name on it. He is not planning any sort of rebellion.'

'Oaths mean nothing to someone like Wheeler.'

'You are wrong, Father. It is not an oath. Quakers do not make oaths, as they always speak true. It is a pledge, for the peace of our land, and I know he intends to keep it.'

Geoffrey was momentarily bewildered. Stephen stood there stubbornly like a mule, and Geoffrey felt for the first time a quiet resistance in his son. He did not like it; he knew the humour of mutiny well from his time at sea and would recognize its wormy taste anywhere.

'Are you telling me you found nothing?'

'There is nothing to find. The king will have received his pledge by now.' Stephen appeared

334

somehow taller, more broad-shouldered. He looked Geoffrey calmly in the eye. 'If you do not believe me, send someone else to do your spying for you. In fact, I resign from this duty. I am not going back.'

Geoffrey was stupefied. He gaped at his son, who now was shifting from foot to foot, wearing an expression of open resistance.

'You coward. You are not up to it, are you?'

Stephen stepped forward, his hands clenched into white fists by his sides. 'I am no coward, Father. I have put myself at risk every day for you and your cock-eyed notion, and there is not even a whiff of any sort of plot.' He stuck his chin out. 'Face it, Father, you were wrong. And whatever Richard Wheeler did to thee in the past, it is surely time to let it go and move on.'

And with this astonishing speech, he turned on his heel and stalked off. Geoffrey leaned back in his chair and rubbed distractedly at his forehead with the ends of his cravat. His son seemed to be swinging out of his control. Could it be that Stephen had turned tide and gone over to the Quakers? No, it could not be possible. But he had used that abominable 'thee'; he had heard it plain as plain. His stomach sank. He imagined the look on Lord Esham's face if he was to tell him Stephen was a Quaker sympathizer. Lord Esham had that week sent a missive to enquire about this very matter, and Geoffrey did not want to tell Esham he had made a mistake. No, Stephen must be wrong; Wheeler had always been a soldier. And worse, there was an unsettling feeling creeping round Geoffrey's chest, a dread like a pall of smoke. His son had talked of Wheeler as though he admired him.

Geoffrey stayed there a long while, brooding, the resentment rising in him like floodwater. As he stared at the cold fireplace a draught blew down the chimney, lifted the papers on the side table and blew ash from the pipe tray onto his knees. When Patterson arrived and brought him an urgent message from Rawlinson, he leapt up, scattering flakes of ash, then strode purposefully through the empty, silent house, his boot heels ringing on the flagstones, slashing his whalebone riding crop through the air. His mouth was set in a thin line of determination. The time had come to assemble some men.

While Stephen was arguing with his father, Richard had arrived home to find quite another problem awaiting him. Richard had spent the journey home from the gaol pondering Alice Ibbetson's plight, resolving to visit her husband forthwith to find out who was to defend her at trial and to volunteer himself as a witness to good character. He would ask the Quakers to treat her as one of their own since she had been so good to Hannah. But when he turned into his lane, it was to find a small group of agitated men waiting for him: Ned Armitage from the mill, Benjamin and Joseph Taylor the ploughmen, and Isaac Fuller, the town clerk.

'Word's out that Fisk's men are to collect the tithe stored in the barn this night,' said Ned.

'My cousin's one of Justice Rawlinson's men,' said Isaac. 'Sir Geoffrey Fisk sent word to him – he is gathering a small army together. They are going to take the tithe goods from the barns to Fisk Manor. They will do it by force if necessary, and will not let anyone prevent them – first on Rawlinson's estate, then Kendall's, then Fisk's.'

'What dost thou think, Richard?' asked Isaac.

They looked to Richard for reassurance. He dismounted quickly and bade them come into the house. They sat round the table, hats on their knees.

'They were to take us by surprise and have the goods away before we had time to make a stand, but now word's out, should we gather our men?' Benjamin scanned the nervous faces around the table.

'Well, if we do, it is to be peaceable,' said Richard.

'We cannot win,' said Benjamin.

'No,' agreed his brother, 'they will take it all by force, and there's not a ram's chance of stopping them.'

'It is not a case of winning,' said Isaac. 'It is about witnessing for fairness and right. If we only fought when we could win, what sort of men are we then?'

'I hear what thou sayest,' said Richard.

Isaac looked at the perturbed faces and said, 'Are we all agreed that we won't bow to a hollow church? Won't give our tithe to pad rich men's pockets?'

'And won't let them tell us God only speaks through priests and parsons?' added Benjamin.

'Aye,' said Ned. 'The Lord speaks to me every little way, through the barleyfield, and the white clouds, and the way the grain falls sweet from the

337

husk.' His face was red, his cheeks glowing. 'And I need no one to make the peace between the Lord and me, save my own prayers.'

Benjamin and Joseph nodded. 'D'ye know we gave our best fleeces to be given away, yet our wives have no wool to make gloves for the winter.'

Richard nodded. 'What sayest Dorothy to this?'

Isaac said, 'I sent a lad to ride out to tell her, but no word back yet, and he is to ride over to Kendall's place and Rawlinson's. I fear the message is too late for those barns. But there will be time in Netherbarrow.'

'Can we not empty the barns, take back what is ours?' asked Ned.

'The barns are locked and chained and only Fisk's overseer has a key,' said Isaac. 'We cannot break in. That would be against God's law, to steal from another man.'

'But it is not stealing, for it is our own by rights and we are only recovering what has been stolen from us,' said Ned.

They fell silent again, measuring the ideas in their minds. At last, Richard spoke.

'That is a thorny question. But we can make a stand at least. Let us pull together, gather anyone who has goods in tithe which are stored in the barn. We will surround it peaceably and they will have to move us before they can move the stuffs out. They will no doubt take the goods, but there is no need for it to be easy, and we shall stand shoulder to shoulder for the cause.'

Richard's words roused them from their seats.

'I'll go tell them at Meadow Farm,' said Ned.

'And I'll to the tannery,' said Joseph. 'We will

meet you there directly.'

'Aye,' said Richard. 'It is a pity Sam could not be here – I left him a while back at the crossroads. We'll not catch him now. I know he would have wanted to make a stand alongside us.'

'Thou hast taken a shine to that lad,' said Isaac.

'I can send my Elizabeth to ride out to Burton for him,' said Benjamin. 'Happen he will get here in time to stand by us after all. We will need a good many for our purpose – and there is more safety in numbers.'

'Remember,' said Richard. 'No weapons. Things can happen in the heat of the moment and we have all forsworn that path.'

'As thou sayest,' said Ned, ducking under the lintel and raising his hand in farewell.

'Let us ride down together,' said Isaac to Richard. 'We can call at the Brewers' on the way.' Richard followed him out; he would make a late call on Thomas Ibbetson directly after their peaceful protest.

Chapter 28

Stephen dressed himself for dinner in his accustomed blue silk suit, tabby waistcoat and white silk hose, and added the powdered wig that made his scalp hot and his forehead itch. How his father stood it, with his condition, he could not imagine. He eyed the rumpled moleskin suit, lying where he had left it on the bed, with regret. He would not

339

be putting these clothes on again, and he felt an unexpected pang at the thought. Over the past week he had turned it over and over in his mind until he had finally come to a decision. He reached over and stroked the soft animal-like material of the breeches, where they were worn at the knees from the saddle, then picked them up in his arms and held them a moment before releasing them back to the embroidered coverlet.

He had stood up to his father for the first time in his life, and he still could not quite believe it. In fact it was not he, Stephen Fisk, as he was reflected now in the glass – with the gold lace cuffs and beribboned wig – who had stood up to his father. It was Sam Fielding, the Quaker, who had stood up boldly and spoken his truth. When his father had asked him if he was a coward, it was Sam who had answered. Stephen would never have dared to stand up for himself. He was elated, but knew this could only be short-lived. He had seen his father's mouth set into a hard line when he addressed him as 'thee' and knew recriminations would be coming.

In these clothes he did not feel so confident. They made him feel like a lapdog, fit only to be by the fireside. They made him walk differently, like a fop, and he had to be careful not to trip over his heels. In Sam's clothes he had the freedom to run and ride like a gale; he felt upright and open like a man should.

He would not return to spy on the Quakers. They deserved better from someone they had welcomed as a friend. He would miss Richard Wheeler, and would never be able to explain to

340

him his sudden absence from the meetings, or how much he had valued his company, but it was better this way, for he could not go on with this double life forever. Sooner or later someone would find out and the pigeons would fly.

When he went down for dinner, it was to find himself alone in the dining room. The long table was set for two but there was no sign of his father. Two trenchers were laid out side by side next to the bowls of vegetables, the meat, the bread and salt crock, but they were untouched.

As he was alone, he repeated the grace he had said at Richard's house, and this small act of rebelliousness brought a smile to his lips. He expected the long, half-stooped figure of his father to appear any moment, but the house was still, barely a creak of a floorboard. Eventually he rang the bell. After the fourth attempt to summon him, Patterson entered, frostily, with a foot barely inside the door.

'Have you seen my father?' asked Stephen. 'He has not dined yet and the meal is growing cold.'

'He had to go out. Rawlinson sent for him. To the tithe barns.'

'Without his dinner?'

'He said to leave it out alongside yourn.'

'Did he say when he would be back?'

'No.' Patterson swept up Stephen's empty plate with distaste. 'Maybe soon. But I guess there's trouble. He rode out earlier with a great army of folk, and they say the Quakers are guarding the barns.'

Stephen was already up. 'When?'

'Maybe an hour ago by the glass, but you'll not catch them now, not on your old nag–'

341

But Stephen was already halfway down the front steps, despite his clothes. He hurled his wig off as he went, caring not that it fell into the wet. He took a rapier from the weapon rack in the yard and shoved it into his belt. No matter what Patterson's opinion of his horse, he needed something reliable. The horse remained placid as he threw on the saddle and bridle and struggled into the saddle in his too-tight breeches. He kicked the horse on with such ferocity that she sprang forward almost unseating him.

He cursed his father. To deliberately leave him there, eating mutton at home, when there was a skirmish down at the tithe barn. He had been kept out of the way on purpose. His belly lurched at the thought that there was going to be trouble between Richard and his father. Whatever was going to happen, he needed to be there. He thought of the white scar on Richard's chest. He would not wait idly at home.

The track to the tied cottages was narrow and the hawthorn hedges ripped at his thighs, but he could hear men shouting even over his hoofbeats. The sky was dark and a distant rumble of thunder warned of an approaching storm. The clouds massed dark grey above. Over the hedge he saw a bank of sand-coloured smoke drift into the air to join the rolling cloud – too dense for chimney-smoke, not nearly black enough for stubble-burning. He urged the horse faster. As he rounded the corner he saw what appeared to be a corn dray and a haycart, now well alight, and the silhouettes of a confused group of men on horseback surrounding them.

A shadow of a man bolted out of the back of the barn and started to run across the field, a man with an unsteady gait, half bent over, struggling to run uphill, but one of the riders must have spotted him and a single musket-shot rattled the air. The man seemed to hang in mid-air, then fell where he was and lay still. Stephen dug his heels into his horse's ribs, urging it on. A sense of dread engulfed him.

Another group of riders was approaching from the north side; he could hear the clatter of hooves and wheels. It must be the constable and his men from the garrison – he could see their gun-belt buckles and the glint of their sword hilts – and there could be no mistake as the carriage lamps lit up the distinctive black box-carriage with its barred windows that trundled behind.

He spotted his father on horseback near the burning wagons and galloped over to him through the wafting smoke.

'What's to do, Father?' he said, breathlessly.

Geoffrey looked him up and down as if he were a farmhand and he was assessing his fitness for work.

'We caught the Quakers emptying the tithe barn,' he said, 'telling everyone to take back their dues. When we tried to stop them they torched the wagons. We have driven them back inside.' He pointed at a group of men gathered round the black mouth of the barn. 'Rawlinson's over there keeping them secure. But the constable's here now, so there should be little need for you.'

'One of them ran out the back, Father, and was shot down.'

'He was trying to make a run for it,' he answered curtly. 'Resisting arrest.'

'But–'

'He can serve as an example – perhaps now the rest will stay inside.'

He left Stephen and cantered over to Constable Woolley. Stephen could see him gesticulating, moving some men forward towards the entrance to the barn, whilst others were sent around the back. Stephen rode forward to the front of the barn, peering through the darkness, looking for Richard. He waited just behind one of Rawlinson's men. Rawlinson recognized him and nodded to him over his shoulder.

'None of them will see their houses again, I'll warrant. Your father won't have dissenters on his land,' he said.

'Come forth, and give yourselves up,' his father shouted from his horse.

The barn remained silent and dark. He repeated his command, but when nothing resulted, he drew the men together to discuss what to do next.

'Send in the constable's men,' said Rawlinson.

'I do not think any of us should go in there, it smells like a trap. They will be armed.'

'They will not be armed, Father, they have taken an oath not to fight,' called Stephen.

His father looked back at him as if he were something unpleasant. His mouth twitched.

'How much hay is left in the barn?' Ignoring Stephen, he turned to his overseer.

'A fair amount, say a half-acre.'

'Then we will give them a taste of their own smoke.'

He cantered over to a group of horsemen and ordered them to dismount. They dragged the smoking dray over and hastily pitch-forked the flaming sacks through the open door. Anything left still burning from the two wagons was thrust inside. The quiet erupted into men's shouts and women's cries. Two village women came running to the door but Stephen saw his father nod to Rawlinson, who raised his musket to his well-padded shoulder and let loose a shot at their feet. They let out a piercing cry and jumped back, eyes and mouths wide with shock.

'Close the doors and bar them,' shouted his father from his horse, 'they'll soon be begging to come out.' At this more people surged forwards towards the door, but the men were ready and leaned against it inching it closed. Several of the constable's men dismounted to lend their shoulders to push. The big wooden door finally creaked shut.

'Quick! Get the bar on!'

It took two men to heave the heavy wooden bar into place, and the door was still vibrating with the hammering of fists when they moved away. A curl of smoke crept from under the door and the door stopped shaking. It was followed straight-away by the noise of banging on the back door, followed by screams of panic as the realization that they were locked in began to bite home. A man's voice was shouting over the wailing.

'Use your coats! Beat it out with your coats!' It was Richard yelling instructions, but there was so much coughing and shouting that his voice was almost drowned out. Smoke was beginning to seep

345

from the slit windows at the side of the barn as the flames took hold of the dry chaff and straw within.

Stephen drew his horse up alongside his father. Even from this distance the fumes were acrid in his nostrils. 'Enough,' said Stephen. 'That's enough. Let them free.'

'A little longer. They need to learn their lesson once for all.'

The heat of the fire was now rippling the air, the smoke pouring like waterfalls from under the rafters. The door began to rattle violently and the noise of shouting and coughing grew louder.

Stephen jumped down from his horse and raced towards the men by the door.

'It is enough! Open the door,' he shouted, and the constable's men began to move towards the barn.

'No,' came a familiar voice. 'Not yet.'

The constable's men retreated uncertainly, awaiting Geoffrey's orders. The hammering and shouting in the barn suddenly ceased. Flames were visible licking from the slot windows and the cracks in the roof tiles were lit up orange. Good God in Heaven, thought Stephen, they would burn alive.

Stephen grabbed one of the constable's men by the arm.

'Come on! Before we are too late!' This seemed to break the spell. The constable's men came to their senses and ran forward to help open the door. The heat had swollen the wood and it would not give. There was not a sound from within. They jerked and heaved, muscling underneath with their shoulders to lift the bar.

346

'Push!' shouted Stephen.

It slid awkwardly out from its housing and they wrenched it away. They hauled the doors open. A blast of hot air buffeted them and they were blown back, shielding their faces.

The fire blazed up the walls, but it was pale behind the wall of heavy smoke. Not a man inside was left standing, they were all lying face down, their clothes the same colour as the smoke, all crowded close together in the centre of the barn. There were women there, and children too. At the sight of the children, Stephen found his throat constricted.

He turned to the constable and wordlessly shook his head. The constable dropped his eyes and looked discomfited. Stephen covered his face with his arm and took a deep breath, then waded in through the smoke. When he reached the first body, a woman, he grasped her by the shoulder and turned her over. Astonishingly, she began to cough, her chest racked by gulping at the air. He half lifted her and she struggled like a new-born colt to stand upright. As she did so, all the rest of the bodies began to rise, to quiver and shake with coughing. It was like a scene from judgement day as one by one they stood and, arms around each other, made for the door into the sweet night air.

The fire was still burning fiercely up the walls, but they must have cleared a well in the centre and huddled together there. They lay close to the ground with rags wrapped around their faces where there was still air to breathe. Stephen's eyes smarted and his throat burnt. All around him people coughed and choked and half carried each other out of the door. He helped a woman with terrified eyes drag her small boy outside, and recognized her as one of the women from the meetings at the Hall.

About twenty people emerged from the barn, most bent double or crawling, without their coats and racked with coughs. Once outside, they took in great lungfuls of air; they were almost indistinguishable in the dark because they were black with smoke; some nursed burns where they had tried to put out the fire with their bare hands.

When he turned to go back in, Richard appeared from the haze. He would recognize him anywhere, even though he had a kerchief tied around his nose. He was walking slowly with an old man leaning up against him. He recognized Old Ned Armitage, John's father, from the flour mill.

'Sam, my friend,' Richard said, his voice cracked with smoke, 'thou art here after all. I am glad to see thee.' He clapped Stephen on the shoulder. 'Canst thou find this man some water?'

'I'll try,' he said. 'Richard, the constable's men—'

'The water first, Sam – time for the rest later.'

Stephen remembered his horse, where he kept a flagon of water in the saddlebag.

'Stephen.' His father's voice was loud and imperious. He turned to look guiltily over his shoulder where his father was picking his way down the slope on his fine-boned horse.

He turned to face him. 'Come away now, Stephen,' said his father. 'If you want our land to prosper there is no place for soft hearts.' His father pointed to the crowd of gagging and retching people. 'They are lawbreakers, they would

348

steal what is rightfully ours.'

'Sam?' Richard said, looking direct into his face with his steady brown eyes. Stephen flinched as though he had been struck; he looked down at the ground.

'Stephen. Go on home. We do not need your help, now. Tell Patterson to have something ready for me – these looters have made me miss my dinner,' his father said.

'Sam?' asked Richard again. 'Elizabeth told me she could find no Sam Fielding in Burton. Tell me this is not so.' His voice was tight. Stephen dragged his eyes from the ground and looked up at him in mute appeal.

'I can see he had you fooled.' His father laughed, but it was mirthless. 'This is my son, Stephen.' He looked at Richard contemptuously. 'And you would do well to remember it. He will be squire here after me.'

Then he turned to Stephen and said, 'Tithes will be paid here, as is the law of the land. And there has clearly been wilful damage to my property.'

Stephen wished the ground would swallow him up. Richard stared at him in disbelief before he turned away to go over to the other Quakers.

Rawlinson arrived then, with his men.

'Never fear, Geoffrey, they will be taken to gaol until they can be brought to trial for these offences,' Rawlinson said. He rode over to the Quaker group and dismounted, shouting for the constable. 'Bind them.'

The group of men and women did not move but let themselves be bound or chained.

'Do we have to take them too?' asked one of the

349

constable's men, seeing Rawlinson roughly dragging a little boy to his feet.

'The children too,' said Stephen's father. 'It is better they learn early. Besides, I do not want orphan children begging at my door.'

'There are too many to take in one wagon,' said Rawlinson. 'What shall we do?'

'Take this man first,' said Geoffrey pointing at Richard, who was still propping up John Armitage. 'My son tells me he is the man who planned this little rebellion.'

Richard's eyes travelled over Stephen's blue breeches, hardly stained with smoke, his fine gold lace cuffs, his heeled shoes with silver buckles, unmarked by mud. A look of disgust crept over his face.

'I took thee for an honest man.' Richard's words were charged; they cut through the air like a bolt of lightning, straight into Stephen's heart. 'But thou hast betrayed me. Betrayed us all. Half killed us for a few sacks of corn.' He nodded at the rapier hung at Stephen's side before saying scathingly, 'I see thou art truly thy father's son.'

Stephen looked away.

'Stephen,' his father said, 'your horse is wandering loose up there. Go fetch it down before it breaks a leg in its reins.'

'Wait,' said Richard. 'Hast thou seen Isaac? He ran out the back before the doors were closed. We heard a shot. Hast thou news of him?'

Stephen swallowed. He could not speak. His eyes were full of tears.

Richard's eyes darkened and his face turned stony.

'Son, your horse.'

Stephen ignored his father. 'I would not harm thee,' he said to Richard, and it was Sam blurting out his words. 'I am not who you think I am,' he said miserably, trying to explain but knowing it to be hopeless.

Richard threw him a look of contempt. 'Get thee out of my sight.'

Stephen turned away and walked quickly up the hill. He heard his father's voice shouting his name but he ignored it. His name no longer felt like it belonged to him. When he looked back it was to see Richard jostled into the carriage along with Ned Armitage and the Taylor brothers, the tallest and strongest-looking men of the group. By the time Stephen was astride his horse, the prison cart had set off down the track and the fire in the barn was reduced to a glimmer. The smell of smouldering straw filled the air, bitter like a draught of aloes.

Stephen turned the nose of his horse upwind and opened the gate to the top field. He rode slowly, searching the ground, until he saw the slumped figure lying motionless on the ground. Even before he dismounted and turned him over, Stephen knew who he was – he knew the round horn buttons on the tweed coat very well, for he had noticed one was missing, the buttonhole empty, at last Sunday's meeting. He knew the brown twill breeches and the old-fashioned boots polished to a high sheen.

Isaac was already stiff, and his face was set in an expression of surprise. His eyeglasses were missing and it made him look younger. Or perhaps it was just that his wrinkles were gone now, his face smooth, as if his cares had melted away. A wound in his neck had drained his face of blood so that he was white as the moon which hung above – a lopsided quarter moon.

Stephen sat down next to the still figure, wondering where all the words, all the stories, all that life had flown to. He recalled Isaac inviting him to his very first meeting at the Hall, and his familiar drone as he talked at the daily meetings. Isaac always brought news of other Friends, characters like Naylor, the heretic, news of Fox's trial and how the followers in the south stood up for him in court, tales of bold Quaker women preaching in far-flung places of the globe. This man had gathered them all together and brought them into the chilly meeting room, breathed flesh into them with his speech, so that Stephen and all the others saw their pictures, vivid and life-like, felt for them as if they truly were their brothers and sisters.

Now Isaac was dried up, cut off from his source. Stephen knelt next to him and prayed. His tears continued to seep out, but whether from smoke or emotion he could not say. He prayed for Isaac's soul to be delivered unto heaven, but he prayed for himself too, for he felt it was his fault Isaac was lying there, all breath stopped. True, he had not fired the shot, but he had told his father that the Quakers intended to hold the barns, and precipitated this tragedy.

Isaac meant no one any harm; he had likely been unarmed, peaceable, standing up for his beliefs, and perhaps he would have negotiated if he had been given the chance, been given the chance to talk. For that was what he did best. What had made him run like that, this old man, with his bandy legs and back bowed from penning ledgers?

'You silly old fool,' Stephen whispered, but his words were full of affection.

Stephen closed the waistcoat over Isaac's chest, fastened the five remaining buttons, laid him out as straight as he could. As he did so, the only noise was the sound of the horse pulling on the grass and chewing contentedly, unconcerned. Its placid munching made Stephen feel suddenly that all the ills of the world were brought about by him and men like him. Richard's face loomed in his mind, full of confusion, looking to him, Sam. But Sam did not exist. He had only ever been make-believe. He must reconcile himself to being Stephen Fisk. That was the truth of it. Richard's words echoed in his head. 'Truly thy father's son.' He saw again the look of utter revulsion on Richard's face when he realized who he was. Stephen let out a great howl of pain, like a wounded dog.

Chapter 29

Alice held Hannah close as she read from the small tract. The candle Richard had brought burnt steadily, standing on a ledge formed by an ill-shaped stone that jutted out from the damp wall behind them. It cast a faint yellow glow in the hitherto greenish dark. This illumination had been both a joy and a horror, as with increased light they were able to perceive the full squalor of their surroundings.

Hannah's wound was terrible to see, her face a ruin of blood and bone. Hannah had so far not dared to explore it with her fingers – and Alice had forbidden her to do so, warning her the dirt on her fingers might cause the wound to fester. But the real reason was she feared that if Hannah should know the true extent of her injuries, she would lose all hope. Already the fever came and went; some nights Hannah was wet with perspiration and delirious, fighting invisible demons of fire, or calling out raggedly for the Angel Michael and his flaming sword to dispatch her into the next world.

In the small flickering light Alice saw with repugnance the ticks on their clothing, the beetles that crept from their midden, the scattered rat droppings and the mould. When Richard Wheeler had brought them a meal it had hurt their stomachs, so hungry were they, and they struggled to keep it down. But both women were as pleased with the other gifts as with the sustenance. Striking the flint was such a familiar ritual that when Alice first heard the ring of it, it made her feel human again, and aroused in her a renewed sense of dignity.

The light, small though it was, was cheering.

''Tis a sign of the Spirit,' said Hannah.

This simple light set Hannah straight away to murmur prayers, then later to a rapt contemplation. She listened intently where she lay, one hand clasped tightly to the other where it poked out of the makeshift sling. On occasions Alice feared she was dead, for when she prayed she

354

entered a stillness so attentive she appeared to have been sculpted from marble, as though a word from the Almighty might strike her, even through these impenetrable walls, at any moment.

When Alice had first picked up the tract and fingered the embossed cover, the frontispiece announced it to be *A Compendium of Repentance;* the subtitle was 'A short description of the Key which opens the *Divine Mysteries,* and leadeth to the *Knowledge* of them'. Alice was indignant when she read the title.

'Does he intend to lecture me even now?' she said to Hannah, and put it down to take up the more familiar Bible.

'Oh please read it to me, Alice. I have no book-learning, and Richard must have thought it would speak to us.'

'If you're sure then. I want hope, not the fear of hell and brimstone.' She began to read it aloud.

The chapbook said that 'the in-spoken word of grace draws all, even the most ungodly, if he be not altogether a thistle'. Alice took hope from the words, 'even the most ungodly'.

However, no comfort was to be had from the parson's visit. It was brief and he looked as though he was there under sufferance. A pale, slight man who looked to be shrinking inside his clothes, he outlined the facts of the case to Alice with an air of impatience. He told Alice that Sir Geoffrey Fisk was to give evidence at the trial, but that he did not wish to visit her where she was confined. Her husband would be present too, but probably would not be called as a witness as his evidence could not be relied upon. He also stated that she had a poor prospect of being released and she would likely hang.

This gloomy news was imparted with no trace of emotion. He was dubious when she had protested her innocence and advised her to set herself to repent. She was told to kneel whilst he said a perfunctory prayer asking God to drive out evil from her heart, to which Alice replied a frustrated 'Amen'.

But he had refused to pray with Hannah, or to fetch a bone-setter or herbs for her condition. His view was that Hannah had already given her soul over to Satan, and so was not worth even prayers.

'How can he call himself a man of God?' Alice was incredulous. 'He who lacks all human charity?'

Alice was so angry she picked up the tin plate that had lain dry and empty for more days than they could count and threw it at the door. It clattered to the ground, barely dinted, and the noise was thin, muffled by the thick walls. She began to kick at the door, thudding over and over with her boot.

'Please stop,' said Hannah.

Alice aimed another vicious kick at the door, before propping herself up against the wall. 'But, Hannah, you heard him. I am condemned before I even have a chance to say a word.'

'Thou wilt have thy chance at the trial. Have faith,' came the weak reply.

'God must have deserted me. Why else would I be here?'

'God never turns away one who truly wants to

know him.'

Alice sighed. She did not share Hannah's trust.

'Richard said he will find a way; he will rally my friends and they will help us,' said Hannah. 'He is a man of his word.'

'Why should any of them help me? They do not know me.' She paused. 'And, Hannah, I have not been honest with Mr Wheeler, and he knows very well I have lied to him. Why should he attend to me now?'

'He will help thee, because thou art my friend, and because I will tell the Friends thou hast a good heart.'

'Oh, Hannah. If only.'

But there was really no choice. Lacking all other friendship, she would have to put her trust in Richard Wheeler – if anyone was an instrument of God, then perhaps it was he. Hannah had explained about Richard's conversion – that he had voluntarily given up his land and his house to pursue a life of honesty and peace, an action Alice found extremely difficult to comprehend.

She still missed her large childhood house, her fine things; all lost in the war, vanished in a roar of smoke and flame, an idyll torn from her by Cromwell's men, the very ground on which she stood. She envied Richard Wheeler the choice; at least he had that, whereas she had simply been displaced along with anyone else who opposed the Puritan way.

Alice began to pray, not the way she was wont to pray before, but in Hannah's way. She opened out her heart, listened with all her might for an answer, still and sober, as if her life depended upon it, which, she thought grimly, it probably did. No answer came, but in her mind's eye she saw the lady's slipper, where she had originally seen it, innocent then, the flower head quivering slightly as she felt the touch of the breeze on her face. As if indelibly printed in her thoughts, she saw again the pale blue sky, the vivid green of the grasses, and recalled Wheeler's smiling face as he heard her first exclamation of delight. The flower had remained always the same, she realized, it was she who changed, her own thoughts and moods that shifted, rolling in and dispersing like clouds. All flowers were like this, she thought. Preserving a lost innocence, outside man-made time, the flower of a thousand years ago repeating itself over and over to every generation, reminding the world of nature's order.

Whilst the candle wavered over her silent kneeling form, she remembered how she had felt when she had first taken the orchid secretly from her basket in the dark summerhouse, how it already seemed to be diminished away from its natural habitat. If she had listened more carefully to herself, she would have realized then that her world was dying. Her first action had set in train a series of unstoppable events, so that now the flower was likely to die of drought; there would be no more lady's slippers, and she alone was responsible.

She considered how her talent, her enthusiasm for painting, her desire to control and perfect nature had somehow come to turn into its opposite. Perhaps this was the way of the world – that an innocuous desire can become a lust by only a small sleight of hand.

She picked up the Bible, peeled open a page at random and began to read.

No man can serve two masters.

The familiar words of St Matthew. When she came to the verses, *Consider the lilies of the field, how they grow; they toil not, neither do they spin,* a salt tear trickled down onto the page. Something began to soften and let go inside her, something that had been frozen a long time. She must be at peace, there was nothing else left for her to do. Her tears were not her usual noisy, dramatic outburst, but a thing of beauty, a mixture of pain and pleasure.

Later, she read the verses again out loud to Hannah, whilst they had light, for the candle was guttering and they must save the others for the morrow.

Hannah murmured, ''Tis good to hear thee read.'

Alice continued: *'Take no thought for the morrow: for the morrow shall take thought for the things of itself.'*

Chapter 30

'Beg pardon.' Ella elbowed her way roughly to the front of the crowd where she could get a better view of the passing procession. Today was the day of the quarter assizes and most of Lancaster had turned out to watch, so there was not much room on the narrow streets. Ella wanted to position herself on the hill leading to the castle, where she would be able to see the cavalcade wend its way up. This was always the slowest section of the route as several of the men were very elderly and the whole cavalcade had to pause whilst they caught their breath. But this was the best vantage point to get a look at them, so it was popular.

A tall woman in a voluminous shawl tried to block her with her shoulder, reluctant to lose her front-row place, but Ella pulled a face at her and wormed her way past. She felt herself to be a cut above, now that she was dressed in a warm woollen dress befitting her new position as housekeeper to Thomas Ibbetson. She had cajoled and pressed him about a new dress as soon as she had started to live in. She withheld her attentions until he gave way, though she had decided to go to the seamstress herself – he would have had her in some dark, unbecoming servant's colour.

She looked down at the fine lawn chemise jutting out over her bosom, and at the full warm skirts of a bluish-grey, like the blue of the Welsh slate on the church roof. She was sure Thomas had meant her to have a grey like a wet Maundy Monday, but when he saw her in her new dress it was not on her shoulders long enough for him to disapprove. She smoothed her hands down the bodice and assumed an air of superiority, glaring up at the lofty woman whom she had forced to shuffle aside.

The town bells pealed out, the eight-note toll repeating over and over, signalling the arrival of the sheriff's party, with all the judges and dignitaries arrayed in their scarlet robes and full-bottomed wigs. Amongst the parade Ella was quick to spot Justice Rawlinson, his paunch almost bursting out of his robes, and pug-nosed Constable Woolley from her home town of Netherbarrow. Following the office-bearers was the Commission of the Peace – made up of the local gentry, who strutted past in all their finery, feathered hats perched on their heads despite the drizzle, pastel-coloured embroidered vests making a bright splash beneath their top-coats.

Ella craned her neck and saw Sir Geoffrey Fisk approaching, with his friends Sir John Fairfax and Lord Kendall, poor old soul, who kept halting and leaning on his stick, causing those behind to almost trip over him. They paused right in front of her and she managed to catch Sir Geoffrey's eye and throw him what she hoped was a winning smile. Sir Geoffrey ignored her. He turned his eyes sharply away and chivvied Lord Kendall into movement by grasping him firmly by the arm and propelling him forward – quicker than he would have liked, judging by his protestations – up the hill.

Ella knew she had been snubbed but she did not care. She turned away, picking up her skirts, thinking to hurry up the hill and try to catch sight of them further up. As she squeezed past the tall woman she came face to face with Tom and Audrey Cobbald.

'Thought it was you,' said Audrey. 'You might have let us in.'

'They have moved on up,' said Ella, noticing for the first time how down-at-heel the pair looked.

'Best place now will be near the gates but we will be lucky to find a perch.'

'Woolley was round yesterday, asking us about what we saw on the night of the cuckolding,' said Tom. 'But we kept mum about what we were up to. Told him we were out celebrating a birthday. All of us have done the same. None of us want to be branded as trouble.'

'What else did you tell him?'

'The truth – that we saw Mistress Ibbetson bending over the body with a knife, clear as I see you now.'

Audrey nodded. 'He asked us if we were sure of it, given that it were dark. But I told him we saw her face plain, and that she had run off away from us like a dog with its tail between its legs.' Her face held a kind of appeal.

Ella reassured her. 'Just the same as we all did.' She was satisfied; she was even beginning to believe she really had seen the body of an old woman in that ditch. After she had claimed to see it, six more of the villagers, including Audrey and Tom, had unaccountably confirmed they too had seen the mistress bending over the body.

'They are to call us as witnesses,' said Audrey, looking proud at the prospect.

'What about him?' asked Tom.

'Who?' said Ella.

'The master. Is he going to stand for her?'

'No,' said Ella, shortly. 'He stands against her.'

Tom and Audrey looked at each other and shook their heads, as if this was hard to believe, then looked back to Ella for more information. She kept her mouth tight shut. For Thomas had

362

refused her in his bed, and had gone to the gaol to ask after his wife only that morning. He had returned looking haggard, saying they would not let him see her until after the trial. He had shut himself in Alice's chamber and would not admit her. But there was time yet to work on him. If he went against her, she would withdraw her attentions, and she had discovered he was a man of strong appetites. She changed the subject by motioning at Audrey and Tom to follow her up the hill.

As they trod on the heels of the jostling crowd, accompanying them to the gates, they heard the noise of raucous shouting as a great surge of angry people pressed their way up the hill, led by a huge fellow and several scrawny bird-like women. Ella and the Cobbalds were just in time to dodge out of the way as the crowd swarmed towards the gates.

'What's going on?' said Audrey.

A woman called back, 'It's Margaret Poulter's son. He's sworn to see Mistress Ibbetson hang, and her head on a stake like them others up there.'

Ella raised her eyes to the top of the ramparts, where the decomposed grisly remains swayed on their poles like lightless lanterns, a halo of flies, as yet unsated by blood, buzzing around each one.

The day after the burning of the tithe barn, Stephen woke with his eyes dry and his throat like parchment. He had arrived home late, stumbled through the dark corridors to his chambers and fallen into bed, still fully dressed, too tired to think. In the morning light he saw the sheets were tangled from his restless movement. As he sat up in his creased breeches and rumpled coat, the blankets slid to the floor in an untidy heap. In amongst them he made out the brown moleskin of his Quaker clothes, which he had left lying on the bed before he had gone down for dinner the night before.

He stood and rubbed his hand over his face. His clothes reeked of smoke. The night's events came to him in a strange rush. He sat down hard on the bed, the wind knocked out of him.

Eventually he got up, washed half-heartedly and changed into another suit of clothes. He did not feel like shaving and could not find his wig. When he went downstairs to the dining room, his eyes prickly and his limbs stiff and sore, his father was reading dispatches from the city. When he saw Stephen enter, unshaven and pale, he frowned at him blearily from over his plate.

'I am called to the assizes,' his father said, 'but there is much to be done here. Go to the overseer and tell him to get the tithe barn cleared and swept. See if there is anything that can be done with those wagons or whether they are past repair.'

Stephen stared at his plate, though he did not see it. A clink as his father set down his knife, and said, 'Stephen. Put last night behind you. The troublemakers will be tried over the next few days and then sentenced.'

'What will happen to them?'

'They will be charged with treason.' Stephen looked up to see his father watching him to see his reaction. Treasonable offences were punishable by death, and they both knew it. There was a moment's pause before Geoffrey continued. 'They will get the punishments they deserve, of course.'

Stephen watched his father refill his plate with kidneys and eggs, and load his fork before taking a sloppy mouthful and wiping his lips with the corner of his napkin.

'I have decided we will sail for New England the day after tomorrow,' said his father. 'The *Fair Louise* was bound for the plantations anyway on a trade passage, so it will be a fine opportunity for me to show you our land there. And it will do us both good to get away from Westmorland for a while.'

Stephen started and sat back in his chair. 'What's this? Are you telling me I am to sail with you?'

Geoffrey nodded, his mouth full.

'No, Father.' A flush spread over Stephen's cheeks. 'I'm not leaving. I know what you are trying to do, and it's no use.'

'You need to get to know my holdings abroad, or how will you manage them else? Of course you will come with me, we will travel out together.'

'I won't go.'

'Now, Stephen, don't be so damned awkward. It is all arranged.'

'Then unarrange it. I'm serious, Father. I am not leaving Westmorland.'

His father wiped his hands on his napkin before speaking. His lips were tight. Two red spots of anger flared in his cheeks. 'In that case we will see how useful you are on the estate. I will tell the overseer you will give the orders this morning for the clearing of the tithe barn. And you will go with him to collect compensation for our losses

365

from the families of those responsible.'

'But—'

'It is high time the men saw you taking more responsibility – after all, you will be master of Fisk Manor one day and the people must learn to bend to your word, just as they do to mine.'

'No.' The word was almost a shout. 'I do not want to be like you.' His father blenched. 'Fear runs ahead of you like a snake. I want to earn their respect through fairness, not rule through terror.'

'Are you telling me the people do not respect me?'

Stephen saw the wound in his father's eyes but he pushed the knife in further.

'They laugh at you. They point behind your back, and scratch themselves and call you names. But they would not to your face because they fear your bullying ways.'

His father sat stock still a moment, then stood, swaying slightly.

Stephen went on, his voice rising. 'I do not want this mausoleum. I do not want to see people grovel and squirm wherever I go. You wanted a different son, one you never had, and you cannot force me into his mould. Why could you not see me?' He pointed to himself. 'Me, Father?'

His father simply stared, a look of incomprehension on his face. 'But you have had everything,' he began.

'Everything? Did you ever ask me what I wanted? Did you really want to know me, what sort of a person I was? No. You never have, and I don't suppose you ever will. We're finished, Father.'

Stephen strode from the room and back to his

chambers. There, he ripped off the moiré suit, the buckle shoes and the shirt with Brussels lace cuffs and picked up the brown moleskin trousers.

Once dressed, he surveyed himself in the glass. Sam Fielding looked back at him and smiled. He left the house, tacked up his faithful bay mare and put her in traces to pull the wood sled up to the top pasture.

An hour later he rode slowly into the yard at Lingfell Hall for the morning meeting. Sam dismounted and waited. Before long the small band of subdued Quakers had assembled, fewer now that many of their company were in gaol. They gathered around the sled, where Isaac lay, his face appearing peaceful in the morning sun.

Stephen listened as Dorothy said a few words. Then the company fell silent.

Stephen breathed a long sigh and let his hands fall loose by his sides. The weight that had been lodged under his ribs for as long as he could remember, that restless unease in the pit of his stomach, was suddenly gone. He rested in the silence, empty, yet full in spirit, knowing he had finally come home.

Chapter 31

It was the middle of the night when Alice was roughly dragged from the cell and fastened into a set of hand irons, which hung from a neck brace in a position that made it impossible to lower her arms to rest them without jolting her neck or wrists. She had no time to embrace Hannah or wish her well, for she was sleeping when they came, and she was stumbling half out of the door before she realized what was happening to her. But she heard Hannah's voice calling with all her strength after her, 'God be with thee, Alice,' as she was pushed down the corridor with the cold muzzle of a musket at her back.

When she was thrust out into the morning air she screwed up her eyes, blinking through the gauze of her eyelashes, for the light dazzled her after the dark of the cell, even though it was hardly dawn and the sky wet with drizzle. In the yard was an uncovered cart made up of a flat platform with high hurdles as sides. Several other bedraggled, raw-boned prisoners were already standing inside, and had probably been there some while as they were soaked with rain.

The gaoler jabbed at her from behind with the barrel of the musket when she struggled to climb into the cart, but the prisoner in front reached out his calloused hand as far as he could to haul her up. She smiled her thanks at him, for old habits die hard, and he smiled briefly back at her with a tight mouth. She guessed few of them would be smiling after the verdicts were read.

The journey to the courthouse was mercifully short. Alice kept her back straight and her eyes downcast despite the hubbub surrounding them as they passed through the busy streets. Every first-floor window seemed to house another vociferous heckler, who would emphasize his or her opinion by throwing down culch or the dregs of swill buckets down upon their heads. Her dress was filthy and the bodice hung loose in a way it had never done before. Her boots were grey with mildew; they looked like someone else's feet, not like her own at all. She resisted the temptation to look up at the harrying crowd that followed them, jeering and throwing missiles. Something hard, like a stone, cracked into her temple and she reeled, then winced, but remained nonetheless fixed, ignoring them.

Outside the courthouse, the cart rattled to a stop and Alice felt herself grabbed violently by the arm. Unbalanced she fell forward, nearly toppling over the side of the cart. A woman screamed at her, words that were coarse and unintelligible, grasped a handful of her hair and, wrapping her fingers in it, tried to jolt her out of the cart. Alice cried out and pulled away, to find herself looking into the wild-eyed face of a woman incensed by pain and hatred. For a moment she feared to be consumed by the crowd and torn limb from limb, but a group of soldiers pressed in and forcibly lugged the distraught woman away, still screaming. Alice stood shakily, heart thumping, blood racing like quicksilver in her veins, haunted by the woman's malevolent expression.

When the back hurdle was unlocked and they could descend, she looked up briefly and caught a glimpse of the assembled people. There was a man close by, his face bright with curiosity and expectancy, and filled with thinly veiled avarice. The crowd was almost as ragged and ill-fed as the prisoners. After a life of scraping and service to their superiors, most people loved to hear a death warrant; it somehow made them feel more alive. She saw the people pointing, and heard the swell of the whispers, like a wavebreak on shingle, as she raised her head. Her eyes combed the crowd desperately for Richard or any of the broad-brimmed hats of the Quakers. But there were none. Quickly she lowered her eyes again and gripped her hands tightly together to prevent tears. She had hoped to see a friendly face; her husband, a neighbour, someone who knew her well – someone who would reassure her that the nightmare was over and they were going to take her home. Home to her airy summerhouse with the jar of paint brushes stood in the sunshine and the vase of sweet-peas on the table.

'Do you promise on this holy book to tell the truth, failing naught, and that it shall be the only truth?' Justice Lackwood of London, who looked as if he should have retired long ago, held out the scuffed Bible on which she was to place her hand.

'I swear,' she said clearly, for the room was packed to bursting, so much so that the smell of unwashed linen gagged in her throat. Even the nosegays carried by the justice and the jurors could not mitigate the stench of sweat, and the air throbbed with an almost palpable air of agitation.

'You are indicted with the murder of one Margaret Alice Poulter. How do you plead?' He glanced perfunctorily in her direction. She was startled, and looked back into his fish-like eyes, watering in his yellow face.

Her own name. Margaret had her own name.

Alice took this in before replying firmly, 'Not guilty.' The room buzzed with outraged whispers.

'And also with the murders of your sister, Flora Longley, your father James Longley, your mother Anne Mary Longley, and divers people unknown?'

'Not guilty.' She was firm. How could she confess to murders of people 'unknown'? It was absurd.

She looked at the jurors, who were seated at a long table to her left. They shook their heads and leaned in to confer, their dusty, white-wigged heads close together. They were a sombrely dressed group – all old men, be-whiskered, their pursed lips working as if chewing on invisible cud.

When they asked her where she had been the night Margaret died, she told them the truth. That she had been out cutting flowers and had got back late. When asked if anyone could vouch for her, she said there was no one, except the villagers who had been out on the wagon. It sounded lame even to her own ears.

One by one the witnesses were brought. Alice watched the drama unfold as if it was a stranger they referred to and not herself at all. She could barely grasp what was being said, it was so outlandish. The first witness was Ella, who took to the stand proudly as if she was indeed a strolling player on a stage, smiling around at the packed benches and the galleries, smoothing her glossy brown hair on her shoulders. She looked different. Alice saw straightaway that she was dressed becomingly in a slate-blue dress with an improbably white chemise.

Alice's downcast eyes took in her own filthy

371

skirts and she immediately saw the contrast between them. She knew she no longer looked to be
mistress of this maid, nor of this situation. But she
was not going to be made sport of by this sow's
purse. Determinedly, she drew herself up taller,
looked at Ella straight, her eyes never moving
from her face as Ella began her testimony. If
indeed it could be called a testimony, riddled as it
was with lies and suppositions and slanderous
implications. She listened to Ella reel off a series
of accusations, which would have been pitiable
were it not for the way the jury hung on her every
word – outrageous claims, such as how she had
turned good milk sour, made ale go black, caused
women to miscarry and men to keel over and die.
How she prayed to the Devil; how she had poisoned her own sister, mixing the noxious poisons
in her summerhouse.

Eventually Ella was asked about the night
Thomas went to dinner at the Fisks'. Alice remembered the bizarre cavalcade that had passed
her in the night and heard Ella describing it as a
birthday celebration. The prosecutor asked Alice
why she had not accompanied her husband to
Fisk Manor, and she replied that she no longer
wished to dine with Sir Geoffrey because of a
disagreement. When asked what this might be, she
replied that 'it was a disagreement over business'.
The prosecutor returned to question Ella further.

'You are quite sure this is the woman you saw
wielding the knife on that night?'

'Oh yes, milord. For I know her very well. I were
her loyal maid and servant these past eighteen
month, and now I am keeping the house going as

best I can.'

Alice stared at Ella for a moment, uncomprehending. 'You? Back in my house?' She began to protest. 'I do not want you in my house.' She managed to keep her rage under a lid. 'I tell you, from this moment forth, you are dismissed from my employ.'

As Alice spoke, Ella's voice cut over hers. 'You cannot dismiss me, mistress. I don't take orders from you no more, only from the master.'

'And we all know what sort of orders they will be,' said Alice bitterly.

'Are you calling me?' Ella shouted. She turned to the justice with indignation. 'Sir, she is blackening my character.' She widened her eyes. 'Her – the woman who has poisoned a babe and cut the entrails from an old woman.'

'You vixen.' Alice lost her temper; the words flew out of her mouth before she could prevent them. She was silenced by the banging of the mallet on the table and the justice's cry.

'We will have order. Remove that witness from the stand and call the defendant's husband, Thomas Ibbetson.'

Alice turned and appealed to the justice, raising her arms in a gesture of supplication. 'Milord, it is all fabrication. I was out gathering flowers. I did see the procession pass by me, but I would never have harmed Margaret. She was my friend.'

There was a muffled reaction from the gallery, which was hastily quashed by those others who feared missing the justice's response.

'I said, hold your peace. Call Thomas Ibbetson.'

Alice heard the call go out for Thomas, a

booming voice outside. The crowd craned round behind them, anxious not to miss a glimpse of the unfolding action. Alice searched the pews for his familiar balding head. Despite their recent differences, he would surely vouch for her. His name echoed again in the corridors outside the room, until the court official returned and whispered briskly to the judge.

'Thomas Ibbetson does not appear to be here, so we will proceed without him.'

'But, sir, surely I have the right...' Alice pleaded that she wanted her husband present, but at the same time there was a commotion in the stalls at the front where Ella was still being escorted to her seat.

'He will be here, sir. Give him a little more time,' shouted Ella, standing up and calling out despite the two people either side attempting to restrain her. 'He said he would be here.' Her voice tailed off. 'He was to say that–' The crack of the justice's mallet silenced them both. He pointed to Ella.

'If you disturb us once more you will be put below in a cell. Hold your tongue.' He turned to the jury. 'If Ibbetson cannot grace us with his presence at his own wife's trial, then we will proceed with the next witness. Constable Woolley, please take the oath.'

When Woolley had been sworn in, Alice saw the clerk bring an object wrapped in a piece of black cloth to the jury's table and place it before them.

'This is the knife you found at the defendant's house, is it not?' asked the prosecutor.

'Yes, sir, there were three of us present when we found it – concealed in the back of a drawer in

Mistress Ibbetson's summerhouse. You can see the blood on it right enough.'

The clerk unwrapped the object and Alice caught a glimpse of a large hunting knife with a curved blade and a bone handle. She had never set eyes on it in her life. The members of the jury passed it along the table, most holding it at arm's length with distaste, and then it returned to the clerk.

'Hold it aloft,' said the justice. There was a gasp from the crowd at the size of the blade.

'Lord have mercy.' A woman's quavering voice rose above the uproar. 'It is a gutting knife. You killed my sister with this? Like an animal?' A large man was holding onto her arm, trying to quiet her. 'Shush, Hetty. Let them get on with it. She will hang soon enough.' Alice recognized the tortured eyes of the woman who had tried to drag her out of the cart.

Alice stammered, 'But how did it come to be in–?'

'Be silent,' cut in the prosecutor. 'Three people will attest that they found this in a drawer in your summerhouse. A building for which you, and you alone, have the key. How do you account for that?'

'I have no idea, perhaps one of them put it there.'

The justice laughed. The whole room took his cue and erupted in guffaws.

'Are we to believe that Justice Rawlinson, Constable Woolley and the eminent Sir Geoffrey Fisk would conspire to pervert the course of justice? Is not the more likely explanation that you hid the

375

accursed object yourself?'

Alice was unable to answer, and was forced to swallow the unpalatable fact that her guilt was a foregone conclusion. She watched with a sinking heart as one by one the villagers gave their testimony. She found it impossible to believe that the safe haven she had lived in for so many years had turned tail and become another place completely, where all those she had known and loved were ready to turn traitor.

She endured the testimonies, as one by one they corroded any remaining dignity and redrew her as a different woman. Every ill in the village was somehow attributed to her, from breech-birth lambs to chimney fires. It seems she never passed anyone by without some disaster should befall them, as barley makes malt. She was an evil influence. This from Sir Geoffrey Fisk. Surely a man of his intelligence would refuse to believe these outrageous claims?

He took the oath impatiently, as though he could not wait to get it over, rushing through the affidavit in stuttering haste. He appeared uncomfortable on the witness stand but answered all the questions briefly. It appeared he had been called upon to witness to her character, and she found herself horrified by the picture he painted.

'Yes, she went into a decline after her sister's death.'

'As one who knew her well, do you think—'

'Oh, I did not know her too well, she is a difficult woman,' interjected Geoffrey.

'Is it likely then,' went on the prosecutor, 'that she was suffering from grief, in your opinion, or could it have been remorse or guilt?'

'Well, it is difficult to say. But she kept painting portraits of the dead child, as if she would make amends and bring her back to life.'

Whispers ran round the gallery.

'May I ask what your relationship was to Mistress Ibbetson?'

'She painted wild flowers for my clients on commission.'

'And you had a cordial relationship?'

'Not of late. Mistress Ibbetson's work had become somewhat unpopular. She became erratic, subject to moods and vapours. The quality had gone from her work.'

Here Alice protested, but was warned by the judge to keep quiet.

'I no longer wished to continue my association with her. One cannot afford unreliable associates in business,' finished Geoffrey.

'And do you think, as others have asserted, that she has been seduced by the dark powers?'

'That I cannot say. Except that my horse always refused to go near her house – and on several occasions transactions over her paintings have gone mysteriously awry. Lord Shipley has thrown away the work he commissioned; he lost both his sons in a carriage accident since having them in the house and swears Mistress Ibbetson's paintings are the cause of his misfortune.'

'We cannot admit hearsay in court. Confine yourself to your own opinion, please. Have you any evidence of sorcery?'

'Not actual evidence, no, but then sorcery is just that, is it not? Invisible, except in its results.'

The jurors conferred some more. Alice tried to catch Geoffrey's eye. Did he not realize he was condemning her with every sentence he spoke? But Geoffrey continued to stare studiously ahead into the middle distance, scratching at his sideburns and tapping his foot. The noise of his heel was loud in the stuffy chamber.

'No further questions.' The prosecutor turned with eyebrows raised to the judge, who was in the process of opening a silver snuff-box. He plucked out the powder and placed a pinch on his hand, from where he snorted it noisily into his nostrils. 'Call the next witness,' he said, before sneezing.

Geoffrey glanced her way just once before striding out of a side door, but his face was cold, set, unreadable.

The scrivener's quill scratched on, setting Alice's teeth on edge, noting it all.

The last witness was Betty Tansy, the cook. Alice resigned herself to more hurtful insinuations. As Betty took the oath, Alice did not even raise her head. She was ashamed of her bedraggled and coarse appearance. The evidence was stacked like firewood at her door, ready to blaze up when the next witness should drop the taper. She shrank away, fearing to hear more bruising words from an old friend.

'You should all be ashamed of yourselves.' Betty glowered at the assembly and took a deep breath. 'I have been in service to Mistress Ibbetson these five years, and found her always to be godly,' she said, defiant. 'A more caring woman I have yet to meet. She never killed her little sister – she nursed her, and comforted her. She was well near destroyed when she died. And it's rank nonsense to say she's a witch.'

'Are you dismissing the testimony of your neighbours, then, Goodwife Tansy?'

Betty looked hesitant. 'I don't know about that. But my hens stopped laying one week and I did not look to witchcraft for the answer. I fed them better and brought them in earlier at night and they soon perked up. Seems to me, too much is being laid at her door that don't belong there.'

The room was now full of whispers, a noise like wind through trees.

'But on the night in question, you were out on the wagon with the Cobbalds and the rest of Netherbarrow, were you not?' The prosecutor paced back and forth, his hands folded behind him under his coat-tails.

'Aye. I did see Mistress Ibbetson right enough. She was bending over something in the ditch.'

'Was it the body of Margaret Poulter?'

'It could have been – but then again, it might not have been. It was dark.' Further rustling from the benches and muffled talking caused the justice to admonish the people to be quiet.

'What of the knife? Did you ever see her with this knife?' The prosecutor pointed to where it lay on the bench before him.

Betty stuck out her chin. 'That knife could belong to any one of us here. Ask them – go on – how many of the men own a knife exactly like this one? With a bone handle and all?' She looked round the room, a pugnacious glint in her eye. 'How do we know it is hers? I know I've never seen a knife like that in her house. She had a little penknife for cutting flowers and such. Not one like this. Nor her husband. What use would they have for such as that?'

'I think we know what use she made of it.' The prosecutor shared the joke with the crowd. 'Are you quite sure you have not seen this before?'

'I didn't say I hadn't seen one. Like I said, I've seen many a knife exactly like that one – my lad has one, and most of his friends too, and I dare say half the men in the village. But I've never seen one at the Ibbetsons'.'

Alice's eyes were full of tears. Dear Betty, she was the only one who would vouch for her.

Betty stood up straight and valiantly went on. 'And another thing. You don't want to believe everything that Ella Appleby says. She's a conniving–'

'You old cow!' shouted Ella jumping up out of her seat. 'What have I ever done to you? You plague-ridden old–'

'Enough!' The justice's voice silenced them. 'It is not Ella Appleby who is on trial here, but Alice Ibbetson. Kindly keep to the point.'

'That is the point,' said Betty stubbornly, refusing to be browbeaten.

'But you did tell the constable earlier that you saw the accused in a violent argument with the deceased only last week?'

'It was just a disagreement, such as we all have sometimes.'

'Other people's disputes do not lead to murder, though, do they, Goodwife Tansy?'

The prosecutor waved a signal to the clerk, who brought forth another black-covered bundle. The noise in the room increased as people shuffled or leaned forward to see what the cloth might contain.

'Show them to Goodwife Tansy.' The clerk let the cloth drop to the floor to reveal a pair of yellow satin shoes.

Alice's hands came up to her mouth. The clerk held out the shoes by the heels so that Betty could see them.

'Well, if you do not recognize the knife, do you recognize these?'

Betty looked imploringly to Alice, and Alice nodded. Whatever the cost, the truth was all they had to hold onto in this world turned bedlam.

'They are Mistress Ibbetson's.'

'And these stains—' he held out one of the shoes – 'we have already ascertained that they are blood – they were not there before?'

'No, sir. I never saw any marks on them afore now.'

'So you have no idea how the marks got there?'

Betty shook her head. The judge went on, 'Or that they were found by Ella Appleby, hidden in your kitchen, on the morning after the murder?'

'That's not true! I hid them before that after I had taken the—'

Alice tried to speak up but was immediately silenced by the judge. 'Quiet. Or I will have someone stop your mouth.'

The prosecutor went up to Betty and with his face close to hers asked, 'Did you help Alice Ibbetson by finding a hiding place for these after she had murdered Margaret Poulter?'

Those on the front row of seats with Ella began

381

to boo and hiss and cat-call, shouting insults.

'No, no.' Betty became more and more flustered. She looked to Alice in confusion. Then loudly, above the hubbub, 'No, I don't know anything about it.' She looked back to Alice, distressed. The prosecutor dangled one of the shoes from his index finger.

'Look at the blood-stained shoe, Goodwife Tansy.' He turned to the jury. 'Surely a lady with nothing to hide would simply leave her shoes in her closet?' He wagged a cursory hand in Alice's direction. The jurors nodded one to the other and whispered between themselves. 'You may leave the stand, Goodwife Tansy.'

'But I'm not done–'

'That will be all.'

The scrivener paused from his writing and dipped his nib into the inkwell, ready for the summing up.

Justice Lackwood's voice was devoid of feeling, like reading a list of groceries. 'I ask you to consider all you have heard, and indeed there has been a fine body of witnesses for the prosecution. Any one of the offences is a hanging offence, so be certain of your decision before you return your verdict. Weigh in the balance all the testimonies you have heard today. Consider also, before you reach your final verdict, the evidence of the knife and of the lady's shoe. I trust you will reach the right decision. All rise.'

Alice was returned to the holding cell to await the verdict. The holding cell was crowded with damp prisoners; the smell of urine permeated the cold air. They stood, not because the floors were running with water, as in the gaol, but because there was no room to sit. They were packed closely like skittles in a box, all the women together, lank-haired and filthy.

Alice wondered if Hannah was on her way by now to the courthouse. She worried whether she would manage to stand up for the journey. All the Quakers were to be tried in the afternoon but she fretted that Hannah might not be able to survive rough treatment. Her husband, Jack, would be in court too for the trial, and it was this, the prospect of seeing her husband again, that had shored Hannah up.

Alice had long since given up hope that Richard Wheeler would arrive with the help he had pledged to her. She should have known his friendship would not stretch to a thief and a liar, no matter what Hannah said. There had been no sign of him at the trial. Maybe after all, she thought bitterly, he has thought better of his promise, and does not wish to become associated with a woman accused of witchcraft and murder.

When they called out her name again, she was surprised. She guessed it was less than one hour of the clock. Were her supposed crimes worthy of so little consideration? She had to extricate herself from the press of bodies and, as she did so, one woman took hold of her hand and squeezed it tight, making the sign of the cross in front of her.

'God save you, mistress, good luck.'

When she emerged into the courtroom again, flanked by two guards, she could see brisk trading going on in the hall; peddlers were still selling tobacco and oranges, others hawking the usual grisly pamphlets detailing the crimes of notorious felons. There was much tattle and jesting as she was led up to the dock.

'All rise,' said the clerk, and the congregation rose as one body, with scraping of boots, jostling and elbowing, whilst the procession of the jury followed by the frail-looking Justice Lackwood filed in. All eyes were nailed fast to their faces, Alice's included – all hoped to discern from their bearing a clue as to the verdict. The jurors took their time sitting, lingering to whisper to each other as they slid into position behind the table.

'Spokesman for the jury, have you reached a verdict?' asked Justice Lackwood, wiping a dripping nose and squinting at them under lowered brows.

'Yes, it is unanimous.'

'Alice Ibbetson, you are accused of the murders of Margaret Alice Poulter and of Flora Longley.' Alice stared ahead at a spot in the wall over the heads of the crowd but her hands were tightly knotted together. 'Do you find the defendant guilty or not guilty?'

There was an expectant hush.

'Guilty.'

The room erupted as spontaneous cheering broke out in the gallery. This could not be happening. Up until this moment there had always been hope of reprieve, some small faith in the triumph of truth over falsehood, in the righteousness of English law. Alice almost sank to her knees, but caught a glimpse of the white flash of Ella's chemise above the blue dress. She would not fall before her, would not give her the satisfaction.

384

The judge was continuing to speak, to add the word 'guilty' to a longer list of supposed crimes, but his words fell empty around her after the first pronouncement. She clung onto the table, her veins standing out on her thin hands, and remained shakily upright as the justice placed the black cloth over his wig. There was silence then, for although everyone knew what the gesture signified, all wanted to hear him speak the words.

As he spoke them, it was as if she had lost her hearing. She heard nothing, merely saw the faces of those she knew suddenly loom vivid from the rest of the pack – Betty, with her hand over her open wailing mouth, Sir Geoffrey, his familiar long, thin face half hidden, his hand over his brow, head downcast towards his knees. But sharpest of all was Ella, tossing her hair back from her face, showing her white throat, brazenly watching Alice through narrowed eyes, a self-satisfied smile playing on her lips. It was as if Ella was illuminated, every detail keen as cut-glass; Alice could not even blink as Ella hefted up her fine new skirts, turned away and swaggered out through the open door into the fresh air of the street outside.

Chapter 32

Geoffrey exited the courtroom, his heart beating like a hammer, his underarms damp with sweat. That expression on Alice Ibbetson's face when they said she would hang – it sent a peculiar feeling along his spine, as if he were a dog and all the hackles were standing on his back. He went straight across the road to the Ring O' Bells tavern and ordered a flagon of ale. Many other people had had the same idea and soon the little taproom was full to overflowing with a noisy crowd, all vociferously discussing the titbits of the case.

'Ah, Geoffrey. There you are.' He looked over his shoulder at the sound of the voice. It was Robert Rawlinson in his best suit, his face red above the white cravat. He had been acting as usher for the proceedings and was keen to dissect the case with a fine blade. Geoffrey found he had no taste for it, to hear over and over the minutiae of the evidence.

'I am sorry, Robert, I am on my way,' he said curtly, and pressed past him. At the door he found his path blocked by two old women. He tried to force his way past but there was no room, they were literally shoulder to shoulder. He rammed one of them hard and her ale washed over the edge of the glass and down her front.

'Say pardon,' said one of them indignantly. Geoffrey ignored her and pushed against the door, but it would not swing open.

The woman brought her wizened face close to his. 'A bit of courtesy costs nothing,' she said.

He noticed the faint outline of her skull, pink beneath her white hair, and the room began to swim around him. Her face seemed to take on Margaret Poulter's, dark beneath her hood. He had to get away.

Geoffrey tried again to push the door before realizing that it opened inwards. He pulled it and blundered through, hearing it slam behind him. On the pavement, he stooped to be violently sick.

Ella had taken her time in the bar of the Ring O' Bells, revelling in being the centre of attention. Thomas must have been stricken with cold feet, she thought. She had been nervous about his testimony, although she had told him of the discovery of the bloodstained knife. He would maybe take it hard – the dishonour of being associated with such a wife. Perhaps that explained his curious absence from the trial. Ella had almost, but not quite, forgotten she was responsible for the whole trial, so taken was she with playing out her part. But Thomas would come round, if she warmed his bed right.

Afterwards she travelled back in a carriage with the others from Netherbarrow, alighting at the crossroads to walk back through the village to the house. She was in truth a little nervous about telling Thomas the verdict. Her stomach fluttered. It was getting on for dusk but the lamps had not yet been lit and the houses appeared gloomy with their black windows, the trees and shrubs in the gardens almost bare except for one or two shreds of leaves still clinging to the branches. There was a nip in the air and the fine rain had given way to a murky fog.

She pulled her new shawl around her. It was a good thick wool, dyed a sumptuous berry colour. She felt the warmth of it around the back of her neck, her fingers teasing the soft tassels. A week ago when she had asked for it Thomas had asked her whether there was any cheaper sort to be had. She had cajoled, and bullied, and pouted, and finally he had smiled good-naturedly, said he couldn't be bothered to argue any more and reached into his pocket for the coins. Ella had almost loved Thomas at that moment, but not quite as much as she loved that shawl, its warmth and colour, its soft texture, its luxuriant fringe.

Ella walked more briskly, her pattens clopping on the cinder paths. She wished the hanging was over. In the back of her mind she knew a woman was about to hang for a crime she probably did not commit, but that thought seemed distant, disconnected from here and now. Alice Ibbetson's fate was nothing to do with Ella's walk home through the misty lanes, was quite unrelated to the feel of her soft wool dress and shawl, a thousand miles away from the warm fires of the house and Thomas's waiting and urgent embraces. It was as if she had put Alice into a magic cabinet inside her head and waved a wand to make her disappear.

The only slight apprehension was that someone else might discover the real killer before the hanging could take place and Alice be pardoned, but that seemed unlikely as no one had come forward before now. She could not imagine going back to being a mere maidservant, or giving up her new clothes and her place in the master's bed. Those things had always been hers by rights. That other life she had had before, well, that was a mistake on the part of the Almighty. She had always known it was this she was born for, to be comfortable, to grow old and fat with a man who could provide a good solid living. If he was dull, then so much the better, she would make sure he

388

would have eyes only for her, that she, and only she, would have access to his cock – and his purse. Then she could get her sister Sadie away from Da, provide a proper place for them both.

The lingering idea that the real killer, whoever he may be, might still be abroad somewhere was a sobering thought, and Ella glanced right and left as she hurried along. The fog was thicker as she went over the bridge by the river, but now she could see the lighted windows of the house ahead of her, and twin lamps as if on the side of a carriage. She wondered who could be visiting, for Thomas always rode, never took the carriage. As she got closer she saw that all the rushlights in the house had been lit. The news of Alice's impending execution must have travelled ahead.

She went up the front path and opened the front door. This small act gave her great pleasure, for previously she had been used to going around the back through the dark passage between the wood store and the yew hedge. She hooked her shawl on the pegs behind the door. Several of Alice's things still hung there, a wide-brimmed hat, a navy shawl, a bee-keeping gauze and a parasol. They would have to go, thought Ella.

'And who might you be?'

Ella jumped – the woman's clipped voice had startled her.

'Ella.'

The woman looked her up and down, questioningly.

'The housekeeper,' Ella was obliged to continue.

'Come along then, we will need you. The

surgeon is with Mr Ibbetson now. I'm the vicar's wife, Mrs Goathley. There was not a soul around when the alarm was raised, except that half-witted scullery maid, and she was about as much use as a pig in a basket.'

Mrs Goathley led the way into the parlour where the local surgeon and barber was bending over Thomas. Thomas was propped up with cushions in a boat-backed chair. The physician had hold of a curved bottle and struggled to administer some kind of drench.

'Help me hold up his head,' he said, beckoning impatiently at Ella.

Ella hurried forwards and took hold of Thomas by the shoulders. 'Master,' she said, looking into his face, 'what's the matter?' Thomas was grey with a faint blueish outline to his lips. His face sagged, one side of his mouth hung open, a string of spittle like a cobweb dangled to his collar. His eyes were opaque. He showed no sign of recognizing Ella. Ella turned to the doctor, angrily. 'What's happened to him?' she said.

'An attack of the dropsy,' said the doctor. 'The scullery maid found him lying on the floor. He must have been there since this morning, poor man. He could not get up again or tell her what happened. Now, take hold of him and tilt his head back for me.'

Ella went round the back of the chair and, resting his forehead in the crook of her arm, drew back his head. The skin near his ear was stubbled and rough, and clammy with cold sweat. She let his head drop back onto the cushion and rushed to kneel in front of him. Putting her hand on his knee, she looked into his face.

'Master,' she said in a rising panic, 'Thomas!'

She implored Mrs Goathley, who was standing rigidly to one side. 'Tell me he'll be all right.' She did not answer, so Ella pawed at her, grabbing hold of a handful of her sleeve. 'He will be all right, won't he?'

Mrs Goathley detached Ella's hand from her sleeve and dropped it as if it were something odious.

''Tis too early to say. We will see what this drench will do for him.' Ella stood whilst the doctor poured a stream of thick liquid into the back of Thomas's throat. Thomas struggled and coughed and tried to speak, so most of the liquid fell out of his mouth and down his vest front, making a foul-smelling brown stain. Mrs Goathley took one of the protruding gloves from his pocket and mopped and rubbed at the stain.

'Leave him alone!' snapped Ella. But Mrs Goathley was already stepping away with distaste, wrinkling her nose and frowning. Ella noticed his breeches were damp too, and there was a faint whiff of urine.

'Master,' said Ella, moving round proprietorially to hold his head, 'be still now. The doctor is giving you some physic to make you well again.'

Thomas did not respond, but Ella pulled his head back and the dose was administered again. This time the doctor clamped his jaw shut whilst Thomas writhed and made noises like a mare in labour, until at last he lay still, his eyes dull and his mouth slack.

'He will be quiet now. But we need to get him

upstairs to his bed. You – housekeeper, go down to the alehouse and bring back a strong man to help me.'

'No,' said Ella. 'I'm staying here. I'll not leave him.'

The doctor sighed and raised his eyebrows to the vicar's wife. 'Mrs Goathley, be so kind as to go down the lane and fetch help.'

Mrs Goathley opened her mouth about to protest, but then, seeing the mutinous look on Ella's face, nodded, squashed her hat back on her sparse brown hair and went out through the open door.

The doctor began to put away his equipment in his greasy holdall, the bottle of leeches, the bone spatulas, several dark glass bottles, the tweezers and the blood-letting scalpel. 'How much help is there in the house?' he said without looking up, his grey wig lowered over the task of fitting so many objects into such a small bag.

'Myself. April, the scullery maid, and a stable lad that tends the master's horses. Our cook's just done the dirty on us and quit.' The physician looked up as if expecting more, and Ella added, 'Lottie Jennings helps out when there's a need.'

'There'll be a need,' said the doctor. 'It looks severe. He'll need nursing. There's no telling when he might be up and about again, if at all.'

Ella stared at him. She did not know what to say. 'You mean, he might die?'

'Best to send out for his next of kin anyway. He will need someone to take charge of his affairs. Mrs Goathley told me about the shocking business with his wife, that she's to hang. My physic

392

may not be a match if there's sorcery involved. The outcome is much more – how can I say – unpredictable.'

From the chair in the corner came a low bleat. Ella rushed over. Thomas leered at her, his face purple, trying to speak, but his words were thick and indistinct. She leaned in to hear better what he was trying to say, and his left hand shot out and clutched her by the wrist. His face was contorted down one side, the other flaccid and useless. His speech would not come, his lips unable to form the letters, his hand squeezed the bones in her wrist till she thought they might snap like kindling.

She dragged her hand away just as the door opened and the purse-lipped Mrs Goathley and the farrier arrived. The last time she had seen him was the night of the cuckolding. This evening he was sober and rubbed his calloused hands together.

He approached Thomas's chair and doffed his cap. 'Mr Ibbetson,' he said.

Thomas lay inert in the chair, not responding.

The doctor exchanged a meaningful look with the farrier, and they approached the chair. 'Come on now, sir,' said the farrier.

The doctor and the farrier levered him up with difficulty, for although the farrier was strong as a bullock, Thomas had always been well fed and portly, and he was now a stupefied dead weight. They threw his arms around their shoulders and hauled him up the stairs by the armpits, his ankles catching and banging on every step. Ella and Mrs Goathley followed, picking up the rolling coins from his pockets and his eyeglasses. Finally the men dumped him onto the bed and left him there. Mrs Goathley and Ella looked on from the landing, Mrs Goathley sucking on her own lips as if on a lemon.

As they came out of the room, the doctor nodded to Ella. 'Get him changed and into his nightshirt. I will call on him the morrow to see if my physic has taken effect, to bleed him if necessary, and to see how he does.'

Ella regarded the lifeless figure on the bed. 'Yes, sir,' she said.

'Oh, and try and find out if there's a relative with access to his funds. I will need paying for my duties.'

Ella inclined her head, having no intention whatsoever of sending for any relative. As far as she knew, Thomas had a mother and a twin brother somewhere in the south, but the mother was rumoured to be a proper termagant and the brother cut from the self-same cloth. The last thing Ella needed was to have them both here, lording it over her and telling her what to do. No, she would take charge herself, and if there were any bills to be paid, then she would make sure she got the wherewithal out of Thomas to pay them.

Mrs Goathley smiled thinly at Ella. 'When his family have arrived, we will see you in church, no doubt. I will ask my husband to remember Mr Ibbetson in his prayers. You know you can call on us for help at any time.'

Ella was shrewd enough to know that this speech was purely for the physician's benefit.

'Thank you, ma'am,' she said with over-obvious deference, curtseying so low that Mrs Goathley coughed in embarrassment.

When they had gone out through the front door she slammed it behind them and clattered up the stairs to the bedroom. Thomas had not moved. He lay there looking up at the ceiling, a bubble of saliva on his lower lip.

'Thomas,' hissed Ella, 'speak to me.'

He made a gargling sound, but no words came.

'Thomas,' she repeated, shaking him urgently by the shoulders, 'what is it? Just tell me what ails you, what I can do?'

Thomas flailed his one working arm in her direction and mumbled something unintelligible. Ella strained to understand him but could make no sense of his words. They were like bedlam talk, just sounds, not words at all.

She manhandled him out of his coat and vest, cursing the stiff buttons, and rolled him over onto his side to force his limp arms through the sleeves. By the time she had done this, she was out of breath. She removed his sodden breeches, discovering with repulsion that he had soiled himself too. She left him with his breeches round his knees whilst she went for water and soap, exposing his white legs, bristling with gingery hairs like a hog's back.

When he was passably clean she dragged the counterpane from under him and threw it over his chest, then she deposited his wet clothes in the pot under the bed. All this she did in a daze; her arms and legs moved, her body bent at the waist to the task, but she could not force her thoughts to arrange themselves in any logical order.

'Sleep now,' she said woodenly, unsure whether

she was addressing Thomas or herself. 'Happen you will feel better the morrow.'

But if Thomas heard her he made no reply, except his breath, a hoarse irregular sound, like the gushing of water from the village pump. She watched him dispassionately for a moment before she went to the linen press and took out some freshly laundered sheets and fetched a feather palliasse from the trunk in the hall. Then she made up the truckle bed in the room where the child Flora used to sleep. It was clear she would not be needed in Thomas's bed tonight.

She did not sleep well. She thought of the mistress sleeping her last few nights on this earth. Soon she would be swinging like a sack of grain, her thoughts silenced, her heart cold and still as a river rock, and it was she, Ella, who had made it happen. She marvelled at her own power, but trembled, for she knew it was wickedness. Yet why did it not feel wicked? She ought to feel something, suffer some sort of remorse for what she had done.

Ella tossed in the sheets, listening to Thomas's breath rising and falling in the next room, praying he would recover quickly. For what would become of her if he were to die? She would have nowhere to go, and no position. She thought of her father and the dark attic where her sister still slept in soot-stained sheets, imagined her cowering in the blanket when she heard Da's footsteps. She smelt again the drink on him, dreaded the thwack of his leather belt. A swell of compassion for her sister filled her eyes with tears. She must find a way to get Sadie out of there, away from

Da, to find her a place somehow.

When the faint light of morning came, she heard the clunk of the key in the back door and knew it would be April, the scullery maid, come to light the fires ready for the day's cooking. Betty the cook had resigned. 'I would not lift a finger for you if you were the last human being on this earth,' she had said after the trial. 'You are a lying, thieving bitch, and by rights it should be you strung up on the gallows. I hope you rot in hell.'

Ella had tossed her head, defiant, and said, 'Cooks are two a penny. And your food stinks. Master wanted rid of you, anyways.'

Betty's face had grown red and hot then, and she had slapped Ella sharply across the cheek. It stung like blazes, but Ella stayed fast, like a statue, watching Betty hobble painfully away on her bad leg.

So today there would be nobody to cook, except herself and April. Ella roused herself and dressed hastily, running down the back stairs. April was fiddling with the coals, for the fire had gone out and needed relighting. She jumped up guiltily as Ella entered. Ella ordered her to get a move on. She would have April make Master some tea and a tempting breakfast. Thomas loved his food – a platter of bacon and eggs would soon get him up and about.

The fire took a long time to get going. They had to huff and puff at it with the bellows, and twice start afresh with new kindling. By the time it was going, they were both hot with the effort and covered in smuts. When the breakfast was ready Ella hurried up the stairs with the tray, leaving

April eating downstairs at the kitchen table.

'Breakfast, Thomas,' called Ella cheerily.

There was no answer so she pushed the door open with her foot and took the tray in. She set it on the half-moon table by the window and threw open the shutters to let in the day. The heavy tapestry curtains around the bed were still drawn, and when she pulled them back she could see the humped figure of Thomas lying on his side, still in his shirt the way she had left him. His beard had started to grow and showed as a stain around his jaw; his shaved head appeared incongruously pasty and freckled without his wig.

She called him gently and he opened his eyes, trying to sit up and speak. One side of him seemed to be lifeless, as if drained. With difficulty she heaved him semi-upright onto the pillows, shoving a thick bolster behind him to stop his head lolling back. Realizing he would not be able to cut up the bacon for himself, she began to cut it for him. A stream of angry noises came from the bed, grunts and groans and mumblings. When she fetched over the platter and made an effort to feed him, he nearly knocked her over trying to take hold of it. He had no control over his one threshing arm and she had to snatch away the plate before it ended up on the floor. After several such frustrating attempts, she held the plate aloft away from him.

'Thomas,' she said, through gritted teeth, 'you must let me feed you, or you won't get any breakfast at all.'

She saw then how he slumped back, passive. She spooned the egg and bacon into his mouth like feeding a baby. He could not even chew so she had to push it down his throat with the spoon, and even then most of it dribbled down his chin. The egg was cold and congealed into clots before she had managed to get even a half of it down his throat, and as she reached to mop his chin with a napkin, she saw his loins heave and heard the splutter as his bowels voided into the bed. The stench filled her nostrils and made her gag. She put the napkin over her nose and fled, dropping the greasy plate on the counterpane. When she got halfway down the stairs, the napkin still over her face, she met April coming up.

'Is he better? Has he finished his breakfast?' asked April.

Ella pushed past her, her voice cracking.

'Go up and see for yourself,' she said.

For the second night Ella did not sleep. The doctor had been and bled him but it had made no difference. In the cold dark, Thomas bellowed incomprehensible sounds like a man possessed of unquiet spirits. He howled the same word over and over. It could have been her own name, 'Ella', but lurking in the back of her mind was the insidious thought that he was really saying another name. Ella shivered in the thin light of her candle, unsure whether he was calling for her or for his wife, and unable to go in and face him. When she had ventured in with his lunch, his eyes had throbbed with accusation, and it was the intensity of his look that made her baulk at going back into his room.

She paced up and down the kitchen with her hands pressed over her ears, her heart hammering in her chest. What was to become of her? It had all been for nothing. She had sent a woman to her death, and it had all been for nothing. Or rather for this man, who instead of supporting her had turned into a blabbering baby. A vision of her future life swirled before her eyes and with it came the stink of sweat and urine. It must be her punishment. She had sent a woman to hang, and this was her reward.

The ghastly sounds continued until she could stand it no more. She flung open the door and reached the bed in two strides. She grabbed hold of his collar and shook him.

'Stop it,' she said, 'for God's sake, be quiet.'

He opened his mouth to let out another sound, but she was weeping now, tears that came from nowhere, dripping onto the sheets. 'Why can't you just be quiet?'

The sound came from his lips again like the cry of a harpooned seal. This time Ella was sure of the name. In a fury she caught up the bolster on the end of the bed and raised it above his head. Thomas's eyes followed her and his mouth stayed open in a small 'o' of surprise. Ella felt her world crumble into small pieces, each piece infinitely slow. She saw her hand, dark against the pillow, its fingers hooked like claws around the white linen. But before she could bring it down, the creases in Thomas's forehead unaccountably dropped away. She watched his lips part to make a small grunt and she paused, mid-movement. She leaned over and put her cheek next to his mouth. There was not a whisper of air. Faintly, in the distance, a cock crowed, though it was still dark, marking the beginning of a new day.

Still clutching the bolster to her chest, as if holding it would somehow hold her together, Ella moved to the window. Outside there was a glow on the horizon. Dawn. She felt nothing. It surprised her. No sorrow for his passing. But she knew there would be a hue and cry as soon as they knew he was dead, and that there would be no place for her when his brother arrived, except as the butt of his boot.

She must get away from here. She started for the door, but then turned back. She would need some things to sell. In a panic she lunged for the silver candlesticks on the dressing table, but in the dark she knocked one over and it clattered to the ground.

The noise of it startled her and she realized she was trembling. 'Get a grip, girl,' she said under her breath. 'Think. Just think.' It was as if her thoughts were tangled like brambles; she couldn't unravel them. She plucked the one thought that made sense. She had to go somewhere far away, where they could never catch up with her. The Devil was on her heels, searching for her soul, and he already had hold of her skirts.

'Oh, Jesus,' she groaned. 'Sadie.' Her heart heaved.

She could not leave her sister behind.

Twenty minutes later Ella ran down the lane, her petticoats flying, followed by a smaller figure, stumbling, trying to keep up. They disappeared into the Ibbetsons' house but emerged fifteen minutes later as the church clock's sonorous tone struck six. The mule's bridle jingled as it was harnessed. They loaded the trap with trunks and cases, baskets and bags, like a rag and bone cart, talking in urgent whispers. Ella helped Sadie into the front seat, clucked her tongue and slapped the reins against the mule's neck so it was set trotting down the lane in a great hurry. And all the while, the Ibbetsons' front door creaked back and forth in the breeze, the draught blowing cold into the empty hallway.

Chapter 33

The crowds outside the courthouse had waited hours to see a glimpse of the witch as she was brought back up the hill to the castle gaol. But they were to be disappointed, for Alice was transported under escort in a covered wagon that rattled on uneven rickety wheels through the crowded streets. She was closeted along with two others who were to hang, both of them men. So this was English justice. She was not so quick now to condemn the bedraggled men in front of her; rather she looked upon their downcast eyes with sad empathy.

She smiled at the young man, who could not have been more than sixteen years old and was shivering uncontrollably so that his thin shirt fluttered on his chest. She did not know what their crimes were and she did not ask, but she was glad all three of them were protected from

402

the jeering crowd that ran alongside, battering on the sides of the lath walls.

'Lord have mercy,' she said under her breath as the hammering threatened to turn them deaf. The young man crouched into the corner like a wounded dog. At the gaol they were separated from her and she was thrust, still looking back over her shoulder at them, into another cell.

Foolishly she had thought she would be returned to Hannah, to the familiar cell with its jutting ledge for her hidden candle, the candle she had left with the flint and the worn buckskin-covered Bible. The new cell was of course no different to the first – it still stank like a latrine, the walls still oozed with damp. But the fact that it was a different cell, and the prospect of spending her last two nights alone, propelled her into deep despair and caused her to weep with frustration. She had assumed Hannah would be given another custodial sentence, that she would be there for comfort in the last hours. But the cell was empty, just four sets of leg-irons rusting against the wall.

Surprisingly, they had not manacled her, and there was a slot window projecting a thin sliver of light. She stood on tiptoe to peer out through the narrowing aperture of the stone wall. It looked out directly into the yard where the towering silhouette of the ramparts was partly visible against the grey sky. Perched on the crenellated but crumbling tower were a couple of crows, nodding their heads in a macabre dance. The cast-aside, dismembered remains of some poor man, who had been quartered and left to rot in the yard, lay in full view. His head was missing –

presumably on the pike above the gates, and his legs were set at an odd angle, the sole of one foot visible, white as wax beneath a blood-soaked cuff.

She shuddered and withdrew into the cell. She remembered the faces of the two men from the wagon. After the trial they had measured them all for coffins before putting them in the cart, and she had heard tell that the condemned had to walk past the line of cheap dealwood boxes on the way to the gibbet.

She surprised herself by hoping she would be the first to hang. She did not want to witness the sounds of her companions' last moments, their pleas for mercy. But then again, she desired not to give them more cause for fear either. What if she were to break down or cry out? It would terrify that young man. Would she be able to step up to the scaffold calmly, or would fear overtake her on the journey and would she have to be dragged? She knelt down on the damp stone, a weight of dread about her shoulders. She must prepare herself.

Her lips moved reciting the Lord's Prayer, but it was an empty prayer. The words seemed ridiculous. She would have no more need of daily bread, though her trespasses certainly needed forgiveness. And if there was a paradise, she knew she did not deserve to enter it. She realized that her life before had been a kind of earthly paradise.

Alice took out the little chapbook from her waistband. It was dog-eared now, but it reminded her of Hannah. She smelt it. Wondered if it might retain the scent of Richard's tobacco. But it smelt only of damp paper. She took it to

404

the window to read.

He should examine whether he is really worthy of the high title of Christian; he should examine his whole Life, how he has spent his Time, said Boehme.

She had lived her life like a blinkered horse, only seeing her own view, all other views invisible to her. Small wonder then that Thomas had so little affection left for her, that he could not even bring himself to appear at the courthouse.

She recalled coming out of the summerhouse one morning to find Thomas on the doorstep about to come in, and she had immediately turned and locked the door behind her as if to shut him out. His face turned from open and smiling to hurt and closed, but she had ignored it and brushed past him on the path as if he were of no more account than the butcher boy.

Maybe there was already a shadow over her even then. As soon as she had stolen the flower. She shuddered. Her preoccupation with the lady's slipper had taken hold of her, setting in its wake a train of events that had led her here to this cell.

She looked anew at her surroundings. She had thought herself observant, but she had never really seen anything before. The stones were laid so precisely overlapping, the evidence of someone's neat labour. She wished she had her paintbrush now. Where there was light near the window moss was growing, vibrant green, soft, with spindly tufts like antennae poking out from the rounded cushion. She put out her hand to the wall and felt the cold stone and the place where it gave into the velvety moss, grateful to be alive, for each moment of presence.

For when she was dead, even these stones would cease to exist.

'Move along now.' Paucett's loud voice outside the cell interrupted her contemplation. She heard the clanking of leg-irons and coughing. She stood up and went to the barred hatch in the door to see what might be happening outside. She was just in time to see another bunch of prisoners bundled and bullied along the narrow corridor – four or five men, none of them wigged, some greying and some younger with thick heads of hair. Their bodies blocked the light from the doorway but they went in quietly enough, the only voices being Bubb and Paucett the gaolers, who prodded them in the back with muskets and made the sort of noises drovers usually made when shifting recalcitrant cattle. There was a strange smell in the air, like smoke; it reminded her of her garden bonfires but there was an undertone of the branding iron's singe about this particular scent, like burnt wool.

The gaolers released the men from the leg-irons, clapped the cell doors shut and locked them, the sounds echoing along the hollow corridors. Alice could no longer see anything so she returned to the window to look out at the sky's darkening hue, to catch a glimpse of her last sunset skies, to hear the sweet trill of birdsong. She was aware of men's voices talking, a soft hum of polite conversation. A familiar enough sound in a withdrawing room after dinner, but almighty strange to hear it now, where it was inconsonant with the surroundings. She moved back to the door to hear what they might be saying but the muffled voices were too low. It was clear to Alice they were not ruffians or footpads from the tone and cadences of their voices, so she called out to them through the door.

'Hoy there! Is there anyone there?' Of course she knew there was, but even in these bizarre circumstances she thought it might appear disrespectful to have been listening.

'Hoy!' she shouted louder.

A man's eager face appeared at the window opposite. She saw him turn back to the others, hissing, ''Tis a woman.'

'Is it one of ours?' said a voice.

The man looked back at her, scrutinized her a moment, then turned back. 'No.' He called out to Alice, 'Art thou all alone, miss?'

'Yes,' said Alice. 'But I was with my friend Hannah Fleetwood. She was tried this afternoon – I was hoping for news of her.'

The man half disappeared from the aperture and she could hear him saying, 'She talks of Hannah, she's asking after her.'

A broad hand wrested him away and another face filled the window.

'Alice,' said a familiar voice, 'is it thee?'

'Richard,' said Alice faintly. 'What has happened?'

His eyes glinted in the darkness, searching her face.

'The trial,' he said, 'what of–?'

'Guilty,' she said before he could finish.

'When?'

'The day after tomorrow.'

He was silent then a while. They looked at each

other through the bars, their faces searching to say what no words could fathom. 'I would have come,' he said finally. 'We all would. But we were arrested by Fisk and his men...'

'I know,' she said, although she hadn't, but her words told some other truth. 'But what could you have done? They had it decided beforehand.'

'I would have vouched for thee–' Someone from behind interrupted him, and she heard him say, ''Tis Alice, Mistress Ibbetson from Nether-barrow, the woman I told you about.' And she felt a warm glow spread through her – she had not been forgotten, he had told his friends after all.

'You promised to rescue me, Richard Wheeler,' she said loudly, until his face reappeared, 'and what use are you to me now?'

His face was serious, until he saw that hers was smiling. 'I suppose I am not much of a hero,' he said, 'arriving too late to save thee.'

'But you are here now,' she said, 'though I doubt there is much you can do for me in there.' She looked into his brown eyes, saying softly, 'The time for recriminations is done. We must be gentle with each other. We neither of us want cause for regret when my time comes.'

He gazed at her, amazed at her calm demeanour. 'Thou hast made thy peace with God?'

'I have made my peace with myself,' she said firmly.

'Tell me,' he said, 'tell me everything.'

When he had heard her whole story, Richard told Alice about how he and his friends had tried to make a stand against the payment of tithes, and how some from a neighbouring village had taken it upon themselves to break in and retrieve their goods, and it had turned from a peaceable protest into a nightmare, with old Isaac dead, and many others half choked to death in a blazing barn. He recounted how they had been summarily imprisoned, separated from their wives and families. They were to be tried later in the week at the quarter sessions on a count of treason – a crime punishable by death; the accusation had been made by Sir Geoffrey Fisk and Robert Rawlinson, the Justice of the Peace. Their chances of acquittal were negligible.

He had not told her about Sam's deception, for he was angry with himself for being taken for a fool and he did not wish Alice to see how unwise he had been. He told her he did not know what had become of Hannah, but suspected she would be held with the other Quaker women in separate quarters, and not with her husband, Jack, of whom they had seen and heard nothing since their arrest. He was unable to comfort Alice; her voice broke with distress when she said she and Hannah had become like sisters.

Alice had listened to him talk, her soft grey eyes never leaving his face. The wall sconce soon failed, and when darkness fell he could just see a faint glint from her irises. When the night was full and black, he had had to ask:

'Thou art still there?'

And she had answered him, 'Yes, as long as you are there, for there will be time soon enough for me to sleep.'

Later in the night they had both slept a little, but the cells were cold, and Richard's friends were also

409

restless, unable to find a comfortable position for their bones and morbidly full of fear. The next day the men organized a meeting for prayer in the cell and Richard asked Alice if she would join with them. She agreed, and he hoped the sound of their voices as they spoke out, and the depth of silence in which they found themselves, might reach her cell and move her, as it moved him.

Strangely, this meeting of the Friends did not bring him any lasting consolation; his thoughts were all with Alice. He chewed the facts of her trial over and over, denouncing the jurors in his head and wondering how such a travesty could have come about. He could not bear to think about the morrow, when Alice would be taken away to have the life squeezed out of her, never to return. He paced back and forth in his cell in frustration, trying to think what to do. It challenged all his convictions that such a thing could happen to an innocent woman. Yet in himself, he was sure that a higher power did exist. Had he not been stricken with it himself?

Those few left at the morning meeting at Lingfell Hall would be remembering them, he was sure, but then he knew what they did not – that no provisions would reach them, and that visitors were only received if they could grease Paucett's palm with coin, something the Quakers, with their meagre and honest lifestyles, seldom would think to do.

Richard continued to move restlessly about the cell.

'Sit thee still, Richard,' said Ned Armitage. 'Thou art driving us all to the end of our patience, with thy constant shuffling.'

'I cannot help it. I cannot think how to help her.'

'Perhaps it is a lesson to thee to accept it, as we must accept our own fates, which are just as surely coming,' said Ned.

'I cannot accept it. But I will sit, if my walking offends you all.' He sat down heavily against the wall. 'But I just wish I could do something.'

'Being a friend and a comfort, that is not so little,' said Ned. 'Better to help her accept it than to rail against it, so she might have peace in her last moments.'

Richard sat quietly then, seeming to take in his words; it was only his restless drumming fingers that betrayed he was still churned up, the anger boiling in his chest.

It was whilst he was sitting like this that he heard the clang of the gates at the end of the corridor being unlocked, and approaching footsteps. He peered through the barred window and could just see young Bubb, the silhouette of his halo of curly hair, and behind that, the broader, bulkier outline of Paucett's sleeve as he followed him, and the scuffing sound of his heavy boots, which he hardly bothered to lift off the ground. He could also hear another sound, the tapping of heels behind them. It must be Dorothy. When they got to his door, he saw Paucett's doughy, moon-shaped face loom in the window. 'Here it is, sir,' he said to the person behind him. 'A visitor,' he leered through the hatch.

Paucett moved away, and a gentleman in a white powdered wig and three-feathered hat approached.

411

'Mr Wheeler,' said the man, in a formal tone.

Richard did not recognize the man but he recognized the voice. He withdrew slightly from the window.

'Sam,' he said, bitterly. 'Or is it Stephen?'

He looked different, not just the clothes, but different in the face, clearer, more open. He held up his finger to his lips indicating Richard should be quiet, then turned to Paucett and said in a loud voice, 'You may leave us. I have some business to relay to Mr Wheeler concerning the ill they have done my father, and my father's rights to compensation.'

Paucett's mumbling voice replied, 'You will find me by the first gate, sir, when you wish to go up.'

Stephen watched Paucett go. As soon as he was out of earshot, he put his face back up to the opening and said, 'Richard, I did thee wrong. But I want to make amends.' Seeing Richard's face, unmoved and silent, he continued. 'I have been to the Hall this morning and seen Isaac buried properly, the way a good man deserves. And I have asked Dorothy to try and get good lawyers for thy defence–'

'What about thy father?' said Richard.

'He knows nothing of this. I am here out of friendship, and because thou art the first genuine friend I have ever had that liked me for myself, and not because I was my father's son.'

'Thou hast deceived us all, Sam.' Richard shook his head. 'We thought thou wast a man touched by the Spirit.' Richard remembered the scenes of terror in the barn and his voice took on a crisp tone. 'Why art thou here?'

Stephen cast his eyes downward, then looked up, his face twisted with pain. 'I cannot pretend to be a holy person, indeed thou knowest I am not. But I want to be Sam Fielding, I want to be the person thou thoughtest I was...' He paused, his voice breaking. 'Just tell me something I can do. I can try and get thee out of here, bribe the judge, stand up for thee against my father...' His words trailed away.

Richard looked at the impassioned young man standing before him. How naïve he was, how little he knew of the world, and their way of life, to even suggest he should bribe the judge. For the first time, he really saw Stephen, his youth, his inexperience, and realized that he himself had been guilty of ascribing to him a self-possession that had never been there. But here was this young man, eager to help – a sudden hope sprang up in his heart.

He grabbed hold of the bars of the window. 'There is something thou canst do,' he said, 'but not for me. For Alice. My fate is as yet uncertain, but she is to hang tomorrow.'

Stephen looked hesitant then, but Richard pushed on. 'She is innocent, Sam. She is lodged in that cell over there.' He pointed, and watched as Stephen looked over to the iron door behind him.

'Thou must find a way to help her.' Seeing him still unconvinced, he said, 'Please, Sam. There is nobody else. I can do nothing, but I cannot bear to think of it, such a waste...' Richard felt a lump come into his throat and he swallowed hard to compose himself. 'Please say thou wilt try?'

Stephen's eyes betrayed his uncertainty. 'But

she is already condemned – I might not be able to do anything.'

'As long as thou hast tried – then that is all anyone can do.' Richard looked into Stephen's worried face and saw the weight of responsibility settle there in the crease between his eyebrows. 'Thou art a true friend, Sam, I know that.' He extended his hand, rough and calloused with blisters, and Stephen held out his smooth dry palm. Richard squeezed it hard.

'Paucett,' Stephen called imperiously. 'I have had enough of this stinking pit. Take me aloft.'

Chapter 34

At nightfall Lancaster seemed to be suspended over the estuary like a bright string of beads, all the house lights twinkling, the cabins on the ships with their windows ablaze with candles, casting long fluctuating stripes of gold onto the surface of the river. Here by the wharf waited the traders and schooners, ready to sail on the late tide, their gangplanks still lowered, their bellies still being filled with barrels of saltpetre, woollen goods, leather hides and pallets of slate.

From the top of the hill Stephen could see the ships' masts on the northern shore – a swaying forest, for the sheets were still furled, and the ropes and moorings made the familiar creaking and clanking sound as they stretched and moved with the water's swell. There was a stiff easterly breeze, which would mean a good fast turnabout. Already he could see a small rowdy group of hands gathered near the jetty by the Flying Fish tavern, presumably hoping to be taken on as crew by those vessels lacking the full complement. He saw the flaring of their pipes as they sat on the moorings and smoked, and he heard their laughter and rowdy voices as a group of girls paraded past intent on their age-old trade.

Stephen could make out his father's ship, towards the end of the moorings where the water was deeper. He knew both his father's ships well; this one was the *Fair Louise*, a flute of Dutch design. His father had added a figurehead with yellow hair and a bright blue drape only half covering the round breasts that jutted forth, their strawberry nipples exposed to the breaking waves. Around her neck hung a necklace of white-painted wood, carved in to shells. His father's other ship was the *Anne-Marie*. The names of his father's ships made him uncomfortable – he had a feeling they were named for his whores, and his thoughts turned sadly to his mother, from whom he'd heard nothing more since the day she departed. He assumed she was settled somewhere in Ireland, and hoped that Hetherington was treating her well.

He watched for a moment as the crew scurried back and forth loading the *Fair Louise* with fleeces from the upland herds, cloth, barrels of liquor and crates of provisions. His father was to sail for New England tonight, which was fortunate as he would be well out of the way if, God forbid, anything should go amiss.

Stephen had still flatly refused to sail, and his

father had become so overwrought, so lacking in reason, particularly since the assizes, that Stephen had been unable to bear another quarrel with him. Stephen felt nerves jangle in the pit of his stomach. He took a deep breath and exhaled audibly before he reined in his horse and turned its muzzle back towards the town.

The convolution of narrow streets with their overhanging windows was like a black labyrinth, the shanty houses leaning up against the castle walls as if huddling there for warmth. Here were doorways that could hide footpads or other ne'er-do-wells, and Stephen had a quantity of money in his pouch, taken from his father's desk drawer.

But he rode on, safe, or rather somewhat nervous, in the knowledge that he was armed. He had taken his pair of flintlock pistols, a present from his father on his sixteenth birthday, from their case in the gunroom, enjoying the look and feel of the inlaid brass mounts chased with spiralling fern-like designs, and the solid weight of the barrels in his hand. He had begun to prime them from his powder horn when he had heard his father's horse returning, so he had slunk silently downstairs and out through the kitchen entrance to the stables. What his father did not know was that he had no intention of returning to Fisk Manor. Dorothy had told him he could stay at the Hall.

Now he was glad he had the pistols loaded and ready, stiff in his gun belt. He also had a small sword slung over his back and a needle-dagger in his sleeve. A voluminous dark blue cloak rested across the pommel of his saddle, a garment so hideously old-fashioned his mother had long since ceased to wear it and had abandoned it in her closet, but he knew he might have need of it in the hours to come.

He had sent word ahead, and when he arrived at the small market square the closed sedan chair awaited him, a fine black lacquerwork affair with gold lines around the window. One of the liveried attendants opened the door and seemed to notice nothing out of the ordinary as they handed him into the compartment. He gave his orders and the contraption lurched into motion. Inside, he removed his sword and laid it by his feet underneath the cloak. He took off the gun belt carefully, for he was aware that movement from within might cause the men to stagger or fall. The two pistols he pushed down inside his wide-topped leather boots, folding lace cuffs over them. He was wearing his most costly outfit, of watered mulberry silk, with tan doeskin gauntlets and a neat wig under a large wide-brimmed hat. In his bag he carried a scroll he had penned that afternoon, pressed with his father's seal, and a purse with a large quantity of coinage.

His stomach was fluttering now as he watched the windows of the houses pass by, the hanging wooden signs of the butcher, the tailor, the mercer, and then the huge stones of the castle walls. Outside the prison gates he was set down and he handed one of the attendants a card with his father's name printed thereon, and a half-crown, and sent him to the small door. A moment later he felt himself hoisted up, and heard the large gate creak laboriously open and then close behind him.

He stepped out and told the attendants to wait

for his return.

'Ah, Paucett,' he said, waving his glove at him as the lumpen figure of the gaoler approached. 'My father bade me return with this writ. I am to deliver it to that dog Wheeler. My father fears he cannot put trust in his serving men, these days.'

Paucett looked at him appraisingly. 'You were here earlier,' he said. 'I thought the face was familiar.'

'Stephen Fisk, Sir Geoffrey Fisk's son.'

Paucett blew out through his teeth, his cheeks puffing out like bladders. 'Night visits are most unusual, sir. It's quite against the regulations to let visitors have access to the cells.'

Stephen waited, guessing what might come next.

'That is, unless ... unless a small consideration might be made for the privilege, sir?'

It was evening when Richard heard the barred gate opening and footsteps outside his door. He saw the yellow light from the rush-light in the corridor creep in through the bars, followed by Paucett's face. 'Five minutes, that's all.' Paucett's lips opened, but then he gave a short grunt, a look of surprise in his soft-boiled eyes. Richard made out a gloved hand holding the barrel of a pistol to Paucett's neck.

'If either of you try anything, I will blow your brains out.' Richard recognized Sam's voice, although he could not see clearly what was going on. Even now, Richard could not bring himself to think of him as Stephen Fisk.

'Sam?' called Richard.

Paucett tried to twist around and at the same

418

time Richard saw Sam's lace-cuffed hand come out armed with the scroll-ended butt of the pistol.

'No!' shouted Richard, his head close up to the window.

A dull thump as the pistol butt bit hard into Paucett's skull.

'There's no other way,' came the reply, at the same time as another plaintive voice from Richard's cell shouted, 'What's happening?' Richard's cell-mates were jostling behind him, unable to see because Richard's head obscured the window.

'It's Sam Fielding–' said Richard, but did not finish his sentence for Paucett let out a groan and his eyes rolled upwards in his head before the thud as his body hit the ground outside, the keys at his waist jangling against the wet flagstones. Richard looked past him into the corridor to see Bubb frozen to the spot, staring open-mouthed at Paucett. Paucett was face-down like a whale, heaving slightly as if he would get up but had forgotten how. Then he lay still.

'If you move an inch I'll blow you to bits,' said Stephen, his voice quavering, cocking his pistol and taking aim at Bubb's chest.

Bubb held his hands up, his eyes darting from side to side searching for a means of escape, but the corridor was a dead end; they all knew the only way out was the way they had come in.

'Sam ... Stephen.' Richard tried to get Stephen's attention, but Stephen was too occupied with holding Bubb at bay. Richard banged on the door with his fist, calling again in frustration.

'Stephen! Not like this–'

'Just let me do what I must,' Stephen shouted

in the direction of Richard's door, and wielded the heavy pistol with renewed determination. Bubb turned pale under his freckles.

'Get the keys.' Stephen pointed with his other hand to the iron ring, half visible under the expanse of Paucett's grubby shirt. Bubb held his hands above his head and crept towards Paucett's great carcass. He tried to pull at the ring by the jagged keys but they were buried under the mound of flesh.

'I can't reach them, sir,' he whined.

'If you do not, I will blow you both to kingdom come,' Stephen said.

Bubb struggled to roll Paucett over onto his back.

'I'm sorry, Richard, it was the only way,' Stephen said, glancing sideways again at the door.

Bubb had extricated the keys and was sidling along the corridor.

'Look out! He's going to–' Alice's voice rang out a warning from the other side of the corridor, just as Bubb dodged past him towards the stairs. Stephen put out his foot and Bubb fell headlong, cracking his cheek on the ground. Instantly Stephen leaned down and pushed the barrel of the gun up to his temple.

'Open the door,' he said grimly, gesturing at where Richard was looking out. The key grated in the lock and the door opened. Richard pushed his way out into the corridor, followed by his curious and bemused companions, who looked in horror at Paucett's motionless body. Ned Armitage bent over him to look more closely, feeling for a pulse in his neck.

'By God's grace, he's only stunned,' he said to Stephen, clapping him reassuringly on the back.

'The other door,' said Richard impatiently, 'open this one.' He had taken hold of Bubb by the arm. 'Alice is in there, we have to get her out.'

Stephen brought his pistol up to Bubb's temple who wordlessly handed over the bunch of keys. When Alice's door swung open she faltered a moment on the threshold, looking at the crowd of men jostling in the corridor, but then she stepped out to join them.

'Help me!' shouted Richard to his friends. 'I have had an idea.' He was dragging Paucett by the feet into Alice's cell. Between them they hauled his dead weight inside. Stephen pushed Bubb in after him and locked the door, turning the key with a satisfying clunk.

'In mercy's name, sir, don't leave me in here with him.' Bubb's face at the window was white. 'He'll do for me.' He kicked at the door, wailing. 'Please, I'll do anything, just don't leave me here with him.'

'What on earth–?' Richard turned back to see Stephen was stripping off his boots and breeches.

'Get undressed,' Stephen said, 'give me thy clothes.'

A few minutes later and Richard was dressed in the mulberry silk. The silk suit was a little too tight but Richard certainly carried the outfit well, even the wig and feathered hat suited him. Stephen felt instantly at ease in Richard's worsted breeches and smoke-stained shirt.

'Take this purse, and this...' Stephen offered Richard one of the pistols.

Richard shook his head.

'There are guards by the front gate, thou mayst have need of them.'

'No. I vowed I would never take up arms again.'

'For God's sake, man, thou needst not shoot them, just wave them about, like I did,' said Stephen. 'Hasten thee, or she will hang tomorrow.'

Alice was waiting mutely, as if in shock, her arms thin and white in the greenish-yellow light. Reluctantly Richard took the weapon in his hand and hid it inside his coat.

'My attendants are waiting with the chair, but they do not expect a woman,' said Stephen ushering him into motion. 'Put Alice inside and walk alongside thyself. There is a cloak lying there for her to wear, and a sword – and a dagger–' he turned to Alice – 'in case anything should happen and thou art recaptured.'

Alice nodded to show she knew the full implications of that dagger. Richard squeezed Alice's hand tightly. Stephen saw their eyes hanging on his words and looked down, suddenly shy. 'There is a passage booked for you both on the light schooner, the *Noblesse* – it is bound for France.' His voice was choked with emotion. 'May God be with you both.' The other Quakers hurried forward to thump Richard on the back, to embrace him or press his hand.

Within Alice's cell a great roar and rattling alerted them to the fact that Paucett had come round. A torrent of foul language ensued, with kicking at the door.

'Make haste,' said Sam. 'He will surely bring the guards.'

'What about thee?'

'I'll take my chances with the rest of the Friends when I have opened all the doors ... now go!'

Alice held tight to Richard's hand, in a state of perfect obedience. Suddenly she was free from her cell, and the prospect of life, even if only for a few hours, was intoxicating. His hand was firm around hers as they hurried through the dingy passageways.

As soon as they had reached the top of the stairs, Paucett's yammering was fainter, like a rumbling in the stomach of the building. The yard was still dark, for the moon was a quarter, and the watch lanterns only illuminated a small patch where the guards stood. 'Walk slowly,' Richard whispered, and they strolled to the sedan chair, still waiting by the gates.

Richard placed his arm around her shoulders, so that in the gloom it was the white plumes of his hat and his white lace cuffs that glowed bright and threw her drab and filthy appearance into shadow.

The attendants said nothing as she was helped into the carriage. She closed the curtain across the window and the bumpy ride began. After only a few steps there was a commotion and running feet behind the carriage, and a shout, 'Wait!'

The chair swayed forward and stopped. She rummaged on the floor for the cloak, wound it over her shoulders and dragged the hood over her hair. She found the sword, felt along the cold metal blade for the round boss of the hilt, then slid her hand into the curved guard, ready, dreading the thought she might have to use it.

'Sir,' said a breathless voice. 'You dropped your glove.'

'Thank you,' she heard Richard say. 'Tell the gatekeeper to open the gate, will you.'

'Yes, sir.'

The man's feet moved off with a clink of iron against stone and she was hoisted, swung suspended in the air once more. The grinding of the windlass and a chain running through pulleys. They were opening the gate.

The conveyance lurched forward and she heard the grate of the portal against flagstones, but then winced as the ear-splitting clangour of the prison bell drowned out all other sound.

The sedan jolted to the ground.

Richard's face appeared at the window. 'Hurry,' he said, opening the door and grasping her wrist, throwing off his hat at the same time. 'Get out.'

It was a tussle to climb down in the heavy cloak and her limbs were weak; he had to half drag her out of the door.

'Run!' He pulled her towards the massive gates, which were just beginning to squeeze closed again. She looked over her shoulder and saw the yard full of scattered men, charging hither and thither in a blur of disorder. A noise like an explosion filled her ears, then came the stench of powder. She did not dare look back again but fled towards the gate, holding tight to Richard's hand, seeing nothing but his mulberry back and the narrow shrinking opening to the outside world. Another explosion of shot bounced off the wall in front of them and the fog of smoke partially obscured the closing gate. When it cleared she saw there was a guard running towards the gateway, armed with a musket.

'Make way, in the name of the king!' shouted Richard, waving the pistol. The soldier looked momentarily nonplussed, pausing as they raced towards the gate. Alice felt Richard's hands almost lift her off the ground to propel her through the vertical crack before the soldier raised his musket to fire at point blank range. Richard flung himself through just as the musket ball sliced the edge of the gate, sending a shower of splinters and powder into the air.

Alice crouched low next to the wall, panting and breathless, as the gate finally shut. The bell was still tolling. A mist of smoke rose up to vaporize into the night sky and the spasms of firing within boomed out over the town.

Richard looked into her face, pulling her back to her feet, his eyes asking her how she fared. She reassured him with a brief smile and followed him, fleet-footed, down the steep cobbles, through the rabbit warren of streets towards the landing stage, where they could see the strip of silver water holding the land together like a belt of mercury. Several ships were already headed out towards the sea, their sails cracking as the bluff wind filled them and drew them westwards.

At the top of the steps they looked back to where the crenellations of the castle were occasionally thrown into relief by feeble flashes of continued gunfire. Alice found her legs were shaking, her heart tattooing behind her ribs. She staggered and almost tumbled down the steps. Richard drew her towards him to support her. He held her close to his chest, his arms wrapped about her waist, her head resting in the hollow of his shoulder.

He drew away to look at her. 'The search parties will be out for thee, when they know thou art gone,' he said. ''Tis not safe to remain here. We had best take that passage, as Stephen said.' He squeezed her arm in wordless comfort before leading her down the steps. 'We must hurry, for the tide is turning and the ships will be heading out. Yet neither must we arouse suspicion with our haste.'

They walked briskly along the wharf, looking for the *Noblesse*. There was a large crowd on the quay, getting ready to sail with the tide, and no one paid Richard and Alice any attention. They walked to the end of the stone jetty but still could not see the *Noblesse*.

At length, Richard paused to ask one of the men carrying a basket of salt herring.

'The *Noblesse*? Why, she's just sailed. You've missed her.' He pointed to a collection of small dots out towards the horizon. 'That's her with the red pennant.'

Alice sagged. A grey hopelessness swamped her. Richard turned her to face him.

'I'll not leave thee,' he said. His forehead was creased with worry. 'We will find another passage.'

'She's sailing on the hour,' said the man with the salt herring, 'the flute, over there.' He pointed to the dark hulk of a merchant ship across the other side of the bridge, still lying quietly in its berth.

'Thanks to thee,' said Richard. They weaved towards it, in and out of the tradesmen, keeping it in their sights. Alice was acutely aware of her dirty clothes and scuffed boots beneath the blue velvet cloak. Her hands clung tightly to its folds to hide what was beneath.

'Over there!' The noise of running feet spun her around.

'Richard–' she stopped him short with a hand on his shoulder – 'the guards have seen us.'

He turned instantly – the metal helmets of two guards could be seen running towards them, dodging through the bustling activity on the quay.

Richard and Alice ducked down into the crowd.

'Now,' Richard said, and he set off at a run, tugging at her arm. They sprinted into the darkness, across the arch of the stone bridge towards the flute that was just about to heave to. The oars were out, the tow boats and ropes ready. The silhouettes of the heads of the crew could be seen bobbing above the rails as they went about their business. Two coopers in wide canvas breeches had just wound the capstan to hoist the last barrels of ale aboard.

Alice heard the sound of running feet but did not dare look behind her. They raced up the stone platform and onto the gangplank. Two roughhands stared at them as they hauled themselves aboard by the rope rail, then exchanged glances and shook their heads before hauling on the pulleys to raise the plank. Richard held Alice's hand in a firm grip as he shepherded her quickly across the deck, weaving between the teams of men loading grain into the dry stores.

'This way,' he said hurrying towards the rear of the ship. 'We will find the Master and, God willing, buy passage.'

She followed his broad back but paused as the world around her began to swivel on its axis. There was a bellow from the quay below and she glimpsed a cluster of black uniforms and the glint of helmets. Quickly, she ducked her head and hastened to catch up with Richard. The sailors at the rails looked up from their work and leaned over to see what the commotion was, but only for a moment, for the land was gliding away from them and once the vessel was moving there was no stopping her – above, a crack of canvas announced a small sail unfurling into the wind. The sound caused her heart to leap in her chest.

She picked her way between the ropes and pulleys to where Richard was speaking to a sailor coiling ropes about a peg. The sailor jabbed his finger wordlessly towards a short stout man with a bristling moustache. Under a hanging lantern, the Master was giving orders to the dishevelled-looking sailors grouped about him. When he saw them approach he looked at Alice with disbelief. Alice saw his look and hurried to Richard's side. The Master frowned and was already addressing them.

'You are not one of my men,' he said, 'nor even a sailor by the looks of you.'

'Good evening, sir,' Richard said with a nod. 'We missed our passage, but just caught the tide with thee. Tell me, where are you bound?'

The Master's eyebrows lowered and he shook his head. He opened his mouth, about to speak, but Richard carried on, 'We can pay for our berths,' and held out the bag of coinage Stephen had given him.

'I don't like women aboard. I won't have them. They cause nothing but trouble,' the Master said.

'I am Richard Wheeler of Kendal, and this is my spouse, Alice. I will vouch for her.' Alice felt heat rise to her face, and not just because Richard had an air of authority and directness about him that made him difficult to refuse.

The Master tried again. 'I tell you, I don't like it, it unsettles the men. By rights I should have you put to shore.'

Alice thought of the guards waiting on the quay. Richard squeezed her hand.

'Sir?' A man appeared at the Master's shoulder. 'What is it?'

'Bo'sun's found another split in the topsail, he needs more men on it.'

The Master gave a heavy sigh. 'I haven't got time for you now, I've better things to do. Fetch a boy,' he said to the sailor. 'I can't have women berthing with the men, can I? I'll have to see if there's space. It's not usual, sir. Women are unlucky.' He shook his head.

'Thanks to thee,' Richard said, opening the purse, 'we appreciate it.'

'No, I'll not be taking your money, you'll need to make yourself known to the owner for that. I don't know what the drill is for paying passengers. The boy will show you to his quarters. Where is your luggage?'

Alice caught Richard's eye, but fortunately the Master did not wait for an answer. A small boy in a brown knitted cap and filthy jersey skidded to a halt on his bare feet. The Master turned and gave the boy orders. The boy nodded.

'Over here,' said the lad, holding up his lantern and beckoning to them with a scrawny hand.

Richard bowed politely, although the Master had ceased to pay them any attention, and followed the boy. Alice swayed behind them, her feet uncertain on the shifting boards. They went past the helm to a small wooden door with a carved surround and green oilskin over its glass panel.

'Here it is,' the boy said in a loud whisper, 'but if I were you I'd hold off till after dinner. He's got a right temper on him and he's sleeping now.' The sound of a rasping breath could be heard through the door. 'He won't take kindly to being woke. Come on, I'll show you where you can berth.'

The boy took them down some slippery wooden steps beneath the quarterdeck to where there were two small plank doors side by side in the gloom. 'It'll have to be this one. Owner's son was to have this one, but he's not coming. Next door's the Master's.'

The boy handed Alice the light and stepped aside to let them enter.

Richard held a coin out to him. 'Thanks for thy advice.'

The boy snatched the coin. 'No trouble. Thank ye, sir,' and ran off, leaving the door creaking back and forth. Alice stepped in and looked around her.

She went over to the port window and peered out through the smeary bubble of glass. The glimmer of fishermen's cottages passed by their flank, then the rocky promontory of the headland and an expanse of flat pale sand, grey in the cloudy moonlight. Richard came to join her at the window.

'That's the last of England,' he said. 'They will not catch us now.'

And he lifted her off her feet like a small child and swung her round.

'Put me down at once,' she said. But she was smiling.

Chapter 35

Geoffrey's heart lifted as the slate of sea widened before him and the land became a mere smudge of tiny lights on the coastline they had left behind. He was glad to be cuffed by the cold air; he knew that after a few weeks at sea his skin always felt cooler and sleek as an otter under his silk shirt. The almanac had predicted fine weather and a stiff breeze out of harbour, so the prospect of the many weeks at sea was very pleasant. He smiled, suddenly carefree, for he was leaving his woes behind him, leaving the dark clouds of Westmorland for the sunshine of Virginia.

When it had occurred to him he could take ship again, it had seemed like providence. He knew that in some sense he was running away. He needed to be as far away from the gibbet at Lancaster as possible; he could not have stomached being present when Alice Ibbetson was hanged. Could not bear the sound of it. Even as a boy he had a ghoulish fear of the hangman in his black

431

hood. It had given him the night-terrors thinking he lay in wait for him under his bed.

He shivered, and not just from the chill of the spray. With Alice Ibbetson's death, the old woman's ghost might be tempted to creep out from her cold resting place. He fancied she knew exactly what he was doing every day, almost as if she was following him – an invisible, but in-extinguishable, malevolent presence.

Geoffrey looked up. There was a reassuring number of men on the topsail spars. Maybe she would not be able to reach him on this table of water. Here the men treated him with the respect he deserved and there would be no women with whom he need concern himself. He would have sturdy male company and could forget the troubles of Westmorland. He would meet with Fairfax in Virginia, have a look at his estate.

There were rumours the king was soon to give Fairfax a proprietary colony, and who knows, Geoffrey thought, if he were to ingratiate himself with Fairfax enough, he himself might yet be awarded a swathe of land rather than having to purchase it from Lord Baltimore's portion. He would invite Fairfax to dine; he would certainly prove to be a more interesting companion than the ship's Master, who hardly spoke a word, and when he did could talk of nothing but wind and water.

With a light step, he went down to his familiar sea-going chamber, creaking slightly like a baby's bassinet – with its comfortable leather chair, its fixed escritoire and delightful collection of objects from around the world. There on the shelf above his cot, with its wooden rail to keep them from falling, were a Dutch porcelain pipe with a silver mounted lid, various drinking vessels from Moorish lands and a curved dagger from Spain with a tooled leather handle.

On another shelf near the stern windows sat his books, including the obligatory large Bible and atlas, and his botany volumes, next to his own nocturnals and mariner's quadrant. He liked to amuse himself by double-checking the progress of their passage. On the starboard wall hung a framed compass-rose and a collection of pressed butterflies from the Caribbees, their iridescent wings glimmering in the light of the hanging lamp, which rocked gently in its counterbalanced housing.

He idly took down a sword from his collection of arms. His swords were arrayed in a sunburst effect on the wooden wall. He made a few thrusts and parries, pleased with his swordsmanship, before sliding the rapier back into its housing and pressing his eyes to the porthole. The blur of the coast was now so faint as to be almost imaginary.

He rang for a boy and sent him to fetch his meal. It felt good to be aboard, to be giving orders again. After a meal in his cabin of salt-pork, bread and beans, he felt the infernal itching returning, so he unpacked his leather case and drew out one of several phials containing the lady's slipper extract. He brought the O-shaped neck of the bottle to his lips and drained it, grimacing at the taste and smell. He was ready with his flask to take a nip of rum to counteract it. After wrapping a blanket around his knees, he sat down in his chair and closed his eyes, listening to the noise of the miniature world of his ship – the lowing of the milk-cow from the hold, the familiar clunk of something heavy rolling on the poop deck above and the distant shouts of the conning officer giving directions to the helm.

The rocking motion and the warming effects of the food and rum soon had him dozing in his seat; he slept with his head tilted back, his mouth open. He did not hear the bells for the change of watch or the slap of the sail. Instead he fancied that his ship had sunk underwater, down to the sea bed, where the mast turned into a gallows and Alice Ibbetson was hanging there, her naked feet swinging above his head.

Alice stared out of the window at the undulating horizon. It was calm but the swell under her feet was an unfamiliar sensation; already her feet longed for solid earth. The cabin was cramped but clean. It smelt of damp wood and had no furnishings except a locker set into a bench, a fixed washstand and a single bare berth which lay along one wall. On it was folded a single canvas hammock for the hooks in the roof beams. Richard had gone up on deck to buy blankets and linen from the ship's stores and already she missed his steadfast presence. She felt vulnerable when he was not by her side.

Earlier he had asked the boy for water and more light, and she was able to wash herself at last. She noticed how her shaking fingers looked red and coarse against the fine porcelain of the bowl. The water was salty and stung in the small cuts in her fingers. They were no longer soft and

434

white but looked like the hands of a maid of all work. She thought fleetingly of Ella, but the thought pained her, so she resolutely put it aside and paid attention to the act of washing her face.

The wooden door opened and Richard stepped over the threshold, ducking his height under the lintel, his arms full of blankets, a basket of other items balanced on top. She turned from her washing and reached out her hand to pull a corner of a linen cloth from the basket. She rubbed vigorously at her face.

'If I am supposed to be your wife, then I suppose I must take pains to be clean, at least,' she smiled.

'I surely would not choose such a troublesome wife as thee.'

He was making jest, and they both laughed, but there was a moment's silence before he spoke again. A moment where both saw clearly what they had not seen before.

'As my wife,' he said to her softly, 'I would have kept thee safe at home and made sure nothing could harm thee.'

Tears sprang to her eyes from a deep well inside her. The cloth fell to her side.

'Come here,' he said softly.

He put down the basket and reached out towards her, closing his arms tightly about her waist. The tears came. But then she found herself yielding, pliant like a tender young shoot, her back arched, her face upturned to his. When he kissed her, it was long and slow and sweet, his lips soft and warm against hers. And there was a stirring in her breast and the heaving world seemed turned

435

to silence by his kiss. It was he who pulled away first, his eyes beseeching. 'I have not offended thee?'

'No, Richard. I think I have wished it for a long time but without knowing it, since the very first time you smiled at me. In the miller's. Do you remember?'

'I remember your face, and something in your eyes. A light there that catches me somehow' He took hold of her face and looked down at her. 'It still does.'

He reached for her again, and she felt him press towards her and his face come down to cover her throat with kisses, whilst her hands grasped his hair as she sought to bring him home to her. She heard herself moan with pleasure as an exquisite tingle mounted in her thighs and she pushed her hips towards him. His hand was on her breast-bone, where her breath rose and fell in gusts, she felt him move against her, hard, through the soft petticoats.

He guided her over to the cot, where he began to untie the laces from the side of her bodice, with the sort of concentration one might use if engaged in a very delicate act of calligraphy. She watched the laces slide away through the holes and hang in his broad fingers, his head bowed to the task, and was strangely moved. Her breath came quicker as the bodice slid slowly from her shoulders, and his hands rubbed over her breasts through the fine lawn of the chemise, her nipples hardening as his kisses drew nearer towards them. Finally his mouth was on her nipple and her hand was wrapped in the silky skein of his

436

hair. She pushed towards him, the place between her legs wet and wanting.

He reached out to touch her face. 'Your husband? I would not want...'

'Hush,' she said then, moved by his earnest expression. 'Who knows what tomorrow may bring. Yesterday I thought my life ending. But today it seems it was a beginning, for I have found you, I have found *thee*, and if it be one more hour or one more day in thy company, I am content.'

He smiled then and kissed her neck, and the ship creaked gently as they took their pleasure of each other for the first time.

The rap on the door made them both start. Richard stood up quickly, tugging on his breeches, and went to listen at the door. 'Who is it?'

''Tis the steward's boy, sir,' came a high-pitched voice from without. Alice pulled her bodice back over her shoulders, flustered, her eyes never leaving Richard's face.

'The Master requests you at his table. At the next bell, sir.'

Alice mouthed to him, 'What shall we do?'

He shook his head. 'Thank you, boy,' he said loudly through the door. 'Thank the Master, but tell him the lady has not yet found her sea legs and we must unfortunately decline his invitation. Perhaps tomorrow.'

'Yes, sir.' They listened until the footsteps had died away. Richard then opened the door and looked out, before shutting it and barring it firmly against intruders.

'I am not ready to share thee with company,' he

437

said. 'Happen the owner of the ship can wait until the morrow for his payment. After all, we cannot go far unless we wish to swim.'

She did not even smile. 'Richard, I am afraid.'

'We are safe here.' He reached for her hand. 'Or leastways as safe as anyone else on this voyage.'

She paused a moment. A deep unease gnawed in her belly but it was a feeling she could not name. 'I don't know. I suppose I am just not used to the sea. And I am as much afraid of gaining a new life as I was of losing it.'

'Thou wilt find thy sea legs soon enough. 'Tis hard to get accustomed to at first, I know.'

'It is not that. It's like an emptiness, leaving England behind. I have nothing left, Richard, nothing to offer. Only what I am standing in.'

He grasped hold of her shoulders and looked at her steadily.

'That is enough for me. Thy life. It could so easily have been otherwise. I will not leave thee, I promise. We will face what life brings together.' He dropped his eyes a moment before speaking again. 'I cannot hold it from thee any longer, the ship is not bound for France, but for New England–' She drew back and made to protest, but he stayed her. 'There are Quakers there who will help us – old Isaac used to talk of them. It is not so bad. We can make a fresh start there, build a new life for ourselves.'

'But I know nothing of Quaker life, only the few things Hannah told me.' She turned away, agitated. 'I cannot start to imagine it, I'm not ready to even think of it.' She pressed her palm to her forehead. 'The other side of the world. I have

438

never been out of my little England before. And besides, I am not so devout as Hannah. I am not sure I am fitted for that life.' She moved away, twisting the lace of her bodice in her fingers.

'You know I would never press thee to become one of us. But we have no choice, and in a way it is good, for it would be hard for thee to return to England, to be always looking over thy shoulder. In New England thou wilt be a free woman in a free land. A new start – for us both.'

He reached over, curled his fingers into hers and squeezed them, his eyes searching hers. She looked down at his broad palm and her own hand lying trustingly there. She must have faith in providence. She reached her other hand around his neck and pulled him down towards her. The boards under her feet tilted slightly and she shifted her weight to compensate. He took her in his arms and clasped her close.

'I love thee, Alice,' he said.

Chapter 36

After his afternoon nap, Geoffrey awoke feeling nauseous and disorientated. He had slept too long and now he forced himself to step up on deck to take some air, where he zigzagged from rail to rail, looking blankly out to sea. His headaches were now severe enough to stop him in his tracks or cause him to hold his skull between his hands and rock back and forth like a lunatic. Since waking he had alleviated the pain with rum, so that now it was a mere throb like distant thunder.

Under the brisk easterly the ship forged ahead like a white-capped mountain, shouldering the waves aside, the water pouring from the canvas, the breeze singing in the tautened ropes. Spray whipped across the deck in the eddy of the mainsail, the deck a-tilt, so that all movement became a lurch from handrail to rope in the slippery film of salty water. Rain was falling now, insistent and blinding, from a sky devoid of stars.

He climbed the narrow steps and breathed in the smell of salt from the top deck, leaning over to watch the tips of the waves slip by in flashes of white. He held onto the rails and looked out beyond the prow to the inky line where the sea joined the sky. The rain stung his face.

He always used to love the ship's motion, the sense of riding on such a huge depth of water, but now he was unsettled by the constant movement, and irritated that it made him bilious. He had hoped another spell at sea would improve his health and clear his mind of the nightmare of the past few weeks. His life was falling asunder. He had never thought he would see the day when his son would disobey him. He did not think Stephen had the guts.

Geoffrey hurried below. Although he had an oilskin cloak, he had no desire to fetch it and subject himself to the sheeting rain when he could lie on his bunk below and read *Pinax Theatri Botanici*, a fascinating manual by a Frenchman which listed species of New England plants. He was determined to follow in the footsteps of the famous

Tradescant and find and list further wonders – ones not already collected by the French.

As he turned the pages he could not cast Stephen from his mind. He thought back to the embarrassing scene in the dining room where Stephen had virtually called him a tyrant and dared to imply he was a laughing stock. Stephen's words had hurt, but he had decided to forgive and forget, and make a new start with his awkward son. He had tried everything to persuade Stephen to take passage with him but to no avail. Even at the last minute Geoffrey had thought he would come round but, frustratingly, despite his best efforts, at the turn of the tide Stephen had been nowhere to be found. Patterson and the dairymen had searched the whole estate, but the old brown nag was missing from the stables so it was clear enough he had purposely ridden out. So to Geoffrey's bitter disappointment he had been forced to take ship alone.

He was angry with himself – he suspected he had been too soft with his son. A few months at sea would have got rid of Stephen's heretical Quaker notions. But he was damned if he was going to let Stephen rule his life, dictate to him what he should and should not do. When it had become clear Stephen was to stay in Westmorland, he had called on Rawlinson and enjoined him to take Stephen under his wing – tutor him a little, whilst he was away. Rawlinson had said Stephen was a grown man now, and perhaps giving him his trust, and a measure of responsibility, would make a man of him. Geoffrey hoped he was right. Rawlinson was no fool; he would keep Stephen on the straight and narrow. And Stephen would return to his senses soon enough – no sane lad would turn his back on an income of forty pounds a year and a house like Fisk Manor.

Eventually, chewing on his lip, Geoffrey took up a quill to pen a letter to him. A six-month absence was always a risk in these uncertain times, and he hoped Stephen was home by now at the manor, safely under Rawlinson's eagle eye. He dreaded he might go back to London to drain the coffers of his inheritance – or, even worse, that he might be hanging about with the scullions at the Hall. Rawlinson had promised him the fire-setting Quakers would be tried and sentenced, so perhaps that would quash Wheeler's treasonous sect for good.

Geoffrey sharpened the quill and dipped it in the ink. 'My dear Stephen,' he scratched, but then paused, wondering how to continue. He did not know what to say, had no idea where to start. He realized he had never written to his son before. Emilia had always done it. He blinked, surprised. His eyes were wet.

He gritted his teeth, lowered the quill into the ink again and wiped it on the lip of the bottle. He must demonstrate affection to his son, put difficulties behind them, guide him away from these ranters and bad influences. It was something he had never understood, why he and Stephen were unable to see eye to eye. Even as a child, Stephen seemed bred of different stock.

Geoffrey remembered that when the Nether-barrow Hunt arrived at a kill, the other boys would be eager to be first there, to have the sticky blood smeared upon their cheeks, and he would look out for his son hoping to see him jesting amongst the throng – but Stephen was inevitably the last, left limping behind the field, his knees flapping aimlessly against his horse's flank, his face pinched with fear.

He cast those thoughts away and instead imagined the two of them managing the estate together, constructing a vast trading network of ships and sugar colonies, putting away quantities of gold against future calamities, such as another war. Father and son together. Slowly he began to write, filling out his dreams, his pen scratching unevenly across the paper as the ship listed from side to side.

He had a sudden idea, and paused mid-sentence. He put down his pen, stood up and went over to the locker. He would make some purchases from his New England friends. When he returned home he would surprise his son with a gift of some land of his own for a tobacco plantation. His own plantation! That would surely whet his interest. And he would purchase some well-seasoned negroes to labour on it for him. Stephen could have charge of them, to accustom himself to giving orders and managing a workforce.

Inspired, he took out papers and charts from his locker, choosing a rolled map of the new territories. He undid the ribbon and spread it out on the escritoire with two lead blocks to hold it flat, for the ship was pitching more now, and he could hear the clap of the waves against the sides and the shouts of the men calling 'Belay'. The gloom below had intensified, so he lit a small lantern and stood it on the edge of the desk, the better to see the itinerary. His eyesight had failed him of late, words often danced about on the page and his headache made it difficult to concentrate.

The last time he had been in St Christopher in the Caribbees, he recalled, he had visited a sugar farm. He had been most impressed with the vast numbers of dusky men cutting like an army through the canes, and had heard that the same technique had been adopted in New England for tobacco. He was fascinated by the blackness of their skins, their flat noses, their loose limbs, the way they needed no rest but moved inexorably along the lines like the black shadow on a sundial. The crops were made fast in half the usual time. He saw no reason why these advanced methods should not eventually hold good for his own estate, and the economics of it were plain. Stephen could arrange the building of their quarters and later sort out the gangs for threshing and ploughing. In this new age Stephen would soon prosper, and he, Geoffrey, would be free to explore his horticultural and scientific interests in his sunset years.

Now with the map in front of him, he laid out his route in his mind, progressing down the coast to the large estates in St Mary's and Jamestown. There he would be able to buy a portion of land for Stephen. He looked closely at the map, seeking a plot close to his own. He earmarked two possible positions in his mind. Once he had made his purchase, he thought, he would check his own plantations, relax and dine in a reasonably civilized fashion, and return refreshed, a few days later, to his ship. From these holdings it was a week's sail to the remoter parts of Virginia, where he would take armed expedition to forage for new plants and extraordinary exhibits before returning to Providence, from there to load his more regular cargo of rice and tobacco.

As he looked at the vast tracts of blank land laid out on the map, the edges fraying into the unknown, the petty world of England grew far away and, with it, the hanging of Alice Ibbetson – for by now, he thought with relief, it was over, and she was surely at peace. The old woman's ghost must have been blown away by the fierce winds and salt spray of the ocean. Here was his little empire, moving steadily towards a new world.

Geoffrey's shoulders began to lower, the tension bled away, his head nodded again over his chest. He rested his forearm over the crenellated coastline of New England, as if to protect it, and sank his long face into the crook of his elbow. He inhaled the subtle smell of the wind from the fibres of his green velvet coat, let his eyes close. Within a few moments he was asleep. Several hours later he half woke, found himself scratching, so took another dose of his remedy. Still dressed, he stumbled to his bunk, fell down onto it and began to snore.

As the graveyard bells rang out, he dreamt his tobacco plantations were full of crawling insects, like ants, that scuttled across the land devouring everything in a black tide.

Chapter 37

Richard lay in the dark in the narrow cot, Alice's hand clasped in his, her head on his shoulder. He held her loosely, feeling the back of her ribs expand and contract with her breath. She was heavy-limbed and warm, sleeping peacefully. From his position he propped himself up on one elbow to look out of their salt-smeared window for any sign of land. Of course that was foolish, he knew. But it was what everyone did on board ship.

He looked down and twined one of Alice's fine coppery curls in his fingers; they were ebony in this light. They had eschewed the hammock and gladly slept in the same cot despite the lack of space. It felt natural, inevitable, like a coming home. She had opened herself to him trustingly, and so he had found himself gentle, respectful, despite the urgency of his desire. Having seen her so near to death, the want in him for life was intense, but also the search for life's deep secret in her eyes. He had been surprised by his own nakedness; it was as if in the previous years he had forgotten his body was there at all. He stretched his cramped bare limbs like a new-born.

A great crash of something falling on the upper deck roused him from his thoughts, and woke Alice, who moved to cling to him more tightly.

'Hush, dear one,' he said. 'The sea is rough, there may be a storm coming.'

'Should we rise?' she asked sleepily, pulling him close.

'No need,' he said. 'I am sure this vessel is built to withstand any storm. But it may get more blustery yet, and the sea swell more fierce. I had best secure anything loose in the cabin.'

He slid out of bed and hitched on his breeches. He made to stow away the wash-jug and basin just as the ship began to keel more violently from side to side. With difficulty he crossed back and forth to the locker, carrying a shaving mug, the chamberpot, a water flagon. When it was done, he climbed back into bed. Out of the porthole he could see the oily surface of the sea coming up towards them, followed all too soon after by the gaping black hole of the sky.

As the night drew on, and the ship's timbers began to moan and the sails whipped louder, he lay beside her and prayed silently, asking God for a safe passage, and for deliverance – not his own but hers. He assumed that God would be disapproving of his lust, but to his surprise his conscience remained untroubled. He was following some inner law of natural behaviour, and as he prayed he discovered that his God had changed, become more forgiving, more accepting of him. It was a great wonder to him. He realized he had prayed to many different ideas of God through his lifetime. How strange it was, that each man's God seemed to be his own unique creation.

The ship heaved and rolled through the night in heavy seas. Richard had to go above decks to vomit but Alice seemed unperturbed by the motion. When he returned she was asleep still,

447

her face pale, almost luminous, against the dark blankets.

The hammer of the rain stopped. Curious, he pressed his face to their cabin window again to see the skin of the sea stretched out into the distance, like the back of a great black dragon arching its spine. He paced the floor, restless and unable to sleep, making plans in his mind. Stephen had loaned them a large amount but he worried it might not be enough for their needs. He took up writing materials and calculated the likely cost of the passage, and worked out what essentials they might be able to afford to give them a start in the New World. He wanted to prepare, for he worried that Alice was bound for a rough life, not of her own choosing.

His eyes kept returning to her sleeping figure – he relived the breathless passion of the night before. He could still feel her touch as if newly branded on his skin, the way his body tingled beneath her fingers, the softness of her lips. She had pressed her mouth tenderly to his scar, the raised weal that ran down his chest like the mark of a whip. She had not asked him about it, and her tenderness and quiet acceptance of it touched him.

Through the night they had heard the bells for the changes of watch, right enough, but their time was slow and meandering as each uncovered traces of the other's past, the memories interspersed with languorous touches. Richard found with awe that his hunger for Alice, and the fact that he had so nearly lost her, became a desire to look into her eyes and drown there, and this

448

seemed to him to be a great paradox – that his love became the shadow of death, haunting, just beneath the surface of his thoughts.

He climbed back in beside her, cold and damp and still half dressed. He stroked her smooth back. She rolled over.

'Thou art all gooseflesh,' she murmured, rubbing at his arms. 'Here, let me hold thee.' She chafed his hands between hers, bringing them to her lips to blow on them.

'I never thought to hear it, but the Quaker speech sits well with thee,' he said.

She smiled up at him and squeezed his hand. 'Hast thou been up on deck?'

'Seems I left my sea legs in Lancaster,' he said ruefully.

'And we are set to sail to the other side of the world,' she murmured. 'Thou must purchase a new pair straight away.'

'If there's any coin left over when I have paid our passage, then I'll get myself a good strong set, and maybe a spare pair for thee too.'

The next morning Geoffrey peered through the crack of the shutter that faced the deck. From here he could keep an eye on the Master and the crew. He winced and drew back a moment as daylight reached his eyes. Behind the shutter, drops of condensation rolled across the window in diagonal streaks. The morning was chill and misty, the rigging a hazy grey against a whiter sky. The men were hauling in sail.

He blinked. Over by the mizzen he saw the faint outline of a woman's figure climb the steps.

449

She was clinging to the handrail with one hand and carrying a basin in the other. Geoffrey stared. The mist distorted his view through the window. He must be imagining it, there were no women on board. He opened the shutter a little more. The crew ignored her presence and carried on shortening sail. He thought he saw the woman struggle over to the side and tip the contents of the basin overboard, before turning and walking carefully back towards the steps. It was Alice Ibbetson. Geoffrey's stomach turned over. But that was impossible – she had been hanged this morning at Lancaster.

He took an involuntary step away from the window. When he looked again, she was gone and the men were working as before. He flung open the door and rushed outside towards the steps, the cold morning air wet on his face. He stared wildly about him but there was no trace of her. The ranks of men raised their eyes from their tasks to watch him, and under their curious gaze he withdrew sheepishly into his cabin.

He slumped back into his chair. 'Get a hold of yourself, man,' he said to himself, 'she's dead.' He had not realized he would be so affected by the Ibbetson woman's death. It must be the stress of it; his overtaxed mind had conjured up her image, that was all. What time had she died? He could not remember. He shivered, the sudden cold seemed to gnaw at his bones. Perhaps her ghost had come to find him. He told himself firmly there were no such things as ghosts.

He must set to a practical task, stop these strange fancies. He poured himself a double measure of rum and felt its sweet warmth hit the back of his throat. He took his morning remedy as usual. He would finish writing to Stephen. But his hands had a tremor like an old man as he opened the drawer and picked up the quill. He could not uncork the bottle of ink, and when he tried to read what he had already written, it was blurred and, try as he might, he could not bring the words into focus. A shout on the deck above and he thought he heard the crack of Alice Ibbetson's neck as she swung, saw her eyes looking at him in reproach. Was she looking down on him now?

Seized with the feeling of being watched, he let the letter drop quietly back into the drawer. He swivelled his head to look over his shoulder and thought he caught a glimpse of the old woman just inside the door. His heart leapt in his chest. He jumped up but she had melted away, like a mirage. His heart was beating too fast, he thought. If it kept on like this it might burst and he would die, he had heard of such things happening – a man's heart might stop altogether if he had a shock. Two women were in their graves because of him, and they were exacting vengeance.

A panic assailed him. He wanted to pray but no words would come; his ears buzzed, his legs were soft as cotton. When he drew his hand across his brow he found that sweat dewed his forehead; he clutched the raised edges of the desk and breathed in shallow noisy gulps with his tongue protruding from his mouth like a dog. It felt as if his chest was squeezed in a metal band, like a barrel, and he knew if he couldn't get enough air he was going to die.

He grappled along the shelf for his Bible and, clasping it to his chest, threw himself face down onto his bunk. Grunting, he stretched out an arm and dragged his leather satchel towards him across the floor by its strap. Still holding the Bible, he felt inside the satchel for his flask of brandy, and rolled onto his back before emptying the dregs into his mouth.

The act of doing this calmed him, and he willed himself to slow his breath. He crossed his arms across the stiff leather of the book and felt the comforting weight of it pressing down on him. 'One, two, three, four...' He counted a beam on the ceiling with each inhalation. The idea he might be losing his wits terrified him. Once, his hand slid inside his waistcoat and felt the rough skin of his chest through his shirt. His skin was hot, his heart still beating too fast, but the thump beneath his palm was reassuring. The cabin was barely moving now, the slap of the waves turned to a gentle lapping. He stayed on his bunk, rigid, staring up at the ceiling. It was eerily quiet. The uncanny feeling remained, that if he turned to look he would see the old woman sitting there in his chair. He dared himself to look. There was nobody there.

A sharp knock on his door made him startle. The Bible thudded to the deck as he sat up. He reached to the hook for his sword belt and buckled it on. Agitated, he dragged out his sea trunk, flipped it open and found his flintlock. He shoved it into his belt.

It was the Master.

'There's another ship close by, sir. We think she's passed us, but we heard her six bell. Just letting you know we'll have to keep the bell tolling, sir. We cannot risk a collision in this fog.'

As if to punctuate his words the doleful clangour of the bell began. Geoffrey groaned and put his hands over his ears.

'Get out,' he shouted.

The noise vibrated through to his core. Unable to bear it in his cabin, he went out on deck, holding his head. The ship was almost at a standstill, apart from the vague shapes of two men above tugging on the bell rope. He could scarcely see a yard before him. Figures loomed out of the mist and then disappeared into it again. There was no horizon, no sea, no sky, everything seemed to have been swallowed in a white shroud.

He felt his way across the deck, from handhold to handhold, grasping at the rigging as he went. The men were leaning over the rails peering into the fog. He looked up. The bare masts swayed above him like burnt-out trees, the tops fading into nothingness.

Then he saw her again, Alice Ibbetson, leaning over the rail. He would recognize that russet hair anywhere. He rubbed his eyes. She seemed to drift away, down the stairs. He watched her disappear below decks before following her. He stumbled in his haste to see where she went, tripping over one of the big guns, ready in case the French should attack again. He brought himself back to upright, his head throbbing, and set off towards the steps. It was impossible to hurry, for the decks were still awash after the rain, and he cursed as his feet slipped in the wet despite the fact that the ship was barely tilting.

He ducked into the tween-deck corridor and flung open the first door; it banged back against the wall. He caught a glimpse of her standing with her back to him, folding a piece of linen, but at the sound of the door she swung round. Her eyes widened, her hands flew up to her mouth. 'By all the saints...?' She took a step back. 'My God,' she whispered. 'Geoffrey, 'tis thee.'

Richard waited outside the owner's cabin swinging his purse by its strings.

Perhaps he was not in.

After the squally night he was glad the roll of the decks had dwindled to a gentle rock and he was feeling less queasy. He took in a few good lungfuls of air, tasting the salt in his mouth, though the morning mist made it seem as if they were gliding through steam.

Richard knocked again, the rap of his knuckles staccato in the silence. He waited a few more minutes before deciding to stroll down to the prow to stretch his legs. When he set off, the decks were quiet. The ship had taken on water last night and he could hear the sound of men baling below. He walked the length of the deck, lost in thoughts of New England, summoning the maps from his atlas to his mind, musing on the crops of cotton and tobacco.

When he returned, he was about to knock on the owner's door for a third time when faintly in the distance he heard a bell toll.

'Saints preserve us, it's another ship,' said one of the men appearing close by, but then all sound was drowned by their own bell giving its answering call.

Richard went to join the men leaning over the side. They were still, like statues, trying to pierce through the whiteness with their eyes, searching for the other vessel.

'Curse this fog,' shouted the man next to him above the pealing din. 'You never know what's out there. Can't get no bearings without sun nor stars. 'Tis easy to be off course, run aground, see. Or worse, hit another ship. And you can't tell which way she's drifting.'

'Sounds like the bell's coming from over there, behind us.' Richard pointed.

'Could be.' He leaned in to talk into Richard's ear. 'But then it might just as easy be ahead of us. There's no telling in this.'

They looked out again over the rails.

'Were you after Sir Fisk?' the sailor shouted in his ear.

'What?' Richard thought he had misheard him, the bell was still clanging above them.

'I saw you knock on his door.'

'What didst thou say his name was?'

'He's gone that way. Old Scratcher. Sir Geoffrey. Not ten minutes ago, down yon stairs. The Master's cabin–'

But Richard did not catch any more of his words, he was already running across the deck.

Alice clutched the piece of linen to her chest, unable to grasp what she was seeing. The jarring sound from above made it hard to think.

'So it is you,' said Geoffrey, 'but I saw you last night, clear as clear, your feet were swinging ...

you were...' His voice tailed away.

She could barely recognize him. He wore no wig and his face was gaunt and hollow-eyed. He took a tentative step nearer, looking at her as if she were an apparition.

'How did you–' she began.

He recoiled as if she had slapped him. 'Leave me alone,' he shouted, flattening himself to the wall of the cabin, 'get away from me.'

'Geoffrey–'

'Get back.' He looked at her through bleary eyes as if he did not know who she was. He shook his head as if to clear it. Suddenly he lurched towards her and took hold of her arm. She let out a cry of surprise.

'You're no ghost.' He thrust her away. 'How did you get on my ship?'

Geoffrey's ship. She blanched. It couldn't be true.

'You were to swing for me, in my place. For the old woman's death.'

Alice tried to take it in but could not order her thoughts. An instinct made her shrink away from him.

'She's following me,' he said, 'she won't rest in peace. She's on board somewhere. She thinks I don't know but I've seen her, hiding in the shadows.'

'You do not look well,' Alice stammered, 'let me fetch the physician.' She started to move towards the door. She must find Richard, fetch help.

'No,' said Geoffrey, slamming the door behind him. He slid the bolt across. 'I need time to think. I need to think what to do with you.'

A chill went over her. She prayed for Richard to come back. He had gone to the owner's cabin. But the owner was here, so surely he would be back soon.

'You can never go back to Westmorland,' Geoffrey said.

'I am not thinking to return.' Her voice sounded normal, but her lips were dry. She sat down. Her heart was pounding. She must get him away from the door.

'Come and sit a moment, Geoffrey.' She indicated the place beside her.

He did not respond but continued to pace up and down in front of the door. He plucked at the fabric of his breeches with a shaking hand.

'Tell me about your plans,' she said. 'I hear there are many interesting plants in the New World, like the orchid you showed me.' She tried again. 'You recall, Geoffrey, do you not, the orchid we were cultivating together, the lady's slipper?'

'Of course I remember.' His eyes refocused on her as if she were a simpleton. 'It has turned out to be a very valuable medicinal plant, just as I said it would.'

'I am afraid the seedlings will not survive, now I am gone.'

'Oh, but they will.' He gave a hoarse laugh. 'All your goods were forfeit by the court. No, I am growing them on myself. Johnson has care of them whilst I am away.'

'That's good.'

'That idiot constable. He would have disposed of them. Can you believe it? Had no idea of their importance, of course.'

'Come sit down then, and tell me how the plants are faring,' she said.

Geoffrey stepped towards her. His colour had come back and now his eyes were less wild. 'I am taking the extract of nerveroot myself. Look.' He fumbled in his pocket and held out a small phial between his finger and thumb.

'May I see?' If she could only get him a little further from the door. She patted the bunk next to her.

'I have made enough to last until I return,' he said, 'and the new plants are already showing.'

'No, that cannot be right. You must be mistaken, the lady's slippers would not be showing yet, only the–' She bit her lip.

'What?' A fraction's pause before he lunged to grab hold of her shoulders.

She took her chance and ducked out of his grasp. She leapt at the door, tugging to release the bolt, but it was damp and slippery and her fingers could get no purchase on it.

He launched himself at her back and thrust her aside with a force that made her stagger. He put his hands on her shoulders and shook her the way a dog shakes a rat.

'You bitch. Which shelf were they on?'

Alice could not catch her breath to speak.

'The lady's slippers. Which bloody shelf?'

'I don't know–' his thumbs pressed into her neck – 'the middle shelf.'

He gave a howl of rage. Alice choked, 'It was the middle shelf.'

There was a moment's pause before he slapped

her hard across the face. 'No. The top shelf. Tell me it was the top one.'

She did not dare move.

His voice dropped. 'My God. I've thrown them away.' With sudden violence he pushed her back against the wall, pinioning her there with a hand at her throat.

'Stupid bloody bitch. You did not label them properly.'

'Richard!' she cried.

'Quiet.' He clamped a hand over her mouth and manhandled her across the room towards the door. She swiped at the bench for anything to use as a weapon and her hand scattered some papers before it closed around a quill knife. She felt its thin cold edge with her fingers. She jabbed it upwards, but a moment too late. He took hold of her wrist and, bending the fingers back, seized it from her hand.

She felt the needle of the blade penetrate her shoulder as he brought his full weight down behind it. The blow instantly weakened her. She said his name again to bring him to his senses, but felt the suck, and a rush of hot blood, as he pulled the knife out of her shoulder. A mewing sound came out of her mouth. She collapsed backwards.

Perhaps if she lay still he might think he had killed her. She closed her eyes, tried not to let her breath stir her. There was a pause. She strained to hear where he was. The sound of boot heels, then a hand gripped her wounded shoulder. She gasped in pain and opened her eyes. He was leaning over her; his breath had a peculiar rancid odour, the pupils of his eyes were like pinpricks.

'I knew she had cursed me. Cursed me to live forever as if ants are eating me alive. You're both alike,' he said, 'you won't leave me be. But you feel warm. Not cold like her. And you're bleeding.' He stared at his hand before wiping it on his thigh. 'Too much blood,' he said. 'Get up.'

He tried to pull her to her feet. Alice froze as his free hand slid around the back of her neck. The other hand still held the knife at her throat.

'Do you need some company? Shall we let the sea take her?' He seemed to be addressing an invisible audience. He tightened his grip, then released her and stepped away. 'What do you think, Widow Poulter?'

Alice heard nothing – no reply, just the ominous tolling of the bell.

He opened the bolt with one swift movement and dragged her up.

The ship listed sharply to one side. Geoffrey struggled to cling onto her but she took her chance and twisted out of his grip. In a moment she was staggering out of the door and into the corridor. Her legs were limp as sackcloth and she put both hands out to the sides of the wooden walls to steady herself as she scrambled in a panic for the stairs.

A vivid orange flash and a shot whistled past her to smatter in the bulkhead beyond. She let out a cry, for the crack made her ears ring.

The air was thick with the acrid smoke of powder, yellow against the mist. She glanced behind to see him feeling his way towards her, the barrel of a gun still held out before him. My

460

God, he was armed.

She had one foot on the stairs but another flash followed by a deafening blast stopped her in her tracks as a hole exploded into splinters in the ceiling above her. She dropped to her knees under a shower of shrapnel, whimpering with shock, her head covered with her arms. She began to crawl up; she could see nothing but a dense cloud of smoke behind her in the dim corridor. Above her the sky was the colour of whey. Everything seemed to be happening very slowly, as if she was wading through mud.

With horror she felt a tug on her skirts and looked down to see his hand clutching them. She snatched them away and leapt up, seizing the handrail with her good arm to haul herself above deck. She cast about for someone to help her but there was a pall over everything; she could see no one and hear nothing above the ship's bell. The fog was still heavy and all spare men were up the rigging on lookout or baling below after the heavy seas of the night before.

The hazy shape of Geoffrey's head and shoulders appeared from the deck below. She ran to the side rail but he was still coming after her, moving unsteadily through the mist, his gun levelled at her chest.

'Alice!' Richard's frantic voice came from somewhere behind them, at the same time as another voice yelled the all clear. The clang of the ship's bell suddenly stopped.

'Oh thank God. Here,' she almost wept, 'I'm over here.' Her voice seemed small.

'Where?' Richard shouted.

She heard Geoffrey swear under his breath as he stopped, fumbling to reload his pistol. She seized her chance and put the mizzen mast between her and Geoffrey, shrinking back behind its solid girth. Geoffrey spun round, took aim and fired – a shot that ricocheted off the edge of the mast and hissed into the white gloom beyond.

Instantly a figure hurled itself out of the mist and grabbed Geoffrey around the neck. His head jerked back and he let out a soft puff of surprise. Richard's fingers clamped over his as he tried to prise the pistol from Geoffrey's grasp. Geoffrey twisted and squirmed to free himself. Taking a deep breath, he jabbed his elbow sharp into Richard's stomach. Richard doubled over, coughing, but Geoffrey rounded to face him, his hand still caught in the other man's grip.

Geoffrey's mouth dropped open, slack. 'You!' he said.

He tottered back as if winded. Richard seized control of the pistol and threw it to one side.

'Is it not enough but you will haunt me too?' Geoffrey whispered.

'Leave her be. Whatever ill I did to thee in the past, let it rest with me.'

'I will never let it rest.' Geoffrey withdrew his short sword from his belt. 'Not whilst dogs like you still walk abroad, and my mother lies cold in the ground.'

'Hold off, Geoffrey. Let's talk like civilized men.'

Geoffrey made a thrust towards him.

'I will not fight thee. Put away thy sword.' Richard backed away to join Alice.

'Quaker coward,' Geoffrey said. 'What's the

462

matter, did you leave your farmer's homespun at home?'

Richard looked down. 'This is thy son's suit.'

'My son's suit? Stephen?' Geoffrey faltered, bewildered.

'He lent me it.'

Geoffrey stared, and Alice saw the recognition dawn on his face. Then he seemed to make up his mind. He shook his head.

Richard continued: 'We owe him our thanks. It was he that loosed us from the gaol.'

'You lie.'

'He speaks true,' Alice said.

'Shut your filthy mouth, Wheeler's whore.'

'Stephen set all the Quakers free,' Alice said.

'Don't you dare to speak my son's name alongside those traitors.' He made a lunge, stabbing the sword towards her.

She screamed and leapt aside just as Richard threw himself at Geoffrey's legs and floored him, scuffling to pinion his arms.

Geoffrey thrashed but Richard pressed his arms flat to the deck. With a heave, Geoffrey landed a vicious kick to Richard's stomach and rolled free.

Richard floundered, clutching his belly. In the tussle the blade had slipped from Geoffrey's grasp. Now it clattered to the ground and slid away on the tilting floor. Geoffrey snapped round to look. The sword glinted against the floorboards in a puddle of sea water.

Both men threw themselves towards it.

'Hey!' There was a shout from above. Alice looked up. One of the sailors was clambering down the rigging. Distracted, Richard glanced briefly his way and Geoffrey grabbed the sword first by the top of the blade. As Richard reached for it, Geoffrey whipped it away from his stretching fingers. Immediately Geoffrey rammed the hilt up against his jaw with such force that the blade flew from his grip.

Richard landed on his back, his hand feeling his chin. Alice felt sick.

'Help him,' said Alice.

The sailor paused a moment, but hurried away into the fog. She watched as, disorientated, Richard pulled himself to kneeling. Geoffrey lunged for the sword and Richard grunted and twisted his body to dive for it. When his fingers closed around the hilt he staggered to upright.

'An end to it,' Richard said and, holding the blade aloft, ran to the side. He drew back his arm and hurled the sword as far as he could over the edge. He paused a moment, listening for its splash into the blank nothingness beyond.

'Bastard.' Geoffrey had started after him but then spotted the pistol lying where Richard had thrown it down. He bent to scoop it up. Before Richard could turn back from the rail, Geoffrey raised the butt of the gun and slugged it hard into the back of Richard's head. Richard groaned, fell heavily against the side rails, slumped and lay still.

A whimper escaped Alice's mouth.

'Oh God, Richard...'

'Be quiet,' Geoffrey said. 'I'll finish him once and for all.' He unhooked the powder horn from his belt and cocked the pistol to refill it with shot.

'No!' Alice flew at him, knocking the pistol out of his hand. The powder horn and shot rolled away

464

on the floor into the slopping water. Geoffrey watched them roll for a moment, then turned quietly to face her.

Unarmed, he approached a step at a time, holding out his arms towards her as if he would embrace her. She did not dare take her eyes away from him. She slowly began to back away. He sprang forward and she had no time to react; in one rapid movement he grappled her arms behind her.

'Damn you, you bitch, I'll have to finish you first,' he whispered. She winced as his fingers sank into the flesh of her upper arm. He almost lifted her as he hauled her bodily across the deck.

'Richard!' she cried out, but he did not stir and she could see the back of his head oozed blood. 'Please...' She kicked desperately at Geoffrey's legs, but he seemed impervious to her blows. There was an almost tangible animal frisson round him, like a stuck boar.

'Help me,' she shouted, but her voice faded weakly into the mist.

'Quiet!' Geoffrey pushed her up the stairs to the upper deck, his hand tight over her mouth.

Stay calm, she told herself, and look for someone who can help you. Through the fog, the upper deck looked to be deserted. She could hear the voices of sailors below on the quarter deck, see vague silhouettes of figures moving against the white sail aloft as the ship heeled in the mist. There was a slight breeze now and they were letting out sail.

But she was too exhausted to struggle so she let herself be carried towards the stern lantern, a blur of yellow light against the mist, tilting sideways with each heave of the sea. His hand was still over her mouth and was damp with her own blood. A swinging spar glanced Geoffrey a blow to the head. He staggered, and cursed it, but it seemed to cause him no pain, only made him seize her more tightly.

The rigging groaned under the sudden fill of wind. The mist came and went in shreds of white. She was failing, the wound had sapped her strength. The stern dropped away and she saw the void loom fleetingly beneath. The wind blew in her nostrils, suffocating her. Geoffrey spun her round and pushed her harder. Her boots could get no grip and scraped as she slid against the boards, skidding backwards until she was wedged up against the rail, the brass housings digging into her waist.

'Help me!' she cried again, but her voice was faint as a seagull's cry.

She reached for the rail and caught hold, but it was grainy with salt water and her hand was too small to cling on. She felt it slide slowly out of her fingers. With sickening clarity she understood what he was trying to do.

'Please, Geoffrey, no.'

She dug in her nails but he was leaning on her harder now, trying to topple her over the edge. Below the wash rushed by in ragged stripes of white foam. Her back arched over empty air, both hands clutched at the neck of Geoffrey's shirt. She felt the fabric bunch in her hands and her own nails bite into her palms. Geoffrey groaned as he struggled to free himself of her, pushing down on her shoulders.

Suddenly he released his grip, feeling inside his pocket. She fought to regain her balance, clenching her fists round his shirt. Next moment, the quill knife was at her throat.

'Let go,' he said.

The ship was moving faster now and the wind whistled at the back of her neck. With wide eyes she saw Geoffrey raise the knife above her throat. His other hand reached back and closed around one of her wrists. The ship rose up under them.

'Stop!'

Geoffrey turned, distracted.

Behind him Richard held a rapier at arm's length, the tip level with Geoffrey's neck. His teeth were clenched, his expression stony.

'Leave her be.'

Geoffrey flailed his arm wildly, swiping the knife across Richard's face. Alice lunged for freedom, but Geoffrey gripped her by the wrist.

Richard dodged and parried the attack. The rapier slipped and sliced into Geoffrey's forearm, but Geoffrey paid no heed to the gashes in his sleeve. He turned back to Alice, who had sunk to her knees and was twisting, trying to loosen his grasp on her wrist. He looked down on her. He had the eyes of a hound coming in for the kill. He raised the knife above her chest. She heard his rasping inhalation as his arm went up.

Then he stood still, mouth hanging open, as if listening. The knife faltered in his hand. Alice saw a spot of crimson appear on his belly and slowly spread out like the red contours of a map.

The knife dropped to the floor with a rattle,

before the ship heeled once more and his falling weight nailed her to the deck.

Over his shoulder she caught sight of Richard, swaying in the pale light. His face was flushed, his eyes blazing. In his hand he held the rapier; it hung loosely from his grasp, and from its tip droplets of blood dribbled onto his boot like ink. He looked down at it and then threw it away from him as if it were red-hot.

Alice felt Geoffrey move on top of her, heard him groan, felt the sticky warmth of his blood seeping through her clothes.

'Oh God help me. He's alive,' she said.

Chapter 38

Richard dragged Geoffrey roughly to one side and lifted Alice to her feet, holding her so tightly she could feel his heart thud against her ribs.

'What the devil's going on?' One of the midshipmen appeared from below. 'Who the hell are you?'

'Richard Wheeler.' He pointed at the figure on the ground with a trembling hand. 'Help us. It's Sir Geoffrey Fisk, he's wounded. Get him to his cabin.'

The man summoned two deckhands who carried Geoffrey, still groaning, to his chamber. Word soon spread and more curious crew came to his quarters to find out what was afoot. They stood there gawping, taking in Richard's cut and

468

bruised face, and Geoffrey who was breathing heavily, lying on his back on his bunk, the front of his shirt and his fine coat soaked with blood. The men hastened away.

'Help me, Alice,' Richard said, pressing his cuff onto Geoffrey's chest. 'Don't just stand there. We must do something.'

'I won't go near him,' Alice said. 'Don't ask me.'

Geoffrey had ceased to thrash and now moaned and lay twitching like a beached fish. Richard pressed his shirt harder into Geoffrey's stomach to stem the flow of blood. Geoffrey screamed and became distraught, heaving and lashing out until Richard was forced to move away.

Before long the Master arrived to ascertain what had happened.

'What the hell is all this? My men tell me there are shot holes in the tween-deck corridor.'

Richard told him plainly they had duelled over the lady, and that Geoffrey had come off the worst in the fight.

'Are you mad? We could not tell whence the shots came. For God's sake, we thought the other vessel was firing at us. Thank God it was one of our own.' He shook his head with an expression of blank disbelief. 'Damned fool. You put their lives at risk as well as our own with your brawling. What were you thinking of?'

He shouted over to the boy, who stood in the corner, white-faced, transfixed by the sight of Geoffrey's sopping shirt. 'Fetch the surgeon. Quick, now.' The boy ran off.

'Don't say I did not warn you,' the Master said.

469

'Women and the sea are like Cain and Abel, they never meet without that some calamity occurs.'

Richard had unaccountably turned his back to them all. The Master narrowed his eyes, tapped his fingers against his breeches, as if weighing Richard in the balance. Richard ignored him, opening all Geoffrey's shutters to let in the light, and now his attention was seemingly focused on the view out of the window. Alice saw the back of his hair was matted with blood.

The Master looked exasperated. 'Our livelihoods depend on him,' he said to Alice, indicating Geoffrey with a tilt of his head. He stepped towards Richard. 'If he does not live, sir, then understand you will be responsible for the men's wages, will you not?'

Richard looked round, and nodded. His face was haggard, the face of a man grown old.

'Then I will leave you to sort out this unholy mess. The surgeon will tell me his chances, and I hope they are better than they look.'

Alice watched this conversation unfold before her as if it were a long way away. Her teeth were chattering as the cold air sluiced over her. She supposed she must be in shock. Her hands were blue, the heat had shrivelled inwards to her centre. On the wall of Geoffrey's cabin the sunburst display was missing a sword. She knew now where it lay – on the deck, cast aside, the tip dark with blood.

She wanted to go to Richard, but she must pass by Geoffrey, and she dare not. She hated to see Geoffrey writhing on his bed like that, in his own blood, like an animal on a slaughterhouse floor.

But what if he should find new strength, attack her again, reach out and grab for her throat? So she stayed shaking in the corner, not daring to pass him, one hand clutching her shoulder where the flesh-wound was throbbing its own aching rhythm. When the Master and his officers had left, Richard turned to her, in turmoil, his sleeve sodden with a mess of blood.

Richard knelt and peeled Geoffrey's wet coat open and then pressed the fabric of his shirt to staunch the wound again. He spoke into his ear.

'Geoffrey. Geoffrey, can you hear me? The surgeon is coming. Hold on there.'

The vessel hit a wave, and Geoffrey moaned and half opened his eyes. When he saw Richard, his eyes closed again to shut him out. Richard turned to Alice.

'Have mercy. I will not let him die, Alice. We were friends once.'

She nodded, but could not erase the image of Geoffrey's face as he lunged towards her with the knife. She still felt the empty air behind her and the suck of the sea. Her legs trembled beneath her skirts. If she were to open her mouth she did not know if words would come.

Richard saw her hesitation and stood up and made to hold her, his brown eyes desperate. His fingers dug into the back of her neck. 'Oh God, Alice. He's going to die.' Then suddenly he pushed her away. 'Don't come near me. I am cursed with his family's blood.'

'What do you mean?' Her voice was thin and small.

He whispered, 'My men – they killed his mother,

in the days of shaking. They tortured her. Raped her. Oh God, Alice, they made sport with her corpse ... they had lost their senses somehow, God alone knows. But they cut off her fingers, wore her white hair in their helmets – as trophies...'

She looked at him in disbelief. He could not mean it.

'I did not know. It was not on my orders, I mean. I saw her afterwards – it was a charnel house. That same woman who had given me sweetmeats and apples as a boy and welcomed me into her drawing room.' He could barely get out the words, they seemed to choke him. He shook his head. 'I swore then I was done with bloodshed, would fight for peace instead, with the Quakers.' He took hold of her again in an iron grip, forcing her to look into his eyes. 'But look at me,' he said bitterly. 'I see now, there will never be any peace in my breast.'

His eyes were streaming – a salt river running down his face. She had never seen a man cry before. It wracked her to see him like this. She hushed him and wiped his face with her fingers.

'Tell me, is one life worth more than another?' he asked. The bones of his face were stark under his skin, his voice held an appeal, as if he wanted her to somehow absolve him. She knew she could not help him. It was a question she, of all people, could not answer.

'Thou art a Quaker. Look to thy faith. Pray, Richard,' she said. 'Pray for us all.'

Richard sank to his knees on the damp floor of Geoffrey's cabin but did not utter a word. He stayed with his head bowed, his shoulders hunched, like a man awaiting an execution. The neck of his shirt was damp with blood and stuck to his back. She had the absurd notion of wanting to fetch him a dry shirt. Exhausted, she sagged onto the side bench. Her right hand twisted her wedding band round and round on her finger.

The surgeon appeared at the door. Richard helped him heave Geoffrey over and undress him. The surgeon used a scalpel to cut away Geoffrey's coat and shirt, cursing as the constant motion of the ship made steady hands impossible, and Geoffrey himself was moaning – tossing and turning now in a kind of delirium. The lacklustre light seeped in through the windows. When they turned him back, Geoffrey's sodden shirt was slit open to reveal skin that was red and inflamed, a patchwork crusted with scars and lesions, scaly like a reptile. In the centre a deep hole oozed blood. The surgeon looked at Geoffrey's scarred chest with astonishment. Nauseated, Alice put her hand to her mouth.

'I have never seen the like,' said the surgeon, fascinated. 'But the blade has come from behind. I thought you said it was a duel?' He looked at Richard accusingly.

Richard could not meet his eye.

'He meant to kill me,' Alice said, 'he had lost his reason.'

The surgeon sniffed and turned his attention back to Geoffrey. 'No wonder he carried himself so stiff.'

'What is it? Is it a disease?' Richard asked.

'No. He must have had this all his life. I have seen it before, but not so severe.'

'I knew him as a boy,' Richard said. 'He never

473

said anything about it, but we used to make jest of his scratching, the way boys will. He never swam in the river with the rest of us, though, and I always wondered why,' said Richard. 'We thought he was putting himself above us.'

'By the look of it, it caused him much pain. But maybe not as much as this wound.' He fetched out needle and thread and carefully turned Geoffrey over to examine his scarred and crazed back, but then stood away, unsure what to do.

'Will he live?' Richard asked. His eyes were desperate.

'It is too deep and narrow for me to sew,' the surgeon said, at length, 'but we can wash it with brandy, and plug it with cotton and woundwort to stop the bleeding – guard it from festering. But no, not a cat's chance.'

Later Alice would remember this scene as if it were a nightmare – the ship shifting one way and the other on the swell of the sea, the light alternating between pallid grey and greenish gloom, the red of Geoffrey's blood and his screams of pain as the wound was plugged.

Richard was wretched. It was evident in his lined face, the way he winced as the alcohol was poured into Geoffrey's wound, his inability to meet her gaze. The next time she turned to look for him, he had silently left the cabin, but she felt his absence as a relief – his anguish had been an almost physical presence in the room.

When the surgeon left, Geoffrey lay listless on the cot, his scabrous chest bound tightly with a muslin bandage, through which Alice saw a spot of blood was already emerging. She stayed well away from him near the doorway. His chest rose and fell erratically with his breath. Alice had not mentioned her shoulder to the surgeon, but he saw she was in pain and he had helped her clean and dress it with a wad made from a neckerchief. Now it felt as if she had been kicked by a horse. But in truth she barely noticed it, her thoughts were dazed.

Behind her the cabin door banged. 'Why?' said Richard, evidently trying to make sense of it all. 'Why would Geoffrey want to harm thee?'

'Some sort of madness. He was not himself. He kept talking to Margaret.'

'Margaret who?'

'Margaret Poulter, the woman they accused me of killing. We had become friends. Geoffrey must have been involved in her death somehow. And maybe Ella Appleby, my housemaid. But it is all so confusing. I can't make sense of it.' She glanced towards the bed, where Geoffrey lay on his back, his face waxy. 'Don't leave me alone with him though, Richard. I'm afraid of him.'

'I have murdered him,' said Richard, 'even after all my vows, my pledge for peace.'

Alice reached out for his hand. 'In heaven's name, Richard. He would have killed me–' she tugged at his arm – 'and thee. Now let me look at the back of thy head,' she said. But he twisted away from her.

'What am I, Alice?'

She shook her head, unable to fathom the question.

'All my fine Quaker principles, all my talk of God. That's easy enough in times of peace, easy

475

enough when the wolf is not at my own door. But am I different when the time comes? Should I have turned the other cheek rather than raise a hand against another?'

Alice's heart flooded out towards him and her mouth opened to comfort him, but his face stayed her from speaking.

'Tell me–' he came towards her and loomed over her, filled with a sudden rage – 'if I had not acted, would I have been more human? Or less?'

She could not answer.

'I thought I had found God. But look at me.' She bowed her head, embarrassed. He pulled at his bloodstained shirt and thrust it close to her face so that the stench of it filled her nostrils. '*This* is the kind of man I am.'

Alice began to weep. He snatched the shirt away and turned, presenting her with his back, rigid, like a wall.

'Richard...'

'Keep away from me.' She stopped in her tracks, his words were harsh and brittle. 'I should have reasoned with him. I cannot be trusted. I cannot trust myself. I make bold promises but cannot trust myself to keep them.'

'No...'

After a few moments he strode out of the cabin without looking back.

Alice looked over to where Geoffrey lay on the wooden cot. She walked purposefully over to him.

'Is it not enough that you should try to kill me?' she said. 'I wish you would die. You have detroyed us. Richard will never forgive himself.'

Chapter 39

The fog lifted but the sea had become as calm as water in a well; the sails would not fill and the ship bobbed in one place – a cork in a teacup, surrounded by her own detritus. The surface of the water was littered with discarded sacks and floating bottles, excrement and oily slicks of the caulk and tar used for repairs. They had been at sea two weeks. The horizon seemed a long way off – an expanse of dead flat, grey water, topped by a paler grey sky, separated by a vague muddy line.

Over the following days Geoffrey's mind sometimes swam back towards them, and he would look at them with recognition, only to sink again and fall into a deep oblivion. Richard hardly spoke. He spent the nights pacing in Geoffrey's chamber, would not come to bed. Anger was etched on his face but it was turned in on himself, so he closed himself to her. When she touched him, he shook her off with an excuse and walked away. Did he blame her, she wondered? Did he wish he had stood away instead of reaching for a sword?

Geoffrey's madness she still did not fully understand. The man she had once invited into her summerhouse for chocolate was nowhere to be seen. She wondered, tussled it in her mind, finally accepting that she could find no answers. She wished he would die. Meanwhile she went on

477

washing out his bandages, folding and refolding them; she set to, she scrubbed the bloodstained cot, brought in fresh rainwater from the barrels. She wielded a broom to the water on the floor and remembered old Margaret. Alice kept herself cloaked, and her head low whenever she ventured on deck, but she knew the men watched her as if she were a bad omen, blaming her for the lack of wind.

In a few days Geoffrey seemed to shrink, his cheeks sagged, his face was pale and veined as marble and clammy with sweat. He did not open his eyes. He would not get up again, that was clear. She gradually began to see him as the Geoffrey she used to know. Filled with sudden compassion, she knelt by his side and felt his forehead. She dabbed at his face with her sleeve, knowing that, unless some miracle should happen, he was going to die. And yet she was still alive; out of all this, she had been spared, and there was even now a chance for her and Richard. They, at least, had time – something that was slipping away from Geoffrey. Give me strength to make it right, she thought.

One morning she saw Richard take hold of Geoffrey's hand between his palms and rub it, as if to kindle it to life. 'What happened to us, Geoffrey?' Richard said. 'What happened to the two boys who used to fish together?'

All the fight had gone from Geoffrey. He was too weak to move. 'War.'

The single syllable was barely audible. It sat between them with all the pain of the past knotted into its three letters. Alice looked on helplessly. She did not know what to do, was powerless to understand what was happening between these two men. She bit her lip. She was excluded. It was men's history. Richard had said they were friends but it was more than that; she would never be able to understand fathers and forefathers carving out territories for their sons in blood.

'It's over. The war, I mean.' Richard closed Geoffrey's fingers in his own. 'But thou must still fight, Geoffrey. Fight for thy life now.' The vehemence of his words was startling in the quiet cabin. 'I did not want to harm thee. I cut thee down because I feared to lose Alice. On account of love.'

Geoffrey roused himself and opened his eyes. 'Love,' he said. He tried to laugh. His voice took on new strength. 'My son,' he said between faltering breaths, 'he shuns me and talks only of you.'

'No, that's surely not true.'

'It is. You've turned him to your damned Quaker ways.'

'No,' said Richard. 'Stephen will always be his father's son. Boys are wayward. As we were, Geoffrey, when we were young.'

'I am dying. I will never see my son again now.'

Richard shook his head. 'No, old man, New England awaits thee.'

He got to his feet and turned to Alice. His eyes were full of self-reproach. He took a long shudder of a breath to get a hold of himself. 'I swear, I did not know Stephen was his son. Not until the night of the firing of the barns. I thought I could put the bloodshed behind me. I thought to dodge its grip by joining the Quakers. But I am somehow come full circle.'

He returned to kneel by Geoffrey's side, his jaw determined.

'Geoffrey,' he said, and he took hold of the side of the cot with white-knuckled fingers, 'forgive me. I am a fool. Hold fast to life, friend, for we will soon be in New England, and thy plot in Virginia awaits thee, where the air is warm and the land fertile and the fruits drop sweet from the trees, and thou canst rest, and build a fine future for Stephen and thyself.'

Geoffrey nodded, his eyes closed, his breath ragged.

The wind picked up, the cabin toppled from fore to aft and water dripped through the ceiling from the deck above onto Geoffrey's bed. Over the following week, the surgeon came and went, as did the Master. 'By rights,' he had said to Richard, 'I should have you taken off and imprisoned for duelling. But the laws of England have no hold on us here – at sea we are betwixt lands, and we sailors see fit to make our own rules. And I'm prepared to turn my eye from this sorry matter so long as my men are paid.' So the bustle of the ship went on above without them. They were silent, except for their prayers, caught in the thin thread of Geoffrey's life. She marvelled that he could cling on for so long. Alice stopped reaching out for Richard, stopped expecting his touch in return. She watched the man she loved pass the days like a man of wood, blundering from one task to the next, seeing nothing, his gaze fixed on the rise and fall of Geoffrey's chest. It was as if he was willing

Geoffrey to stay alive, not for Geoffrey's sake but for his own.

'Let him die,' Alice prayed at night in her empty bed, 'oh merciful God, let him die, and Richard come back to me.' Then she hated herself, and was more tender with Geoffrey than ever.

In the third week, she entered the cabin to see Richard had procured a flagon of rum. She spoke to him gently.

'Is it for him? Or for thee?'

He swallowed hard. 'I thought he was fighting, but he grows weaker. I cannot let him die.'

''Tis not in your hands.'

He took a drink from the bottle. 'I should have made amends years ago. When Geoffrey and I first spoke harshly to one another. When I decided to support parliament against the king. You know, he thought it a dishonour, he could not comprehend my reasoning, that the common man should be able to govern his own affairs. And I could no more understand him, cleaving to the old order.'

'We all hold to something,' she said, 'some vision, some story of a glorious future. You were both young and full of ideals.' She tried to touch him on the shoulder but he flinched away.

'What use are ideals to any of us now? We are just three more souls in a floating cask, caught in different ways between one world and another.'

Alice took the bottle from his hand. Then she poured water from the lidded jug into a cup and passed it down to him. 'How can we know what lies ahead?' She wiped a drop of water from the lip of the jug. 'We can only deal with what is here

481

before us. And we must let the past lie. Take this cup now, drink, and make sure he sups too, and suffers little.'

'I will not let him die,' he said.

'The world has never bent to my will, and it will never bend to thine. Come away now, let him alone a while.' She held out the cup again.

Richard drank, and said haltingly, 'I do not deserve what I have. I cannot touch thee with blood on my hands.'

'The blood was shed on my account. Do not torture thyself with harsh judgements. Even mortal sins can be forgiven. Jesus forgave the Iscariot, for without him the world would not have been changed.' She reached out and placed her hand on his arm. 'In pity's name, Richard, we are far from home, and do not know what may yet befall us. We have only each other. Thou hast been so cold. As if thou wouldst begrudge me my life. But I miss thee, my love, I am an empty husk without thee. You promised me life, but a life like this is no life at all.'

He took tight hold of her. 'I had lost sight of thee.' He touched her cheek with a faltering hand and said, 'Thou art my strength. I need thee to stand beside me, I am a fallen man without thee.'

He took her to their own cabin and his love-making was hot and urgent, and when it was finished he slept, peaceful at last, his head a dead weight on her shoulder.

The next day she awoke stiff, and when she went up onto the quarterdeck she could hear sounds from Geoffrey's chamber. She pushed open his door and saw that he was sitting, his eyes very bright, a hot flush over his face. His bandage was frayed and bloody, and it was clear he had been scratching for his skin was full of weals. Alice rushed over to him to calm him.

''Tis I, Alice. Lie still whilst I fetch a cloth.'

'What time is it?' He looked around wildly, tried to get up but then sank back, too weak to hold himself up. He fingered the bandage as if puzzled it should be there.

'What time is it?' he repeated, distressed.

''Tis early yet,' she replied, wringing out the muslin into the bowl. She pushed him gently back down and wiped carefully over the scratches with the cloth. He watched her for a moment like a child, but his skin was aflame with fever, the cloth grew warm in no time, and he could not lie still. He rocked from side to side, talking all the while, most of it nonsense, words Alice could not make out. It was clear he remembered nothing of earlier events. At one point he turned to Alice and asked her lucidly:

'Will I die, Mother?'

Alice did not know how to reply, but he became distraught then, shouting out, 'I'm not ready to die. Not yet, the old woman will pull me down, don't let me go yet, I'm not ready.'

Richard, having sensed Alice had risen, arrived at the door, tousle-headed, his eyes still heavy with sleep. Geoffrey stopped his noise and stared as if trying to place him.

'I know you.'

'Yes.' Richard went to him and leaned over, the better to hear. 'It is Richard.'

'Richard.' He lay more quietly, his eyes wandering, accepting. 'Where is my mother?'

'She died a long while back. Lie quiet now and rest.'

Geoffrey slumped back, his mouth contorted in pain. When the spasm was over he said, 'Richard, fetch the parson. I have need of him.'

''Tis all right. Rest now.' Richard brushed the moment aside.

'My mother is calling me,' said Geoffrey. 'I can hear her voice, she has a sweet voice, like the sound of the sea. Please, before it is too late, fetch the parson.'

Richard hesitated. Quakers did not hold with parsons or intercession with God. Alice watched him wrestle with himself, and nearly wept with relief when he finally nodded to her and she hurried above deck to find the cleric. At first the men were rowdy when she emerged from below, but when she asked in distress for the parson they fell silent and respectful. The parson hurried down the stairs, his black robe swinging above bare feet, a warped Bible in his arms.

When they entered the cabin Geoffrey's breath was rattling in his chest. He was blue now around the lips, his cheeks grey with stubble, purplish stains under his eyes.

'He asked for thee,' said Richard to the parson. 'I think he wanted to make his peace with God.'

'Aye. It looks like it is time.' He leaned over close to Geoffrey's face. 'The Lord bless and protect you. You wish to repent, and turn to God?'

There was no answer, the breath began to falter and rasp in his throat. Richard and the parson

484

exchanged glances. Suddenly, Geoffrey's eyes fluttered and looked up.

A word half formed on his lips. Richard spoke the name for him. 'Yes. I'll get word to him, tell him you love him.'

A silence descended in the chamber, a silence bigger than the slapping of the waves and the sound of the spume from the bow. The parson put his hand on Geoffrey's forehead. 'I anoint you thus, so may our heavenly Father show you an inward anointing of the Holy Spirit of his great mercy. May he forgive you your sins and release you from suffering. May he deliver you from all evil, preserve you in righteousness and bring you to everlasting life, through Jesus Christ our Lord.'

'Amen.' Richard's was the only voice.

It was over. Thanks be to God. At last it was over.

Chapter 40

On the day of Geoffrey's burial, the sea was the grey of charcoal, great saddles of cloud hung over the horizon. The ship forged relentlessly through the undulating water. The bell clanged out but the sound was swallowed by the wind.

Geoffrey's body had been wrapped and wound in the sheets from his bed and his canvas hammock. The gathering of hushed crew in their black armbands brought back memories of Flora's wake, but the day of Flora's funeral seemed to lie in a distant history when Alice was quite another woman.

She could not imagine now that she had ever been that person – Thomas's young wife, immaculate in spotless black mourning gown, sorrowing for the loss of her sister. A quite different person stood here now, swaying on the deck in her salt-spattered clothes. It seemed to her now that she had put on a suit, or a life, as the times demanded, and that she had always been in some sense a dissembler. The real feeling of who she was, like a seam of coal, was buried deep inside.

She looked to where Richard heaved the white bundle, heavily weighted with shot, onto the chute. He was labouring in his wet shirt sleeves; no doubt this was considered strange by the crew, given that he was a gentleman. But they stood aside from him with respect nonetheless.

Alice had given up anxiety about the future or predicting what might come to pass. She simply stood, watching Richard struggling, the wet cotton transparent against his forearms. She saw his face as the bundle disappeared over the side, and the involuntary rise of his palms as if he would call it back from where it sank, leaving not a trace behind it, not even a bubble or speck of foam. For hours he stood at the rails, looking back, a silent hulk, oblivious to the activity in the rigging, the winding up of ropes and the scurrying crew.

In the days after the burial Alice was soft with Richard, for she knew the ache of grief herself, and ached with him. She could not help him, she saw that, and it hurt her to see him hide his anguish. He took it on himself to pack Geoffrey's most personal possessions into his trunk – his suits, his fine cambric shirts, his comb and razor. And each time he emerged from Geoffrey's cabin his jaw was set and his face was grey. He asked her if he should write to Stephen.

She had replied, 'No hurry, time enough for that when we reach New England.'

It would be a hard letter to write, and one that would sound like a sort of nonsense had you not been there.

The Master saw no reason not to honour Geoffrey's ongoing trade commitments, which would pass now to his son. Richard had told him that the *Fair Louise* would belong now to Stephen Fisk, Geoffrey's heir. In the weeks after Geoffrey's death Richard had somehow grown to talking of him to the Master. It seemed to help him, to talk with another man, and now they bore each other grudging respect.

A gentle acceptance had grown up inside her. She saw how her life was tied to Richard's by an invisible cord. It tugged at her heart, so that the thought of life without him was unimaginable. And they were so small, on this huge table of water, their lives so tiny. There was something about the ocean that gave everything its proper perspective – a great stillness, for all its continual motion.

The days became routine. Life at sea was full of discomfort, everything was damp; even on fine days the dried salt sucked water into their clothes, but she hardly noticed it. It gave her time to rest

487

and take stock. She needed time to marvel at how her life had turned over like a flipped farthing. She wondered about Thomas, why he had abandoned her at the last, and she wondered about Hannah, but she hardly gave the orchid a thought. It was lost forever. Geoffrey had seen to that. There would be no more lady's slippers in the English woods. She heard Thomas's words echo back to her. 'It's only a plant,' he had said, and at the time she had thought him insensitive and boorish, caught up as she was in her ideals of art and refinement. Now she saw that perhaps he was right – in the grand scale of things, it *was* only a plant.

During the weeks that followed the Master sometimes sat in Geoffrey's cabin, but neither Alice nor Richard could bear to spend much time there. The Master occasionally brought out one of Geoffrey's books or maps, so that Alice grew to appreciate Geoffrey's fine collection of works on natural history, and she and Richard spent many evenings studying his map of the new territories together. In the evenings there was improvised music from the pipes and tabor and the crew told them tall tales about Virginia and the natives there, though many of these proved to be so hair-raising that in the end Richard ceased to ask for them.

The sea took its toll, they frequently had to lash themselves to their bunk, and oft-times she was so terrified by the immensity of the waves that she wished the ocean would swallow them up and have done with it. She hated the miserable diet of ship's biscuit and the way everything tasted of salt. She longed for some honey, longed for dry clothes and the crackle of a wood fire. And she yearned for the green fields of England with an almost physical passion that wrung her heart, but when her thoughts turned that way she would look over to Richard, and the sight of his chestnut hair and thoughtful expression was enough to soften her and make her count her blessings.

She would catch him sometimes, staring down at the waves, a far-away look in his eyes, a slight furrowing of his eyebrows, and know he was thinking of Geoffrey. At those times she knew not to go to him but to leave him with his thoughts, to let the constant conversation of the sea soothe him.

One morning she awoke early, feeling even more restless than usual. She left Richard sleeping and went up onto the deck, staring out behind them at the wake of white foam. Her eyes stung from the brine in the air, her hair whipped round her mouth. She turned to face the prow and inhaled. The air smelt softer somehow; afterwards she fancied she had sensed the damp freshness of the vegetation, but she would never forget the taste of that moment.

'Land ho!' came the shout from the crow's nest, followed by sudden activity on the rigging as the men clambered aloft for their first view of the New England.

She ran to the rails. She was transfixed. On the horizon the blurred outline of the coast appeared as a smudge, almost an illusion in the wavering heat. She looked at it with disbelief, a sense of unreality, as if looking at an illustration in a book.

So many colours and textures after the months

of dark cabins and unrelenting grey seas. The plants so tall and green, the wooden jetty built out of thick timbers with rough bark that was almost red. As they hoved into sight of the unfamiliar harbour with its strange collection of squat timber buildings, Richard came to stand wordlessly beside her. He wrapped an arm around her waist and pulled her close so her head lay on his shoulder.

'There it is,' he said, 'and I cannot tell what kind of land it is. But I hope it is a place of new beginnings, a place to inspire us. A virgin land, where we can build something new with our own hands.'

'What will we do? Find the seekers who have gone before?'

She felt his body tense. There was a long pause before he answered. 'No,' he said, 'I realize now, I can never be like them. The seekers are good people, right enough. But sometimes the world needs fire as well as peace. I cannot live their life, only my own.' She pulled away from him, but he looked into her eyes and said softly, 'I cannot make promises of peace when I may feel called to break them – cannot live by their certainties when life will give me none.'

'But...'

'Maybe in another age, a golden age, we will have no need to protect those we love. Lord forgive me, but I cannot live the Quaker way.'

She moved further away, astonished.

'Art thou done with the seekers then?'

He paused for a few moments before giving his answer. 'I do not know. I have been thinking on it. When I took sword to defend thee, in that

490

moment I came to life – too much control destroys a man. I was more truly myself then, with a sword in my hand, than any amount of digging vegetables in Netherbarrow. It led me to ask whether God is truly as much in the soldier as in a peacemaker, and to try to fathom when soldiering ceases to be God's work and becomes an instrument of terror.'

'I don't understand.' A great fear had arisen inside her.

'When my men butchered Geoffrey's mother, they had lost sight of themselves, turned from God. The house was already surrendered, it was madness – bloodshed for no cause, designed for no end but to cause suffering.'

She heard the passion in his voice. His face was alight with a kind of fierce pride.

'But there is an honour and a glory in fighting. It is life that is holy, not our warped view of God. A soldier aims to preserve the lives of the old and the vulnerable, the women and the children of their homeland – oh, Alice, it is a glory I can taste but cannot express in words. That is what I mean. And that is what I am called to do.'

'But thou hast no land now, but this one. And we have not yet set foot there. And thou art telling me thou desirest more strife? How canst thou speak of such things?' She searched his face.

'I do not know. All I know is that I defended thee with my sword and would do so again. That is the truth.' He turned his face into the wind before returning to place one hand on her cheek. His brown eyes looked into hers. 'Thou knowest, I care for thee so much that I would cut down

491

any man that tried to hurt thee. And I would lay down my own life gladly to save thine. The seekers have taught me one thing – and that is, to search out the truth of ourselves, to see clearly who or what we are. And in my deepest being, I have found I am a soldier. Canst thou love a soldier, Alice?'

She put aside her misgivings and reached up to kiss him. It was her act of faith.

'I love thee whatever thou art,' she said. And she resolved in that moment to be true to her word, although a great flutter of uncertainty hung over her heart. She took in a deep breath.

The *Fair Louise* strained against its anchor, and the timbers creaked as the ropes were flung to the quay to secure her down.

Alice held tight onto Richard's arm as she walked down the gangplank, a little unsteadily, her scuffed black boots reaching out towards the dazzling quay and the painted buildings of the New World.

Epilogue 1695

From the water the dark silhouette of the twin landmarks of church and castle were hidden behind the façade of grey that flanked the quay, but as soon as the horses turned uphill to pull away up to the town, there it was, as if carved from blood-red sandstone.

Time had stood still there; the crenellated tower

of the castle gaol and the neighbouring priory were unweathered by the storms of change, the coming and going of kings and queens, the shift of empires and boundaries. Alice stared and stared at the castle's craggy outline as the carriage rattled its way over the cobbles. From inside she had thought the gaol to be a vast underground territory, like a maze of damp labyrinthine corridors, and she remembered it as black, like something that might house a minotaur. She was surprised to see that it was a jutting protuberance in the landscape, much loftier than she had thought, a grisly red landmark sitting above the town like a crown on a royal head.

After all this time the memory of it had begun to blur, her remembrance of it becoming worn like a washed-out tapestry, but she could not help but wonder if innocent people were even now incarcerated in its bleak vaults. The thought caused her to shudder and pull down the leather blind on the window.

She had hired a post-chaise for herself and her maid and manservant to travel from Lancaster, for she could afford it now, and the sea journey had made her stiff and uncomfortable. Aboard ship, by careful negotiation and by dint of her age she had been able to secure them a private cabin, but after all this time she had forgotten how the incessant dipping and bobbing on the water and the constant struggle to remain upright taxed the body. Despite the autumn chill, Alice had braved the open deck to get the first glimpse of the old port as she drew within sight of land; despite everything, she was surprised to find she still considered it to be a homecoming. The sheer quantity of smacks and barges, the hoys plying their routes to the other tallships at anchor in deeper water took her breath away. The wharf had become a wall of huge stonework buildings with gantries and loading bays, pulleys and cranks to load and offload the cargoes of herring, or wool, or tobacco, or tea. The familiar landmarks were overlaid by new features, which gave the peculiar effect of looking through a mist into the past.

After a night's rest, she asked the coachman to call first in the village to see if she could find Thomas's grave. In the early years she had wondered about him, the mysterious illness Geoffrey had mentioned, and had sent word to him on several occasions by letter but had no reply. Her letters had been stilted and brief. She had asked him to release her from the marriage, to sell her forth, as was the custom. It rankled in her heart, the thought that when she wed Richard she was already in some way wife to Thomas. But when several years had passed with no word, she had written to ask Stephen about him. At first she had been reluctant to ask Stephen for news directly, fearing that his enquiries would bring trouble in their wake. Stephen replied that he had assumed they already knew – Thomas had died some years before. He must never have received her letters.

She rubbed her fingers through her mitts; they were stiff and aching in the unaccustomed cold, and the knuckles were hard as fetlocks. These days her hands were bent out of shape with age, dry and peppered with liverspots. When she looked down on them she found it hard to remember that they had ever been smooth-jointed and rosy.

From the window of the carriage the hedges of Lancashire gave way to the walls of Westmorland. The fields were full of fat wethers and she saw pheasants standing golden in the verges. These sights constricted her throat; she felt her youth sweep in, threatening to overwhelm her with bittersweet memories.

Her house at Netherbarrow had a new whintin slate roof and a front gate made from a wagon wheel cleverly inset. The globed box trees by the door were gone. As she alighted, stepping down awkwardly, holding the doorframe in one hand, several small curious children appeared from around the back and looked up at her with wide-eyed faces, wondering who had come to call.

She explained that she had lived there once and asked if she might walk in the garden. The housemaid shrugged, and Alice nodded back, an exchange that Alice took to be permission. The garden was more unruly and overgrown than when she had left it, but some of the plants she had set as seeds were still there, thriving, all this time after. She ran her hand over a sturdy rosemary shrub, brought her fingers to her nose. She had planted this, not expecting it to survive the harsh Westmorland winter, yet here it was, its pungent tang reminding her of the warmth of New Hampshire. The apple trees had grown tall and thick-trunked, so she wended her way between them down the path towards the octagonal stone building she could see just peeping out from behind the already yellowing leaves.

When she got closer she could see it was in

disrepair. Ivy had grown up over it and seemed to be clasping the building against collapse, its tendrils creeping in through the roof, pushing the slates aside. She stepped inside, felt the sudden rise in warmth now she was out of the wind. It was empty of furniture, there was no glass in the window frames and the door was missing. The sills were curded with bird droppings and the roof beams thick with cobwebs. Alice took in the bare walls, the whitewash mottled with patches of damp. She could not help but admire the patches of pink Indian willowherb sprouted in the corners. She had expected to be moved, to feel something, but the building was an empty shell; the wind and weather must have scoured the place of memory. She looked down. Two plump brown bantams at her feet scratched at some scattered seed and the couch grass in the gaps between the flags. One of the children had followed her down the path and into the summerhouse. 'That one's mine,' he said pointing to one of the hens.

'She's a beauty.'

'You can have an egg if you like.' The boy ran to the back of the summerhouse and came back with a brown hen's egg cradled in his hand.

'It's still warm,' he said, handing it to her.

'Thank you,' she said, opening her bag and gently placing the egg inside. 'That's a lovely present.'

'Are you going home now?'

'Yes. I was looking for my sister but I can see she's not here.'

'Is your sister an old lady like you?'

'No, she was about your age.' Seeing the boy's

perplexed face, she said, 'I am not making much sense, am I? But never mind, my carriage is still waiting. Thank you for the egg.' She followed the skipping figure down the path, without looking back.

The carriage took her to the green, from where it was a short walk along the lanes to the church. Alice scanned the hedgerows for familiar plants from her youth, saying the long unused names as she passed, until she came to the lychgate with its tall yews either side. The wind whistled round the church and inside it was not much warmer. She was not used to the cold now; she had been too long in the warmth of New Hampshire and she felt the draught eat into her bones. In the side vestry the new curate brought her the ledger and laid it out where the light from the domed window would enable her to read it. She took out her eyeglasses, for these days she was never without them.

The book was thick as a coping stone but the pages thin calf-vellum. Each entry had a name, a date and some details of the manner of death. Her finger traced each entry, going back over the years, seeing the black fates of her dimly remembered neighbours written out in copper penmanship and gall.

Here were Audrey and Tom Cobbald, little Lizzie Pickering, the Hardacres and the Armitages. And dear Betty Tansy, the cook, who stood up for her so bravely, dead these twelve years of a fever. The book brought forth the sad ghosts of their smiles, their hard graft, their determination to outwit a death which in the end can never be outrun. Their faces swam before her until her head reeled with people and dates.

Her hands had grown stiff by the time she reached the name she sought: Thomas James Ibbetson, moneylender, right back in October 1660. So he had been dead all that time. Right from the very beginning. She touched the entry with her finger, smoothed it over the grit of the ink as if it might tell her more, but the words were simple, 'felled by the palsy, never recovered'. She wondered who had gone to help him, what had happened. A great pity rose in her, for she had never really found him, the way she had found Richard. He had always been already lost to her in some sense, even when alive.

His headstone was not hard to find. Someone had kept it tidy and tended she was glad to see. She did not go to Flora's grave, for she had already said her farewells, and knew that if she had not found her in the summerhouse she would not find her here.

She left the church then and the horses pulled away from the village, out towards the estuary.

At length they drew in between two stone pillars. Alice was apprehensive. Although Stephen had corresponded, even now she was not sure what kind of a welcome she would receive at Fisk Manor.

'Stephen?'

'Alice!' She need not have worried. He grasped her in an indecorous bear hug. He was much thicker round the waist and his hair was greying at the temples, but the slightly apologetic grin was the same. He was dressed in plain brown worsted and his cheeks were ruddy from fresh air and exercise.

She looked around in amazement at the activity in the yard – there were carts full of turnips, some tethered horses, two goats, two men in broad-brimmed hats carrying what looked to be wet laundry and spreading it out over the bushes, a fish-wagon making a delivery and, on the drive-way, now almost completely grassed over, a group of children chasing hoops and squawking with delight.

Stephen saw her amazement, and said, 'It has changed, I know. People refer to it simply as The Fieldings now. I did not like the idea of it being a manor, it sounds too forbidding. But come, I'll show thee round.'

She followed him while he showed her the schoolroom, the meetinghouse, the almshouse and even a place for caring for the sick. The whole time they were walking he was constantly inter-rupted by people asking him his opinion or his advice, which he gave effortlessly and with good cheer. The great gardens, once formal parterres and grids of mathematical precision, had been given over to root vegetables, and there were a number of women engaged in digging the plot, their skirts hitched about their thighs. Slightly shocked, Alice looked away, but then thought to herself that perhaps her views on a lady's dress might be considered a little old-fashioned these days.

Everywhere was a veritable lather of activity. It made her tired just to look on it, so she was glad when he took her into the quiet, dimly lit drawing room and brought her a handled glass with some dark nettle tea. She was flagging, but the feel of its smooth warmth in her hands and its bitter taste revived her.

She asked after the seekers at Lingfell Hall and was told that after Dorothy died the Hall was repossessed by her nephews and the seekers thrust out. He had offered them refuge at Fisk Manor, The Fieldings as it was now known.

'Hannah Fleetwood, and Jack?'

'Jack Fleetwood died the night he was arrested.'

Oh no. Poor Hannah. Suddenly she felt weak and old. Her hand shook as she reached out to put the teacup on the table. The unfairness of it roused a deep anger within her, but she was exhausted. The anger died, betrayed only by the rise of her chest.

Stephen seemed to read her mind.

'I know. It was cruel. Hannah was never told, not until she appeared in court. But it made her all the more determined to uphold the cause in his memory.' He told her then how Hannah had never remarried, but that she had an inner light that touched all who saw her.

'Where is she now?' asked Alice, seized with a sudden desire to see her.

'The last I heard, she settled with our friends in Barbados in the Indies.' Alice knew she must have looked astonished, for he nodded and continued. 'Thou knowst there are Friends now all over the world.' He leaned towards her, and added, 'And thou amongst them. For without Richard and thee, none of this–' here he opened his arms to embrace his expanding domain – 'would have come about.'

'And without thee...' She did not need to finish, he was waving it away as if it was of no account.

The nervous young man she remembered had gone. The whelp with the be-ribboned breeches that flapped on him like flags from a flagpole had been replaced by this solid middle-aged man whose clothes seemed to be grafted onto his skin as if filled from within. Stephen had a calm assurance about him, a maturity that had not been apparent from their correspondence over all these years. He asked after Richard, and the manner of his death, so she told him.

'Since we moved north to New Hampshire, there has been constant fighting to guard our territories from the French. He was garrisoned in the new fort at Hampton. A native on the French side shot him in an ambush.' She looked down into her lap, reluctant to show him the extent of her pain, which was raw even now. 'It is five years since.'

She looked up again, to see that he had read it in her face.

'He did not die fighting then?' There was a moment's awkwardness.

'Do not disapprove of him,' she said. 'You know he was always a man of action, the way he expressed his love was always through his sword.'

'One man should never judge another. But I know him for a truthful man, and one who examined his heart. It cannot have been easy for him to tell me of the manner of my father's death.' There was a pause, whilst they weighed the past.

Stephen went on, 'My father and I were never close as a father and son should be, Alice, but I like to think he would be proud if he could see me now.'

Alice nodded but kept her thoughts to herself. She had never been able to come to terms with the mystery of Geoffrey. She seemed to have known so many different, conflicting Geoffreys.

So instead she said, 'We should have come sooner. Richard would have loved to see this. But life there was hard and bitter to begin with, we had to dig our existence out of the earth. We fought for it with our sweat and toil. And later somehow we were afraid to return, we feared to lose what was so hard-won – and we were happy as we were, we had our children to think of, and we had put the cold dark of England behind us.'

Stephen nodded. 'No matter. Thou art here now.'

She leaned towards him. There was one more mystery she needed to lay to rest.

'But tell me, do you know what became of Ella Appleby, the girl who used to work for me as housemaid?'

'An odd thing – they say that when Thomas died, she just disappeared. It was quite a scandal at the time. She took as many valuables from the house as she could carry, and she and her sister just vanished. The king's men tried to catch up with her, and there were rumours she was seen in London. But she must have covered her tracks well. There's been no more word of her since.'

'She would be getting on in years, anyway,' said Alice, 'like the rest of us. It all seems so long ago. But I would still find it hard to forgive her.'

'But she was so young. Scarcely more than a child.'

Alice could find nothing remotely child-like in her memory of Ella. But then, Stephen had never met her.

He carried on. 'And in a strange way, without Ella Appleby your future would have been quite another story. She gave thee a life thou couldst never have foretold, just as surely as meeting Richard transformed me.'

They sat companionably, mulling over this thought.

'Wilt thou join us at the meeting for worship tonight?' said Stephen.

She smiled her agreement, and later that evening found herself in the great hall, now transformed into a meeting room. The quiet of the meeting lulled her, the busyness of the day banished by the calm faces. Nobody spoke. Alice looked around and was oddly moved. She understood now what Richard had talked of, the presence he had felt on the field when George Fox spoke. It was the same presence she had felt when she had first seen the lady's slipper, standing so still and alone in Richard's wood.

Her head was heavy, and before long it dropped forward onto her chest and she let her eyelids close. And there was Richard, smiling at her in the miller's, asking the miller for a fair price, his brown eyes oddly familiar in his young face. A while later she awoke to find Stephen's hand on her arm, shaking her gently. Strange – she had not meant to fall asleep.

The next day Stephen offered to accompany her on her carriage ride to the village, but she refused him. For this was one journey she needed to make alone. She left her maidservant at the top of the lane and pushed the kissing-gate open, pausing for a moment on the threshold of Helk's Wood. She took in the speckled lichen surface of the posts, breathed in the dampness of the day. She would want to remember this when she returned to New Hampshire.

Her feet, that had once trod this same route in the dark of the moon, nimble in her pretty yellow shoes, stumbled over the stones and roots in her path. The wood was denser and the way a little more overgrown; the wall was plush with green moss; beech trees dripped overhead. But she recognized the route even after all this time.

At the overhanging branch she put her hand out to the wall to support herself, but in her mind she was still the young woman who had come here thirty-five years ago. The clearing was velvety underfoot. The swish of her skirts scattered the beech nuts as she searched for the right place.

She bent over the spot and began to open the ties on her painting basket. When they had settled in New Hampshire, it was a long time before she had wanted to take up her brush and paints. One day she had been persuaded by a neighbour to visit a local trading fair, and there had been a small display of paintings by the governor's wife. As she walked along the row of paintings, a deep wistfulness overtook her. She realized how much she had missed her drawing, how she longed for the touch of the brush in her hand. She was musing on this when she came face to face with a painting of a lady's slipper. She stopped, her mouth dry and her heart hammering loudly in her chest.

Her friend said, 'Are you all right? You look pale.'

'This flower, the lady's slipper. It reminds me of home. England I mean.'

'I like it too. It is one of my favourite wild flowers.'

'You mean, it grows here?'

'Yes, they are everywhere out in the pastures. They should be easy to find now because the flowers are so showy.'

She had stood there a long while, in front of the picture. The next day she had driven the buggy out to the woods and, sure enough, the dark shadows of the redwood trees were full of lady's slippers, nodding and dipping in the breeze, drowsy bees buzzing as they hovered between one pouch and the next. Not just creamy flowers, but bright yellow and pink ones too. She had been staggered by the sheer numbers, unable to take it in. But then she had started to laugh. She laughed until she cried, until she had to hold on to the ache in her side, until, breathless, she had to sit down on the grass.

She had taken one home to show Richard, and he had stood up from cutting wood, and he had laughed with her and fetched some to plant out back under the plane tree. As the years passed her children had picked them, called them, as their friends did, 'moccasin flowers', put them in jars of water as if they were buttercups and thought nothing of it. But here now, in the dark woods of England, the memory of that one single flower, its beauty and strangeness, flooded back.

She opened the sackcloth in the basket and

drew out the orchid. Her hands were clad in black, just as they had been the last time she was here, except the mourning was for Richard now, not for Flora. Carefully she dug a well for the little plant and lowered it into the ground, tamping down the earth around the roots until it stood sturdy and upright in its leafy setting. She stood up and paused, looking down on it, and inhaled deeply. She imagined the sweet smell of tobacco drifting over the wall. Then she spoke, her voice soft amongst the call of the birds, the Quaker form of address springing naturally to her lips.

She leaned down towards the flower. 'Do well, little plant,' she whispered, 'for thou art far from thy New Hampshire home, and I would not have brought thee, but for love.'

She stepped away then, and hurried back up the path.

In the glade, the rain began to fall, but one flower shone bright against the green like a single star.

Afterword

The lady's slipper orchid is Britain's rarest wild flower. Thought at one time to be extinct, its decline is due to over-collection by botanists and it is found now on a single, fragile, natural site. Recently a propagation programme has been undertaken at Kew, supported by the Threatened Plants Appeal.

More information about this can be found at www.kew.org.

Acknowledgements

First, thanks must go to the members of the Cypripedium Committee who have care of the species recovery programme for the lady's slipper, and in particular Ian Taylor of English Nature who took the time to answer my questions.

I would also like to thank my friends from the MA in Creative Writing at Lancaster University (2007) for getting me started on writing this novel, and especially Vicky Delderfield who volunteered to read the book when it was finished and offer her comments.

Special thanks go to my husband John, the Windermere Book Group, the Thursday Writing Group, and all my tai chi friends for their interest and support.

Lastly, thanks to my agent Annette Green, my editor Will Atkins, and all at Macmillan New Writing for their enthusiasm for this book.

The publishers hope that this book has given you enjoyable reading. Large Print Books are especially designed to be as easy to see and hold as possible. If you wish a complete list of our books please ask at your local library or write directly to:

Magna Large Print Books
Magna House, Long Preston,
Skipton, North Yorkshire.
BD23 4ND

This Large Print Book for the partially sighted, who cannot read normal print, is published under the auspices of

THE ULVERSCROFT FOUNDATION